The Last Night of the Proms

The Last Night of the Proms *is the third book in the Alastair Cameron-Strange trilogy. The first two titles are:*

Click, Double-Click
The Seven Trials of Alastair Cameron-Strange

Also by James Calum Campbell:
Cobra

The Last Night of the Proms

James Calum Campbell

Troubador Publishing Ltd
Unit E2 Airfield Business Park,
Harrison Road, Market Harborough,
Leicestershire LE16 7UL
Tel: 0116 279 2299
Email: books@troubador.co.uk
Web: www.troubador.co.uk

ISBN 978 1 80514 311 6

British Library Cataloguing in Publication Data.
A catalogue record for this book is available from the British Library.

Printed and bound by CPI Group (UK) Ltd, Croydon, CR0 4YY
Typeset in 10.5pt Garamond Pro by Troubador Publishing Ltd, Leicester, UK

To see a World in a Grain of Sand
And a Heaven in a Wild Flower
Hold Infinity in the palm of your hand
And Eternity in an hour.
William Blake, Auguries of Innocence

Now I am become death, destroyer of worlds.
The Bhagavad Gita

And when he had opened the fourth seal, I heard the voice of the
fourth beast say, Come and see.
And I looked, and behold a pale horse: and his name that sat on
him was Death, and Hell followed with him.
The Revelation of St John the Divine Ch 6 V 7– 8

September 6th

I don't know about you, but I have no intention of attending my own funeral. I'll be long gone. Elsewhere. Speaking as a doctor, I'm a strong believer in the ostrich doctrine of preventative medicine. Let the dead bury their dead. One thing I've noticed about the worried well. They take great pains to watch out for the grim reaper and to cut him off at the pass, but they seldom see the direction from whence he comes. Death comes as an ambush, and we are taken by surprise.

Well that's a benison, is it not? In my professional life, because I have always worked towards the acute end of the spectrum, I have seen death come in many forms. Sudden; violent; lingering; protracted; serene; distressing; good; bad. Yet one thing these visitations all have in common. Even when anticipated, they remain in some sense unexpected. I don't believe I have ever met a patient, not even among the suicidal, who woke up on the day of their death, knowing it would be their last.

Yet still… Still there remains September 6th.

There is a car, a sleek black Jaguar, creeping quietly out of a West Highland coastal village, Ullapool, at dead of night, and heading north. I watch it from the air. I follow it, like a drone tracking its progress across the blighted moonscape, briefly hugging the coast, then turning inland to cross Strath Canaird, the driver slowing to glance to his left at the jagged rocky contour of Stac Pollaidh. Will he turn down in that direction and towards Coigach? No, not this time. He keeps heading north, into the wilderness of Assynt, making swift progress now. See the car cross the elegant arc of the bridge at the confluence of Loch Glencoul, Loch Glendhu, and Loch a' Chàirn Bhàin, at Kylesku, to the tolling of a bell. I think of the traverse of that bridge, as a failsafe point. What was that throwaway comment somebody once said to me about a failsafe point? I try to remember, always heading north, towards the edge of the world. North-West Sutherland. This bleak landscape also has a soundscape. It is the sound of a string orchestra in deep mourning, playing a descending minor scale, thickly enmeshed, overlapping, recurring. Over and over again. And the tolling of a bell.

But how can I observe this car's progress from above, when I am its driver? This is an out-of-body experience. Nobody knows where I am, nor where I am going.

I always knew I would return here. I always knew that my first coming here was not an accident. That is surely why my thoughts have ever since kept returning to this place. It is as if everything that had previously happened to me had merely been a rehearsal for this moment, and this trial.

I stole my beloved sister's Jaguar. Dear MacKenzie, forgive me. You, too, don't know where I am, nor where I'm going. And now I remember that throwaway remark that Major Forster cast in my direction.

"I once told you, Cameron-Strange, that there is a tipping point… Stay this side of it, and the failsafe mechanisms apply. Cross it, and the past is irrevocable."

OPENINGS

OPENINGS

I

Somebody at the Maudsley suggested to me the other day that I might be suffering from PTSD. Post-Traumatic Stress Disorder. They said I was in shock. Shock! I rather resent the way that the mental health people have hijacked words like 'shock' and 'trauma' for their own nefarious purposes. 'Shock', after all, is a catastrophic collapse of the cardiovascular system, and 'trauma' is a Greek word meaning wound; that's all. You get too close to 'shock and awe'; you witness trauma, and of course it upsets you. But somehow your upset state of mind itself becomes the shock and the trauma. Well, that's a bit of an indulgence if you ask me. I'm an emergency physician. I'll show you trauma. I'll show you somebody who's really been through the mangle.

Still, that day at the Maudsley, I had the great privilege of observing a very talented psychiatrist at work. Dr Ralph Parkinson could hardly be said to be a low-key individual. He was a large, overweight, untidy man in an off-white suit badly in need of a press. He had watchful eyes and a slow, Melbourne drawl. He hammed up the 'Strine' with his resonant bass voice. Yet, paradoxically, he had mastered the trick of disappearing into the furniture while he calmly listened to the self-serving platitudes of his patient, the sanitised version of the truth applied like fake tan or a cheap cosmetic. It was only when the patient had finally dried up, had exhausted his sump of bullshit, that Parkinson leant forward and undercut it all, with a single, excruciatingly hurtful comment which suddenly left the patient exposed, and at last allowed him to articulate his innermost thoughts. Thus, he was enabled for the first time, even to himself, to reveal his soul.

I have this recurring dream. It relates to April 25th. Anzac Day. It's a recollection from the other end of the world, of Nikki and me trapped in our sarcophagus on board *The Captain Cook*, down at Marsden Wharf on the Waitemata Harbour at Auckland, alone on the vessel that was about to turn into a funeral pyre.

I know what you're thinking. You're thinking I must have suffered another bereavement. And, in a way, you'd be right. There was a fatality on the wreck of *The Captain Cook*. But I get ahead of myself.

There had been a deep subterranean grumble and a thump and a massive spalling pressure wave seemed to engulf us from below. I just remember a very sharp pain in my ears and a persistent ringing as the wreck of the boat gave a great heave and lurched over onto its port side, the side where Nikki's arm was trapped, and rapidly began to sink. Instinctively I'd grabbed one of the two oxygen cylinders Major Forster had left with us, opened the oxygen supply and proffered the rubber tubing with its mouthpiece in Nikki's direction. I have no recollection of utilising the second tank myself but I must have done so. I just remember desperately trying to pull Nikki's left

4

arm from under a giant metal stanchion and, as the ship hit the bottom, sensing some movement and the possibility that I might just free her up. Then came the cluster of frogmen – I don't know how many – but several helping hands and within a minute Nikki was free and we were propelled to the surface. And this episode, the two or three minutes encompassing the detonation, the sinking of the ship, the freeing up of Nikki, and our surfacing, is the substance of my recurring dream.

A propitious outcome? Not entirely. Against orders, a naval rating had reboarded the evacuated ship to retrieve some trivial personal belongings. He was taken to Middlemore Hospital with severe burns. He didn't make it. Personal belongings became personal effects.

I didn't see Nikki for a few days. The army spirited her away, and I was kept busy fielding all sorts of enquiries from officialdom while trying to stay away from the media. About a week after the sinking of the ship I got the briefest of texts from her suggesting we meet at a coffee place in downtown Auckland. It was the same place where Martin Forster and I had met before the incident, kind of a favourite watering hole of mine, at the Quay Street entrance to a mall on the corner of Queen Street. I got there first and sat at a table on the concourse of the mall overlooking the street. I watched her saunter from the west towards me along the pavement. Signature jeans and T-shirt, no limp this time. She had lost her vulnerability. I got up and we greeted one another with an embrace, as we had done before. No difference then. All the difference in the world. For all that I have zero emotional intelligence, I'm sensitive to atmosphere. I can't even call it body language, or demeanour. Just something in the air. I knew immediately and before a word was spoken that we were all washed up. To be brutally frank, she had made this appointment in order to chuck me. At least she didn't do it by text.

5

She sat and stirred her Americano meditatively and then looked at me intently with these gorgeous pale blue eyes.

"I can never thank you enough for what you've done for me. You saved my life."

"You returned the compliment."

"Yes but you did it twice!" She performed some brief *armography* with her left upper limb. "You saved my arm. Thank you so much."

"You're welcome."

Hers was a conventional utterance, something that needed to be articulated. It wasn't insincere, but it was a formal vote of thanks. She might have been called upon to give it on some ceremonial occasion. "It falls to me..." Of course I knew it was valedictory. I suppose if I'd paused to think about it, I would have sooner realised as much myself. I was just a bit slower to appreciate that that which we had had, had not been quite real; it had occurred within a framework of highly unusual circumstances. It was meaningful while it lasted, but had no connection with the lives, the divergent lives, we were about to lead.

Then she dropped her eyes to her coffee and she began to tell me in low tones about the army posting that was very quickly going to take her to Nairobi where she might continue her study of the world's land mines, and her mission to eradicate them. What a difference a day makes. One minute I'm free to hold Nikki, the next she is off limits; and she is all the more beautiful and beguiling for that. It crossed my mind to remonstrate. I could fight this. Wasn't it right to fight it? Faint heart never won fair lady. 'Nikki, please, it doesn't need to be this way...' I could lay out a rationale as to why we should stay together. What do you do? Do you go with your head and your heart, or do you go with your gut?

I decided to go with gut.

"I'll miss you. You take care with them land mines."

"You take care too."

"Stay in touch?"

"Oh absolutely." She said it too quickly.

Be dignified. Keep it together. Don't make a scene. We walked out of the shadow of the mall into the blazing sun on Quay Street. A final embrace. I tried to hold the remembrance of her shape, her scent, her persona.

"God bless." There is no adieu more final than that. I watched her beautiful form drift west along Quay Street. She turned one last time, gave me a wave and a cheeky grin, and called back something her boss once said to me.

"Check six!"

I laughed, sick at heart.

This, too, was my recurring dream.

Do you dream in black and white or in colour?

Colour gets filched out of dreams. And memories. When they are new they are in glorious technicolour. But the archive of memory is, at best, sepia-toned. How else can we cope with the agony of remembering everything? Imagine if your unrequited love stayed with you, year after year, her image forever imprinted in your consciousness, drawn with the same intense hues as on that first day. You go to bed at night and she is the last thing you think of. You wake in the morning and she is the first thing to come into your mind. People who fall in love and marry successfully are sometimes wistful because, while they continue to love, they arc not *in* love. But the agony of unrequited man is that he just cannot fall out of love. He carries a torch, and the flame will just not be extinguished. The extraordinary thing is this: it does not matter what tactics he employs to end his agony. He knows his love is doomed. He might prostrate himself before his loved one and beg her to return. He might make a complete fool of himself. Worse, he might make a nuisance of himself. On the other hand he might be eminently sensible; knowing that his love is doomed, he might resolve to make a clean break. He might avoid her haunts. He might choose another path home. He might distance himself from her friends. He harbours neither grudge nor favour. He never talks about her. He chooses not to think of her. All mementoes – postcards, letters, gifts, photographs, all are destroyed. To fresh fields and pastures new! Absorbs himself in his work with renewed energy. Takes up a new hobby. Gets up to date with all these tiresome chores he usually leaves to the last minute; does his tax return in April; mends fuses, cuts the grass. Catches up with all the old friends he's been neglecting. Goes to concerts, goes to the movies, plays squash, gets fit again, has some fun. Goes out on a date; might even start a relationship.

And you know what? None of it makes the slightest difference. You long to obliterate the pain of your love in precisely the way a dose of morphia obtunds pain; it's not that the pain has gone, merely that it doesn't seem to matter anymore. You long for that. But nothing you can say or do or even think will alter the course of true love. True love has a life and a will of her own, and she is entirely without your power. You can slander her, curse her, banish her, abuse her. You can try to ignore her, mock her, smother her, murder her in cold blood. And none of it makes the slightest difference.

You didn't choose her. You may think you invited her into your life, but actually she gate-crashed. She squatted for a while. You think there were reasons why you liked her. She was 'your type' – tall and slim and outdoorsy and ready for a laugh. You thought you had 'shared interests' – badminton and the hills or Schubert and film noir or origami and Japanese raw fish; whatever. But the truth is that all of that was irrelevant. She was an alien. She might have had a head like a donkey. Love is not the sum of its parts. Love is not an epi-phenomenon. Love is a phenomenon. And, dammit, she will not die. And there's absolutely nothing you can do about it.

The one thing, the only thing you can do that will do you any good, that will save your life, save your soul, is to accept all of the above. It happened. Don't fight it. What's done cannot be undone. Maybe it was fortune, maybe misfortune. It hardly matters. It merely is.

And once you have accepted that, you can begin to get better. You are no longer struggling. For one glorious pivotal moment of epiphany, you are serene. You are once more yourself. It wasn't your fault, nor was it hers. There is no guilt. You have as much right to occupy this universe as she has. It's okay.

From that day on, imperceptibly, the colour in the memory begins to fade.

Don't go back.

Meanwhile, colour belongs to the present. The present is full of the unimagined colours on the Churchillian celestial palate. Not madder-brown, but vermilion. There is a rare neurological condition, a complication of stroke, in which the unfortunate patient loses his sense of colour. He moves in a world of grey tones. You might imagine such an affliction to be less devastating than, say, the loss of movement, the loss of language, the loss through neglect of the left half of one's world. Yet those condemned to inhabit a black-and-white universe describe the horror of moving in an environment that has become sullen and inimical. In a world of colour, you know you are awake. It is not a nightmare. *Corusco, ergo sum.*

I suppose it was in a sense in search of colour that, after Nikki left, I'd called Margaret Rowallan and signed up for the N-MASS post. National Medical Adviser to the Security Services. I'd have dearly loved to clear off ASAP to the Northern

Hemisphere, but of course, it's never as simple as that. I had commitments at Middlemore Hospital in South Auckland, and then the N-MASS post had to be gelled with a consultancy (my first) in Edinburgh. The upshot was that I would commence my UK commitments on July 3rd. I eventually got out of New Zealand in June. I wanted to be on the move, and the thought of the Northern Hemisphere's summer was attractive, but it was all sham activity, ersatz hustle and bustle, a hallucination of travel, in an effort to forget. I had two weeks to kill, so I went to Iceland. Terrible idea. There's an obverse to seasonal affective disorder. The 'white nights' got me down. Iceland is a fantastic place, but the last thing you want to do is go there on your own, especially when you're on a downer. The landscape of Iceland is like the moon. I realised my mistake as soon as I got there. I fished out the dog-eared business card from my wallet with its familiar logo and its iconic jingle:

You don't get what you deserve, you get what you negotiate.

I was relieved to find there was a home number. Somewhere in Earls' Court. I tapped it out on my mobile without premeditation. Thoughtless, really. It was very late in the evening. And an hour later in London. But I had lost all perspective. Frankly, I'd lost the plot.

The phone rang out and then gave way to the click and whirr of some antiquated bedside cassette tape answering machine. There was an absurd background of didgeridoo music, to the rattle of dry bones. I was walking through spinifex in the hot red centre, under a sky of intense *lapis lazuli*. "Ah g'day. You've reached Ralph and Megan's place. After the tone…"

"Yep?"

"Ralph, it's Alastair. I need your help."

"Good as gold mate." He hung up and went back to sleep. Remorselessly I redialled the number.

"Yep?"

"Ralph. Wake up."

There was a grunt. I could hear him turning round and sitting up. Somebody next to him – Megan I suppose – was grumbling, "Tell them you're not on call."

"Ralph, this isn't easy for me." And that was certainly true. Like every other doctor, when it came to mental health, I was at heart a snob. I really despised all these people I'd seen over the years who whinged and whined because they couldn't keep it together. So life's a bitch. Why are you telling me? Get over it. D'you think you're the only one who struggles to get up in the morning? Why don't you go out for a walk and a breath of fresh air, and tell your 'personal demons' to go get stuffed? And now here was I, weeping down the phone, stunted, diminished, vulnerable.

"Ralph, I've lost it. Big time. I'm in a very deep hole. I've tried to climb out and I can't. I need help."

That was the first time in my life I'd ever said that. I wasn't aware of it at the time but, thinking of it now, I wonder if that admission might not have turned out to be the opportunity of my life, the moment when I laid myself open to the possibility, with all its risks, of leading a life for, with, and among people.

There was a momentary pause on the other end of the line.

"Where are you?"

"Keflavik."

He expressed no surprise.

"When can you get back?"

"Tomorrow?"

"Come to the Maudsley. Call me as soon as you get there."

"Are you not going to carry out a suicide risk assessment? You know? Like a 'Sad Persons Scale'?" (Hockberger and Rothstein, 1988. Sex: male. Age: <19 or >45, Depression, Previous psychiatric care, excess drug use, rational thinking loss, single, organised premeditated attempt, no life supports, suicidal ideation. Max score: 15. I scored 10.) I was teaching my grandmother to suck eggs.

"I just have. If you were going to top yourself, why would you bother making the appointment? See you tomorrow." The line went dead.

By the way, I had a slightly odd experience at the airport in Iceland. It was very busy in the terminal building. All the bars and eateries and duty-free shops were crammed with obese passengers and their outrageously oversized hand luggage. I found a gate at the end of a long corridor that wasn't being used and sat there quietly, reading a book of Icelandic sagas to pass an hour. 'There was a man named Ulf...' Then I got up and wandered back down the corridor to the shops and bars and restaurants.

Everything was shut. The terminal concourse was completely deserted. I was the last person in Iceland. I had the notion that all these vanished people had merely been extras on a film set assembled purely for my benefit.

As it turned out, I consulted Dr Ralph Parkinson, Consultant Psychiatrist at the Maudsley, four times. There was a paradox about the trajectory of this extended consult. At the start, he treated me seriously as a colleague and as a professional, but of my role as a patient he appeared to me to be quite dismissive. By the time of our fourth consultation, my status as professional had deteriorated to the level of farce. Meanwhile, with respect to my role as patient, he treated me with the utmost gravity.

Doctor-doctor consults can be fraught, because the patient can have difficulty surrendering his professional credentials and assuming a more passive role. Sitting in Parkie's office in the Maudsley, I felt as if I were a medical student and an observer, trying to remember the architecture of the psychiatric history. Presenting complaint – history of presenting complaint – past medical history – personal history...

Not that Dr Parkinson appeared to stick very closely to this pedestrian trudge. In fact he hardly seemed to direct the conversation at all. He just disappeared into the wallpaper. There was an occasional grunt. He seemed to have the knack of making a usually reticent patient quite loquacious. Now and again he would mutter a few words like a prompt to get the patient back on track. Not that he appeared to mind if the conversation strayed off-*piste*. Maybe he knew this was the area affording the greatest return – at the dangerous edge of things. It was really only towards the end of the interview that his interjections appeared to become more opinionated and proactive. He seemed more interested in one small aspect of the patient's history than was the patient himself. In fact the patient had mainly tried to skirt it. But Dr Parkinson kept returning to it, like a surgeon continually pushing on a discrete area of abdominal tenderness. At the conclusion of the interview, and abruptly, he did the trick of undercutting all the humbug with the single, agonisingly hurtful comment, thus permitting the patient for the first time to drop his guard and speak from the heart.

"So she dumped you mate. There's nothing wrong with you. It's only injured pride. Get over it. Get back to work."

I said to Ralph, "But don't I get a pill or potion?"

"You need drugs like you need a hole in the head. You like the great outdoors don't you? What is it... triathlons you do?"

"Yes."

"Go for a run. Get some exercise."

Parkinson actually made the patient laugh out loud with relief. Of course, that patient, whose fragile barricade of self-preservation he had obliterated with his succinct 'formulation', had been me. Alastair Cameron-Strange.

II

Two months later, on August 15th to be precise, I found myself
in Terminal 5 Heathrow, staring through a departure gate,
across 400 metres of terminal apron, at the squat edifice of an
ancient Boeing 747. I had a momentary flutter of stage nerves,
waiting in the wings for my cue, on the first night. Overture
and beginners. But I was only mildly apprehensive. I believe I
have a talent for brinkmanship.

After the briefing, there had been a flurry of red tape before
I could leave the operations room. A bald-headed bureaucrat
with round gold-rimmed spectacles had talked me through the
proformas.

"Who are you with?"

"Excuse me?"

"Life insurance. Prudential? Scottish Widows? Sign here."

"What is it?"

"The Official Secrets Act."

"Is this absolutely necessary?"

Apparently it was. I had signed the relevant chit and it had been whisked away expeditiously like a credit card docket in a busy restaurant. Simultaneously there had been a flurry of activity at the gate lounge entrance and an entourage surrounding a VIP had trooped in. A middle-aged man, tall, portly, deeply sunburned, looked vaguely familiar to me. He had great unkempt bushy eyebrows above a pair of restless, darting, chestnut eyes. He wore a pair of checked slacks, an open-necked shirt and, incongruously, a blue baseball cap. He might once have cut a handsome figure but he was heavy-jowled and the face was etched with signs of dissipation bordering on debauchery. His movements were rapid and he carried with him a supercharged magnetic aura and the pulsating glow of inner certainty.

He struck me immediately, even from a distance, as a man who could be very charming when things went his way. But underneath it all, he would have a vicious temper. Now he was being fussed over and briefed by a group of civil servants and he wore a fixed expression that was meant to convey intelligent interest, concern, and dynamic decisiveness. A hush had spread rapidly across the room. Chief Inspector Ronnie Slack had whispered out of the corner of his mouth to Chief Superintendent Harry Golightly, "It's the Minister." Golightly muttered, "O Goad."

"All right, Chief Superintendent?" The brown eyes were unblinking.

"Yes, thank you, sir." Golightly had coloured. "Everything under control."

"Splendid! Anything you need, back-up, support, let me know." The man from the ministry flexed his knees and stole a quick glance through binoculars on a tripod trained towards the aircraft beyond the periphery of the apron. He gave a brief tight-lipped smile and moved on. Behind him, a young

Civil Servant with the imperious demeanour of a Gauleiter surveyed the scene in a broad, sweeping glance. His eyes rested thoughtfully on Dr Ralph Parkinson. Parkinson had taken off his headphones and was staring fixedly at his blotter, drumming his fingers, waiting. The Civil Servant turned to Golightly.

"I take it Buenos Aires is happy?"

"I believe so."

"Good. Keep it that way. We've spent the better part of forty years soothing an injured *amour propre*. You know? Mending fences, building bridges. Don't cock it up, will you?"

I saw Golightly's jaw tighten. The entourage drifted away. The Chief Superintendent took a deep breath.

As soon as the Minister had left the gate lounge Parkinson got up, walked over to me, put an arm round my shoulder, and drew me to one side.

"Happy?"

"I'm fine."

"You know you're under no compulsion to do this."

"No Ralph. I need to do this."

He gave me a searching look. "I wish I could tell you more, but I can't figure them out. It's completely anachronistic. They sound like they're stuck in a time warp back in 1982. Making up slogans for the tabloids. 'Argies out. *Gotcha*!' Don't seem to know what they want. Bunch of bogans."

"Bogans?"

"Hoons. Larrikins. Out for a joyride. Fancy taking a 747 for a joyride."

"I didn't know they were still flying jumbo jets."

"Last of the fleet, I gather. Be careful out there."

Major Martin Forster gave me a thumbs-up. As usual, he had that look of mock incredulity on his face as if he had just twigged the Great Cosmic Joke. He raised an ironic, admonitory finger. I said, "Martin, I know. Check six."

At long last, I left the hubbub and descended a moving staircase, carrying a crash box, accompanied by a single uniformed police officer who was taking directions through an earpiece. Together we traversed the last long corridor, an axon extending towards the apron's periphery out of an unoccupied dendrite of the body of the terminal. We entered the last provocatively named Final Departures Lounge. What would I find when I crossed over? What scene of havoc? I quietened my mind. Consider it to be another routine consultation. You are a GP doing your rounds. Just another home visit. A rather unusual house call.

Now there was a delay. Negotiations, apparently, were excruciatingly slow. So I had a chance to review the events of the morning. It had had an inauspicious start. The single yelp of my bedside telephone might have been a hypnagogic hallucination, to cease as abruptly as it had started. I retrieved the receiver into the warmth of the duvet.

"Hello?"

"*Speedbird* this is *Super.*"

"I think you must have the wrong number." I hadn't yet learned to talk in ciphers. I hung up and went back to sleep. The phone rang out again immediately.

"Yes?"

"Dr Cameron-Strange?"

"Yes."

"It's the Metropolitan Police, sir. Stand by one."

I stood by.

"Doctor, it's Harry Golightly. This is an R23. This is not a drill." He added, rather tautologically I thought, "Stand up and put both feet on the floor." I put both feet on the floor and stood up. "We need you at Heathrow. It's a channel seven five hundred. Terminal 5. You're at No 1 Wimpole Street?" Indeed I was. I'd gone down to London to attend a conference. "There's a car with a driver waiting for you outside. Get cracking."

Now it so happens I know what a channel 7500 is. It's terminology borrowed from aviation. It's a squawk code, an emergency code you dial up on your aircraft transponder. There are three of them. 7700, 7600, and 7500. 7700 is a general distress call, a *Mayday*. Perhaps an engine failure, but it could be anything. 7600 is radio failure and loss of communication. 7500 is probably the most sinister of them all. It signifies a situation of mutiny. Somebody else has taken control of the aircraft.

"Somebody hijack a plane then?"

There was a stony and disapproving silence from the other end of the line.

"How big's the plane?"

"Do me a favour Alastair. This is an open line."

"Chipmunk or Airbus?"

"Bring your ID or they won't let you airside."

"Pissed lager-lout or the Baader Meinhof gang?"

The line was abruptly disconnected. I knew I was being a prat, but I couldn't help deflating their cloak-and-dagger pomposity. Everybody in the Committee *sine nomine* had a code name beginning with S. It was a tradition borrowed from the US Secret Service in the heady days of JFK's Camelot. Margaret Rowallan was *Sphinx,* Martin Forster was *Scimitar,* Ralph Parkinson was *Shrink.* Even the Committee's patron, His Majesty the King, was *Saxe-Coburg.* And I was *Speedbird,* because I flew light aircraft. I'd pointed out to them that this might cause no end of confusion because *Speedbird* happens to be the British Airways call sign, but the possibility of sending air traffic control into complete chaos didn't appear to bother them. I shouldn't be telling you this but I'm past caring.

Anyway I'd got up and gone to Heathrow and here I was in my Final Departures Lounge. The police officer raised a finger and absorbed himself in the message coming through his earpiece.

"You're on. Good luck, sir." He raised the Perspex cover over the electronic keypad on the wall, tapped in the code and turned a switch. The departure door slid open. I lifted the crash box and stepped out on to the tarmac. The door slid closed behind me, and I began to walk unhurriedly across the apron. It was 11.30 on an August morning, fresh and breezy. To my right, an eddy current of wind was playing havoc with a spilt bag of rubbish at the edge of a concrete underpass.

I closed my mind to the gallery behind me, the binoculars and the telephoto lenses, the press, and, for all I knew, sniper cover. Now I had left the protective shadows of the terminal and was a lone figure making my way across a deserted expanse of tarmac and windswept grass. Three hundred metres to go. I kept my pace even and unhurried. No doubt I was also being watched from the aeroplane. They would be looking for any unexpected moves.

I focused on the steps which ascended to the rear exit of the aircraft. The perspectives gradually changed until the enormous airframe loomed over me. No-man's land safely negotiated. Now to cross the barbed wire, the redoubts, the parapets, into the enemy lines.

Close up, the 747's enormous bulk was intimidating. I paused at the foot of the steps and looked back across the asphalt desert to the terminal. On schedule, conspicuous in garish orange overalls, the paramedic had commenced the traverse of no-man's land. As instructed, he was alone. He was driving a short, low-slung vehicle with a six-by-six-foot platform behind him, presumably for baggage handling. Apparently the injured patient, a man named Armitage, was not one of the walking wounded. He was no longer fit enough to make the trip on foot. Now for the swap. The injured man was to appear at the top of the steps. We were to pass one another on the courtesy stair, and there was to be no communication. I ascended the steps and kept my gaze rigidly to the fore. No sign of Mr Armitage. Was there a glitch? Now I was at the top of the stairs, on a metal grid, two metres square, twenty feet above the ground.

"Stop."

I did as I was bid.

"Put the case down."

I laid the crash box gently down at my feet.

"Open it."

I snapped open the catches and, with theatrical deliberation, pulled back the lid until it rested on its hinges.

"Step forward."

I moved towards the fuselage. Two things happened simultaneously. Abruptly an arm in a dark green windcheater shot forward, took me by the collar and pulled me indecorously into a tiny galley. My position on the platform high above the tarmac was filled by a bulky black bag, about the size of a man who teetered for a moment on dead feet and then crashed down the courtesy stair with a terrible series of heavy thuds. The crash box was retrieved, and the heavy door was pulled back into position. Now I was hermetically sealed within the quarantine of the aircraft. There was a brief impression of two men, dark-clad and in balaclavas. Then I was blindfolded.

So. This wasn't a game. These people weren't kidding.

"Walk."

The flat, regionless, monosyllabic instructions were delivered entirely without inflexion. A pair of strong hands pinned my forearms to my side, and I was pushed firmly from behind. An impression of a murmur subsided to a silence. The pitch blackness under the blindfold was absolute. But I sensed the curiosity of eyes turning to see the new arrival, rather as a theatre audience might hush to observe a dignitary taking a seat in the Royal Box. In the cabin of a jet passenger liner, with engines shut down and air conditioning turned off, the silence is as thick and as all-pervasive as a London fog. Little sounds, of a seat belt being undone, of a child asking her mother for a drink, were absorbed without any resonance into a black hole of sepulchral stillness. I rapidly developed the hyperacusis, as well as the olfactory sharpening, of the blind. The air was very stale. I tried to imagine the geography of the aircraft. We were walking down the left-hand aisle, the entire length of the aeroplane. How far had we gone? Fifty, sixty metres. The 747 was as big as a cathedral.

Abruptly I was turned to the right, and right again. A stout piece of metal jarred my right tibia, painfully. A voice behind me said, "Tell them the quack's here." The pressure on my arms relaxed.

"Grasp the rail. No funny stuff."

It was to be Business Class. At least there might be room to work.

"Up."

The flat voice faded to inaudibility behind me, and I ascended the stairway alone. It crossed my mind that I might have to leave, hurriedly, in smoke, fire, or darkness. I counted the steps. My last footfall passed through a phantom step and I stumbled, saving myself by tightening my grip on the rail.

"*Hee Hee Hee!*" A high-pitched, cat-like shriek. I awaited my next cue. Keeping a hand on the rail to steady myself, I tried to remember the layout of the upper deck of a 747. Stairway behind; there would be a recess for luggage on my right. Panelling straight ahead, the side wall, perhaps, of a toilet. Obliquely ahead to the left would be a working area for cabin crew, with more luggage space, and a kitchen galley. The Business Class cabin lay behind my left shoulder and, beyond it, the flight deck. I let go of the handrail and groped my way vaguely to the left, reaching a hand behind my head toward the knotted bandana.

"Leave the blindfold."

Now I was turned further to the left and propelled forward by a dull thud between the shoulder blades. I struggled to retain my sense of the geography of the plane. A curtain brushed across my head and neck and fell away behind me.

"Take off your shoes."

Another arid, monotonous soundbite. These brief, featureless instructions were delivered as a matter of policy. Even when the blindfold came off, as presumably it must, I would be run blinkered, on a tight rein. I pinned the heel of my left shoe with the toe of my right and slipped my stockinged foot free. Then I repeated the manoeuvre on the other foot. Tricky for an erect, unsupported blind man. I lurched to the left.

"*Hee Hee Hee!*"

"Shut up, James."

Silence. Now I was being inspected. Sensory deprivation and velvety blackness. Vague flutterings of panic, still a way off, were nonetheless beginning to encroach. I was a butterfly awaiting execution by camphor at the hands of an entomologist. I tried to keep relaxed, my extra-sensory antennae reaching out into the darkness. What did I know about hostage situations, the captor–captive relationship? It was important to introduce some element of human warmth, to have your captors realise that you, like them, were flesh and blood. Then, once the shooting started, if it came down to the wire, they might just hesitate before despatching you to kingdom come. And don't provoke them. Don't be a pain in the neck. Avoid confrontation. Be conciliatory. Keep the temperature down. Do whatever you have to do to keep yourself, and your loved ones, alive. And above all, deep down, beneath all the equanimity and the calm reasoning, retain a sense of self. Don't start to believe in the relationship you are striving to forge. It was fatal to fall in love with your jailer. That type of countertransference even had a name, an ICD coding. What was it again? It would come to me. Meantime, why not start forging a relationship?

"I am Dr Alastair Cameron-Strange. I am an emergency—"

"Shut your face."

The Stockholm Syndrome. That was it.

The sudden grasp of gloved hands on my neck and shoulders made me flinch. I was methodically and expertly searched. The search, of the axillae, the waistline, the groins, was vigorous and uncompromising. It ended at the ankles and feet. I sensed my searcher withdrawing and signifying that the search had been clean.

"Listen to your instructions very carefully." The low-pitched voice was so close to my ear it was like an auditory hallucination generated inside my head. There were no introductions and absolutely no pleasantries.

"One of my men has been wounded. He has a stab wound to his chest. Currently he is being tended by a member of the cabin crew. In a moment you will be taken to him. You will examine the wound. You will carry out any related examination that you consider necessary. You will not address the patient. You will not converse with the cabin crew. Your sole remit is to undertake the examination and report your findings to me."

I found myself struggling to conceal an inappropriate sense of mirth. Something farcical had occurred to me. I was back in the Royal Melbourne doing short cases for the Fellowship exam. "Examine this patient's respiratory system." The wise old men of the College were far more intimidating than this! I bit my lip. I heard the flick of the switchblade and felt its cold sharp steel against my thyroid cartilage, my trachea.

"Bastard finks vis is funny. Bastard finks vis is a *joke!*"

An asthmatic wheeze and the acrid burnt tea-leaf stench of cannabinoids. The inane, hysterical feline shriek had been replaced by a cold rage.

"Why don't I make that stupid smile on your face permanent? Eh? Ear to ear. Then" – there was a gloat in his voice – "I'll set Johnnie on you."

Who was Johnnie?

"That's enough, James. Stop making the doctor nervous. We don't want him to develop a tremor, do we?"

The blade was reluctantly withdrawn.

"You understand your instructions?"

I shook my head. "I need to be able to take a history. I need to talk."

"The conditions are non-negotiable."

There was the hint of an accent. Parkinson had said these people were English. Certainly, the crazy youth with the flick knife who answered to the name of James was English. He might have come off any slummy estate in any number of deprived neighbourhoods. Merry England! A band of stout yeomen. Crispin Crispian, and the fields of Agincourt gone mad. Vile men gentling their condition. We few, we happy few. 1966 and all that. Yet this other voice, the voice of the man apparently in command, this had not been an English voice. There was a lilt.

Irish. Could it be the old trouble?

"All right. My men are currently inspecting your doctor's bag. If it contains no weapons, booby traps, or surveillance devices, it will shortly be returned to you. Meantime, you may see your patient."

"That would be fine."

I had a sense of my captor making an appraising double-take. There was no further comment. I was pushed past the final curtain, into the forward section of the upper deck.

"Remember. No talking." The blindfold was removed.

I blinked and let my eyes grow accustomed to the monochromatic gloom of the cabin. There was no artificial

24

light. What little illumination there was came from the parsimonious oblong cabin windows. The twilight enhanced the scene's hallucinatory quality.

There were three other people in the cabin. Ahead, the door to the flight deck was closed. Before it, a tall and well-built individual in paramilitary gear stood erect with his feet slightly apart and his hands behind his back. I gave him a casual glance. Black, thick, woollen-knit balaclava. A dark green knitted jumper with suede reinforcement at shoulders and elbows. There was a mud-coloured waist belt worn over the jumper. It held on its right side a substantial chamois holster containing a pistol. The rough serge trousers were the same mud colour, tapering to a pair of polished black leather boots. The man stood fixed, immobile, staring rigidly into the middle distance.

The patient occupied seat 19A. On him, the balaclava was a featureless black cowl. He was wearing an oxygen mask attached by plastic tubing to a short cylinder at his feet. Behind the slits of the balaclava, the eyes stared fixedly towards the ceiling as if gazing at a vision. This man had entered the zone of the near-dead. He was walking in a sunlit meadow, drowsy with the heavy fragrance of summer flowers, drifting towards the happy, rippling laughter of beckoning children.

The window seat was positioned by an exit whose passageway afforded plenty of legroom. The seat was in the semi-recumbent position. The man wore the same uniform as the guard to the flight deck, but the jumper, bloodstained, had been cut away, and its remnants lay on the neighbouring seat. The shirt had been unbuttoned but not removed. The cabin crew was kneeling obliquely in front of the patient, engaged in taking his blood pressure with a portable sphygmomanometer, which she had extracted from a medical kit open on the floor beside her. She was a tall slim woman in her late twenties, with black hair in a pageboy cut. She was wearing a protective bib over the black and red hostess uniform as if she were engaged in serving the passengers coffee. She had applied the blood pressure cuff to the patient's right arm and was now pumping the cuff up. She applied the diaphragm of a stethoscope to the patient's right antecubital fossa, and gently released the pressure in the cuff. I watched the pointer on the dial of the manometer. It slid steadily under 100 mmHg and, at about 90, began to pulse almost imperceptibly at a rate of about 130 beats a minute. The cabin crew allowed the cuff completely to deflate. She tore its Velcro binding loose and deftly pushed the stethoscope's earpieces behind her neck. Her gaze shifted away from the patient and drifted up towards me. Our eyes met. Hers were big, frightened, tawny orbs. She would have been an attractive woman if the situation had not drained all the blood from her face. For a second, I was reminded of that painting by Edvard Munch, *The Scream*. I gave her as warm a smile as I could and nodded to show I'd taken in the BP reading.

"Who is it?" It was the questioning tone of a blind man. The voice, West Country, maybe Welsh, was remote and piping. Best get on.

I moved towards the exit door so that I was directly in front of the wounded man, registering his condition in a single comprehensive gaze. The crew member moved out of the way. On the armrest by the window, I found the control for the overhead reading light and switched it on. The man's frame splayed abjectly. The eyes flickered away from whatever they strove to see, heavy, glazed, and hooded. He was in deep trouble. I leaned forward to take off the balaclava.

"Don't touch that."

I was being watched. My invigilator had taken up a position aft, just within the aisle curtain. He, too, was in paramilitary uniform, and masked. Like clones, I thought.

Their relentless restrictions were beginning to irritate me. I quietened my mind and forced myself to trudge prosaically through the conventional format of a respiratory exam. I knelt by my patient. He was just a youth, a skinny scrap of a lad. I must try to establish a relationship, some sort of tenuous rapport with him. I reached out. The eyelids flickered. There is a final commonality about all conscious patients who are decompensating. They share a look of apprehension that even a black balaclava cannot disguise. It is the look of an injured animal sensing something slipping away. He focused lazily on me. I gave him a reticent half-smile with closed lips. The eyes closed in a gesture of acquiescence.

Hands. They were limp, unresisting, grey, cold, and clammy. I glanced at the blue pigment which dully stained the bloodless epidermis across the metacarpophalangeal joints. I am a keen student of tattoos. The knuckles of the right hand said *IRA*. Hmm. Maybe it *was* the old trouble. Funny tatt, though, for a Welshman. The palm was callused, and the nail folds were embedded with dirt. The radial pulse was rapid and thready. The right little finger and half of the fifth metacarpal were missing. Old traumatic amputation. Maybe an industrial injury. Perhaps he'd stuck his hand into a running engine. Something like that.

Eyes. I gently pulled down the right lower lid margin and examined the pallid conjunctival reflections. This time the eyes were preoccupied and inward-looking. The orbs of the pupils were dilated.

Neck. The jugular venous pulse was not visible. There were no palpable nodes. At the sternal notch, the trachea was deviated to the patient's right.

Precordium. Look. Feel. Percuss. Auscultate. The respiratory rate was just short of forty breaths per minute, shallow, ineffectual. A Gamgee dressing had been applied across the area of the patient's left clavicle. I peeled back an edge of surgical tape and glanced beneath. There was a single innocuous-looking stab wound, less than a centimetre in width. Immediately inferior to the dressing, at the second intercostal space and almost exactly in the midclavicular line, a wide-bore angiocath had been inserted into the pleural space. The trocar had been removed, and the cannula had been secured with a piece of surgical tape. The cabin crew must have inserted it. She must have some medical training. She had bought the patient some time.

The heart's apex beat was impalpable. The movement of the left side of the chest failed to coordinate with the patient's respiratory effort. Flail chest. There was a sensation of crepitation beneath the examining fingers. Air trapped in the subcutaneous tissue.

The rest of the examination was academic. I spread my left hand across the left chest and percussed my middle finger. The percussion note was hyper-resonant. I glanced over my shoulder at the cabin crew. I ignored my captor.

"Borrow your tubes?" My voice sounded overly loud in the cabin. There was no recrimination. She unleashed the stethoscope from around her neck and handed it over.

No air entry on the left.

I had broken silence and gotten away with it. I would try again. I said softly to the patient, "Going to sit you up now." The crew member eased forward and carefully supported the patient's left shoulder. I pulled the shirt up from the waistline and examined the pale, scrawny back. Then we eased him back in a coordinated movement. I took the pulse again, this time at the left wrist. It fluttered ineffectually like a sparrow's broken wing. The left hand was even more mangled than the right. The fifth metacarpal shaft and neck were angulated and deformed by old multiple boxer's fractures. It looked as if the patient had a temper and a vicious left hook. The index finger and second metacarpal had gone in another traumatic amputation. This guy had to be accident-pone. The tattooed knuckles on this side said *DIE*, like a scud missile with intimidating graffiti on its warhead. I laid the hand down and smiled at the woman. I was very impressed by her. I guessed she was a trained nurse. She must have relinquished the calling in favour of something apparently more glamorous. Had it been worth it? I stood up.

"I'm done."

"And?"

"Tension haemopneumothorax. I wonder if you could ask the flight crew to release the emergency oxygen supply on the upper deck. We'd better save that oxygen cylinder for the evacuation. And I need my crash box now, please. We can put the drain in here. It should improve his vitals, although I think he's lost a lot of blood. Then we can get him off and to one of the London West End hospitals. Maybe the Hammersmith. The paramedics will know best."

"No."

"Excuse me?"

"Nobody leaves the aircraft."

We stared stolidly at one another. Impasse. Take the initiative.

"Shall we step away from the patient? Would it be possible to step out for a moment?"

Risk it. I slid the aisle curtain to one side and carefully counted six steps towards the rear galley at the head of the stairway. I felt the eyes of my captor boring into the back of my head. How far dare I impose my presence on the scene? Don't push your luck. You may have established some kind of professional high ground, but you're not indispensable.

I stopped, turned, and waited. The eyes behind the balaclava watched me as a leopard might watch a gazelle. The hooded man shrugged indifferently and sauntered unhurriedly down the aisle.

"Yes? What is it?"

"The man is dying. I don't know what this is all about. I'm a doctor, not a policeman. I have no hidden agenda. I can probably ensure your colleague's survival if you stop getting in the way." I thought to myself, I shouldn't provoke him, but you know what? I really don't care. I despise these people.

In the half-light, I felt as if I were looking into the eyes of a panther.

"I thought they'd send in a professor in a three-piece suit. What stone did they find *you* under?" Then he relented fractionally. "What do you need?"

"As I said, my kit, and the oxygen. And I need the freedom to work. I need the woman to assist me. I need to be able to talk to her, and to the patient." I held up my hands, palms outwards. "I'm unarmed. I've no ulterior motive. I'm not army. I'm not security." (A small voice inside my head raised a tiny question mark over this last observation.) "I'm afraid you are just going to have to trust me."

I watched the man in the balaclava weighing it up.

"All right, mister. I'll cut you some slack. But don't call it trust. You may be a doctor. But you are also something else. I can smell it. One step out of line, and the only person getting off this aircraft will be you. In a big black bag."

He allowed the message to sink in.

"Understand?"

I said cheerfully, "That's fine."

"I'll organise the oxygen."

"Thanks. Could you send the crew member back? I need to brief her."

"Don't push it."

I stepped into the kitchen galley at the head of the stairwell and washed my hands in a tiny sink. I took a deep breath and let out a prolonged expiration through pursed lips. I searched vaguely for a towel. She slipped round the corner into the galley beside me, glanced at my dripping hands, retrieved a paper towel from the dispenser on the wall, and handed it to me.

"*Gracias.*"

"You're welcome."

I dried my hands and held out my right. "Alastair."

"Suzanna Fergusson."

"Pleased to meet you."

She laughed involuntarily at the incongruity of the exchanged courtesies. Her laugh had a nervous edge, threatening to spill over into tearfulness. The colour was returning to her face. It was a striking face with clear-cut even features, quick eyes and full lips, a face which reminded me of a stroll down the broad boulevard of the Avenue of the 9th of July and of the tall, haughty, beautiful Latin girls in blue jeans and summer tops with designer labels. At street corners, sad young men in white shirts sat under trees and played poignant tangos on decrepit bandoneóns. This girl might have been born on an Argentinian estancia. Yet this was not the whole story. For now, I sensed the flood of pent-up emotion, the sheer relief at being able to converse with (I hope) a perfectly normal stranger after the hours of fear, coping with the menace, the doubt, the intimidation, the not-knowing. Her hand trembled slightly as she brushed a tear away from her eye.

I said, "You're English, aren't you? I thought I might have to resurrect my Spanish. It's a bit rusty."

"Half and half. My mum's from London, but my dad's Argentinean."

It occurred to me that there was some history about Fergussons in Argentina that I'd forgotten about. "Great job with the angio-catheter. That took nerve."

31

The short, hard-edged laugh again. "I had to persuade them all I wasn't trying to kill him. I hope I got it right."

"Well, it's a self-fulfilling prophecy. If he didn't have a pneumothorax before you did it, he sure as hell has one now."

"Oh God. You don't think…"

"Just kidding. Anyway, he's still tensioning, and I think we'd better try something a little more definitive. What the hell happened to him anyway?"

She glanced cautiously over her shoulder and in the direction of the flight deck. There was no one within earshot. "I'm not sure. I think one of the passengers decided to *have a go* with a Swiss army knife or something."

"He's just a kid. Do we know his name?"

"I heard one of the others call him *Taff*."

"Who are these people anyway? What do they want?"

"Search me. All I can tell you is they broke into the flight deck about an hour from Paris. They confiscated everybody's devices, like phones and stuff, and herded everybody down into Economy."

"How many?"

"I don't know. I haven't been able to go downstairs. One other man came up and spent some time on the flight deck. The one they call Johnnie."

"What was he like?"

She shivered. "Hellish."

"And are the pilots all right? Are they still on the flight deck? So we'll use a thirty-two French thoracostomy tube with an underwater seal drainage system, if you don't mind helping me." I flashed a brief warning with my eyes. She turned casually. The man under the black cowl had returned.

"Hurry up. We're waiting."

Now the crash box was sitting open by the exit door at 19A. The emergency oxygen supply had been released and a series of orange face masks suspended on transparent umbilical cords dangled from overhead like sea anemones. I grasped the mask overhanging 19A and pulled. The flow of oxygen kicked in with a soft hiss. Here was another opportunity to advance ground, to whittle away at the barriers of impersonality and anonymity. I called over my shoulder, "The balaclava needs to come off. Otherwise we won't get a good seal for the oxygen mask."

"I told you already. Don't touch that."

"Give us a break. I can't be doing with this keyhole medicine." I reached a hand out.

"Touch that and you are dead meat."

I don't know what would have happened if the boy named Taff had not defused the situation. He reached up a limp hand and in a single gesture pulled both the old oxygen mask, the one attached to the cylinder, and the balaclava off his face.

"There you go, Doc." It was whispered voicelessly in a single expiration. He had a sharp-nosed, weasel face, pallid and acneiform under a shaven head.

I stretched the fresh mask's elastic cord over the clammy scalp. Our overseer muttered a single flat obscenity. He leaned over the seat. "You tell him nothing, Taff. You hear? *Nothing!*"

There was an inarticulate mutter. I said, "He's past caring." I switched off the portable cylinder's precious oxygen supply, turned to the crash box and began to lay out the items of equipment I needed. I cleared away the debris from the neighbouring seat, 19B, and created a workbench for a bulky light green paper parcel enclosed in cream tape whose oblique black stripes indicated the content had been adequately autoclaved. I opened the parcel without touching anything inside. Thoracostomy set. The overseer watched with flickering eyes.

Without prompting, Suzanna Fergusson repeated the vital signs. She slipped a pulse oximeter on the patient's left middle finger while I busied myself inserting a drip into the back of the right hand.

"Pulse is 125. BP 90/60. Resps thirty-eight. Oxygen sats…" She glanced at the probe. "No signal."

"He's probably too shut down. We'll give him some volume."

She repositioned the jaws of the probe on the patient's finger. I glanced across at her.

"You're a professional. Doctor or nurse?"

"Staff nurse. ICU trained. But it's been a while."

"It's a bit like riding a bike though, isn't it?" I secured the drip with tape, and selected a litre of colloid from the crash box. "D'you want to hook that up?" She did so. I snapped open a vial of local anaesthetic and drew five mls into a syringe.

"Where can we hang that colloid?"

She improvised. There are no overhead lockers in Business Class. She fashioned a cradle out of surgical tape and secured the bag as high up on the wall above the side window as she could.

I glanced at my watch. Just approaching 1 pm. Where had the morning gone? It occurred to me that up and down the country, in the TV and radio stations, the news bulletins would be going out. The story, which in the early hours had been a *shirt-tail* based on a rumour, would have advanced up the rankings and developed into a full-blown front page splash. From all over the country, and beyond, the media men and women would have converged on the environs of Slough and West Drayton, wandering the terminal corridors and scouring the airport perimeter for the best view, the best shot. The authorities would be endlessly harangued for information and, if it were not forthcoming, it would be replaced by speculation. What sort of people hijack an aircraft? Where would they have come from? Syria? Libya? Afghanistan? Iraq? But the

34

men in balaclavas just didn't fit the profile. What about the Argentinian connection? Something to do with the Malvinas – the Falklands? But why would they choose to hijack their own national airline?

Then there was that Irish accent. But this was not the style of even the most radical of the paramilitary groups, on either side. What else? Could it be some form of malignant private enterprise, and if so, what did they want? The pundits, the armchair terrorism experts, and the professors of international relations would have been retrieved from their cloistered Oxbridge colleges and placed under the arc lights of the TV studios. The security people, the ones who had been in this situation before, would have quelled their own irritation and resolved to work with, and not against, the media. One stand-off on its own would be enough of a day's work. Meantime here was I, occupying the eye of the hurricane, but I was completely in the dark.

I picked up the syringe of local anaesthetic and pulled the patient's bloodstained shirt as far clear of the ribcage as I could. On the left side, I palpated the fifth interspace at the anterior axillary line. I cleansed the area with an alcohol swab and said in a soft voice, "Taff, I'm going to pop a little tube in here which will make your breathing much easier."

"Yessir." He was clearly used to taking instruction. So much for informed consent.

"Wee prick now."

I pushed the twenty-two gauge hypodermic under the epidermis and raised a bleb of skin. Then I directed the needle down on to the periosteum of the sixth rib and fanned the lignocaine generously across the proposed incision site. My patient didn't flinch. I withdrew the needle and massaged the puncture site with the alcohol swab. I looked round for somewhere to dispose of the used sharp. Suzanna held out her hand, and I offered her the syringe, plunger foremost. She had improvised a sharps bin out of polystyrene cups. She said, "What size of gloves do you take?"

"Seven and a half. I'll just wash my hands again." I got up and walked back down to the rear galley. This time I was not challenged. At the sink I washed my hands as thoroughly as I could using dishwashing liquid. I dried them again with a paper towel. I couldn't be too precious about surgical asepsis in this environment. I went back to the improvised operating theatre, holding up my hands, relaxed, in front of me. She had peeled apart the sterile wrapping of the latex gloves. I grasped the infolded proximal end of the left-hand glove with my right hand and slipped it on. Then I curled the gloved fingers of the left hand under the proximal fold of the right-hand glove and pulled it well over my wrist.

A glance at the pulse oximeter. The pulse rate was 128 beats per minute, and the haemoglobin oxygen saturation was low at 83%. *Get a move on.* I glanced at the opened thoracostomy set on seat 19B. Suzanna had anticipated me and filled two tiny silver galley pots with the toffee-coloured povidone-iodine solution. I folded a gauze swab within the jaws of a long steel clip and saturated it in solution.

"Cold and wet."

This time, the patient did flinch against the chill of the liquid.

"Sorry."

Our overseer was nowhere in evidence. Maybe he didn't like the sight of blood. I took a chance and said to the boy named Taff, "You're British army, aren't you?"

There was a snort. "Aye. AWOL."

How could he have passed the army medical with hands like these? Still, he could serve as cannon fodder. After all, he still had a trigger finger. Maybe I was doing him an injustice. He might have sustained all these injuries on active service.

I cleaned the area twice, and then surrounded the operating site with a series of sterile green drapes folded into triangles. The glare of the overhead reading light fell to the right of my planned incision site. I glanced up at it and frowned. Suzanna reached a hand up. "I'm afraid I can't redirect the beam."

"No worries."

She switched 19B's light on, with marginal improvement. I peeled away the wrapping of a size eleven scalpel and slid the blade on to the scalpel handle. It snapped into position. As an afterthought I glanced at the crash box. "Any goggles or visors in there?" She rummaged and found a stout pair of Perspex safety spectacles. She secured the frame round my ears and pushed the lenses firmly across the bridge of my nose. "D'you want a mask?"

"Nah. All set?"

I made a generous incision just above and parallel to the sixth rib. The anaesthetic had taken effect. I collected the small amount of bleeding with a gauze swab. Then I blunt-dissected down to the pleura.

"All right, Taff?"

Then from the thoracostomy set I selected the biggest, bluntest clip I could find. I held its handles in the fist of my right hand and positioned my left hand distally on the clip to act as a guard. I inserted the clip into the surgical wound and down onto the pleura just above the sixth rib.

"Some pressure, now."

I pushed, hard, and without inhibition. Several things happened at once. The characteristic deflation *pop* of the punctured pleura could be both heard and felt. Taff's startle reaction came simultaneous with a great *whoosh* of released blood under pressure. I was glad to have glasses on. The lenses were now speckled in bright red. I insinuated my left index finger into the surgical wound and located the hole I had made

37

in the pleura. I removed the clip and mechanically widened the gap with a twisting motion of my finger.

"Thoracostomy tube next."

"Size?"

"Thirty-two, French."

She withdrew the long plastic holder, snapped open its end, and carefully discharged its content onto the thoracostomy pack so that it would not roll off on to the floor. I picked it up and took it apart, removing the trocar completely from its cannula. Then I grasped the cannula at its most distal aperture using the same clip I'd used to puncture the pleura. With my left hand, I relocated the hole I had made. Now I insinuated the thoracostomy cannula through into the pleural space. I released the clip and directed the tube upwards, medially, and slightly backwards towards the site of the lung apex. It immediately filled with blood, which started to discharge on to the sterile drapes. Their green colour darkened. I used the clip again to clamp the tube off at its proximal end.

"Underwater seal drain."

She pulled off the plastic guard over the sterile tip of the tubing and passed it to me. I said, "Shake in time with me!" She gave a single involuntary yelp of laughter.

"Damn! Doesn't fit. There must be an adaptor." I glanced in the thoracostomy set and found the small length of threaded plastic tubing. I secured it within the proximal end of the chest drain. Now the tubing of the seal fitted, snug.

"Suture, please."

"Curved or straight needle?"

"Straight. '0' silk, if there is any."

She separated the cellophane from the paper of the outer wrapping, and I grasped the sterile inner packaging, tore it open, and withdrew the tough thick black silk thread on its atraumatic needle. The silk was enfolded in a series of hairpin bends, and I ran it through between my gloved finger and thumb to obliterate the silk's 'memory'. Then I fashioned a purse-string suture around the thoracostomy tube at the incision site and secured it with a one-handed surgeon's knot. Suzanna had repositioned the big three-litre reservoir of the underwater seal drainage system on the floor of the cabin.

"Moment of truth now." I released the clip.

A torrent of fresh red blood cascaded through the system of tubes, sending billowing clouds of redness into the reservoir. The fluid level in the bottle began to rise rapidly.

"Hmm."

Now Suzanna was using scissors to fashion strips of broad white surgical tape into T-shapes. I took off my gloves – latex gloves and surgical tape usually end up in a glorious fankle – and taped the thoracostomy tube firmly around the sutured incision site. I removed the temporising angiocath from the second intercostal space, fished in the crash box, found a bandaid, and covered the puncture wound. I left the Gamgee over the original stab wound undisturbed. Now the whole of the left side of the chest was a mass of dressings and surgical tape. The proximal end of the thoracostomy tube stood proud of the bandages, and the blood still flowed freely into the reservoir. The pulse oximeter now read saturations of 87% – better, but not by much. I glanced at the flimsy oxygen mask and its tubing hanging down from the ceiling. How much oxygen did these masks supply? What was the flow rate? Probably only two or three litres a minute. They would do well to deliver 30%. Could I jury-rig a couple of them together and increase the flow? I looked down at the reservoir. It had already drained over a litre of blood. If there had been a big bleed, and if the thoracostomy tube was relieving the tamponade effect of the enclosed pleural space, then it was conceivable that the whole intervention could do more harm than good.

Suzanna read my thoughts. She slipped the blood pressure cuff back on the right arm.

"Ninety-nine systolic."

"He's shocked."

"So what now?"

I shrugged. "I guess we play the numbers game. If we drain a litre and a half and it keeps going, he needs a thoracotomy. Can't do that on a 747. He needs to go to hospital. How much fluid's he had? A litre. Give him another." I glanced forwards towards the flight deck, and then aft towards the galley at the stairhead. "Where have our jailors gone? Stay here."

I got up and walked to the back of the cabin. The Irishman and the crazed youth with the flick knife were standing at the galley entrance, sipping hot coffee from polystyrene cups and conducting a conversation in low tones. They stopped talking on my approach. The Irishman glanced at me indifferently.

"Your friend needs to go to hospital. He needs an operation. Will you arrange an ambulance, please?"

"No."

"He's bleeding out. He's going to die."

"It's your job to fix him."

"I've bought him some time. That's all I can do."

"He takes his chances."

"Then at least let me organise a blood transfusion. We need to send a blood sample to a blood bank in one of the London hospitals. Without that, he really has no chance."

"A moment."

Seize the initiative! I said, "I'll get the sample." I turned and walked back to the patient without waiting for acknowledgement or confirmation. The Irishman had lifted a telephone from its bracket on the wall and was now speaking rapidly into it. Who was he talking to? Presumably, a compatriot holding the fort downstairs. Had there been the suspicion of a note of deference in the tone of the man speaking down the telephone? Who was calling the shots?

Suzanna was kneeling by the crash box, scribbling in a notebook. I asked, "Keeping a record?"

"Something like that."

"That's very conscientious." I gathered the remaining unused equipment of the thoracostomy set within its sterile packaging and turned to replace it in the crash box. I fished out a syringe, a needle, and a tourniquet. We were kneeling with our backs to the patient, and I began to whisper rapidly.

"We're going to cross-match Taff. If they buy into this, we'll try to persuade them to make you the courier. Six bags would be reasonable. Send them back with a paramedic. Don't get back on the plane. You've done enough. Tell them as much as you can about the set-up here. I've counted six of them – three downstairs, three up here, not counting Taff. There may be more. Young. Inexperienced, I'd say. Funny mix – mostly local. Don't seem to know what they want."

I glanced round at the patient. He was lying still with his eyes closed, surely in no condition to eavesdrop on a whispered conversation. I turned back to Suzanna.

"Taff's army. I'm sure of it. They might like to follow up on that. What else? Armoury – all of them armed. Mix of pistols and semi-automatic weapons. One other thing. The plane's not wired or booby-trapped, so far as I can see. The army was kind of nervous about that."

"For a doctor, you're very observant."

I took the blood and ostentatiously held up the sample in its pink-topped bottle. I called down the aisle, "I've got the specimen! I suggest Suzanna ship it out. She can explain what's needed."

"No. Write any instructions down, and show me. No funny business. We will send a child. As a gesture of goodwill."

I labelled the sample. I said to Suzanna, "Borrow a sheet of paper from your notebook?" She ripped a page out and handed it over. I scribbled away. I looked up and asked blandly, "The patient's date of birth?"

"What?"

I said, ingenuously, disingenuously, "The lab will not process an unlabelled specimen."

The barrel of a pistol was being pushed into my face. I was sailing too close to the wind. "I'm running out of patience, mister. Show me what you've written."

He laughed mirthlessly. "I can't read your writing."

The letter was handed back, and I placed it along with the sample in a plastic bag. "There." The captor took it and went off, presumably to select a courier. Suzanna said, "What now?"

"We wait."

I glanced out of the cabin window at an uninspiring prospect of disused tow trucks, refuse bins, and asphalt. It had become dull and overcast. Jaundiced artificial lights were coming on haphazardly in the only wing of the terminal building that could be seen from here. I wondered what was happening around us. Had the hijackers made any demands? Was Parkinson making any headway?

I glanced sequentially at the underwater seal drain, the intravenous line, and the patient. The thoracostomy set had drained nearly two and a half litres, and we were into our fourth litre of IV replacement. Under the cabin's artificial lights, the patient was growing less substantial, sprawled on the reclining seat like a discarded effigy. If only the bleeding would stop! I wondered what artery had been hit. Probably an intercostal, maybe the internal mammary. When the cross-matched blood arrived, we could play catch-up resuscitation, but if we couldn't plug the hole, we were throwing good money after bad. I could try tamponading the bleeding by spigotting the thoracostomy

42

tube, but the patient would probably tension again. We were running out of options. Oh, well!

I wondered what was going on inside the flight deck. The sentinel at the door had displayed all the stoic immobility of a guardsman outside Buckingham Palace. I called up, "Hey mister, does anybody else, passengers or crew, require medical assistance? Do you want me to look at anybody else while I'm here?"

The man averted his gaze.

"There must be some other patients."

He said, with finality, "There are no other patients." It was a Scottish accent, smoky and heavily industrialised. A thought occurred to me: 'There once was a Scotsman, an Englishman, an Irishman, and a Welshman...' These people were a joke!

There followed a long delay. I could picture a police car with blue lights flashing and siren blaring, going back into London with the blood specimen, along the Great West Road, running into a tailback on Ellesmere Road in Chiswick, the driver cursing the cars in the queue ahead that doggedly refused to pull over. At the Hogarth Roundabout, traffic would be converging from all sides like army corporals in white singlets doing synchronised headsprings off a box at the Royal Tournament. Eventually, they would get to West Cromwell Road and inch their way through Hammersmith. Next up, there would inevitably be an administrative delay at the hospital's blood bank. The documentation for a blood transfusion has to be meticulous. A major transfusion reaction, giving the wrong patient the wrong blood bag, is what hospitals call a *Never Event*. It just shouldn't happen. Somebody at the blood bank would shake his head and say, "We're just not doing this."

Then, Parkinson would need to get on the phone. If he thought negotiating with a bunch of terrorists was difficult... If he had any sense, he would enlist the help of that bruiser of a government minister. A few caustic words from him, and everybody would be touching their caps. Then the police car with the lights and music would have to make the return journey through traffic that would be even heavier.

Or something like that. I changed Taff's drip bag and put up another litre of colloid. I said to Suzanna, "Fancy a coffee?" She made to get up. I said, "No. Let me. How do you have it?"

"Milk, no sugar."

I went back to the kitchen galley and this time I was observed but unmolested. I fixed the drinks in plastic cups and took them back. She reached up. "Thanks."

I glanced out the window. It was getting dusky. I said, "Sorry they wouldn't let you off the plane, Suzanna. You've done a shift and a half. You're on overtime."

"It doesn't matter. And thank you. I can't tell you how glad I am you're here." There was a tremor in her voice. "I mean, I can't tell you what it means to me..."

"Shoosh already. And likewise. I feel the same about you."

The blood arrived; six units in a bulky, thick white polystyrene chiller. I inserted a second line into the patient's left ante-cubital fossa while Suzanna primed a giving set. Automatically, we had checked the data on the bag. Group O negative – a universal donor, not a universal recipient. The batch number. The expiry date. All in order. We had smiled at the intimacy of the hospital ritual.

"How long were you in ICU?"

"About three years, before I came into this."

"A good move? All that travel and duty-free eau de cologne."

She laughed. "I thought so until now."

We exchanged our potted life histories. I described the Australasian medical scene with some nostalgia. She had also spent time in the southern seas. I learned from her that the Qantas cabin crew referred to the return Sydney-Auckland business commuter flight as a *double-banger*; that two crew members passing on the aisle were required by regulation to pass one another back-to-back and not facing one another – a behaviour known as *fronting*; and that, at the end of the flight, all the liquor that had been opened, known as *ullage*, was discarded down the sink. With such inconsequential discourse, you delineate a personality and begin to construct a friendship.

But we were losing, at the rate of about half a litre of blood per hour. We could replace it with the six cross-matched units and, presumably, cross-match again, but by the time we had replaced the patient's entire blood volume, we would be running into coagulation problems, and the bleeding could only get worse. I debated whether to insert a bladder catheter and monitor the urinary output, but such an intervention was only useful if it predicated therapeutic options. No. It was coming down to the wire. I went back down to the rear galley and addressed my captor without preamble.

"I'm afraid we've run out of options. Either we get Taff to an operating theatre, or he won't last the night."

"Operate here."

"That's impossible. We have no facilities, either anaesthetic or surgical. He would die with the incision. He would——"

The rest was obliterated in a deafening crash and the residual splinter of cascading crockery. The Irishman had punched a hole through the galley's panelling. I thought, 'This man is on a very short fuse. He is losing control in every way. And he knows it.' I retreated to patient and nurse, my own territory.

"How's he doing?"

But I didn't need to ask. I noted the muddy pallor, the frosty sweat. Suzanna looked up. Our eyes met. She slowly shook her head.

From beneath, I could hear the deep-seated rumble of somebody heavy-footed mounting the stairs. There was a brief and irate tirade delivered at the stairhead. A slap abruptly terminated the inane shriek of the feral James, who started sobbing, and blurted, "I'm sorry, Johnnie."

Suzanna's focus shifted. I looked round. I straightened myself slowly. I found myself facing a new captor, this time unconcealed. The man named Johnnie was indeed, as Suzanna had suggested, a man from hell. He was only of middle height, and yet he seemed custom-built as an instrument of hand-to-hand mortal combat. He wore a plain white sleeveless vest, dark trousers, and sneakers. Even in repose, the upper body and lower limb musculature threatened to burst through his clothes. The tattoos bilaterally over the deltoids were brief, explicit, and obscene. From his right hand, bizarrely, hung a cricket bat into whose distal willow segments had been impaled a cluster of stout bristling nail heads. The hair was fair and cut right back into the scalp. There was nothing jokey about the face. The overall impression was of an extremely disagreeable, unpredictable and dangerous psychopath. Yet the sullen grey eyes did not lack intelligence.

Our exchange couldn't have lasted more than half a minute. Over the years, I've come to recognise occasions in my life when a cup offered to me may not be suffered to pass from my lips. Here it was again. Maybe not this time. But sooner or later. Somehow, somewhere, the man named Johnnie would not be avoided.

"If anything goes wrong with this, mister, if there is any glitch, any hiccup, any double-cross, I personally will damage you beyond repair. I will see to it that you spend the rest of your life in a nursing home, being fed chicken soup through a tube. Got it?"

"Yes."

"All right. Get him off."

———
*
———

11.30 pm. What was the hold up? We had lost hours apparently negotiating with the ground the logistics of the evacuation. Suzanna and I together were to stretcher Taff off. A propitious outcome indeed. Thanks very much. Nice doing business with you.

God Almighty, how long does it take to find an ambulance gurney and send it up the stairs? I slid the flimsy grey plastic shutter of 19A's window upwards and looked out. It was pitch black outside, with nothing to see and not even a sense of perspective. Velvety blackness enshrouded the window. But now came a glimmer of light. From a gap in the perimeter fence somewhere abutting the terminal building, an ambulance had crept airside and was edging towards the aircraft at an agonisingly slow pace. I watched the anonymous tall cream-grey vehicle with its rather sinister dark one-way windows make a series of silent, laboured manoeuvres. The ruby tail lights edged imperceptibly towards the foot of the stairs and then came to a halt.

The patient had grown very quiet. The last unit of blood had been transfused. Suzanna had put up a litre of normal saline to scavenge the remaining precious red cells and chase them through the dead space of the giving set. Then she switched the drip off, disconnected it, and secured the intravenous catheter with a luer plug. For the transfer, I disconnected the adaptor of the thoracostomy drainage system and secured a Heimlich valve in its place. To this, I attached a urinary catheter bag to contain any further haemorrhage.

The stretcher had arrived. It was a standard Order of St John Mark 11. I laid its two halves down parallel on the centre aisle and snapped them together by the metal clips at each end. Manipulating the patient onto the floor was easier than I'd anticipated.

Oxygen. I extracted the compact cylinder I'd saved from earlier in the day. I positioned the squat depth charge on the stretcher snugly between the patient's legs, opened the supply with a small spanner, adjusted the adaptor for a flow rate of eight litres per minute, and substituted the giving set with a new Hudson mask.

Then Suzanna covered the patient in three blankets and secured him on the stretcher with the three parallel straps and their standard seatbelt buckles. Thinking of the difficult transit down the stairway to the lower deck, she ensured the belts were firm.

I surveyed the scene. "All set? Mind if I take the lead? It'll be easier on the stairs."

She nodded. "Hope you've done a moving and handling course. Straight back now!"

"Whoa! We're towing the aeroplane." I'd forgotten the IV, still on the back of the patient's right hand, attached to the colloid suspended overhead. Painstakingly, we laid the patient down again, found another luer plug, and disconnected the drip-giving set. One last glance at the scene. The cabin was strewn with the chaotic detritus of a prolonged resuscitation. Somebody else could clean that lot up!

The palaver of negotiating the stairs woke the patient up. During our descent, the public address system went live, and the man with the Irish accent told everybody to stow their tray tables, return their seats to the upright position, and fasten their seatbelts. It was as if we were coming in to land. I suppose it was a method of crowd control. Then, even more incongruously, the message was followed by music. I vaguely recognised it. They must have opted for the classical tape. If it was supposed to soothe the nerves of those with a flying phobia, it wasn't very well chosen. In fact it was rather spooky. Bleak, chromatic, monumental. Surreal and serial. I wondered if it was a tone row. I found myself quietly whistling along with it in an undertone.

It was an odd experience, to return to the lower deck and see that which I'd previously passed through as a blind man. Don't look too interested.

They were using the forward, First-Class cabin as a headquarters. Swinging round at the foot of the stairs and facing backwards, I had a glimpse of flak jackets, weaponry, electronic devices, and three hooded figures. One of them got up and pulled a curtain across and the brief look was over.

Taff's arms had somehow worked themselves free of the blankets and the stretcher's strapping and were flailing aimlessly down by the floor. I paused for a moment to balance the stretcher between my left hand and my right knee while I placed the patient's forearms crosswise across his chest. Now he really did look like a corpse.

The passengers had all been huddled into Economy. The air was thick as gorgonzola. There was a terrible smell emanating from the forward toilets. Any babes in arms? They were often positioned in the front row of the main cabin. I checked. No. An insubstantial shadow in a suit, wearing headphones, preoccupied. The man glanced up indifferently at the passing caravan and returned to his preoccupation, whatever it might be. Then, various lolling forms in attitudes of negligent abandonment. Nobody spoke much. They had probably been instructed to keep quiet.

I glanced at the pulse oximeter. Oxygen sats 95%! Best it had been all day. We were two-thirds of the way down the aisle towards the rear exit. In another minute we'd be off. I gave the rear stretcher-bearer an encouraging smile. She looked calm and composed, and amazingly fresh. She might have been pushing the dinner cart.

If I had not been walking backwards I might have been

quicker to realise that something was wrong. There was a brief commotion behind me, a shriek of terror abruptly terminated by a dull thud, and the metallic clatter of a heavy object being hurled down the aisle. It bounced off my calf with a muffled combustion which nearly blew me off my feet. Then the cabin lights had gone and the aircraft was filled with billowing smoke. Suddenly there was a tremendous eruption of noise from every area of the aircraft.

I abruptly lowered my end of the stretcher and yelled at Suzanna, "Get down!" I was aware of the occupants of the seats on my left assuming the crash position and, beyond them, through the windows and out on the tarmac, the ambulance was now bizarrely flashing its multi-coloured lights and sounding its siren. Men, more men in balaclavas, were disgorging from its back door and running in columns of two up the stairway towards the aircraft's rear exit.

Still clutching the poles of the stretcher, Suzanna had frozen like a rabbit on the highway caught in the glare of approaching headlamps. The ensuing events overtook me so quickly, that they almost seemed to happen simultaneously. A ghoulish, cowled figure had materialised behind my left shoulder. Through the thick, acrid smoke, the headphones and speaker and the night vision apparatus were the antennae and mouth parts of a huge and disgusting stick insect. The alien being focused indifferently on the wounded man on the stretcher and levelled the blunt stub of the automatic at his head.

"No!"

A hand in a thick black gauntlet grasped the blood-filled catheter bag, the Heimlich valve, and the thoracostomy tube and gave the entire apparatus one definitive, terminal heave.

Now the crazed youth with the *cri du chat* scream was rampaging down the aisle towards us. There was a blaze of automatic fire. Suzanna's arms appeared to reach towards me in supplication, before she collapsed. The insect fell across the stretcher, twitching its antennae and clutching its mandible. Its pistol fell on the stretcher and lodged against a remnant of surgical tape. The crazed youth dropped to the floor and lay dead still. Behind him, a man resembling a warrior on a medieval battlefield, wielding his cricket bat mace, closing in for close-quarters mortal combat, bore down on me with a prolonged, enraged scream.

What happened next must have only taken a split second, yet for me, at that moment, the world had gone into slow motion, virtually into freeze-frame, to the extent that I had time to think rationally rather than act purely on reflex. I picked up the weapon of the disabled stick insect soldier and, feeling ridiculous, pointed the barrel straight at Johnnie, the man from hell. I wasn't so much a desperate man, as a hammy thespian pretending to be a desperate man in a lurid melodrama. Yet what else could I do? I pulled the trigger.

III

You are asleep, and you know you are asleep, and you decide to wake. But you cannot. Your eyes are closed and you are blind and your body is paralysed. You make a monumental effort to open your eyes and to jerk your mind-body into wakefulness, the alternative state. But you cannot. You lie as still as a corpse, trying to stay calm, locked in. Panic once more flutters round the edges of your consciousness.

Then suddenly, with a gasp, you find yourself awake.

The sleep state and the waking state can be so totally alien to one another that it is almost as if this body were occupied by two souls, as people in cramped lodgings serially use the same bed, in shifts; Cox & Box. You go to bed late at night full of the day's pity and terror, impatient for the morning, yet you wake to find yourself preoccupied with something entirely different.

The wakeful man lies still and assembles the vestiges of his personality, waiting for the man asleep to vacate.

There were two difficult times of day. The second came around 5 pm. The cocktail hour. This was the first, the retrieval of consciousness in the morning. Sometimes I would wake up and not know who I was. I was just a man lying in a bed. An anonymous cipher. Even the supposedly hard-wired demographic data – name, age, nationality – had been locked away with the whole of my short- and long-term memory.

That morning, for example, I was a man lying on the edge of an enormous super-king Slumberdown in a windowless bedroom. I could not have been restless in the night because the vast acreage of the rest of the bed – I stretched out an exploratory hand – was cold. The vacancy of the bed taunted me.

Then memory came flooding back.

I'd gone to bed furious with my colleagues and the world at large, but I woke furious with myself. Why the hell had I returned to this madhouse? Why the hell had I left a perfectly good job, a dream job for me actually, in a benign country, not without its problems, but at ease with itself, to be admitted to an asylum recently taken over by the lunatics? It was vanity, pure and simple. They'd bought me, without my even realising it. I'd sold my soul for a mess of potage. National Medical Advisor to the Security Services. N-MASS. I'd liked the sound of that. Oh yes, I'm the N-MASS. That was going to look good on the CV. Maybe a young man's job, something to do for a few years while you're up for something slightly crazy, you've got the energy, and you're a free agent. Later on, in pursuit of a quieter life in an academic cloister, when you're ready for a Chair, you might let it go. At the professorial interview the dons will remark, "This N-MASS thing sounds jolly interesting. Tell us about that!" But I would be circumspect. "Can't really go into detail, I'm afraid, but yes, it certainly opened up some very remarkable avenues for me."

What a bloody idiot.

You go to bed impatient for the morning, as if in anticipation of some big event, like sitting an exam, interviewing for a job, getting married; whatever. Then you wake up in the morning and find that you don't want to get up. In your dreams, in your unconscious mind, you have been absorbed in something entirely different. I'd gone to bed determined that as soon as I got up in the morning I'd phone Ralph Parkinson and ask him what the hell had happened. Why had somebody blown the whistle just at the moment when we had at last made some headway, and when three people were about to get off that bloody plane? I couldn't believe it had been Ralph's idea. What were the security services playing at? Then I'd get on the phone to Baroness Margaret Rowallan, who had headhunted me for the N-MASS job, and demand that the Committee *sine nomine* immediately reconvene. I felt entitled to throw my weight about. These people had effectively killed Suzanna. And they had just about killed me.

When morning came at last I was still angry, but all the sense of urgency had gone. I lay in that twilit hinterland twixt sleep and wakefulness to discover that I was preoccupied with a strange incident that had occurred about eight weeks previously, at midsummer to be exact. It had been so odd, that I found myself wondering if I hadn't made it all up – if it hadn't been my own midsummer night's dream. It had been an episode in my life that didn't seem to have any connection with anything that had happened to me previously, or indeed subsequently. It was autonomous, a finished thing, complete in itself, and without ramification. It merely was. So why did I persist in lying there, reviewing the images, as if on a reel of 35 mm film, running the tapes in my head?

In times of crisis in the UK, I find it best to get north of the Highland Boundary Fault Line or, better still, the Great

Glen. After I'd seen Ralph Parkinson at the Maudsley, I'd taken his advice to get some fresh air and exercise and then head back to work. So I checked in for a few days at the Newton Hotel up in Nairn, on the Moray Firth. There was fine June weather, and I'd thought to take a full Scottish breakfast and then burn it off on a walk by the Nairn River over to Cawdor Castle and back. Then at dusk I would go for a run, jogging across the golf links to the long beach on the Moray Firth, then increasing the pace along the firm sand, heading east towards Nairn Harbour, trying not to think too much about Nikki. Time after all is the great healer.

But in fact, early that morning, I was back at the airport at Dalcross by Ardersier. I had a yen to hire a light aircraft and fly out to the far northwest. You might put what happened later that day into the Funny Coincidence Department, but then again, in retrospect, maybe I went looking for trouble.

So I borrowed a Tomahawk for the day and flew it out over the great mountainous wilderness of the northwest of Scotland. The sky was cloudless. You don't get many days like that up there, and it was pure joy to put the jagged ridge of the Cuillin Hills on the aircraft's nose, trim the aircraft out, and sit back to enjoy the view. I flew clockwise round the Isle of Skye. I remember looking down at Talisker Bay on the west coast, at its jagged stacks and waterfalls and steep escarpments, at the tiny paddock between the beach and the big house, and thinking, did I *really* fly a Slingsby Firefly out of there? I must have been off my head.

I crossed back to the mainland and landed on the strip by the railway station above *Am Ploc*, walked down to the village's beautiful secluded harbour and had lunch *al fresco* amid the palm trees.

Late in the afternoon, I took off again. If I'd been sensible, I would have headed east at that point and back to Inverness, but I was reluctant to leave my wilderness playground. I had half a mind to track up and round Scotland's north coast, but the *Notams* I had downloaded at Inverness had told me of some military low-flying in the far northwest, so I decided against it. I only went as far north as Lochinver.

Then, as can happen so quickly in Scotland, the weather closed in. I could hardly believe just how rapidly it turned. I'd grown complacent, with too much flying in the benign conditions of New Zealand. Before I knew it, I suddenly realised that the cloud base was down to eight hundred feet, and my sole reference point was the coastline. There wasn't a single airfield I could divert to in the whole of the northwest. My two-seater trainer light aircraft lacked the instruments for IFR flying. I'd have to track visually at low level down the west coast and get back either to Plockton, or to the strip on Skye at Lower Breakish. I throttled back to seventy knots and put down a stage of flap.

I berated myself. This was the aviator's equivalent of going up a Munro in shorts and T-shirt and a pair of sneakers. Idiot. Air Sea Rescue would rightly give me a good bollocking.

Then it got really bad. I was heading southeast towards Ullapool, just offshore, when the whole of my forward vision became obscured. Nine *okta*, right down on the deck. I turned round by heading a little further offshore and then performing a left-hand, not a right-hand turn. That's important. Never lose sight of the coast, or you've really had it. I looked ahead and realised with a sinking heart that in another few minutes, all the visibility would be gone. I had no choice. I had to make what is known as a *precautionary landing*.

There was the briefest stretch of sandy beach southeast of the Summer Isles, at Horse Sound, abeam the undulating silhouette of Horse Island. Would the sand be firm enough? Might be okay. They land scheduled flights on the beach at

Barra. I lodged it in my mind. The terrain to the north looked less promising. There was some higher ground. I glanced at the aeronautical chart on my knee to check the elevation. 666 feet. Lucky I'm not superstitious. But better turn before you smack into the hillside. I turned through 180 degrees, right-hand turn this time, being driven ever lower.

In the end, I was left without an option. All I had was that postage stamp of usable beach. I didn't even have time for a further reconnoitre. The wind was a northwesterly, and it would have been better to land from the southeast, but I had a notion if I risked another turn, I would lose visibility altogether, so I landed with a tailwind. It was fast and bumpy. I landed as near the surf as I dared, giving my head an almighty smack off the cockpit roof. The sandy surface held, as did my head and the canopy, and to my enormous relief I lurched to a halt with undercarriage intact.

It had started to rain. I remembered again that time my sister-in-law Caitlin Roy and I had landed at Talisker Bay. The conditions had been even worse then, and we had hurried to find shelter. But now I was in the middle of nowhere. I was at a dead end on a peninsula somewhere to the west of Ben More Coigach, and nobody knew where I was. I really ought to have put out a *PAN* call while still airborne, but I'd been too busy flying the aeroplane. Down here, I probably wouldn't get a signal on my mobile. I knew I must get off the beach and find my way to the end of the single-track road by which I might trudge back in the direction of Achiltibuie, knock on a door, and make a phone call. But for the moment, I was happy to sit in a daze and enjoy the sensation of being alive.

I was roused from my reverie by a polite knocking on the Perspex screen of the port cockpit door. A gillie in tweeds and deerstalker peered in at me. I opened the door. The gillie politely doffed his hat. The face was weather-beaten. He was as emaciated as a scarecrow. He said to me gravely, "Good evening, sir. Himself is expecting you. Dinner will be served on the hour. Himself suggests you have time to settle in, bathe and dress, if you please."

Himself?

I was completely bewildered. I said, "I need to make the plane safe."

"Calum will see to that. He has already telephoned Inverness. Search and Rescue have been stood down. Do not discommode yourself. Himself would be delighted if you stopped for the night."

Profoundly puzzled, I followed the man in the tweed suit off the beach in the direction of a hectare of Scots pine. He glided between two sand dunes and led me over a Japanese-style vaulted wooden footbridge which crossed a river in tumultuous spate, its gushing Newcastle Brown waters overjoyed finally to have reached the sea. We slipped under the luscious green canopy and for the first time, I discerned the ancient grey granite edifice that I had failed to spot from the air. We entered a quiet garden and crossed to an ivy-bedecked loggia, which took us to the haha on the edge of a spacious lawn, as fastidiously tended as a bowling green. A pathway in fresh orange cinder running between tiny saplings – they reminded me of Japanese Bonsai – and sculpted hedgerows carried us to the house's main entrance. This was of grand classical design. We ascended some steps and entered a porch between two short columns. On the entablature at the head of the right-hand column, I noted a diminutive plaque that read *Egdon Heath*. At the front door, we were met by the housekeeper, a substantial matron with stern features who nodded briefly and led me indoors. The gillie disappeared.

There was a brief glimpse of a dusky atrium in dark wood panelling. Ahead of me, a grim display of weaponry took the form of about a hundred muskets arranged like a Catherine wheel on the atrium wall. On either side, stag heads crowned with ostentatious antlers, and portraits, presumably of ancient dynastic ancestors, critically observed my progress. I followed the housekeeper into an intensely claustrophobic lift, and we lurched up three floors in absolute silence. We emerged into a long corridor. The only illumination came from a stained-glass window at its far end, towards which we gravitated. I was shown into the last room on the right. It was a spacious and comfortable bedroom with *en suite*. A set of clothes had been laid out across the bed.

I said, "It's almost as if you expected me."

"As you see."

"Thank you very much."

"Dinner is on the hour."

She withdrew.

Still in a daze, I took off my wet things, entered the bathroom, and took a shower. There was Camay soap, Black Lynx shower gel, and TRESemmé shampoo and conditioner. It was a very good shower, a substantial high-pressure overhead deluge at perfect temperature. I was pleasantly surprised. British plumbing is seldom remarkable. I stayed under the hot torrential monsoon fully for fifteen minutes, analysing my situation. Had I really been an expected guest? Of course not! The master of the house had merely noted the unexpected arrival of an aviator in distress and had instructed his staff to offer hospitality. Himself! Must be some sort of laird. Perhaps a clan chief. Somebody or other *of that ilk*. Or maybe even higher. I dried myself with a luxuriantly thick towel in dazzling white, found some Nivea deodorant and applied it. Then I got dressed for dinner. The apparel was formal – black tie. The fit was perfect, down to the polished black shoes. I put them on, thinking, this is very strange! Some gentleman's gentleman must have observed my progress across the lawn, measured me up, and selected the appropriate wardrobe.

I ignored the lift and took the stairs out of curiosity. It was an old house, but there was no evidence of decay or disuse. The dark wooden bannisters, balustrades and skirting boards were entirely without blemish. The thick carpeting – in a tartan I didn't recognise – might have been put down last week. On the ground floor, I was met by a very blonde, very young woman in a pinafore who curtsied politely. "Please to come to this way." She might have been a student from Stockholm, an au pair, on her gap year. She led me to an anteroom, a preprandial cocktail suite, and handed me on to the *maître d'*. "This way, sir." During my whole stay, I must have come across a dozen functionaries, but I never saw the same person twice. The *maître d'* led me through double doors and into the dining room.

It was the sort of place the great Scottish collector William Burrell might have transplanted *en bloc* from some medieval Westphalian *Schloss* and brought home to his Scottish keep. Constance would have said, "For pity's sake, William! Where are we going to put it?" Centrally, there was a magnificent table, in wood burnished almost black, to accommodate twenty diners. The entire surrounding walls and the ceiling were of similar hue, ornately carved in bold relief. There were chandeliers and candelabra. The *maître d'* led me to the foot of the table and pulled out my high-backed chair – it was more like a throne. He fussed over me. I endured the awkward flummery of his laying a pristine white napkin in a substantial triangle across my lap. Then he handed me a menu as thick as a Bible. Apparently, I was dining alone.

"Would you like a cordial, sir?"

I heard myself ask for a gin and tonic.

"Of course, sir. May I suggest the Caorunn small batch? Copper Berry Chamber infused from the Balmenach distillery at Cromdale. It has depth in every detail. They use five handpicked Celtic botanicals."

"Really?"

"Indeed. Bog myrtle, dandelion, rowan berry, heather, and, if I'm not mistaken, sir, Coul blush apple."

"It sounds irresistible."

"Dry and crisp, with fruity floral notes."

"Yes, please. Yes, ice and lemon would be fine." He disappeared. I looked down at the array of silver cutlery, sparkling glasses and goblets. I opened the menu and started to read. It was extremely hifalutin. You know the sort of thing; something along the lines of *Smoked prosciutto pitch blended in an emblazoned coulis farce diabolo…*

I closed the menu. When the waitress came – a young American with a mid-west accent – I asked for French onion soup followed by a sirloin steak, *bien cuit*, with a New Zealand cabernet sauvignon. She took no notes. She rearranged my silverware cutlery according to my order. ("Pardon my reach.") I gave her a smile and said, "Where are you from?" She smiled back, nodded once, and disappeared.

The dinner was remarkably good. Between the soup and the steak, I cleansed the palate with a raspberry sorbet, and I followed the entrée with a simple *glace*. *Quel parfum*? I was intrigued to choose basil. It worked well. The dessert wine was a Muscatel.

For coffee, a young man led me into a neighbouring drawing room. After the dining room's oppressive ambience of dark wood, I was relieved to find myself in a spacious, well-lit, comfortable lounge with a scattering of plush armchairs. Even at midsummer, I was glad of the blazing log fire on the grate. A bookcase caught my eye, and I went over to choose some reading material. C. P. Snow's *The Two Cultures*, the 50th-anniversary printing (Canto, 2008) caught my eye. I took it from the shelf and leafed through the pages.

"I find it rather droll that Snow's Rede Lecture should have been juxtaposed with Leavis' Richmond Lecture."

The quiet, cultured voice made me jump. I'd thought I had the lounge to myself. Somebody was sitting by the fire in a deep brown leather armchair with its back to me. I couldn't see him. I put the Snow back on the shelf and took down its neighbour, *Two Cultures? The Significance of C. P. Snow,* by F. R. Leavis (Chatto and Windus, 1962). I took the volume with me and crossed to the armchair facing my host.

"Unusual bedfellows, wouldn't you say?"

I remarked, "Probably do them both good to bang their heads together." He laughed gently and rose to meet me.

"St John Pennington-Althorp." He pronounced *St John* as *Sinjun* and *Althorp* almost as a single syllable: *Althrp.*

He was an elderly gentleman so slim, so emaciated, as to be cachectic. I surmised he must have some wasting disease. His three-piece Harris Tweed suit hung about him in loose, redundant folds. I shook his hand. "Alastair Cameron-Strange."

"Good heavens, we have enough barrels between us to stock an armoury, Dr Cameron-Strange."

"How do you know I'm a doctor?"

"I can always tell a medical man. It's the facial expression of compassion etched with world-weariness. You couldn't possibly be anything else."

I pulled a face. "Sometimes I'm half-minded to hang up my stethoscope and retire."

"I think not, Doctor. Medicine is a little like Roman Catholicism. Once they have you in their grip…"

I sat down. My host sucked on a pipe with a deep mahogany bowl and a curved black stem of the sort favoured by Sherlock Holmes. I wondered about the pipe. Reading my thoughts, he said, "My doctor has advised me to abjure tobacco. I am obliged to suck on an empty bowl. Will you take a dram?"

He gestured towards a table on which stood, oddly enough in this part of the world, a tall, slim bottle of Irish whiskey. Writer's Tears. It so happens I'm very fond of Writer's Tears. The name initially attracted me, and then I acquired the taste. My sister-in-law Caitlin, who has a liking for whiskey that ought to be discouraged as it is far beyond her years, is fond of hamming up her Dublin accent and declaiming, "Wroiter's tears ah-ha! Wroiter's tears don't ya know..."

An elderly lady appeared from nowhere and decanted the whiskey into two heavy crystal glasses. Himself said, "*Tapadh leat*, Mhairi." The lady asked me, in a form of Gaelic so archaic that I had difficulty comprehending, whether I would take some water. When I declined, she gently admonished me, so I accepted a drop. She presented the drinks to us on a silver salver and then disappeared. I confided in my host, "My father used to say, half and half – plenty of water." He laughed politely. I said, "I can't thank you enough for your hospitality."

He waved a dismissive hand. "A man of my years enjoys an unsolicited visitation."

I took an appreciative sip of whiskey. "Since you guessed my profession, I really ought to hazard a guess at yours. I should say you are a university academic."

He didn't so much blink as close his eyes slowly and open them again. Was it an affirmation? "I confess, Doctor, I have dabbled in natural philosophy. But unlike you, I really *am* retired." Abruptly, he changed the subject, and for a moment, we engaged in small talk, commonplaces about time, place, and the capricious weather. It was only then that I noticed a chessboard on the table between us, with rather ornate pieces laid out ready for play. I glanced at the white king and queen seated on their thrones. Substantial pieces, perhaps ten centimetres in height. I thought the bearded king looked like George V. He had the majestic look of somebody who understood the mystique of kingship, as well as a great deal about public relations. The queen was holding her head in her hand in an attitude of repose. I ventured, "The Lewis chessmen?"

"Indeed."

"I thought they were in the British Museum." He made no comment but stared at me with an expressionless visage I struggled to interpret.

I picked up the black king on my side of the board. It was surprisingly heavy.

"Ivory?"

"Walrus ivory. Species protection had less of a profile in the twelfth century. The pawns are of whales' teeth. Fashioned in Trondheim, although I prefer the theory that they are Icelandic, the artist being one Margret the Adroit."

"Adroit indeed. Some of the expressions are quite comical."

"I wonder if they were intended as a gift. Perhaps part of a marriage dowry? Lost at sea, then washed up on the outer Hebrides, and found in a sandbank in 1831 by one Malcolm 'Sport' MacLeod or, in Gaelic, *Calum an Sprot*. Actually, rumour has it that it was one of Calum's cows who found the chessmen. Mr MacLeod and his family were evicted, and the district given over to sheep."

"In that single sentence lies the tragedy of our nation."

"Santé."

"Slàinte."

"Do you play?"

I said, "I was very keen as a youngster. Played for my school. Board 3. I'm afraid I'm a little rusty." It crossed my mind that the last time I'd played chess was on the pavement of Queen Street Auckland with a seven-year-old Indian kid raising money to travel to an international chess competition. He beat me hollow. Twice.

"Would it amuse you to pass an hour?"

"Why not?"

He picked up two pawns, black and white, deftly juggled them and then presented me with two gnarled closed fists. I chose the right. The pawn was white. I carefully turned the board through one hundred and eighty degrees. Himself mused, "Chess is an extraordinary game. It is so ancient that its provenance is lost in antiquity. It has survived through millennia because its current evolutionary state is little short of perfection. Chess is undoubtedly the greatest game mankind has ever created. But isn't it interesting that the chessboard is not merely a metaphor for competition but for conflict? Chess is all about war. Do you see yourself on that board? Are you a pawn, a foot soldier, or are you, perhaps, the king?"

I picked up a rook and examined it. It depicted a warder, a *berserker*, brandishing a sword and biting his shield. "I don't think I'm this fellow. I'm a man of peace. Can I take the cloth and be a bishop?"

He shook his head. He leaned across and picked up one of my knights, the depiction of a man on a white horse. He waved the piece in front of my eyes and said, with disconcerting emphasis, "This is you."

We commenced. I daresay my opening was somewhat conventional. I said, "I invoke the Nimzo-Indian defence."

"Declined."

Then he changed the subject. I wondered if he was mischievously trying to divert my attention. "To return to Snow and Leavis, you, as a medical man, sit astride science and the humanities. Are you familiar with the Snow–Leavis debate? Are there two cultures? Art versus science? Is the intellectual life of the country riven, and does that hold us back? What's your view?"

Now it so happens I *have* read F. R. Leavis on C. P. Snow,

so I wasn't entirely out of my depth. I said briefly, "I think F. R. Leavis was a snob."

"A snob?"

"Yes. Leavis thought Snow was common. He thought of Snow as a used car salesman trying to sell him a dodgy jalopy. And he really stuck the boot in. There's nobody more cut-throat than a man of letters when it comes to vitupery. Is that the right word? Vituperation?"

"I like *vitupery*. I should call it the *acme of vitupery*. Charles told me he found it very hurtful."

We exchanged pawns. I would gladly have dropped the Snow–Leavis debate, but he wanted to pursue it. "Why do you say snob?"

"Oh, I dunno. Leavis comes across to me as an arbiter of taste so refined as to be beyond the reach of the *hoi polloi*. And he's very defensive. You can tell Snow had struck a nerve. Granted, Snow was probably a pain in the neck, traipsing around cocktail parties asking his arty friends if they knew what the Second Law of Thermodynamics was."

"Ah! The Second Law."

On the chessboard, I began to cultivate a flanking manoeuvre, a salient on the queen's side. He saw it developing, castled on the king's side, and began to build a series of redoubts and ramparts. There was a bit of bloodiness in no-man's land, but it was indecisive.

Mein Host continued. "You are right. I think Charles had a point. The old classical education hardly fits one to a position of leadership in the world of today. I worry, in particular, about our political masters. PPE at Oxford, then a research assistant to some MP. What sort of an education is that? What does it tell you of the real world?"

"Humph."

"But I'm not sure that Leavis truly felt superior to Snow.

I think that, at heart, he was jealous of him, not just of his worldly success, his influence along the Corridors of Power, but of his scientific knowledge. He was jealous of the fact that the intellectual leadership of the world now resides with scientists."

I said lightly, "The mad boffins? God help us!"

"Ah. God." He paused. "Are you a religious man?"

"Not particularly."

Clumsily, I knocked over a knight. Unsaddled! I turned the piece upright.

"J'adoube."

"A church member, perhaps?"

"No. Sometimes, I like to sit at the back of cathedrals. Like Nicodemus, visiting Our Lord by night."

"You have taken out an insurance policy against the afterlife, or its absence."

"Not at all. I have no opinion on the afterlife."

"You don't think the perpetual consciousness *ad infinitum* of Alastair Cameron-Strange would be felicitous?"

"Felicitous to whom?"

"Felicitous, perhaps, to you? Propitious, perhaps, to others?"

"'Let the dead bury their dead.' My business is with the living. There's a good motto for a doctor."

"So what lies at the kernel of your religious quasi-belief? What do you believe in?"

I shrugged. Himself was beginning to make me feel uncomfortable. "Faith, Hope, and Love."

"And a loving God?"

"I do hope so."

"What do you say to people who ask, 'Where was God in Aleppo? Or in Mariupol?'"

"I imagine God might be saying to us, 'You are my hands and feet. Where are you in Aleppo? Or in Mariupol.'"

"Do you imagine such an answer would beguile a scientist? Surely, the scientists have made God redundant."

"The best scientists aren't arrogant. On the contrary, they are humble. I don't trust people who think they are on the edge of discovering the Theory of Everything. I'd say Leavis got one thing right. He saw the potential for science to dehumanise us – the quantification of human souls. I like the motto of the Royal College of General Practitioners. *Cum Scientia Caritas*. If that makes me a One-Culture man, so be it." I didn't know where all this airy talk was coming from, far less where it was going. It crossed my mind that I'd given my head a harder knock off the aircraft canopy than I'd thought. "But science and religion are different entities. They pose different questions and seek different sorts of answers."

"Yet you profess to be a One-Culture man. But don't you see that the essence of the scientific endeavour is…" He paused. "Power."

Now came the counter-attack. It was only to be expected. He was developing his rooks. Heavy artillery. He was building up for a *big push*. I'd been distracted from the activities on the board. Himself had laid a trap for me on my right flank.

I shook my head emphatically. "Scientists – the best scientists – are not interested in power. They pursue lines of enquiry for their own sake. It is an article of faith that the laws underpinning the universe are fundamentally simple. The scientific endeavour is really a quest for simplicity and beauty. Scientists don't try to understand the atomic nucleus in order that they can construct a bomb."

Himself retorted, "That is one of the greatest misconceptions about science alive today. Scientists like to pose as platonic aesthetes, but it was never so. The great scientists are intensely practical. It is a misapprehension that theoretical science precedes applied science – quite the contrary. Galileo started to develop mechanics because people wanted to understand the trajectory of cannon balls. Sadi Carnot started to develop thermodynamics because he wanted to maximise the efficiency of industrial engines. He came to realise that he couldn't construct an engine with perfect efficiency, and there you have it – your Second Law. Faraday just wanted to supply Humphrey Davy with an electric lamp…"

"I think you're pushing the boundaries, there."

"Look at the enormous scientific effort that went into the Manhattan Project and the construction of the A-bomb. Who started it? Einstein. He wrote a letter to President Roosevelt and told him the Germans would get there first if he didn't get a move on. It's just as well he did. I can't imagine somebody as unstable as Hitler would have hesitated to attach a nuclear warhead to a V2."

A grey shadow appeared from nowhere like a wraith to recharge our glasses – a cadaver in black jacket and grey striped trousers. I had the impression of an elderly retainer who had cultivated the art of subservience to a distillation of almost total anonymity and invisibility.

"Thank you, Oswald. You can let yourself out. The doctor and I can manage ourselves from here."

"Thank you, sir. Good night, sir. Good night, Doctor."

The phantom disappeared. Himself said absently, "Where were we?"

"Hitler."

"Ah, yes. Ghastly fellow. At least Lord Dunglass told me that was his impression at Berchtesgaden. The only thing he held in respect was power. Theodore Roosevelt might have managed him. 'Talk softly, and carry a big stick.'"

"Then all that happens is your adversary acquires an even bigger stick."

We suddenly entered a new phase in the conflict, one of

considerable slaughter. The board was beginning to thin out. If this was going to end in a victory, the victory could only be Pyrrhic.

"*Technik* that has been learned cannot be unlearned. You know how this is going to end, don't you?" I wasn't sure whether he was referring to a game of chess or the nuclear arms race.

"You think we're going to blow ourselves to kingdom come?"

"That might be the least of all evils. I see you haven't thought this through."

"How do you mean?"

"Tell me, Doctor. Do you believe in Manichaeism?"

I think it was when Himself raised the spectre of the Manichee that I suddenly wished I had never embarked on this conversation. I wondered again if I'd banged my head harder than I'd thought.

"The struggle between Good and Evil? I try not to dwell on it. I shy from apocalyptic visions."

We exchanged queens. Now the board looked bare. It was a mud bath, and a blood bath, like the Somme. What is the point of utter devastation? And what use is a world without women?

"You are not alone there. Indeed, I rather suspect that it is I who am, with one or two close associates, alone. Therefore, I hesitate to share my apocalyptic vision with you. If I do, then you will have joined a very small and select group of individuals in the world, in this world, who appreciate it, who sense its inevitability."

I had the unnerving sense that I was attending a job interview, that I was being tested as to my suitability for a post which carried with it considerable responsibility and a heavy burden of secrecy. I might have been a Cambridge undergraduate, getting the tap on the shoulder. Abruptly,

I decided I wanted the chess game to end. Perhaps I would resign, excuse myself, and go to bed. But the game remained evenly matched. And I did not wish to be a rude guest.

"Go on."

"We have seen how scientific progress has gone hand in hand with the concoction of increasingly sophisticated engines of war. First, the club, then the axe, then the sword, the bow, the gun, the explosive, the petard, the incendiary, all the way down to our present-day arsenals and their manifold weapons of mass destruction. What next?"

"I dread to think!" I looked across at the wizened, haggard form in the armchair. The shaded lamp above his head seemed to detach his head and shoulders within their own pool of light, and this spectral apparition seemed to tilt and hover above the chessboard. It was an absurd notion, but it crossed my mind that I might have been drugged.

"What next depends upon the next breakthrough in physics. Our physicists are engaged globally in a concerted effort never before witnessed on earth to discover the Grand Unified Theory that will reconcile the physics of the very small with that of the very large. Quantum Electrodynamics and General Relativity will become as one. The four great forces of nature, gravity, electromagnetism, the weak nuclear force, and the strong nuclear force, will all be seen to obey a single unifying law, which might be written as an equation on the back of an envelope. I sometimes think the great mystic poet William Blake must have had some premonition of such a unification when he wrote the opening quatrain to his *Auguries of Innocence*…

> *To see a World in a Grain of Sand*
> *And a Heaven in a Wild Flower*
> *Hold Infinity in the palm of your hand*
> *And Eternity in an hour.*"

I said lamely, "There you have me."

"There is your beauty and your simplicity. The Holy Grail of physics – the Theory of Everything. Once we have the Theory of Everything, we have the keys to the universe. We will understand its creation, and therefore, we will be able to recreate it. We will have become as God.

"But…" He held up an admonitory finger.

"By the same token, we will also be able to destroy the universe."

I very badly needed to go to bed. I felt prodromal as if I were about to fall ill.

But we had moved into the perilous endgame. There are four possible outcomes to a game of chess. You can win, you can lose, you can draw, or you can reach a stalemate. Personally I rather favour a draw. While defeat is miserable, victory is always tarnished. What joy is to be had from humiliating your opponent into a state of unconditional surrender? No. I believe in keeping lines of communication open from the earliest possible moment. Ultimately, every conflict resolution has to be political.

There is something peculiarly hellish about checkmate. There is no regicide in chess. Whenever you put the opposing monarch under attack, you must announce your intention. Moreover, His Majesty cannot be ambushed through his own carelessness. If he walks into a trap, you chivalrously point it out and allow him to escape and take another route. No. There is no sudden death for the king. What remains for him is a dawning sense of the inevitable as the dark forces close in. Gradually, his lieutenants around him dwindle in number. The white king gets forced back to the edge of the board. His back is to the wall as the black men close in around him.

But what then? Is he slaughtered? No. He is left standing on the board in a position of entrapment, confinement, and incarceration. Mate. He is left in a state of perpetual durance. He is left to rot in some lower Dante-esque Circle of Hell. He has to face the horror of standing with his back to the wall, left without recourse, and with the knowledge that he has run out of all options. He can hasten this fate – resignation is always possible – but he cannot avoid it. This cup will not pass from his lips.

Yet I wasn't at that final stage yet. I still had options. A lone white pawn was inching its way painstakingly down the left flank of the board. If it could only reach the enemy trench, then it might suffer a metamorphosis, it might be queened, and then anything would be possible. I began to invest a lot of emotional capital in the progress of that pawn. I began to think of the pawn as a triathlete engaged in an Iron Man event, his heart full of terror because the stakes were so impossibly high. He had to reach and infiltrate the enemy encampment. He just had to.

Himself continued in that smooth, beautifully modulated RP accent I was beginning to detest. "When I was a boy, I used to wonder at the mystery of Creation. I suppose we all entertain such thoughts at one time or another. Why does anything exist? Why is there anything at all? Why is there not… nothing? A nothingness so vast that it cannot be alluded to because there is nothing to allude to it. I confess I terrified myself with this vision – if such it can be called – of pure nihilism. There isn't even a nothingness in the sense of void. Void implies space, and already you introduce physical concepts – dimensions in terms of length, depth and height. If such a void exists, does it exist in time? Is the void infinite? Does it have substance?

"So you see, physics deals with the most fundamental concepts known to us – length, mass, time, etc. We already know that these concepts are infinitely queerer than we had supposed. You might slip in and out of a black hole in a millisecond to find the universe had aged billions of years! What can that possibly mean? If we can find out, then we are in a position to switch it off if we so choose. You understand? It's the ultimate suicide vest. Time must have a stop. Do you see?"

Our conversation had become profoundly disagreeable to me. I had presumed that in the Manichean Universe, Himself was on the side of *the good*. Now, I was less sure. He fixed me with his hypnotic glare. "You must see that the ultimate destination of all scientific enquiry is the construction of a Doomsday Machine."

"You mean, like Dr Strangelove?" I was still struggling to get Himself off this apocalyptic mumbo-jumbo. It sounded to me like deranged claptrap.

"Nothing so trivial. A Doomsday Machine does not merely destroy the planet. It destroys... everything."

I found I had taken a violent dislike to my host.

That game of chess ended in a stalemate. I did queen my pawn. It collapsed at the end of its forced march like a triathlete on the finish line and at the end of his tether, awaiting his regnal metamorphosis, only to be captured. *Zugzwang*. Now there were only a few figures left standing on the board – a distilled situation. I remember my white knight performing its awkward L-shaped manoeuvre in a vain attempt to shield and protect his liege-lord. Vain? Was it an inspired move or serendipitous? Perhaps it was an act of divine grace. Or maybe Himself made a mistake. Either way, we suddenly found we had reached an impasse. Left without recourse. Gridlocked. Yet both our kings, the great antagonists, black and white, were still alive. Stalemate.

I slept very badly that night. My dreams were full of foul fiends and flibbertigibbets. I harboured a deep resentment towards St John Pennington-Althorp that he should have disturbed me with such a black vision of the *ordor essendi*. The poor man must be off his rocker. Shouldn't be too hard on him. Surely, the man is ill. Surely, he has a terminal disease. Maybe he's got cerebral metastases.

Sometime very soon, I'm going to be the principal player in an endgame.

IV

On August 22nd, exactly a week after the Heathrow hijack incident, the Committee *sine nomine* reconvened in an anonymous grey building off Storey's Gate. It was like a convocation of Druids at Stonehenge at the summer solstice. I still hadn't fathomed the origin, nature, and purpose of this ancient Witenagemot beyond the fact that apparently it, or something like it, had been on the go for at least 1,000 years and that it had always found favour with the monarch. I suppose that that, to some extent, explained the archaic make-up of the 'Witan' with its combination of the military and the ancient estates and professions. It certainly went some way to explaining the nature of the order of ceremonies. In my naivety, I had imagined we might have plunged immediately *in medias res*, and conducted a post-mortem, literally a post-mortem, on the fiasco that had occurred at Heathrow precisely one week previously. Not a bit of it.

Operation *Whetstone* (who makes up these ridiculous

names?) was right down at the bottom of the agenda, next to *Any Other Competent Business*. Not only that, barring a brief nod and a tight-lipped smile from Margaret Rowallan, and a searching look from Martin Forster, I was studiously ignored. New kid on the block. I was the invisible man. As we took our seats, I did have a brief, inconsequential, yet deeply mysterious chat with my neighbour, Lord Chief Justice Forteviot Dunning.

"Anent the north, where's your Skye retreat?"

"Croft nine and a half, Camustianavaig. It's my cousin's, actually."

"Lovely part of the world. I'm Scotch myself, you know." (He said, "Scutch.") "Is your cousin a feuar?"

"Sorry?"

"Or perhaps croft nine and a half was granted in sasine."

"Which?"

"Infeftment."

Baroness Rowallan called the meeting to order. Zoe, the visiting facilitator from Deloitte Touche Tohmatsu, tucked her shapely calves in their dove-grey leggings under her toned buttocks and invited the group to adopt a similarly negligent pose. This was an exercise in conciliation through mindfulness. The policemen, Golightly and Slack, slouched compliantly. The intelligence people, Hotchkiss and Braithwaite, hardly changed their demeanour at all. Parkinson? Parkinson might have nodded off and snored loudly and offensively. But Parkinson's chair was vacant. Civil, the very model of a modern major general, stared angrily into the middle distance, rapidly flicking a pencil in mid-air.

Zoe had us all introduce ourselves and let the group know something about which we felt passionate. "Christ, it's like *Watch with Mother*," muttered Civil. Zoe's passionate interest was for *Save the Children*. She did not enlarge upon it. There was a palpable easing of the tension which had suddenly gripped a group so burdened with the habit of concealment.

"I'm Margaret Rowallan," said the Chair with the complete self-assurance of one born to lead. "I have the honour to chair His Majesty's Committee *sine nomine*. Passions – I'm terribly fond of my garden."

The litany went on. Chief Superintendent Golightly volunteered that he helped to run a youth club in London's East-End. He coloured as he said it, and the intelligence people, detecting sincerity like a bad smell, stared contemptuously at him. Hotchkiss had the chilly demeanour of a functionary of the *Sicherheitsdienst*. He spoke in the breathless whisper of the late Cardinal Ratzinger. I wanted to translate everything he said into German. *Mein Hobby? Haben Sie schon einmal Bogenschießen gemacht?* After the meeting, nobody could quite remember what his sidekick Braithwaite had said. Passions? Hobbies, maybe. Philately, cricket, crosswords, etc. I noticed he was wearing the same garish sports jacket in strident broad checks, a clashing striped shirt and a kipper tie that was almost incandescent. If he ever appeared on TV, the BBC would have to issue an alert to those prone to epileptiform attack. "We should warn you there is flash photography in this report, which also features Jonathan Braithwaite."

Major Forster gave his details in clipped tones as if he were giving up his name, rank and serial number to the enemy.

"And… your passion?" Zoe tilted her head at him with a frown.

"Shakira."

Civil gave a low, lecherous chuckle and carried on waggling his pencil.

"General?"

"I am General Iain Civil," said the small, ruddy man in sharp, staccato tones of suppressed rage. "I am Officer

Commanding, His Majesty's armed forces, Scotland. I have a passion for committee meetings which stick to the agenda and come to the point!"

So. Since I'd last seen him, he'd been promoted.

I was the last person to introduce himself. "My name is Alastair Cameron-Strange. I am a consultant emergency physician. I'm passionate about a group I chair, DAMASK. Doctors Against Muddle and So-called Quality, with a capital K." It was supposed to be a light-hearted remark. Nobody laughed. At the far end of the table, the Air Vice-Marshall and the Rear Admiral, *Spitfire* and *Scud*, sat in inscrutable oracular silence. *Whetstone* had been a land operation, nothing to do with them. Best leave it to the frocks. The lord chief justice had resumed his nap, and the archbishop appeared to be in prayer.

Now Zoe had produced a quire of A4 in mauve, and she was passing handouts round the table. Civil said suspiciously, "What's this?"

"Team building."

He scanned the paper briefly. "Oh for pity's sake!"

I can't remember what the table top exercise was all about. Something about constructing a bridge to an island using inadequate lengths of plank. I'd switched off. It's the only time I can ever remember being on the same wavelength as the general. I just remember Zoe wrapping up her session and excusing herself, then the Chair trudging through the rest of an agenda that meant nothing to me. I thought, with increasing bitterness and indignation, of the late Suzanna Fergusson.

"...think Dr Cameron-Strange performed outstandingly throughout *Whetstone*." This from Chief Superintendent Harry Golightly.

"It was like giving a gun to a boy." General Civil spat it

out. "I always said he was a loose cannon. Gung-ho. Margaret, I told you he needed to spend six weeks at Aldershot." Either Civil hadn't noticed I was present at the meeting, or he couldn't care less either way. "Where's Dr Fanshawe anyway?" He was referring to my predecessor.

"Dr Fanshawe no longer sits on this committee."

"First it's Fanny, now it's Parkie. What's wrong with the medics? Picking up their balls and going home."

"Dr Fanshawe has reached his ceiling."

"What are you talking about? A first-class quack. Why I'd trust my own son to him. Fanny's the only civvy street blighter worth having a drink with has ever served on this committee." I couldn't figure out whether Civil was being deliberately rude or he was just too stupid to notice.

"Dr Fanshawe," said Margaret Rowallan patiently, "has an appointment with the General Medical Council following an unfortunate incident in his Harley Street rooms involving a fifteen-year-old boy."

Civil blinked. "Then I suppose we're going to have to put up with this cowboy." (I remained invisible.) "I still think a basic course could have dispelled some of that pinko rot. Nothing a bit of square-bashing couldn't have knocked out of him. Break his spirit on a yomp on the Brecons and then give him a good beasting."

"Oh yes, the army's good at that," said Golightly. "This is all nonsense. The doctor came through with flying colours." I was grateful for that.

Jonathan Braithwaite smirked. "The operation was successful but the patient died."

"Thanks solely to the cackhandedness of the military." I began to sense the Chief Superintendent was my ally.

"Now look here," said Civil, "I'm not having that. The *Whetstone* assault was a brilliantly executed operation.

Collateral damage to one civilian in an aircraft of 400 people is frankly an outstanding result. You can't make an omelette without breaking eggs."

"I suggest you pop across to Cockfosters and tell that to Mr and Mrs Fergusson."

"Gentlemen," said Margaret Rowallan.

"Whose bloody idea was it anyway," said Golightly with uncharacteristic anger, "to mount that bloody assault?"

"Gentlemen, I've already said that I don't want this meeting to degenerate into a *Whetstone* shouting match."

"The trouble with *Whetstone*," said Civil, "was the same trouble that all these operations share – an ambiguity over the line of command. We got the order to go – a correctly encoded order, mark you, and we responded."

Golightly protested. "There was no ambiguity over the line of command. As with all of these operations in peacetime, the operation is run by the police. The order to *go* did not come from me, nor was it at the behest of the Metropolitan Police's Chief Negotiator, who has seen fit, understandably in my view, to resign over this matter."

I chipped in, "I should like to know who issued the order to that soldier who dismantled my patient's chest drain. The patient was hardly a threat."

Civil said, "If you run with the craws... And *that soldier* paid a heavy price. Don't expect any crocodile tears from me."

Major Forster reasoned, "Well, if the command didn't come from the police, that suggests to me that we – both the police and the military – were being run blind on a *need-to-know* basis. There was probably a hidden agenda that had evolved at some point during the scenario. There was an escalation. A degree of mission creep."

"Mission creep," muttered Civil contemptuously. "Some clever dick's buzzword."

"What I'm trying to say," Forster continued patiently, "is that the order to *go* must have come from Whitehall."

All eyes turned to the end of the table.

"The Civil Service," lisped Hotchkiss, choosing his words carefully, "does not make independent political or executive decisions." There was the faintest trace of irony. "We serve under the command of our elected masters." The thick twin lenses of the round spectacles focused unswervingly back at the chairperson.

So! It had been a government intervention. Now, eleven pairs of eyes were staring back at the Baroness. As a peer, she had not been elected, but she was a member of the government and, of late, one of its principal spokespersons in matters relating to national security. But looking in her direction, I felt quite sure that she did not know the provenance of the order to storm the hijacked aircraft at Heathrow seven days previously. I found it frankly incredible that the principal senior players in the operation were similarly ignorant. I looked down the table at Hotchkiss' quiet composure. It suddenly occurred to me – Hotchkiss *knew*. Margaret Rowallan asked him, "Was it the Home Office?" I'd heard they'd been snooping around Heathrow all day. They were always hanging about Heathrow's corridors, looking for bogus asylum seekers. Hotchkiss gave a non-committal shrug.

"MOD?"

"Not MOD."

"Were there any ministers on site?" The question was directed at the Chief Superintendent. He coughed nervously into his fist. "Sir Roger Hollis did make a brief appearance."

"The Enterprise Czar?"

"Just a cameo role," said Forster.

"What was the point of that?"

Golightly shrugged. "Military expertise, I s'ppose. Special knowledge of the Argentine."

"Of course. His war record. But still, what was his *role?*"

"The support, I dare say, of a cabinet minister."

Forster said, "Was this under the direction of Downing Street? Does this thing go right to the top?"

The question was unanswered. I think it was during that strange meeting that I began for the first time to understand how Blighty worked. Public life was an elaborate gavotte. People rehearsed a highly stylised choreography which purported to protect the commonweal but was really designed to build a personal career and sustain a lifestyle. The purpose of being on the Committee *sine nomine* was to be on the Committee *sine nomine.* The mission statement of the Committee (never articulated) was to ensure its own perpetuation. In so doing, and because the Committee represented a single rivet in the 'ten thousand rivets in free formation' that was the Ship of State, that Ship's perpetuation was also ensured. It could sail on through whatever rough seas *events* might stir up.

Finally, Baroness Rowallan invited me into the conversation.

"Are you giving evidence to the Select Committee, Doctor?"

"This afternoon."

Forster said, "Mm. Good luck with that."

"Your point, Major?"

"I wonder if the doctor realises just how vulnerable his position is."

I felt like an elderly relative at a social gathering, deemed too decrepit to be consulted or to make autonomous decisions. Does he have sugar in his tea? I said, with frank irritation, "Well why don't you ask him?"

Now the eleven pairs of eyes were swivelling in my direction.

"Why should I be vulnerable?"

"Vulnerable because you are isolated. With the death of the

Fergusson girl, your own depositions will be uncorroborated. And you don't belong to any pressure groups. You have no affiliations. You don't strike me as a clubbable man. You're not police, not army, not civil service. You're a Kiwi bloke. Down your neck of the woods, the individual can travel far. Here, we hunt in packs. Have you tumbled to the fact that you currently stand alone in a country with one of the most finger-pointing cultures of blame on the planet? Let's face it, *Whetstone* is going to collect more brickbats than bouquets, and you, Good Doctor, are the ideal scapegoat."

Margaret Rowallan said frostily, "Don't be ridiculous. The purpose of a Select Committee inquiry is to establish the truth, not to offload any systematic failures on to the shoulders of an individual. Besides, Major Forster, you are mistaken when you say Dr Cameron-Strange is isolated. He is, after all, a fully-fledged member of the Committee *sine nomine*. He—" The Baroness' eyes swivelled in my direction. "Forgive me Doctor; *you*… You are part of the Witan. You have our support, and it is unconditional. Just remember that, especially if the going gets rough. Hold it in your mind, and above all, keep your cool."

"Oh yes, he's good at that," growled Civil. "I'd as soon confine him to barracks. Toilet privileges only."

"Don't pay any attention to the general." Said with a patrician smile. "He routinely defaults to curmudgeon mode. But really, he's a pussy cat. And you have nothing to fear from the Select Committee."

Martin Forster contrived to widen his eyes and drop his jaw without opening his mouth. Then, in an apparent non-sequitur, he said, "Where did you learn to shoot, Doc? I suppose if you were brought up on a Northland farm, you might get exposure to firearms." He mused to himself, "They're still hunting wild boar in the Coromandel."

Then, to the Committee at large, "Did you see the autopsy of the man from whom Dr Cameron-Strange was obliged to defend himself?" He took out a single sheet of paper from the left-hand breast pocket of his khaki uniform shirt. He unhurriedly unfolded it and spread it out on the table. He briefly scanned the pathologist's report relating to the deceased body of a male Caucasian aged between 35 and 45 years, weighing 182 pounds. He read out, *"In my opinion, death resulted from massive intracranial damage secondary to a single bullet wound to the head. The entry wound forms a well-defined circular aperture, 4.5 mm in diameter, exactly in the median plane of the frontal bone, two cm superior to the glabella and five-point three cm anteroinferior to the bregma. The projectile is thought to have passed postero-inferiorly in the median sagittal plane to exit at the lambda, destroying almost the entire occiput and considerable portions bilaterally of the parietal and temporal bones extending as far anteriorly as the pterion."*

Major Forster found it difficult to conceal a degree of relish. Margaret Rowallan said impatiently, "I don't know what that means."

"What that means, Baroness, is that our good doctor here, in addition to all his other attributes, is an incredibly good shot. He exhibits Olympian accuracy and a steely nerve. If you ever want a change of profession, Doctor, you might consider the role of hired assassin. You know? A professional hitman."

V

I found it difficult to obliterate the stark imagery of my final moments on board that cursed aircraft: the men with hidden faces, the smoke, the shouts, the terrible engines of war and, over and over in slow motion, the outstretched supplicatory arms of my stretcher-bearing companion. Now, I sat in a gloomy corridor in the Palace of Westminster and awaited my summons. So far, they'd kept me here for an hour, enduring that uncomfortable mix of boredom and edginess. In a flashback I found myself back once more aboard that 747, amid the panic and the mayhem, the smart of the tear gas, and my ineffectual attempts to resuscitate the hapless doll-like creature that had up until a few moments previously been my companion, colleague, and helpmate. One minute she was flesh and blood, the next she resembled one of these *Resuscitation Annies* you took out of a box like a hypermobile ventriloquist's dummy. I remembered my desperately futile attempt at one-person CPR in the cramped and smoky aisle of the jet. Suddenly, I had been pitched unceremoniously onto an evacuation chute and had found myself wallowing on the tarmac outside in a welter of heaving panic-stricken bodies. There was no possibility of regaining access to the aircraft. Amid a barrage of parade ground shrieks, we had been shepherded hurriedly into the terminal building like a confused flock of sheep surrounded by yapping dogs. There, I had been corralled in a bare room in dank pastel shades and told I would have to wait for *counselling*. I couldn't get it across that I wasn't a passenger but a duty doctor.

"You'll just have to wait your turn, luvvie. You're not the only special case, you know." This, from a squat woman in a boiler suit. "Even doctors get post-traumatic stress."

I had grasped her by the lapels and said to her in a husky voice, "If you do not take me to Ralph Parkinson right now, I will throttle you." She had burst into tears and, I subsequently learned, had been given a cup of tea and sent home. I'm not proud of it.

But Parkinson was nowhere to be seen. The old order seemed to have been supplanted. The military and anonymous suits from Whitehall were everywhere. After half an hour, a deep resentment set in my mind. I hung around long enough to ascertain that seven hijackers had been *taken out* – they said – in an operation that was already being described as *very clean*. And *surgical*. All these ghastly euphemisms. The political class uses them all the time. *Discretionary wars* and *extraordinary rendition* and *enhanced interrogation* and *collateral damage*. Even describing them as euphemisms is *ipso facto* euphemistic. They are bare-faced lies.

I'd had enough. I identified myself to a police officer and curtly explained where I could be contacted in the event of my being needed. The constable made a note and politely enquired how I was travelling.

"I'll take the Tube."

"I wouldn't. Not in those clothes, sir. Let me get you a taxi."

I looked down. I was covered, head to toe, in her blood. It was that picture of me, in lurid colour, which appeared the following morning in many of the London newspapers, broadsheet, tabloid, and online. I'd got caught by the paparazzi just as the taxi pulled up at the kerb, after the manner in which media people doorstep the PM outside Number 10.

"Was it a successful operation, Doctor?"

"Shambles. Absolute bloody shambles." I thought, that'll come back to haunt me. But at that stage I was past caring.

Now, I would have to give evidence before the Select Committee, no doubt hostile to me following the circumspect reportage of *The Times*. "An Edinburgh Royal Infirmary emergency physician was yesterday highly critical of the handling by the authorities of the Heathrow hijack incident…" It was after that report that I stopped reading the papers. I really wasn't clued up on the media speculation as to why *Aerolíneas Argentinas* Flight 301 had been hijacked. What had it been all about? Four days after the event, the Sunday papers and the reviewers on the BBC's Sunday morning flagship news programme were full of theories – the idle speculation of the chattering classes. But already, the news junket was moving on. I wondered if the Select Committee had reached a formulation. Perhaps I would find out. Or, more likely, I would be kept in the dark.

The enormous door to my left finally swung open. "Dr Cameron-Strange? Would you come this way, please?"

The cross-party Select Committee sat behind an extensive series of desks in the form of three legs, two straights and one curve, of an athletics track. The fourth leg was replaced by a single long rectangular table, slightly separated from the track, behind which was placed a single chair. In the area surrounded by all the desks, the field of track-and-field if you will, sat another squat secretarial bureau and two chairs, but they were unoccupied. The desks around the race track were littered with loose-leaf folders and sheaves of notes. By contrast, the rectangular table was bare, save for a bottle of water and a single glass.

Behind stood several rows of chairs in regulation municipal green. These were full of people, but I had no idea who they were, whether they belonged to government departments or whether the meeting was open to the public. The long isolated desk on the race track pattern I had to myself. It was thus designed to give the interviewee a sense of isolation and vulnerability. But even then, I wasn't particularly intimidated.

I hung my jacket over the back of my isolated chair, sat down, and surveyed the Committee. Like the Committee *sine nomine*, there were thirteen of them. Nine men and four women. I had imagined that this would only be a fact-finding mission and that all I had to do was tell the truth. Questions had already been asked in the House. Still, the brief and remit of this committee were restricted by the fact that there was an inquest pending, and Ms Fergusson's family wished to take the British Airports Authority – for lack of a better target – to court. Now everything was *sub judice*. It was apparently impossible for ministers to comment in anything other than a general way. His Majesty's Opposition lambasted the treasury bench in the usual fashion. Not since Winston's Sydney Street jaunt in 1911 had His Majesty's Government interfered to this extent in the execution of law enforcement. And so on.

My appearance began in an unfortunate way.

"Mrs Thornicroft."

"Thank you, Chair." A severe woman with a monocle, a hooked nose, and thin lips had me establish my credentials. I'd never previously seen a woman wearing a monocle, and I found myself unable to stop staring.

"And your last qualification, Doctor. What does FACEM stand for?"

"Fellowship of the Australasian College for Emergency Medicine."

"That's Casualty, isn't it?"

"*Casualty* is not a term commonly used in antipodean medical circles."

"Accident & Emergency, then."

"My specialty is Emergency Medicine."

She paused and perused her notes, and I realised she was looking at my CV. How had she managed to get hold of that?

"So, after a brief flirtation in this country with medicine and surgery, you went Down Under to pursue Cas."

She's having a go at me and my specialty. Why?

"Now, Doctor, you have described in your deposition statement the dramatic manner in which you were summoned to attend a patient on board a hijacked aircraft at Heathrow last week. You felt obliged to make, shall we say, an heroic intervention. Is thoracostomy a technically difficult procedure?"

"Not particularly."

"But it is highly invasive."

"I would not describe it as highly invasive."

"What? Stabbing somebody in the chest not highly invasive?" Mrs Thornicroft had excellent voice projection. She addressed the room at large without diverting her eyes from me. She had a ranting, hectoring tone. She sounded like Mrs Thatcher.

"Inserting a tube into the pleural space is not *stabbing somebody in the chest*." I was getting irritated already.

"Isn't it? I dare say the procedure was a little tricky in the cramped confines of a passenger airliner."

"Not really."

"Oh come now, Doctor! You are too modest. But it is

possible to strike a major vessel and to cause severe bleeding while inserting the tube; is that not so?"

"I don't believe that was the case. I used a blunt dissection technique. It's very safe."

"Yes. But it is *possible*, is it not?"

"Yes, but—"

"And more likely, working in an unfamiliar environment, in poor lighting, and so forth?"

"I really don't think this is relevant to the case on hand."

"Just answer the question, Doctor. My point is that procedural complications are more likely to arise in suboptimal operating conditions. Isn't that the case?"

"Yes, that's true."

"Yes, thank you. Wait there." She made a note.

In court – and this felt like a court – when you are a medical witness, an expert witness, and counsel attacks you, sometimes you have to remind yourself that, after all, it is not you who is on trial. I reminded myself of that fact now.

"Hugh Standish."

My next interrogator was a comfortable, jovial-looking man. I recognised him as a cabinet member without a ministry. A Minister without Portfolio. He wore half-moon spectacles and had an owlish way of looking over them towards me. He was about to commence when an anonymous Civil Servant on his right squeezed his arm, passed him a document, leaned in, and briefed him *tête-à-tête*. I was reminded of an ancient BBC comedy show concerning the shenanigans of a cabinet minister, an incompetent bumbling oaf shortly to become PM and his Machiavellian permanent undersecretary. "The point about tragedy," said Harold Pinter, "is that it is funny, and then it is no longer funny." Yet Hugh Standish did not come across to me as a bumbling oaf.

"I'm sure the Committee would wish to offer you its

thanks, Doctor, for your efforts, albeit in vain, on board AA Flight 301." Slain by the morganatic compliment.

"...and also for taking time from your busy schedule to assist us in our deliberations today." Did I have a choice? After these courtesies, it would be as well that I brace myself for the unforeseen.

"I needn't take up much more of your time. In retrospect, doctor, it would have been better to have evacuated your patient straight away. What's your preferred terminology? *Scoop and Run? Load and go?*"

I shook my head. "The intervention was indicated. Besides, *Scoop and Run* was never an option."

"How so?"

"Because our captors would not have permitted it. As it was, it took us the better part of the day to obtain their consent for an evacuation."

"Did you offer the *Load and Go* option as an alternative to chest drain insertion?"

"No, not as an alternative."

"Ergo, you cannot be sure such an option would not have been taken."

"No I can't be sure. But—"

"Yes, thank you."

"Hang on a sec—"

"Nothing further."

I turned to the Chair. "Sir, I—"

The Minister without Portfolio interjected as if he were adroitly helping somebody avoid a socially embarrassing *faux pas*. I was the inebriated uncle at the wedding reception who insists on singing 'My Way' with the band.

"Dr Cameron-Strange, nobody is *blaming* you." He had a sudden thought. "Oh – just one thing. Meant to ask you. What is Damask?"

"Sorry?"

"Damask. D-A-M-A-S-K. Is it a secret organisation?"

I frowned. "How did you know about that?" DAMASK had been a throwaway remark. It had come off the top of my head, once, and once only, in the confidential setting of the Committee *sine nomine*.

"I take it it's an acronym. What does it stand for?"

"It's nothing. It was just a joke, a one-liner." I was conscious of the fact that I was sounding defensive.

"Won't you share it with us?"

I shrugged. "Very well. Doctors Against Muddle and So-called Quality." I added, "With a capital K." A ripple of laughter went round the room. The next series of exchanges took place in jocular mood.

"You're not a fan of Quality?"

"Not if it's spelled with a capital K."

"And what about the quality control relating to Operation *Whetstone*? Quality with a capital K?"

"I couldn't say."

"But Doctor, you already have. You described it as 'a shambles, an absolute bloody shambles.'" I'd been right. That remark was returning to haunt me.

"It looked pretty shambolic from where I was. Maybe I was just too close to the action."

"Well, the Committee is grateful for your candour, Doctor. Where do you imagine the problem lay?"

"Now that I really don't know."

"Not at the coal face, we gather. The problem was managerial?"

"In the broadest sense, yes, I suppose so."

"You *suppose* so?"

I shrugged.

"It's a default position with you, though, isn't it?"

"Excuse me?"

"Blaming management. Here, you've got form. You don't think much of management, do you?"

A great weariness descended on me. I had lost track of the train of thought, the nature and purpose of the argument. But now I was on my guard. A year ago, I might have agreed with him and said, "No, I don't think much of management." Now, I was more cautious. I said, "I've worked with some excellent managers in my time."

"Yes, thank you."

"Hector Harcourt-Beasley."

My third and last interrogator was a young patrician with aquiline, supercilious features. I cast an eye over him. High flier. I'd do well to hold myself in readiness for a surprise ambush and then an attack of the utmost ferocity. In my slow-witted way, I remembered that Mr Harcourt-Beasley also had a high public profile. He was Chancellor of the Duchy of Lancaster. Historically, that office had served as a naughty step for ministers who had, in one way or another, blotted their copybook. I recalled that Winston had occupied the position after Gallipoli. Yet even I, in my ignorance of public life, knew that Hector Harcourt-Beasley was a Man on the Up, being flagged as a future Prime Minister even while he was still in his thirties. He was one of these high-profile public figures known simply by his first name. The Fourth Estate just referred to him as Hector. Everybody knew who that was. He had assumed the role of Chancellor of the Duchy and rebranded it. The Chancellorship had become a badge of honour for somebody rapidly ascending the *slipper slope* towards high office and rewriting the rule book for himself as he went.

"We come now to the manner of death of a 40-year-old man who has subsequently been identified as" – Harcourt-Beasley consulted his brief – "Mr Johnnie *Mad Dog* Johnstone, of No 18B, the Sluggins, Southsea, Portsmouth, a man in whose violent demise, Doctor" – Harcourt-Beasley looked up – "you were instrumental. Would you accept, Doctor, that in discharging a firearm on board Flight 301, you were exceeding your brief?"

"Yes." I was stupefied.

"Prior to the event – just prior, in fact – had you not specifically given your word to the men with whom you were negotiating that there would be, to quote from your deposition" – Harcourt-Beasley's voice assumed the leaden irony of heavy quotation marks – "'No glitch, no hiccup, no double-cross'?"

"Yes, but—"

"Had you been issued by the security services with any remit or brief aside from that of issuing necessary and immediate care?"

"No."

"Have you at any time received formal training in the use of firearms in situations of interpersonal conflict?"

"No." I was growing sullen. Passive aggressive.

"I see." Mr Harcourt-Beasley indulged a pause to allow the room to apprehend that I had been enmeshed in some ghastly administrative, technical, and executive blunder.

"You are, Dr Cameron-Strange, a signatory to the Official Secrets Act?"

"Yes."

"Can you, therefore, explain to the Committee how it is that you felt free, following the evacuation of Flight 301, to describe Operation *Whetstone* as" – the voice assumed the inverted commas again – "'a shambles, an absolute bloody shambles'?"

"Because that's exactly what it was."

"You mistake my point, Doctor. It is not that you were not entitled to hold a point of view, but that you were not entitled to noise it abroad, the more so as your own recourse to violence has rendered your position vulnerable."

"That's nonsense." My temper was going. I was disinclined to hold on to it. "I hardly think a throwaway comment as non-specific as mine constitutes in any way a breach of privilege or a contravention of the Official Secrets Act."

"It was just something you said in the heat of the moment."

"Indeed it was!"

"Understandable in somebody who was emotionally fraught?"

"If you like."

"Ah, but it's not a matter of what *I* like, Doctor. Of course, you were on a short fuse for more reasons than one."

"Excuse me?"

"Believe me, Doctor. I do not wish to intrude on private grief, but is it not the case that, even prior to last week's unfortunate events, and for a protracted period of time now, you have been in a state of emotional lability?"

I appealed to the Chair. "Sir, this is intolerable. I came here with the intention of telling not just the truth, but the whole truth. I don't know what's going on, but what is being projected here, piecemeal, is a travesty. I had recourse to self-defence simply because I had no option. If I hadn't, I would not be here giving this evidence. God knows I derive no satisfaction in taking away the life of any person, young or old, but the fact is that these people had killed one colleague, disabled a soldier, and were about to kill me. Frankly, none of you is asking the right questions. What was the motivation of the people who took over the aircraft? Were they acting alone? If not, who was directing operations, and why? What was their purpose? What did they hope to achieve?"

"Doctor," remarked the Chair, "in case it has escaped your notice, you sit before a House of Commons Select Committee.

It is we who sit on this side of the table who ask the questions. You are only required to answer them."

For the first time, I took in the occupant of the chair. He, too, was vaguely familiar to me. It took me a moment to realise that I had seen him before. He was the cabinet minister who had appeared briefly in the operations room at Heathrow during Operation *Whetstone*: Sir Roger Hollis, the Enterprise Czar. "Just a cameo role," Forster had said. I looked at him again with curiosity, remembering the weathered, sunburned face, heavily lined and with bags under the icy eyes. He certainly hadn't had any *work*. Sir Roger had a rich, melodious bass voice and a courteous smile. I noticed he never blinked. I suddenly wished I'd paid more attention to the newspapers, had put in some preparation for this *viva voce* examination, had studied my adversaries – for that was now how I thought of them.

Sir Roger Hollis reiterated, "Just answer the question, Doctor."

"I forget what it was."

"Mr Harcourt-Beasley?"

He rephrased the question with careful annunciation, a tinge of regret in his voice.

"Isn't it the case that during the recent past, you have suffered not one but two losses, following which you have had to receive psychiatric treatment?"

I heard myself say, "That question is not worthy of this committee. I decline to answer it."

The Enterprise Czar leaned forward and tapped his pencil on the desk. He sat centrally on the curved section of the track opposite me such that we faced one another directly.

"Doctor, this is not a Court of Law, but you are expected, if not obliged, to answer."

As recently as three months ago, I would have told them all where to get off. I would have told them – actually,

I *did* tell them, or people like them, where they could stuff their ruddy trumped-up briefs and what they could do with their ingratiating, oleaginous, pompous, self-satisfied smug bloody… and so-on-and-so-forth. But I had undertaken self-imposed DIY classes in anger management. And I didn't want to give them the satisfaction. Instead, I took a deep breath and counted to ten. I looked round the assembled company, resting my eyes on my interrogators. Who was calling the shots? The ogress Thornicroft? No, she was an acolyte and not a priest. It was the Chair and the two other cross-examiners. It occurred to me that, in a cross-party Select Committee, the Government, indeed one wing of the Government, was overrepresented. Standish, Harcourt-Beasley, and Hollis. The so-called Gang of Three. His Majesty's Opposition called them *The Three Amigos*.

"I see. The Minister without Portfolio, the Chancellor of the Duchy of Lancaster, and the Enterprise Czar. This is a stitch-up, isn't it?"

"That's *enough*!"

"Why are you doing this? Why?" I left the question hanging in the air.

Sir Roger Hollis was not entirely unruffled. There had been a quick flash of temper there when he had snapped, "*Enough*!" It only lasted a second, and he brought it quickly under control. When he next spoke, it was to make sure that I knew my place and stayed within it. I had seen it all before in the schoolyard. The bully who realises his intended prey might just be a suicidal maniac, and quietly retreats while saving face. The Gang of Three were like birds of prey who'd decided the lamb might not be so sacrificial after all. The talons seemed visibly to recede. Not the *Falconidae*, and only that power to clutch, of the weasel coot, merganser, and smew.

"You're just a bit-player, aren't you?"

We stared one another out. I was so glad I'd finally managed to keep my temper. If I hadn't, I might have missed that split second when Roger Hollis had betrayed his innermost thought. He might think I'm plebeian, and he might have the lowest contempt for me, yet for just a moment, I saw something else. Just a trace. It was *fear*. I was hardly surprised. Sir Roger was a bully. Perhaps the deepest motivation that drives a bully, the ultimate *sine-qua-non* of his whole mode of being, is fear.

VI

"You're just a bit-player, aren't you?"

Beethoven's string quartet no 14, in C sharp minor, Opus 131, is undoubtedly one of the greatest pieces of music ever written. I would certainly take it with me to my desert island, and if Roy Plomley (as it were) were to ask me which one of my eight discs I would *save from the waves*, this would be it. Not that he'd be likely to ask. How can I be a castaway if I am cast away already? I am an invisible man now that I have decided to quit medicine. I guess it was the only thing I was ever any good at, but I can't continue when I know I am surrounded by a zone of chaos, when people who dare to come close to me find themselves on a sticky wicket, all the more so when I try to help. "I am become death, destroyer of worlds." I need to say to these people, "Don't come near. I spell trouble." Best if I keep out of everybody's way. I will go up to Skye, to the tiny croft in Camustianavaig, and disappear.

I desperately wanted to get out of London, but I couldn't.

Too many debriefings to attend, like Morbidity & Mortality Meetings. Too many post-mortems. I wanted to get back up to the clean air and the sanctuary of the *Gàidhealtachd,* where I could stop awhile and think. Instead, here I was, stuck in Metropolitan La-La land, in central London, touristy London with all its iconic imperial landmarks crammed into the area delineated by the yellow Circle Line, north of the river, shaped like a gin bottle on its side with its neck pointing to the east.

I was holed up in a room without windows somewhere in the bowels of the Royal Society of Medicine, No 1 Wimpole Street. This was the designated headquarters of the National Medical Adviser to the Security Services whenever business took him to the capital. From here, I would go for aimless walks or rides on the Tube. I remember at the time there was a dark BBC drama on TV that concerned British politics in the 1930s. Its strapline appeared on the sides of the red London buses and was plastered over all the hoardings beside the endless moving staircases of the London Underground. *Who Runs Britain?* It was all about Whitehall mandarins like Sir Robert Vansittart and his mysterious colleague at the Central Office, Ralph Wigram, a man with a limp, who at great personal risk leaked information to Churchill during the wilderness years. Wigram was appalled by the rise of the extreme right in Europe, by Mr Baldwin's bland insouciance, and Mr Chamberlain's smug self-confidence that he could outwit Herr Hitler. Life got so black for Ralph Wigram that it is said he could see no way out. Did he take his own life? If he did, then he was driven to despair because his political masters could not see and did not know that they were in mortal danger. Only Winston knew. And Winston would go on to the end.

I couldn't get that strapline out of my head. *Who Runs Britain?* Certainly not the Committee *sine nomine.* The thing about Britain, in the thirties but perhaps even more so now, is that her institutions are so mired in obfuscation that nobody really knows. This is what hapless colonials like Ralph Parkinson and me discover when we accept a job here. We are run blind, remotely, on a *need-to-know* basis. We have been recruited by an ultra-secretive organisation and we don't know who our control is, far less the ultimate destination of the chain of command. We each operate in our own personal, bespoke silo, and we have no idea what other silos may exist.

The Wigmore Hall is just around the corner from the Royal Society of Medicine, and the most remarkable string quartet in the world, The Arnold Bax Quartet, was playing. If I didn't go, my twin sister would give me a hard time. She had become an A-Lister. Anne MacKenzie Cameron-Strange. She was growing apart from me.

Bit of Schubert, bit of Mozart. Very nice. I stayed in my red velvet seat during the interval, musing. Aisle seat, half-way down the shoebox hall of marble and alabaster. Hold that thought.

People often say Beethoven's late quartets are *difficult*, but I've never found that to be so. Of course, they are profound, but I've never thought of them as being in any way inaccessible. They are just incredibly beautiful. I have this theory that just before Beethoven composed the first movement of the Op. 131, he heard, or perhaps played, Bach's fourth fugue from the first book of the 48, *Das Wohltemperierte Klavier*. Like the Op. 131, it, too, is in the key of C sharp minor. Of course, it, too, is fugal. Even the thematic subjects are similar, the first in their chromaticism, the second in the architecture of their *cantabile*.

Now here they came, emerging from the anonymous door stage left for the second half of the concert. The Baxes: Raphael Preller, Dominique Moulin, Anne Strange (her viola name), and Malcolm Broadsword. A full house in what is surely the greatest chamber music venue in the world. Rafa is what every quartet needs: a great, inspirational, virtuosic solo violinist. Dominique had gotten over her crush on MacKenzie, much to my sister's relief. She had even taken up with a new guy. I thought Malcolm looked a bit pale and uncertain when they came on. I recalled MacKenzie had sought an opinion of me.

"He's not right. He's getting dizzy turns. And… I dunno… he's *vacant*. It's affecting his playing."

"Tell him to visit his GP."

"I've tried that, but he's too pig-headed. He won't go. Can't you speak to him? He knows you. He trusts you."

"MacKenzie, I've quit. I've retired."

"Bollocks!" She was angry with me.

The Baxes took their seats, arranged their music, tuned, and sat in silence. I realised they were waiting for the green light. BBC Radio 3 lunchtime concert, live. I've often marvelled at the classical music world's maintenance of the conspiracy of silence that is essential in a live concert if the spell of the music is not to be broken. Of course incontinent coughing can be the bane of the performer's life, and occasionally a mobile might go off, or somebody's hearing aid whistle. I did once hear an audience member at a Glasgow concert shout out, "I don't want to hear any more of this classical pish!" But that's my point. Such interruptions are extremely unusual. Here we are in the Wigmore, at the start of the Op. 131, and a deep silence has descended upon the hall. Now Rafa will raise his violin and introduce that sustained, protracted, adagio theme; Dominique will echo it a fifth lower, MacKenzie a fourth lower, and Malcolm… Imagine if, just for the hell of it, I got up from my chair, walked down the aisle to the stage, leapt up onto it, and, before Malcolm could touch bow to string, I wrested his cello from his grip, laid it on its side on the floor, then wrested Malcolm from his chair and laid *him* on his side on the floor…

Why ever not?

I got up and sauntered down the aisle until I was within two metres of my sister. I put both hands, palm down, on the stage and leapt on to it. I was aware that MacKenzie, while still iterating the C sharp minor theme, was watching me with big, frightened, dilated eyes. I walked over to Malcolm Broadsword and released the neck of the cello from his clammy grip. His bow fell to the floor. I lay the cello on its side, carefully. After all, I didn't want to damage it. Then I grasped Malcolm round the torso and kicked his chair rather noisily backwards and out of the way. Then I swept Malcolm sideways in a passable jujitsu manoeuvre and decked him, left side up, with his left leg crossed over his right, bent at the knee. I heard a cry of dismay from the audience and the ensuing hubbub. Clearly, somebody with a mental health issue had decided to disrupt proceedings.

The Royal Society of Medicine is not to be confused with the Royal Medical Society. Though Martin Forster declares me not to be a clubbable man, I'm a life member of both institutions. The RSM is an august London institution full of medical academics and elder statesmen. The RMS on the other hand is an Edinburgh undergraduate medics' club with its HQ on the first floor of the rather unprepossessing Potterrow Building opposite MacEwan Hall. You might think the RSM is weightier than the RMS, but in fact the Edinburgh undergraduate society is far older than its London counterpart, it gained royal patronage far earlier, and in many ways has had a more distinguished membership over the years.

From the Margaret Street entrance to the Royal Society of Medicine, you enter a foyer with the reception desk ahead of you, the restaurant on the left, and the bar on the right. I was sitting quietly in the bar at 5 pm nursing a G & T, when I saw my sister enter the foyer, approach the desk, and speak rapidly to the receptionist. I saw the receptionist gesture in my direction and I thought, now I'm for it.

MacKenzie marched into the bar and sat down abruptly opposite me.

"What the *hell* do you think you're playing at?"

"Hi, sis. Would you like a drink?"

"You can't just interrupt the Baxes like that. You can't. You can't cause utter chaos and then just walk out of the building."

"I've always found that if called upon to be a Good Samaritan, the best thing to do is to step in, make a difference, and then walk away."

"You certainly made a bloody difference!"

"MacKenzie, it was you who told me that Malcolm's not well. Of course, you're quite right. In case you hadn't noticed, while you were playing the opening bars of the Op. 131, Malcolm was unconscious. He had fainted. No blood to the brain is not good. All I did was put him in the recovery position."

"And then you buggered off? What kind of medical consultation is that? Call yourself a doctor?"

"No."

"What?"

"I've hung up the stethoscope. I'm done."

"That's completely ridiculous."

"Besides, you couldn't have been short of help. Audience with a middle-class grey-haired demographic at the Wigmore. Place would have been awash with doctors."

"Yes, but Malcolm wouldn't be attended to. I told you, he won't be told. He doesn't really know what happened. He thinks somebody from the audience assaulted him, which, in its way, is true."

"Did you cancel the rest of the concert?"

"No, we took five, and then went back out and played the Op. 131."

"Did Malcolm get through it?"

"More or less. Bit shaky, but we got there."

"Well there you go, no harm done. But Malcolm should go and see his GP."

"I told you. He doesn't have a GP. Do you know what really hacks me off about all this?"

"I've an idea I'm about to find out."

"It's the fact that you know. You know what's wrong with him, don't you? And you're just sitting there with that fucking awful smile on your face."

"What makes you say that? What makes you think I know?"

"I just know you know. Caitlin calls it telepathy."

"Caitlin's full of nonsense."

"But I'm right, aren't I? Look me square in the face and tell me I'm wrong."

"If I knew the diagnosis, I wouldn't be telling you. Secrecy of the confessional."

"Crap! Utter bullshit! You're not his doctor. You're not even *anybody's* doctor, according to you. You can't have it both ways. Meantime, you're harming him through neglect."

"Not at all. I'm more than happy if you tell Malcolm that your brother strongly advises him to seek medical advice."

"This is all pure rubbish. As you bloody well know. Of all the pig-headed, intransigent, contrary things you've ever done, this takes the biscuit. This is all about Suzanna Fergusson, isn't it?"

"Of course it is! Just in case it has escaped your notice, I'm leaving a trail of death and destruction behind me wherever I go. No more. I'm going to go up to Camustianavaig to tend my flocks."

"And I suppose you think that's noble and self-sacrificing, don't you? Identifying your own shortcomings and taking yourself out of the equation. Do you think it's selfless? Well, let me tell you, you are a smug, conceited, pompous, lily-livered coward!" There were tears in her eyes.

"Don't feel constrained to hold back."

"You suffer a setback. A colleague dies as a result of someone else's incompetence, the powers-that-be choose – for whatever reason – to scapegoat you, and you just fall over and quit. Look. I've got a big gig coming up at the Royal Albert Hall. Biggest gig of my life. I'm absolutely terrified. It would be lovely to sidestep it and carry on playing the viola part with the Baxes in Haydn quartets. But I'm not going to do that. I'm a viola player. Rather a good one. I'm not going to bury my talent in the ground. But you just have. I suggest you dig it up and do something useful with it. Let's face it, you're a one-talent man. It's all you've got."

"All right, that's enough. What do I need to do to shut you up? Malcolm's got Shy Drager Syndrome."

"What's that?"

"Look it up. I tell you what. I'll bend over backwards, just this once. I'll write a letter of referral to a Professor of Neurology I know. He has rooms a hundred metres from here. He comes down from Edinburgh and consults once a week. I'll write the referral letter in such a way that the Prof will see him this coming Tuesday morning. All Malcolm needs to do is phone and make an appointment. The Prof's a pompous git. Ego the size of Manhattan, posh suits, drives a wank-tank of a posh car and all the rest of it. But, though I'd never tell him to his face, it so happens he's a damned good neurologist. His name is Angus MacTaggart."

VII

I went to Suzanna's funeral. I nearly didn't. I tried to talk myself out of it. I'd thought, what's the point? It's not as if I really knew her. I'd just be a blight on the occasion. I just couldn't see myself offering emollient words of commiseration to her people. "I'm the doctor who failed to look after your daughter and get her safely off that plane. Come to think of it, I was the key player in a botched operation. Sorry about that. Nice to meet you."

Besides (I argued with myself) that bloody Committee *sine nomine* are showing up *en masse*. The cops and the army will be there. Uniforms always add a certain respectful solemnity to such occasions. It'll be like Remembrance Sunday. They'll all be wearing their gongs. Somebody from the government will say all the right things. I'm really quite superfluous.

But in the end, I went. The funeral was in Cockfosters. I took the Tube – northern terminus on the Piccadilly Line. I suppose I just had a gut instinct that, for me, it had nothing to do with her family and friends, or the security services and the politicians, and everything to do with a brief and intense relationship. I was just going to slip quietly into the church, incognito in my charcoal suit, and tell Suzanna how sorry I was.

I got there early, but already the place was full. It made anonymity that bit easier. An usher, a pale young man, handed me an order of service. He said, "Thank you for coming." Younger brother, maybe? But I don't think he knew who I was. I sat in the obscurest corner at the back of the church. The organist was playing J. S. Bach. A family group joined me in the rear pew, and we nodded wordlessly at one another. I occupied myself studying the order of service. There was a portrait photograph of Suzanna looking lovely in an academic gown at a graduation ceremony. Suzanna Constanze Fergusson. And her dates. She was twenty-seven. More pictures – of a fun-loving girl, various sporty outdoor pursuits, in nurse's uniform, in cabin crew uniform, and with a handsome young man.

The coffin was borne in and placed before us at the altar. Six bearers, five men and one woman, followed by an extended family group. Her parents looked stunted as if suddenly and violently diminished. The youngest members looked frightened and bewildered.

The congregation were invited to rise to sing a hymn. Hubert Parry's *Repton. "Dear Lord and father of mankind, forgive our foolish ways."* I tried to sing it, but my voice kept cutting out. Kindly words of consolation from the vicar. "We come here to grieve and to mourn but also to celebrate the life…" But how could celebration be remotely possible? You might say that of someone who had lived a long and full life; you might even say it of someone whose life had been tragically cut short by illness, so long as the event had not been too sudden. But how could anything come out of *Aerolíneas Argentinas* Flight 301 that was remotely celebratory?

A prayer.

A Bible reading. Romans 8. "For I am persuaded that nothing on heaven and earth…"

And now the vicar was inviting a family friend to give the eulogy. I didn't catch the name. Kathryn somebody. She was the one woman who, along with five men, had borne the coffin in. I saw a tall girl dressed in black rise from a side pew and walk unhurriedly to the lectern. From the back of the church, I couldn't see her very well. Younger than Suzanna. She was carrying a slim satchel in black leather. From it, she extracted a single sheet of paper and laid it on the lectern. She took in the congregation with a scanning glance of appraisal and then smiled briefly at the family group on the front pew. I had the impression of a strong and capable person who had taken on a duty because no family member felt up to it. They would simply have crumbled. But the girl named Kathryn was up to the task, and she would not crumble.

It didn't take me long to realise that the Fergussons had chosen their eulogist well. I was vaguely aware of an unobtrusive North American accent, not brash, possibly Eastern seaboard, that conjured an image of the golden colours of a New England fall. It was the voice of Cordelia, somewhat low-pitched but perfectly audible.

Her voice was always soft, gentle, and low…

Something about the delivery, the rhythmic sense of timing, the clarity of enunciation, was hypnotic. Some people can hold an audience and engage attention. There was utter silence. Kathryn furnished us with Suzanna's biography in a way that was informative, sometimes surprising, sometimes amusing, and, while being neither mawkish nor sentimental, was always poignant. It was only towards the end, when Kathryn was describing her own friendship with the deceased, that she seemed in some danger of losing her composure. Suzanna was still nursing when they'd first met. In fact, Kathryn had been her patient in the ICU. Later, they shared a flat. It was when she told the congregation that Suzanna had recently agreed that she be Kathryn's bridesmaid that she paused in silence, waiting until the threat of a tremor in the voice had subsided. During that brief silence, she cast another glance across the congregation, and though it may have been my imagination, it seemed to me that her gaze alighted on me, and I felt pretty sure that she knew who I was.

Another prayer. More words of consolation from the vicar. And a closing hymn. *Engelberg.* Charles Villiers Stanford.

"We know that Christ is raised and dies no more."

The committal was to be a brief family affair. Then all were invited for refreshments to a nearby hotel. I decided to pass on that. We went out once more to the strains of J. S. Bach. A sizeable queue formed to shake hands with the family group. I slipped out of a side door and wove my way between the headstones of an ancient church graveyard. Something made me glance back at the exit through which I'd come. Kathryn, the eulogist, the pallbearer, the girl in black, had appeared at the doorway and was watching me. She was still carrying her soft leather case. She raised a hand, and I waved back. Then she raised a forefinger. It was a piece of mime. A minute of your time? We walked towards one another and met amid the gravestones.

"Doctor?"

"Yes."

"Kathryn Hathaway."

We shook hands. I said the most inane thing: "Nice name. Shakespearean." She smiled resignedly. I know I ought to furnish you with a description of Ms Hathaway, but, d'you know, I scarcely noticed. I was in the condition of the three-time *unrequited man.* I was in a monastery. Of course, I vaguely registered that she was attractive, but I deliberately avoided eye contact. Afterwards, I wouldn't have been able to tell you the colour of her hair, or her eyes, or much else about her. If I'd passed her in the street five minutes after our meeting, I wouldn't have noticed her. I didn't want her to enter my consciousness and reside in my memory. I didn't want to establish a connection. I didn't want to find myself trampling roughshod across anybody else's life. First, *do no harm*. All I wanted to do was take the Tube to the other end of the Piccadilly Line, get on a plane at Heathrow and get the hell out.

She asked, "Are you coming to the hotel?"

"No."

"In that case, can I buy you a coffee? There's a place round the corner."

"No, thank you."

"I have something to show you. It won't take long."

"I'm a bit pressed for time myself." I looked pointedly at my watch, aware that I was being monumentally rude.

"It's important." Abruptly, she unzipped her soft leather case and extracted a slim, hardback notebook with a pastel, floral cover. She opened it on a bookmarked page and handed it over. "Probably best if you read it."

"What is it?"

"Just… read it. Please."

I looked down stupidly at the neat, feminine, rounded handwriting in turquoise ink. It took me a moment to realise that Suzanna had written this letter to her friend while on board the aircraft. I had even seen her writing it. I had said, "Keeping a record?" and she had replied, "Something like that." She had penned it over the course of several hours during the brief snatches of respite she had taken while tending to her patient. She must have finished it shortly before her death. It was, therefore, the kind of letter people sometimes feel compelled to scribble hurriedly to their loved ones, with the realisation that they are on board a vessel that is doomed. I started to skim-read the entries, but then I found myself leaning up against a massive gravestone, reading carefully, word for word, verbatim.

Dear Kat,

    I am writing you this letter in the hope that you never have to read it, or maybe I'll show it to you, and we can laugh over it at your hen night – in which case, the writing of it is futile. Perhaps not so futile – it's helping to steady my nerves.

    I won't tell you the frightful fix I'm in – that will be common knowledge soon enough. Besides, if I don't go into detail, and the men in balaclavas take a look, maybe they won't get mad with me again. Patient's calling – got to go…

    10.30 am – had to carry out a procedure. I was scared stiff – couldn't stop my hand shaking. Never done it before, but I've seen the docs do it, and I guess it's really quite easy. Anyway, it seems to have helped a bit.

    I think they're trying to negotiate a doctor on board. I wish they would. I feel so lonely.

    11.45. Doctor's arrived. He seems to know what he's doing. Thank God.

    1315. We've been busy! I'm feeling much better. Can I bring this guy to your wedding? He's quite dishy, actually. And he doesn't seem too bothered by the men in balaclavas. The more decisive he is, the more feckless they seem. I'd better keep my mouth shut.

    1830. Long, long delays. Our patient's failing. Balaclava men have no bloody idea what they're doing. Not the foggiest. That's what's so frightening. I dunno. Kat, I'm beginning to get a very bad feeling about this.

2315. At long last! We're on the move. I'm a bit nervous. Before, I'd got kinda resigned to – don't know what. Still, we can't stay on board forever. I guess it'll be all right. I'm going to stop now 'cos I've got to help Alastair. See you next Friday.

Promise.

Love you, girl.

Suzie.

I gazed abstractedly at the signature. I carefully closed the notebook and handed it back. Kathryn Hathaway placed it back in her satchel.

"I need to know why my friend had to die."

"Good luck with that."

She said to me very directly, "Will you help me?"

"I don't see how I can."

"You were the last person to see her alive. You were uniquely placed."

"I was in the eye of the hurricane. Anybody who watched the ten o'clock news had a better idea of what was going on than I did. Honestly, I had the worst view on the planet."

"What did these people want? Were they really just out for a joyride? National Front declares war on Argentina. Do you buy that?"

"No."

"You were the only member of the security services to have accessed that aircraft before it was stormed. You must have picked up something."

"I was just a bystander giving *necessary and immediate care* at the kerbside."

"You said the whole thing was an *absolute bloody shambles.* Don't you want to know who was responsible?"

"Look. I'm just a humble emergency physician." (Could

I even lay claim to that?) "I'm quite good at diagnosing and fixing people. I'm hopeless at administration, and I'm not particularly interested in politics. All these big noises at Heathrow – I hope I never see any of them again. I'm very sorry for the Fergusson family. I feel terrible about what happened to Suzanna. I thought she was a lovely person. I don't know what the authorities were thinking of. It looked to me to be a complete balls-up. But believe me, I'm the last person on earth who would know how to bring somebody to account for it all. I'd like to help you, but I honestly don't think I can."

Her candid eyes just kept gazing at me unswervingly.

"I see."

She did not attempt to hide her disappointment. She opened her mouth as if to say something and then closed it again.

"I see I've taken up quite enough of your time. I have to thank you for interrupting your busy schedule to listen to me." There was no hint of irony.

"I'm sorry if I've wasted your time."

"Not at all. I'm glad to have shown you Suzie's letter." She motioned vaguely towards her bag. "I think she liked you."

Suddenly, I felt very bad about the whole thing. "What are you going to do now?"

"Get along to Suzie's wake, I guess. I'd better get going. Thanks again for your time."

"Good luck."

"Goodbye." We shook hands again.

"Oh! Good luck with the wedding."

She said absently, "Oh, that. It's off."

"Postponed?"

"Cancelled."

She started to walk away.

"Ms Hathaway."

She turned. "Yes?"

I reached into my wallet and extracted a business card. Like a blind man reading braille, I felt the embossed motto of Dr Ralph Parkinson under my fingers. I glanced down at the logo and the legend. It was like a rebuke.

"You don't get what you deserve, you get what you negotiate…"

"This is the man who was in charge of the negotiations at Heathrow that day – at least until he was overruled."

Had I any right to do that? Hadn't Parkinson done precisely what I was doing and got out? Maybe I was sending Ms Hathaway on a wild goose chase. Parkie had gone walkabout.

She took the card without enthusiasm. I might have been dealing with a hypochondriacal patient, one of the worried well, endlessly troubling her doctor about some nebulous complaint. I, in desperation, was referring her for a specialist opinion simply to get her off my hands. Wistfully, she read the legend on the card.

"Call him. He's a good man."

"Thanks. There aren't many of them around."

VIII

Royal Society of Medicine,
1 Wimpole Street,
London W1A 4WW
Friday, August 24th.

Professor Forbes Pearson
Department of Emergency Medicine
Royal Infirmary of Edinburgh
Little France
Edinburgh EH16 4SA

Dear Forbes,

I write formally to tender my resignation from my consultant post in the Department of Emergency Medicine forthwith.

Recent events have made it abundantly clear to me that I am not as effective as I used to be, and need to be, at the front line of acute clinical care. I am not as sharp. Frankly, I have lost my clinical edge.

Although I felt rather hostile toward the House of Commons Select Committee charged with the Operation *Whetstone* inquiry, I realise on mature reflection that much of their implied criticism is perfectly valid. Any competent emergency physician handling any form of patient extrication knows that he must make a careful assessment of the situation with regard to health and safety, his own and that of his colleagues. In this, I am afraid that I let Ms Suzanna Fergusson down very badly. The thought that I might find myself in another similar situation, and that another individual should meet a similar fate is, to me, intolerable. Accordingly, I believe it would be better for everybody if I take myself out of the equation.

Medicine has always been, for me, diagnostic, in particular, the elucidation of the plight of the undifferentiated patient through the beautiful and sacrosanct medical consultation. If I cannot undertake this, then medicine holds nothing for me. It is for this reason that I have decided to leave the profession altogether. Hopefully, after a period of reflection, I will find myself able to embark on a new and entirely different career, although, for the time being, I have little idea what this might be.

Please don't be angry with me. My beloved sister's wrath is already too much to bear. And please don't be sad for me. This is for the best.

I have asked that this resignation be with immediate effect. While I appreciate this might cause some minor disruption with rostering, I really do not believe you would wish me, in my current frame of mind, to be a part of what is an exceptional clinical team. I would only be a liability.

I send Dorothy my love. I will always be profoundly grateful for your kindness, your mentorship, and, indeed, your friendship. I think it unlikely that I will remain in the UK for much longer, but I do hope that at some future time, we will meet again and perhaps look back on this period with a degree of detachment but also with fondness. Until that time I am, and will remain

Believe me
Your grateful friend,
Alastair.

THE MIDDLE GAME

IX

I laid my letter of resignation, sealed, stamped, and addressed, on the lip of the red letter box's aperture, and paused for a moment. Then I pushed the letter into the box. There, that wasn't so difficult! I couldn't help noticing that the embossed royal *imprimatur* on the box was the cipher of Edward VIII. There aren't very many of these. I, too, was abdicating. Or, like a Prime Minister, I'd taken the short walk out of No 10 to the podium on Downing Street and told the world I'd be gone by lunchtime. Quick trip to the palace, and that's it. Total eclipse. History. The removal van's already round the back, loading up all the accumulated junk, salvaged from all the dead years' filing cabinets, drawers and cupboards. Isn't it strange that the higher your station, the quicker you can vacate it? Most of us, having made up our mind to go, then have to endure – what? – a month, three months, six months? – of the daily grind working our notice. We retire to our cells every night and etch another score on the wall. Every Friday we run a diagonal score through the four verticals we have painstakingly carved out between Monday and Thursday. Then on Monday we start afresh with another quintan construct until we have scratched out four, twelve, and then twenty-four of them.

Now that I'd decided to quit, not just the Committee *sine nomine*, not just the Emergency Department at Edinburgh, but the whole rickety shebang of medicine, I felt a tremendous sense of relief. Even a surge of Hope. A new beginning! The world was my oyster! What a fantastic opportunity. You're still a young man. You can reinvent yourself. There's still time. There's nothing you can't do if you're minded to do it. Aviation was the obvious choice. I'm twin-engine instrument-rated. I've got a swag of hours in the logbook. I could apply to the major airline companies and do a jet course. How dare my sister tell me I'm a one-talent guy? Besides, I'm rather on the side of that guy in the parable. Wasn't he just taking care of his resources? I don't see why he had to get it in the neck.

But anyway, I told myself, there's no hurry. I have a little money in the bank. I can take a moment or two to make plans. I could travel for a bit and just let life evolve. Be open for business. See what falls in my lap. Take a gap year! I never took one after school. Better late than never.

Of course, I might not be able to make as clean a break as I'd like. I'd written to my boss, and the die was cast, but still, I was obliged to meet him face-to-face; anything else would have been a craven act. Then I'd need to shut down my Edinburgh life (again). That would take a while, and who knows? – Forbes might insist on me working my notice. But I didn't think he would. He wasn't a vindictive man.

I had another reason for coming back to Edinburgh. Mindful of Ralph Parkinson's advice to get some exercise, I'd got a wild card for the *Crazy Auld Reekie* Triathlon, which was a bit of a fluke as I hadn't been on the scene for a while. One kilometre swim in the Royal Commonwealth Pool, a ten-lap bike ride round Arthur's Seat in Holyrood Park, and then the really crazy bit – a run up the seven hills of Edinburgh. It's nuts because you can take the seven summits in any order and run between them by any route, so long as you go through the checkpoint on each top (you're microchipped) and don't take a ride in a taxi in between. You end where you began, at the Royal Commonwealth Pool forecourt, under the frowning buttresses of Salisbury Crags. You had to sign a disclaimer before racing, just in case you ran under a bus. One of these days, Health & Safety would put a damper on it. I signed up for it.

The field was limited to ninety-six competitors, with a very early Sunday morning start to avoid traffic and tourists. It was a staggered start because there are only eight lanes in an Olympic Pool. I was surprised to be given the purple running singlet of the elites and to go off in the first batch. What was my goal? Podium finish? Unlikely, to be honest. If I could come in in the middle of the pack, I'd be quite happy.

I drew lane three for the swim. I'd wanted to avoid the side lanes, where you were liable to get swamped by everybody's wash. And I wanted to conserve my energy, just stay in touching distance with the front. But it was a strong field, and I found myself exerting myself to keep up. I came out second last.

And had a fairly clumsy transition on the Commonwealth Pool forecourt, identifying my bike and struggling into the bike shoes before charging off past Pollok House into Holyrood Park. On this hot day of a particularly scorching summer, it was going to be a killer. I hurtled downhill past the Scottish Parliament on my left and then Holyrood Palace, getting up a head of steam and setting a rhythm along Queens Drive and past St Margaret's Loch. Then it was the first of ten brutal ascents up to Dunsapie Loch. Here the road levelled out to a winding plateau, taking me round the southeast flank of

Arthur's Seat before plummeting back down at suicidal speed to the roundabout at Powderhouse Corner. A quick tap on the brakes to hold the road, and then off like the wind again back down towards the Parliament before doing it all over again. On the second ascent, I stood on the pedals and concentrated on the biker ahead, closing in and taking him at Dunsapie. Into sixth place! Don't let up; establish the lead on that rider as you round the plateau and then give yourself a breather with a brief freewheel on the downhill. At Powderhouse, a marshal obligingly held up a placard bearing the number 3. I swept by and into the third lap.

Now, a stroke of luck on the ascent. The guy ahead of me had a puncture. Don't look a gift horse in the mouth. I moved into fifth place and held it all the way back round to Lap 4. Now I wanted a period of consolidation. The other elite riders clearly felt the same. I tucked myself into the purple peloton. I didn't want to expend too much energy fighting my way further up the field only to find myself dead beat for the run. The field was getting busier as the later starters were beginning to crowd the road. Lap 5. Keep in touch. Don't let them run away.

I held my position for two laps, slipped back into sixth on Lap 7, and climbed back into fifth again on Lap 9 – only one more murderous climb to endure. There was no further change. Everybody was gearing up for the sharp left turn at Powderhouse back to the Commonwealth Pool and the last transition.

It went well. Park the bike, off with the bike shoes, and on with the running shoes. What a relief to be into the run. This was my strong suit. Fifth place and plenty of gas left in the tank. Everybody was heading for Blackford Hill, but I craved solitude and went back into Holyrood Park. The Hawse, Hunter's Bog, Haggis Knowe, St Anthony's Chapel… So I began that strange traverse, flitting like a ghost across the precipitous city.

I wasn't quite alone. There was a single purple vest ahead. I knew him. He was a fell runner with the spare build of a whippet, named Chris. I dug deep for a steeper climb and caught him as we accessed the twin peaks of Arthur's Seat from the north, and we exchanged a few words. I remember asking him, "You gonna win this?" and he cast an eye northwards across the Firth of Forth and over to Fife, shrugged, and said, "Maybe." Then we passed through the checkpoint and went our separate ways.

I charged northwards off the hill with reckless abandon. St Margaret's Well, Holyrood Abbey, Croft-an-Righ, Regent Park, the old Royal High School, St Andrew's House, Calton Hill. Two down.

Suddenly I was in the zone. It only happens to me occasionally. It's a trance. You no longer need consciously take another stride. Somehow it all happens automatically and at maximal efficiency. You are on automatic pilot. You couldn't do it any better if you tried. And, for as long as you remain in the zone, there is no pain. It is almost an out-of-body experience. Your mind, your imagination, can depart and fly to any remote location it chooses. It's not that you lose touch with the race. You still have to identify hazards and you are constantly making and taking decisions; but somehow your mind is working on two levels and is free to soar.

I slipped down into the underbelly of the Old Town and entered my own private world. I found myself thinking about a brief news report, barely a column inch I'd chanced to see in *The Daily Telegraph* a couple of days before the race. I don't normally take *The Telegraph*, but I'd picked one up while having a coffee in Blackwell's bookstore on South Bridge.

Sir Roger Hollis, the Enterprise Czar, has dismissed the suggestion that Operation Whetstone, *the response to the hijacking of* Aerolíneas Argentinas *flight 301, was heavy-handed. In a* statement, he said, *"The security services bent over backwards to allow time for a peaceful resolution. When the attending doctor – clearly out of his depth – proved incapable of retrieving a casualty after twelve hours, the Special Forces had no choice but to force the issue. Our hearts go out to the family of Suzanna Fergusson, but we cannot allow..."* I'd dismissed *Whetstone* with a grunt of impatience and stopped reading. After all, I'd walked away. None of my business.

Market Street, the Mound, Ramsay Lane. A guy dressed in saffron robes was practising levitation outside the *Camera Obscura*. How did they do that? I was a pushover for magic. The Castle Esplanade was fairly heaving, but I slipped up the left side under the stanchions of the temporary seating for the International Military Tattoo, identified the checkpoint, and said, "Hi." Three down. Now for a long run out west to Corstorphine Hill, the outlier of the group of seven.

Princes Street Gardens, and a safe transit over Lothian Road. Funny how that brief statement in *The Telegraph* from Sir Roger Hollis rankled. Why should I care? Hadn't I washed my hands of the whole business? Then, I nearly got run over by a tram on Shandwick Place. *Pay attention!* Palmerston Place, Belford, Ravelston Dykes, and the long slow ascent west past Mary Erskine's and into the lane transecting Murrayfield Golf Course. I thought again of the Big Bruisers on the Select Committee. Standish, Harcourt-Beasley, and Hollis. The Three Bloody Amigos.

It was always a relief to leave the city streets and enter parkland. At the head of the golf course, I veered right and scrambled up on to a rough path that took me to the checkpoint just abeam Clermiston Tower. Four down. Past halfway! I turned south and re-entered the mean streets. Saughtonhall, Balgreen. Next stop, Craiglockhart. I took my well-rehearsed route across Slateford Rail Junction and the Union Canal and headed for the campus of Napier University. The road map and my stream of consciousness were as one.

The Minister without Portfolio, the Chancellor of the Duchy of Lancaster, and the Enterprise Czar. The alt-right. Despite their polarised position, they exerted huge influence within their party. Many people considered them a government in waiting, Standish the Chancellor, Harcourt-Beasley the Foreign Secretary, and, of course, Hollis, the Premier. What a shower. I pushed them angrily out of my mind.

I nicked through a gap in a hedge, accessed a path, and abruptly turned left up a steep grass slope towards my next checkpoint, the summit of Wester Craiglockhart. I was just behind the old Craiglockhart Hospital, where Wilfred Owen met Siegfried Sassoon during the Great War. Once again, I'd left the hustle and bustle of city traffic for the peace and tranquillity of parkland.

It seemed that out of battle I escaped...

I rounded a curve in a path nearly obliterated by gorse and almost collided with the spare form of Chris the fell runner coming the other way.

"Hiya!"

But he didn't reply. He was frowning with concentration. Here was I reciting Wilfred Owen poetry to myself. Stick with the programme! It occurred to me that, while I was running the seven hills anticlock, Chris was going clock. After Arthur's Seat, he must have headed for Blackford. That would mean he had four down with three to go. So had I. I held that thought in my head for the two more minutes it took me to reach the Craiglockhart trig point. Now I was five down with two to go. It crossed my mind I might be doing quite well. I headed for Braid Hills.

Merchants of Edinburgh Golf Course, Greenbank, Braidburn Valley, Comiston Road, Riselaw, Braid Hills. Follow the bridle path that will take you up on to another golf course. There's the radio mast near the trig point summit. Checkpoint number six.

One to go. After that, all I had to do was run back to the Royal Commonwealth Pool. But a tricky piece of navigation was coming up: to cross Blackford Glen without getting lost in a welter of broom. I'd rehearsed the paths. Left, right, left, right, left over a footbridge, left again, right and upwards, and I'd be on the skirts of Blackford Hill, still on automatic pilot. I was thinking about Suzanna's eulogist. What was her name again? Anne Hathaway? No, that's Mrs Shakespeare.

Kathryn. I ran across a meadow, through a gate, turned left and right, and began an ascent up steep wooden steps towards the Royal Observatory. The apparitions populating my wandering thoughts drifted into the background, and I found myself concentrating again on the mechanics of the run as I emerged from my trance. It was beginning to hurt. I rounded the shoulder of the hill to access the trig point from the southeast.

There, to my great surprise, were Forbes and Dorothy Pearson, my sister MacKenzie, and my sister-in-law Caitlin. Support! What a boost! I suppose, after all, I do have a remnant of a family. Of a sort. I experienced a warm inner glow. Caitlin was on her mobile. She started to jump up and down. She yelled at me as I passed, "The leader's just gone on to Calton Hill. You're lying second. Knock 'em dead!"

I managed a wave and a grin, turned for Observatory Road, and once more dug deep. I had a mile and a half to run. My opponent had less, but while we both had an incline to negotiate, his was the steeper. Moreover, his was the busier. He might get snarled up. I'm in with a chance! But here's another opportunity to screw up the route. At the bottom of Observatory Road, don't turn left, turn right, that's the trick. Then take first left onto Lussielaw Road, then it's just a little jink across Mayfield onto Suffolk Road and, at long last, Craigmillar Park Road. Hare up Craigmillar Park until it changes its name to Minto St, then turn right onto Salisbury Road and there, across the Dalkeith Road a hundred metres ahead of you, is the Royal Commonwealth Pool and, on its forecourt, the finishing line. There's tape across the finishing line, and it had yet to be broken!

I was vaguely conscious of the grey man standing at the bus stop at the corner of Minto Street and Salisbury Road. Middle-aged, obese. God, he looks awful. I thought, is that man decompensating? I glanced back, just as he slumped to the pavement. Who shall I be? The priest or the Levite?

No. Be the Good Samaritan.

I stopped and went back.

First, have a thought for your own safety. He's on the pavement, clear of the kerb, lying prone. I knelt by his side and eased him over. I pushed a knuckle into his sternum and said, "Are you awake, mate?"

He wasn't.

I felt for his carotid pulse. The first aid manuals don't recommend it, but hey, I've had training.

Unconscious, pulseless, not breathing.

Start CPR.

I rolled him supine and got on with it. I thought, 'Give him fifty compressions and then see if you can get some help.' A small crowd gathered. Somebody said, inanely, "Better not touch him." I looked up and said, without stopping the chest compressions, "Anyone got a mobile? Dial 999, ask for a blue-light ambulance and say there is a cardiac arrest at the corner of Minto Street and Salisbury Road. Got it?"

Then we had a great stroke of luck. Allison Stewart, Charge Nurse at Edinburgh Royal ED, was kneeling beside me and saying, "Don't you ever stop working?" Better still, she had a resuscitation mask in her bag. She must be in the habit of carrying one around with her. She tilted the patient's head back, put the mask over his nose and mouth, got a good seal with both hands and started to blow periodically through the tubing, timing her respirations with my compressions.

There's nothing much else to do in basic CPR. The important thing is to keep going, without interruption. The ambulance was impressively quick. Maybe six minutes from the call. We knew the crew. A paramedic said, getting the defib pads on, "You two! Must be this guy's lucky day." It was indeed. He was in ventricular fibrillation. He only needed a single shock at 200 Joules to get him back into sinus rhythm. That was when it got a bit tricky. He had, after all, suffered a hypoxic insult. He was what we call *combative*. We stuck a line in and gave him a pulse of midazolam, and that solved the problem. Then it was a question of *Scoop and Run*. The Infirmary is only five minutes down Dalkeith Road, with blue lights.

So I never did finish the *Crazy Auld Reekie* Triathlon. But you know what? I was quite happy. During the episode on the pavement, during the ambulance ride, and during the ED stabilisation and assessment, amid all the teasing and ribaldry, I was very happy. Must have had something to do with all these circulating endorphins. Incidentally, our patient walked out of hospital one week later, neurologically intact.

There's no better way to sort out your life than to go for a run. I thrashed my body to bits, twenty times up and down the Commonwealth Pool, ten times round Holyrood Park, and then up and down the seven hills of Edinburgh, and by the end of it, I knew that I always was, and always would be, a doctor. I didn't care that I hadn't finished the race. I had the odd notion that it had always and only been a training run for something else, something that would turn out to be far more taxing, and far more important.

Then I draped a Crunchie-bar wrapper space blanket over my shoulders and set about hitching a ride back up to the Commonwealth Pool. But first I found a phone and called my sister-in-law on her mobile.

"Did you win?"

"Haven't finished yet. I guess I'm going to be last. Besides, I cheated. I hitched a ride. I'll be disqualified."

"What are you rabbiting on about?"

"I'll explain later. Is Forbes there? Can you put him on?"

"Hi boss. No I'm fine. Something came up. Look, can I ask a favour? I sent you a letter. Should be on your desk on Monday. Could I ask you not to open it? Could you shred it? Thanks so much! See you on Monday."

X

Have you ever had that ghastly experience of being within earshot of people who don't know you are there, and who are talking about you?

"Your chap Cameron-Strange," said Professor Angus MacTaggart, "I gather he's been through the mill." I could see MacTaggart cast his eye across the splendid array of finger foods on the white tablecloth, courtesy of Boerhinger-Ingelheim. He carnivorously heaped his plate with chipolatas and mini sausage rolls. Chairing the Monday lunchtime Grand Round has its perks. "Is he all right?"

Forbes Pearson remarked briefly, "He's fine."

"I gather he was put under a bit of pressure by the Select Committee after that Heathrow rumpus and rather lost the plot."

"That's not true. He simply spoke his mind. Frankly, I think the cross-party Committee were monstrously insensitive."

"It's an ocker trait, though, isn't it? Contemptuousness."

"Dr Cameron-Strange is not an Australian. His father was a New Zealander, and his mother was Scottish."

"Antipodean, then. There's an arrogance there. The British establishment does not warm to it."

Forbes Pearson held the complacent gaze of the Professor of Neurology and said evenly, "Dr Cameron-Strange has my full support. I back him one hundred per cent."

"Well, Forbes, I hope your instincts prove to be well-founded. He may be an impulsive lad, but we do need the odd bright spark down in Cas."

I could see my boss take in a sharp breath and then bite his tongue. I really must learn how to do that. MacTaggart is a back number, a medical prehistoric monster. He doesn't believe in Emergency Medicine, and thinks *Cas officers* are better off as foundation year two juniors putting in a few months' purgatory stitching up the scalps of drunks, drug addicts, and sociopaths. He happily pays lip service at the Committee level to the concept of advancing the Emergency Medicine cause, but when it comes to diverting funds towards that cause, for example, from the coffers of Internal Medicine, then he is inclined to bend the ear of management with another story. So MacTaggart and Pearson cautiously fence around one another across the boardroom mahogany expanses. One of these days, the knives will come out.

But not today. Forbes Pearson diplomatically changed the subject. "What's on the programme?"

"Big noise from the Mayo. 'Myalgic Encephalomyelitis – fact or fantasy?'"

"*Médecins Sans Frontières* will be on the edge of their seats for that one."

I was back in harness and glad to be so. And my other job, the N-MASS? The Committee *sine nomine* had adjourned for the time being, and I'd put it on the back burner. Occasionally, there would be a reference to *Whetstone* in the newspaper – it was usually a caustic remark from Sir Roger Hollis – and my stomach would briefly churn. Best to stick with Plan A, dump it, and concentrate on the day job. It had always been a bit of a dodgy set-up. I meant to call Margaret Rowallan and hand in my notice. I just hadn't got round to it.

Later on that day, over afternoon tea (Russian Caravan – smoky and peaty, with notes of *Romeo e Julieta* Havana tobacco, and Islay single malt – he's such a tea jenny), Forbes, his nose buried in *The Scotsman* muttered, "Good gracious."

"Hmm?"

"The RAF have strafed a hiker up at Cape Wrath."

"Accidentally or on purpose?"

"What would you imagine?"

"Nothing would surprise me."

"Drone strike."

"What the hell are they doing with drones up there?"

"Practising, I suppose. 'Police Highland,'" intoned my boss, "'became aware yesterday evening that a lone hiker had been seriously injured on the Durness Peninsula, about three miles southeast of the Cape Wrath lighthouse. It is thought he may have strayed inadvertently onto an MOD practice firing range that had gone live. Following the accident, a medevac helicopter retrieved the casualty, a 30-year-old man, and transported him to A & E Raigmore Hospital in Inverness. He was subsequently transferred, in a critical condition, by air ambulance to the Queen Elizabeth University Hospital in Glasgow. The hospital issued a statement that the casualty had died in theatre at around midnight. He has not been named, but next of kin have been informed. There has been no statement to date from MOD. However, Sir Roger Hollis, the Enterprise Czar, has called for the immediate and permanent closure of the Durness Peninsula to the public.'"

Ah. The Enterprise Czar. Sir Roger, turning up again in my life like a bad penny.

Forbes continued reading. "'This incident is liable to intensify the current spat ongoing between Westminster and Holyrood. To date, the Durness Peninsula has been only periodically closed to the public during MOD operations. MOD training activity is escalating in the area, and the British Government wishes to close the peninsula entirely to the public. This proposal is opposed by the Scottish Government, who wish to develop the area as a tourist destination. However, as defence is a reserved and not a devolved matter, it seems likely that members of the public will no longer be able to access the northwest tip of Scotland.'"

I said, "I've never been out there. Have you?"

"Once, about five years ago. Dorothy and I went. Rather an uncomfortable trip. It was very choppy, crossing Durness Sound in an open boat. Then, we boarded a minibus. It was eleven miles to the lighthouse, and it took an hour. That tells you something about the state of the road. Just a track, in such a state of disrepair it was positively dangerous. Health and Safety? I don't think so. And there's not much to see when you get there. The scenery's wild and spectacular, but there are precious few amenities. We got a coffee and a bun, but it wasn't exactly *Pret A Manger*, and Dorothy couldn't find a loo. I just used the *machair*. Strangely, there's an old, dilapidated Lloyds Insurance building. They used to watch the ships coming round the top of Scotland and they would telegraph London and change the insurance policy. But really, it's all falling to bits. The fact is, MOD prefer it that way. The more neglected the place, the less people want to go, and the more MOD have it to themselves. I have to say we felt like interlopers. We were there under sufferance."

"That's a bit sad. Now that it's going to be off limits, I'd rather like to go take a look."

"Ha! Thrawn and contrary, as usual. But you're too late." He read again from the newspaper. "'Following this incident, MOD has closed the site until further notice.' I doubt if they'll be in a hurry to open it again."

"Hmm."

I'm always drawn to the edge of places. In New Zealand, Bluff is the Land's End equivalent. But, really, the bottom edge of NZ is the southern tip of Stewart Island. It's true wilderness. Nobody goes down there but the occasional fisherman or trapper. I once took a Cessna 172 across from Invercargill and flew all the way down, circling these ancient granite tors, Gog and Magog. I remember looking down at the undisturbed bush that covered the terrain all the way down to the shoreline and thinking that if I had an engine failure, I would have no option other than to ditch. Then I remember the weather closed in, and I felt a bit spooked. I was the last man on earth. I headed back for Invercargill.

At the other end, at the northwest edge of North Island, lies New Zealand's Cape Wrath equivalent, the lighthouse at Cape Reinga. It is a very special place for me. There used to be a coffee shop and a post office up there, but that's all gone now. Still, at least the place is open and accessible, and now the road up is sealed and good all the way. That's as it should be. I didn't like the idea of the northwest corner of Scotland being closed. It struck me as being authoritarian and paranoid.

Funny that Sir Roger Hollis should be poking his nose into this matter. First *Whetstone*, and the *collateral damage* to Suzanna Fergusson, and Sir Roger was there; now this incident on the Parph, and another death of an innocent bystander – and there was Sir Roger again! I suppose this was why *Whetstone* and Cape Wrath got conflated in my mind. It was that contrast between New Zealand being open and Britain being closed that further nudged me to revisit *Whetstone*. I pondered the similarity between the late Suzanna Fergusson and that hapless hiker who had been gunned down in the remote northwest. There would be a bit of fuss and to-do in the papers, and then it would all die down again. The media juggernaut would get distracted by something else while the great Ship of State lumbered on.

That afternoon, I was back in the boardroom. ELSCOMF – the Emergency Liaison Standing Committee on Moving Forward. I couldn't believe it. Same long table, same pompous chairman, he and I at opposite ends, MacTaggart to lead the speeches, and me to toast the monarch. And exactly the same committee. Last time round, I'd learned their names by rote. See if I can remember them... MacTaggart Hargreaves Horne Worthington Doctor Gaskell Gawkrodger Pearson (my boss turned up this time) Campbell Clotworthy Bach Partridge...

...and me.

Another committee of thirteen. Funny how, in the two parallel universes of my professional life, I sat on two committees of thirteen, the Committee *sine nomine* and ELSCOMF. I might easily get the personnel confused in my mind, mix up the agendas, and inadvertently betray a confidence. But being back on this committee was like time travelling, as if I'd never been away. ELSCOMF is reconvened. It must be some terrible mistake. Yet there was one difference. Whereas before, they had looked at me with an expression somewhere between mild amusement and pained indulgence, now they were all staring at me as if I were a rattlesnake. All except MacTaggart. No eye contact there. He kept his eyes down on his blotter, glued to the agenda.

"Item 12: Dr Cameron-Strange, 'A new way of working.' Alastair, haven't you presented this before? Complete, as I recall, with rather bizarre *son et lumière.* "

"No. I just retained the title. This is new material."

"Ah. A *new*, new way of working."

"Indeed."

MacTaggart sighed. "You have the ear of the house. We are all agog."

I'd prepared a statement. I suppose it was going to come across as a bit of a rant. But Forbes had always encouraged me, as far as the hospital was concerned, to get political. I brandished my copy of the morning paper.

"With monotonous regularity, *The Scotsman* publishes the same old ghastly 'A & E' (sic) story, and here it is again. 'Targets missed as patients facing four-hour wait at A & E.' Apparently, for the week ending July 9th, 88% of patients were disposed of, one way or another, within four hours. The *target* is 95%.

"Personally, I couldn't care less. That's not why I find *The Scotsman*'s recurring piece so dismal. Rather, it's the assumption that spending time in 'A & E' (the hopelessly anachronistic terminology says it all) is intrinsically a bad thing. That is because everybody knows 'A & E' is a squalid poor house for drunks, drug addicts, 'inappropriate attenders', the poor and needy, the accident-prone, the crazy, the violent, the feckless, and other assorted casualties of life. The Acute Assessment Unit, on the other hand, is for people who had the gumption first to attend their GP, who in turn deemed them worthy of appropriate referral. No four-hour rule there! Medicine in the UK is utterly class-ridden. It's hardly surprising. All the doctors have gone to private schools. The entrances to our hospitals are run on an apartheid system based on snobbery, in which the most vulnerable in our society are treated with contempt.

"It makes me laugh when shadow health spokespersons try to make political capital out of missed targets. As if their lot could do any better. Politicians need to stop trying to micromanage the health service and concentrate on producing more hospital beds, more doctors, and more nurses. Meanwhile, the doctors need to abandon ancient rites of hierarchical tribalism and create a true specialty of Emergency Medicine.

"In short, I think Acute Medicine and 'A & E' (yuck), should...

"...amalgamate."

There was a stunned silence. MacTaggart broke it.

"Preposterous."

I glanced down the table. I've become fascinated by the dynamics of committee meetings, by the way motions and initiatives can stand or fall on the basis of a single remark – often dismissive – from a person of power and influence. I wasn't going to let this thing be nipped in the bud. Not without a fight. At least throw it open to the floor. I said, "What does management think?"

Leslie Horne said, "Blue sky thinking!" Eugene Gawkrodger concurred. "There are no sacred cows." Clotworthy was less impressed. "I think we should carpark this for the time being."

They were feeling their way. MacTaggart addressed my boss with evident irritation. "Did you know about this, Forbes? Or is this another blast from a loose cannon? Can't you keep your juniors under control?"

"With respect, Angus, may I point out that Dr Cameron-Strange is not junior. I'm delighted to say he has been offered and has accepted his first consultant post. He brings to it – and to us all – a wealth of experience gained from all over the world. I think we should explore some of these issues a little further. Besides, in case it has escaped your notice, his approach is conciliatory. He is, after all, offering you an olive branch."

"I should say it comes complete with thorns and nettles. Just exactly how is it going to benefit the Acute Assessment Unit if it is suddenly swamped by an influx of undifferentiated and hapless humanity? I'm not against Casualty. On the contrary, I'm an ally. Believe me, you have a place. You fulfil a role. And part of that role is to provide a buffer that protects the rest of the hospital and allows the hospital to function in an atmosphere of calm. Your role is analogous to that of the General Practitioner in the community. It is to separate the wheat from the chaff. Despatch the coughs and colds. Otherwise, the entire hospital will end up in a soup of snot! Casualty Officers need to be able to triage out the inconsequential, recognise significant pathology, and direct it to the appropriate specialty. That is why the four-hour rule is so important. We mustn't have patients languishing under the care of junior doctors unequal to the task."

Prof Pearson said, "That's strange, Angus. I thought emergency physicians existed to provide optimum care to decompensating patients."

"Decompensating patients are best dealt with by a team approach, by physicians, surgeons, anaesthetists and intensivists."

I re-entered the fray. "I wonder if I might expand a little on my idea, particularly to delineate the way in which it has evolved."

Horne and Gawkrodger said virtuously in unison, "We'd appreciate it."

But I never got the chance. We got interrupted. The board room door opened, and Faith, my favourite ED charge nurse, popped her head in.

"Alastair. Phone call."

"Could you take a message?"

"He says it won't wait."

"Who is it?"

"It's the palace."

"Which palace?"

"Buckingham."

"Is this a wind-up?"

Forbes said, "Take the call, Alastair. We'll talk about you behind your back."

"See Forbes. I *told* you this wasn't going to work."

Forbes squeezed my arm, gave me a mischievous smile, and whispered, "It's good to have you back." It crossed my mind that Forbes might have sneaked a quick peek at my letter of resignation before he shredded it.

As I went back along the corridor to ED with Faith, I said to her, "It's that intensivist bastard Galletly again, isn't it? The last time he did this, he was imitating Ambulance Control. Train crash. He told me the bus for the annual outing of the Haemophiliac Society got stuck on a level crossing and hit by the annual outing of the Osteogenesis Imperfecta Group. The first ambulances will be with you in ten minutes..."

"I don't think it was George."

"The time before, he was a policeman at a student rave in Marchmont. 'Somebody's put ethylene glycol in the punch...' If there's one thing I can't stand, it's a practical joker."

I took the call.

"Dr Cameron-Strange? This is Hoppy Metcalfe, equerry to His Majesty. His Majesty wonders – and if you have a prior commitment, he will perfectly understand – but he wonders if you would be free to join him this coming weekend at Balmoral."

"George, that's the worst fucking RP accent I've ever heard in my life."

"He has been keen for some time now to entertain the Committee *sine nomine*..."

"You sound like the late Brian Sewell. Or Sir Isaiah Berlin. *Nobody* speaks like that, not even in Buck House."

"It would be, if you take my meaning, a walk in the afternoon."

Code for *Witan*. George wouldn't have known about '*Walk In The After Noon*'. My heart sank.

"Mr, er, Metcalfe, forgive me. I'm terribly sorry."

"Sir Hopcroft. Hoppy's fine."

I said lamely, "I thought you were somebody else."

"Can you make it?" Hoppy was entirely unfazed. Maybe he had a long experience of people assuming he was winding them up.

"Yes. Yes, of course."

"If you come up on Saturday morning by train, I'll pick you up at Insch – 11 am. Ballater was so much more convenient, but unfortunately, it went on fire. Would that suit?"

Yes, it would suit. We exchanged courtesies and the phone call came to an end. I carefully replaced the receiver on its cradle and sat staring at the telephone in bemused silence. It still could have been that practical joker Galletly. These days, scams of all kinds are getting increasingly sophisticated. But no. This was the real deal. I had a premonition that I was about to enter, albeit briefly, a world that was entirely alien to me, and therefore not quite real. I already knew I would look back upon it afterwards and wonder if it had really happened.

But in the meantime, I was living in the present. Sir Hopcroft Metcalfe's phone call reminded me of the man the day before who had collapsed at the bus stop on Minto St. Fate had interrogated me. "Well? Are you, or are you not, a doctor?" And now it was a guy with a daft name like Hoppy, equerry to *Saxe-Coburg*, who might as well have asked me, "Well? Are you, or are you not, the National Medical Adviser to the Security Services?" I'd thought, if I'd thought about it at all, that I was at heart a republican, but I rolled over like a puppy looking to have his tummy scratched. Just like that. Pathetic. Hmm.

Could still have been that bastard Galletly.

XI

"...and on the rainy days, he took the lift back up to his penthouse on the fifty-first floor." Caitlin sat on the hearth rug in the lotus position, rocking to and fro, her gorgeous long red hair dancing about her shoulders. "But on the sunny days, he got off at the thirtieth floor and walked the rest of the way up the stairs."

"The stairs are on the outside of the building," volunteered MacKenzie, "and he wants fresh air and exercise."

"Wrong!"

"The lift's solar powered," said Dorothy Pearson, and then abruptly changed her mind. "But then he'd have to get off on the wet days, I suppose."

"Something to do with the structure of the well of the building," said Forbes vaguely.

"Nope. Give up?"

I made a suggestion. "I missed the first bit, but it sounds to me like a dwarf with an umbrella."

There was a momentary silence followed by a chorus of catcalls and boos.

"The thing about my brother," said MacKenzie, "is his mind is so lateral that it's off the edge. He gets the answer before he's heard the question."

"Well you should know," said Caitlin. "You are telepathic, aren't you?"

"No," I said firmly. "We're not. Is this *Lateral Thinking* you are playing? Do you want to solve a real one? This really happened last year in Australia."

Caitlin uncrossed her legs and sat forward on her knees. "Okay. Go."

"You are walking through the charred remains of a forest that has been destroyed by fire. You come across the dead body of a scuba diver right in the heart of the bush, complete with a charred wet suit and melted oxygen cylinder."

"Goodness," said Dorothy Pearson.

"Don't tell me," said MacKenzie. "He was picked up out of the sea by a helicopter filling up one of these water buckets."

"Correct."

"Did that really happen?"

"Who knows in this day and age? Could be fake news."

"How bizarre."

Caitlin remarked, "I guess it just wasn't his day. Any other ones from real life, Ally?"

"How about this? A doctor boards a 747 to retrieve a patient." (Dorothy pulled a face and gave a little gasp of dismay.) "On his way off, they put on some *Musak*, and everybody gets murdered."

"Andrew Lloyd-Webber!" (I should say Caitlin is a musical snob.) There was laughter.

"Okay," said Caitlin. "A man parks his tank outside a hotel in Mayfair. He goes into the hotel and ends his life."

"Ah!" said Forbes. "Did he throw himself out of a window? He's a stockbroker."

"Why do all these conundrums involve death and destruction?" said Dorothy in a tone of outrage.

"Defenestration," said Forbes, "is the preferred mode of demise of the bankrupt."

MacKenzie snapped her fingers. "Monopoly."

"Yes!"

Party of six. They were assembled in the Pearsons' Moray Place flat, spacious as an embassy, in the heart of Edinburgh New Town: Forbes and Dorothy Pearson, and Caitlin Roy, up on holiday with her latest boyfriend, whom she had met at the NYO – a percussionist and a pianist who was about to go up to Cambridge to study mathematics. Such it is to be multitalented. Which college? Jesus. I remember he had an absurd Anglo-Saxon name. Caedmon Ambrose-Pedoe. He was just a stripling of a lad, pale, ascetic and emaciated. He looked like a younger Ian Bostridge. Who else? My sister, up for the Festival, and her new man, Howard Perfect. He was considerably older than she. Thirteen year age gap. I knew vaguely of him as a Massachusetts captain of industry. He had a company that made some tiny engineering component like ball bearings or something. It seemed an utterly prosaic calling, but it had made him very wealthy. He was a philanthropist with a love of music, and a benefactor of musicians. I'd met Howard once before. He was a tall, well-built and handsome man whom I'd been fully prepared to detest. But I was appalled to find I rather liked him. I'd teased my sister about him. "How's the King of Balls?"

"To whom do you refer?"

"Howard the Ballmeister."

MacKenzie raised her eyes to the ceiling. "You're jealous."

And, of course, she was absolutely right. No, not in any

inappropriately incestuous way, but it was almost preordained that I would be biased against my twin sister's suitors. Nobody was good enough for her. I'd paid little attention to her string of boyfriends because I knew she did much the same. Music was just too big a part of her life. There wasn't much room for anything else. She didn't like to get distracted. I was always going out with absolute strangers and rendering myself vulnerable to the unrequited state because I was addicted to *xenoerotica*, the thrill of the beauty that is other. She had always recognised the folly of it all, the time-wasting of it, and she had firmly pushed all that stuff out of her life. Of the pair of us, she was the stronger. But now that she had made a career for herself, now that she was established, even on the cusp of eminence, things were different.

As soon as I met Howard, I knew he would be a contender, all the more so because he had a life of his own, and it was a life outside music. When I met him, I had a hunch that he was going to give up the ball bearings (he'd made his pile; they'd served their purpose), enter public life and go up to Capitol Hill. He'd be a senator. There was no guessing where he and MacKenzie might end up. Howard Perfect. It was indeed a perfect name for him. This quiet, unassuming man was precisely the one who might turn my sister's life upside-down. I had a premonitory vision of a white picket fence in Kentucky bordering a driveway sweeping up through the blue grass where the thoroughbreds grazed, towards a white-pillared mansion that Thomas Jefferson might have built. Here, my sister would calmly and without regret put her Stradivarius back in its case and hand it over to her most gifted pupil.

Then Mr and Mrs Perfect would found a dynasty. You would see their names on the *Virtuoso* list of donors to the Symphony. Mr and Mrs Howard Perfect. There would be the Perfect Trust, the Perfect Bequest, the Perfect Fellowship and the Perfect Foundation. In twenty years' time I'd be getting my annual Christmas card with the round robin digest of the achievements of the next generation of Perfects. Reince's football scholarship to Yale has opened all sorts of doors, and Missy can't wait to get to Oxford on her Rhodes scholarship. At the end of the day, there would be the Perfect Legacy, for all to peruse, within the hallowed cloister of the Perfect Library.

I revolted against it all. I sent my twin sister a telepathic message. *Whatever you do, MacKenzie, don't stop playing. Marry the guy by all means. I'll even give you away if you like. But just make sure he knows you are not entering his world; he is entering yours. Just make sure he understands it's a ménage a trois: you, him, and a Strad.*

Party of six. I saw all this as I entered Forbes and Dorothy's gracious Georgian living room. There they were, bathed in a pool of light. I paused for a moment in the shadow, about to make it a party of seven, an odd number, a prime number. I had the sudden absolute conviction that I would always turn a party into an odd number. I would always be a lone passenger on a tram in a suburb, preoccupied with some musical worm and some situational puzzle while, in some other universe, people were leading a life.

And yet I knew it was a conceit and an indulgence to imagine that I was in some sense cursed by fate. The fact is that – at least for the moment – I had no desire to *settle down*. The idea of founding my own dynasty in Edinburgh, of all places, just seemed preposterous to me. I'd spent half a decade here completing my medical degree and doing a swag of house jobs, and I never had any sense that I belonged. It's true that I found somebody here before I lost her, and that our story started here, but I think we both knew instinctively that we were in transit. The idea that I might start all over again here and find an Edinburgh girl with that slightly superior Edinburgh look, that we might plan a life here and put in an offer for a villa on Henderland Road (at some fantastically exorbitant price), handy for our daughter when she went to St George's, that we might build up a middle-class circle of middle-class friends, couples, like Rupert and Angela, Adrian and Deirdre, Fergus and Gareth, that we might time-share in Madeira and go on holiday with Paul and Melissa, that I, greatly encouraged to do so by my new wife, should join a racquets club and work out with *best friends*, join Murrayfield Golf Club, that I might sing again in the choir of St Giles, that I should chair the hospital's medical ethics committee, that Fiona and I (I've just christened this putative new wife) should plan a safari in Botswana and come back with thousands of picture of elephants and giraffes with which to bore our social circle, then go off to the Grand Canyon and Yosemite and do much the same again, endlessly absorbed in the images on our tablets, that I should (like the Perfects) sire a dynasty so that I could send out these relentless Yuletide updates on the relentlessly upbeat progress of our issue...

Utterly impossible.

No. I would remain the reluctant wedding guest, and when Caitlin married somebody with a name like Caedmon Ambrose-Pedoe, the seating plan would put me beside some bald-headed bank managers and ladies of ample girth, left to wonder dimly why I wasn't down at that rowdy table with all the other young bucks.

At the end of the evening, I knocked diffidently on Caitlin's door, and she yelled, "*Entrez!*" Caedmon had been assigned to another room. Forbes and Dorothy had rooms enough to assure propriety. I glanced at her furrowed brow and said, "You look tired. Are they overworking you at school with these endless SATS tests? Maybe you're moonlighting at the doughnut."

"Doughnut?"

"GCHQ."

"No. It's just exam fever."

"In August?"

"Holidays are an indulgence and a thing of the past."

"You poor bastard. Who'd be a young person nowadays? You're cannon fodder for some Minister of Education with a mad gleam in his eye and a cunning plan to outwit the Chinese. I expect you work a sixteen-hour day."

"Seventeen. Give or take."

"Why has the woodman carved these scars
"Across that which should be so clear and bright
"Like the matelot's phare on the frozen ice?"

She hazarded, "Whitman? Eliot?"

"Cameron-Strange. Hot off the press."

"Time for my annual bedtime story."

"Aren't you getting a little long in the tooth for this?"

"Long in the tooth? What am I? A mare?"

"I should say you are more of a yearling. With a fancy name. Madame Bovary."

"No thanks! I seem to recall Mrs B called on the apothecary and ended up poisoning herself. Please, can I be Fandango?"

"The 2.30 at Kempton Park, Fandango, 2-1 favourite."

"Fandango is Tuppence's horse."

"Tuppence?"

"Tuppence Pennington-Althorp. She's on my lacrosse team. But dressage is her big thing. She's training for the Paris Olympics."

Well, with a name like that, she could hardly do otherwise. I had a vision of a tall young woman, beautiful if somewhat horsey, immaculately turned out in a pink jacket and beige jodhpurs. If she carried a riding crop, she would look like a dominatrix.

"Well, good luck to Penny Tuppington-Althorp."

Caitlin giggled. "Not Althorp. Althrop. But you're right. She prefers Penny."

"Threepence Tuppington-Penny. She's inflating."

"Far from it. Thin as a stick. She models. On the runway, she's Penny Althorp."

"Ha'penny Farthington-Groat."

"You always go too far, don't you?"

Then I remembered. The gentleman I met – or maybe dreamt I met – up in Wester Ross on a midsummer's night; his name was Pennington-Althorp. There can't be too many of them in the phone book. I asked Caitlin, "Do you know anything about her people?"

"The Pennington-Althorps?" She screwed up her nose. "Scottish aristocracy. Her grandfather's a duke or something. Somewhere on the west coast. Could it be Rothesay?"

"Unlikely. I think that's the Prince of Wales."

"Nothing would surprise me. I believe the Pennington-Althorps are very high. Is it something like *Accent* or *Ascent*?"

"The Duke of Assynt?"

"That's the guy."

"I think I may have met him. It's a small world."

When I left Moray Place that night, I found that *The Telegraph*'s column inch on *Whetstone,* the one in which Sir Roger Hollis had put me in my place, still preoccupied me. I was mixing it up with a game of charades. The dwarf with the umbrella going up to his penthouse, and so on. They are called *situational puzzles*. They don't make any sense at all until you indulge in a single creative act of *lateral thinking* that renders the solution glaringly obvious. I'd pitched *Whetstone* as a situational puzzle just for some black humour, a sick joke, but I suddenly realised that that was precisely what *Whetstone* was: it was a situational puzzle. Not only that, but I was the only person who could solve it because I was the only person who had been there. Hadn't that girl with the Shakespearean name, the eulogist at Suzanna's funeral, said as much? All I had to do was conduct a thought experiment, to revisit that cursed aircraft and go over the sequence of events in my head, and I would be able to solve the conundrum. This I felt confident I could do, for I am blessed with an eidetic memory. But did I want to do it?

Fate was interrogating me for a third time. First, the man at the Minto St bus stop. Are you or are you not a doctor? Then Hoppy. Are you or are you not the N-MASS? And now, it was that Hathaway girl. Are you or are you not going to get to the bottom of *Whetstone*?

So here I was, back at my apartment in Thirlestane Road, top flat, looking out over Warrander Baths. On an impulse, I fired up my laptop and drafted a letter.

The Editor
The Daily Telegraph
August 27th

Sir,

I think the Chairman of the Commons Select Committee overseeing the inquiry into Operation Whetstone is being a little disingenuous in concluding that the agency overseeing the hijack of Aerolíneas Argentinas Flight 301 merely wished to open old wounds in the South Atlantic. The perpetrators may have been a hapless bunch of anachronistic buccaneers nostalgic for past glory, but their sponsors, whoever they may be, must surely conceal some more sinister motivation. I regret that I was unable to assist the Select Committee in exploring this more fully. But then, I'm just a bit-player.

However, I intend to give the matter some further careful thought.

Sincerely…
Dr Alastair Cameron-Strange
National Medical Advisor to the Security Services.

It took me five minutes to write that email. Because I imagined I was just doodling, I didn't edit it or agonise over it in any way. I sat and read what I had just written, and there was Fate at my shoulder again. Well? Are you, or are you not, going to send it?

In retrospect, knowing what I know now, it was a crazy thing to do, writing that letter. If I were going to revisit *Whetstone*, it would have been far more sensible to go undercover and stay there. But here I was, by implication, about to announce my intention to all and sundry. I suppose it was vanity; I didn't like to be dismissed as a *bit-player*. I ran a quick spell check, but then I did pause before pressing 'send'. It was, after all, a Rubicon moment. It was an open letter addressed to Sir Roger Hollis announcing, in some way that I didn't fully comprehend, that I was an antagonist, perhaps even a foe. Once I sent it, there would be no going back. Still, why should I be apprehensive? How many letters does *The Telegraph* get every day? They probably wouldn't publish me. The whole thing was still *sub judice,* and they wouldn't touch it with a barge pole. And even if they did, probably nobody would pay the slightest attention. I was just flying a kite. I would pitch it up into the air and wait to see what happened.

Who ordered the storming of AA301? Who runs Britain? Yes, that's the question. But did I really want to ask it? I was under no illusions. Frankly, I didn't think I would get anywhere. And I would be taking a considerable personal risk. I would be joining the Awkward Squad. I would become a thorn in the flesh of the British Establishment or at least a substantial portion of it. They wouldn't like it. As a result, I would certainly come under attack. It would initially take the form of psychological warfare. They would try to wear me down. If I grew stubborn and intransigent, the attacks would become more personal. I could expect to have my reputation besmirched. I would be scorned, mocked, repudiated, and vilified. Well, bring it on. I will bolster my well of inner resource by reading the Beatitudes. *Blessed are ye, when men shall revile you, and persecute you, and shall say all manner of evil against you falsely...*

Sooner or later, it could get really nasty. Ultimately, if I persisted that long, the attacks might even become physical. Was I prepared for that? Would it be worth it? How far was I prepared to go? It might be then that I would ask myself, why are you doing this? Why do you care? Wouldn't you rather wash your hands of the whole bloody lot of them? That might be when the doubts would set in. My resolve might be weakened by my loved ones, acting as unwitting Job's Comforters, distressed by my pig-headed bloody-mindedness. Forbes would tell me to pack it in and just come to ED in the morning and work a shift. The elder statesmen of the hospital would get exasperated with me again. Yes, it had all happened before. Bringing the hospital into disrepute. David Walkerburn, my lawyer, would come as close as his cautious and circumspect persona would allow, to issue me with some words of friendly advice. MacKenzie would say, with tears in her eyes, "Don't you care that you are hurting those close to you? Okay, I told you to keep practising medicine, but I never told you to become a martyr!" That would be the hardest of all.

Caitlin? No, dear Caitlin would be the one who would stand by me through thick or thin. That was because, in many ways, Caitlin and I were so alike. Caitlin had a devil-may-care, to-hell-with-it approach to life. She was every bit as crazy and off her head as I was.

So here we go again. 'You're taking the bastards on again. You haven't a hope in hell, and you're on your own, but you're going to take them on.'

I read through my letter to *The Daily Telegraph* one more time. As an afterthought, at the end of the letter and under my name and position, I appended, somewhat mischievously, *Chairman, DAMASK (Doctors Against Muddle and So-called Quality – with a capital K)*. I took a deep breath and pressed 'send'.

XII

A doctor boards a 747 to retrieve a patient. On his way off, they play some Musak, *and everyone is murdered.*

The *Telegraph* published my letter.

Of course, the bit about playing the *Musak* was nonsense. Yet I was not entirely dismissive of it. I couldn't remember the music that happened to be playing on the aircraft's sound system when we tried to get Taff off. Yet, it always seemed to be on the tip of my tongue. I had an idea that if I could retrieve it, I would also retrieve the atmosphere of the whole episode, and that, in turn, would help me to remember that which was staring me in the face but which I was overlooking. "You see," remarked Holmes to Watson, "but you do not observe." In Blackwell's bookshop on South Bridge, I sipped coffee and went over my situational puzzle. Think laterally! What is it you are missing? What is directly before your gaze, that which you failed to observe?

With respect to *Whetstone,* the narrative that had evolved

in the papers I found entirely unconvincing. A hapless bunch of skinheads from Portsmouth and Hastings had decided to open old wounds in the South Atlantic and teach the Argies a lesson. They were like Japanese soldiers who had disappeared into the Manchurian jungle in the summer of 1945, who had never heard of Hiroshima and Nagasaki, and were still fighting the last war. They were like a bunch of football hooligans throwing tables and chairs across the plazas outside the estaminets of continental Europe just because they enjoyed nothing more than a good punch-up.

But I'd seen them. I alone had seen them. They weren't like that. They were like a unit of Special Forces who had been dropped behind enemy lines, who had been cut off, and then had been disowned and abandoned by their masters and left without recourse. Why?

It crossed my mind once more to call up the Witenagemot's chairperson, Baroness Margaret Rowallan, *Sphinx*, and ask that the Committee *sine nomine* be reconvened. But I immediately dismissed the idea. There was a mole on the Witan. That remark Mr Hugh Standish had passed while serving on the Parliamentary Defence Select Committee proved it. He knew about DAMASK. Now, DAMASK was trivial; DAMASK was a quip; it was nothing at all. Nonetheless, he knew about it. That meant that at least one person on the Committee *sine nomine* was bad at confidential. For all I knew, confidentiality-wise, the entire committee might be as porous as a sieve. Yet my instinct told me that there was one mole. Just one.

Who was it?

I jotted down in my diary a dozen code names of the Committee membership. *Sphinx Sword Scimitar Spitfire Scud Super Slacker Spook Sports-Jacket Silk Somalia Speedbird.* I excluded our patron, *Saxe-Coburg*. And I excluded *Shrink*. Parkinson. Neither had been present at the meeting. That left twelve possibilities, including myself. I suppose I might have blurted the name *DAMASK* out elsewhere. But I didn't think so. *One of the twelve.* A Judas in our midst.

It had to be *Sword*. General Iain Civil. I could just hear Civil getting on the blower to Sir Roger straight after the Witenagemot adjourned. "Roger, it's Iain. The medic's on his way across to the Select Committee. Impetuous young whippersnapper. If you want to put him on the spot, get one of your chaps to ask him about DAMASK. Some sort of quack-based anarchists' think tank. Sure, he'll dig a hole for himself. Cheerie-bye."

I put a circle round his name. Just a hunch. It wasn't exactly evidence-based. Just prejudice. He didn't like me and, I suppose in consequence, I didn't much like him. I reminded myself to give the matter a little further thought. But in the meantime, at any rate, my enquiry was going to remain private. DAMASK, for the moment, would remain a college of one.

I opened up a *zapiska* – the old Soviet name for a dossier – on Sir Roger Hollis. Hollis was key. Hollis had gone out of his way to justify the storming of AA301. My gut instinct was that he was responsible for the decision, that it was he who had fired the starting pistol. Could I prove that? And even if I did, I would just be left with another, far bigger question, the question that preoccupied Ms Hathaway. Why? What made Sir Roger Hollis tick?

If I wanted to understand his motivation, I needed to understand the man. I already knew him to be a man of many parts. His influence was everywhere. He was widely referred to as the *de facto* Deputy Prime Minister. He himself was dismissive of such a notion. He characterised himself as a dutiful public servant. Occasionally, the government would use him when they wanted to air something unpalatable. He was adept at defending the indefensible. He seemed impervious to criticism. He would come out and do a short piece to camera expounding some piece of humbug, entirely unfazed by any cognitive dissonance in the burden of his argument, whatever it might be. He had issued a statement on the unfortunate demise of Suzanna Fergusson, and now he was doing a piece on the unfortunate demise of a hiker strafed by the RAF on the Durness Peninsula. He almost used the same script. "Our hearts go out to the family of this unfortunate man..." That was why I conflated *Whetstone* with the Parph of Durness. Every time I thought of AA301, I thought of a drone over the lighthouse at Cape Wrath. Since I found myself in Blackwells, I bought a slim text about the Durness Peninsula, ordered a second coffee, and read up about it. I had that vague sense of guilt that you experience when you are supposed to be studying some dry subject, and you allow yourself to be diverted towards something more entertaining. I skim-read, taking notes as I went.

> *Gaelic Am Parbh. A cape in the Durness Parish of the county of Sutherland. The most northwesterly point in mainland Britain. Separated from the rest of the mainland by the Kyle of Durness. Two hundred eighty square kilometres of moorland wilderness known as the Parph. The first road across the Parph built in 1828 by the Lighthouse Commission. The Parph now used as a military training area by MOD. Live firing range. The name Cape Wrath derived from the Old Norse hvarf or turning point.*

(I liked the notion of Cape Wrath as my own special turning point. A fulcrum, *un point d'appui*. I remembered something Major Martin Forster had once said to me. "There is a tipping point. Stay this side of it, and the failsafe mechanisms apply. Cross it, and the past is irrevocable."). I continued my skim-read.

Cape Wrath once populated by several crofting communities, dwindling by the mid-nineteenth century to a handful of shepherds, and by the mid-twentieth century to some thirty souls. Small school at Achiemore with about ten pupils closed in 1947. The area now almost entirely depopulated.

The Lighthouse: built in 1828, and, at the end of the nineteenth century, a Lloyd's of London signal station to track shipping around the Cape.

During the Great War, RMS Dunottar Castle *fitted out for wartime service as* HMS Caribbean. *On September 27th 1915, she foundered off Cape Wrath. A tow by* HMS Birkenhead *failed. Fifteen souls perished.*

Sea cliffs (Torridonian sandstone and Lewisian gneiss) rise to nearly 1,000 feet above sea level at Clò Mòr. There are sea stacks offshore – Stac an Dunain and Stac Clo Kearvaig (also known as The Cathedral) and a reef, Duslic, just north of the Cape. To the east, Garvie Island (An Garbh-Eilean) is a target for live firing by the military.

Inland lochans include Loch Airigh na Beinne. Plant species include heather Calluna vulgaris, juniper Juniperus communis, and ferns.

The lighthouse manned until 1998. A Category A listed granite tower with a semi-circular base. The light visible from twenty-two nautical miles.

Military use... (I scanned this briefly). *Naval gunnery range – multi-service NATO training area – live ordnance deployed including 1,000 pound bombs – control centre at Faraid Head, Balnakeil. 2002, a shell landed eight miles off target and one mile from houses. 2008, live ordnance destroyed 137 acres of heathland… Adverse effects on nesting birds, and lambing; noise pollution for residents.*

2012: MOD considered purchasing Cape Wrath Lighthouse, and surrounding area, from the Northern Lighthouse Board. The Durness Development Group, wishing the area to remain open to the public, opposed this with a petition raising thousands of signatures. MOD dropped the idea.

Climate: Oceanic (Koppen Cfb) with occasionally a Fohn effect.

Landscape largely untouched by man; wide diversity of wildlife, including red deer, fulmar, hooded crow, rock pipit, golden eagle, cormorant and gannet. On the cliffs, nesting colonies of puffin Fratercula arctica, razorbill Alca torda, guillemot Uria aalge, kittiwake Rissa tridactyla and fulmar Fulmarus glacialis. Marine species include porpoises, seals, bottle-nosed dolphins, sea squirts and sponges.

Clifftop vegetation: scurvygrass Cochlearia officinalis. Clifftop sand dunes and montane habitats…

Cape Wrath sounded to me like a beautiful, beguiling, and mysterious region. I badly wanted to visit. But since the demise of that hiker, it had become sequestered. It was taboo.

From Blackwells, I went down to the National Library of Scotland and took down from the reference shelf *Who's Who*, a book in red covers as bulky as a car battery.

Hollis, Sir Roger Albert VC KCBE, born Weymouth, Dorset, January 31st 1955, educated Winchester School, and Baliol College Oxford 1973–1976 (PPE). President,

*University Union. Military service 1978–83 (Paratroop
Regiment). Active Service the Falkland Islands 1982.
Married Imogen Gould 1984. Two daughters, Patricia
(b. 1985) and Ursula (b. 1987). Founder and Company
Director The Conglomerate 1984–2000. Elected MP
Easter Wessex 2001. Junior Minister Ministry of Defence
2010-15, Enterprise Czar 2015–. Interests include
hunting, fencing and horse racing. Address: c/Athenaeum,
Westminster, London W1.*

My goodness, he had a Victoria Cross. Cast from the
gunmetal of a cannon used in the Crimea. *For Valour.* It was
the gong to surpass all gongs.

What was his act of valour?

I borrowed a library computer and tried to research
it online. But I kept coming up against a brick wall. It had
been conferred following some action outside Port Stanley in
1982. But Hollis had been in Special Forces, and the citation
was confidential. That only made it all the more intriguing. A
senior cabinet minister who, as a young man, had carried out
an act of heroism on behalf of his country. Yet, of its nature, he
must remain reticent.

Holding a VC, even if with becoming modesty, you don't
routinely append the letters to your name, you don't pin it to
your lapel (except on Armistice Day), must be like holding in
your wallet some sort of platinum credit card reserved for the
top ten in the Forbes rich list. It would be an eternal meal
ticket. It would open every door for you. Politically, it would be
the equivalent of an obliterating nuclear arsenal. Imagine if you
tried to oppose Hollis' views on defence. Who was the public
going to side with? A chocolate, armchair strategist, or the
real deal? He would be feted in the States. "Honoured by his
Queen…" They just loved that stuff. Hollis would be skilled

at deploying his heavy artillery. He would never flaunt it; he would take pains merely to hold it in reserve. Other people would play the VC card on his behalf. The BBC interviewer would say, "You are in a far better position to tell us what today's soldier needs than most of us..." and he would wave a dismissive hand. "This has little to do with me personally. Rather, it is the force of the argument..."

I must find out a little more about that VC.

Then there was his company. I looked up *The Conglomerate.* It turned out to be an amalgamation of companies with a vast portfolio of enterprises, whose management had been passed to daughters Patricia and Ursula so that the cabinet minister would have no conflict of interest. I thought of The Conglomerate as an onion with countless layers. You peeled one away, and another was revealed. It was like a diamond-studded series of Russian dolls by Fabergé. One of its subsidiaries was named *Holistic Proprietary.* I gathered that it was a pun on the name Hollis. It implied something multifaceted, perhaps The Conglomerate in a microcosm. I wondered how removed Hollis really was from his business interests. The Conglomerate was said to be held in a *Blind Trust.* What did that entail? Something else to research. I went on to the Holistic website and got a UK contact number off the home page. I dialled the 0800 number on my mobile.

"...come to Holistic Proprietary. Press star now."

I did so.

"You will now hear four options. You can make your selection at any time. For insurance services, press one. For travel services, press two. For hotel and conference bookings, press three. If you would like to speak to one of our operators, press four."

I pressed 4.

"Our operators are currently experiencing a high level of

demand. Please hold, as your call is important to us. You can also contact us via email…"

I sat back and listened to Mozart 40. I envisaged, somewhere in New Delhi, an open-plan office as big as an aircraft hangar. The fluorescent strip lights illuminated row upon row of telephonists seated on swivel chairs beside serried ranks of computer screens in oblique, ergonomic rows. The dark satanic mills had gone offshore.

"Holistics you are speaking with Karen how may I help you?"

I'd got the location wrong. Karen was probably in Bristol. "Good morning. I was looking to obtain some comprehensive advice on money management."

"May I put you through to Stocks? Pension planning?"

"I'm not sure. What I would like to do is sit down face-to-face with someone who could advise me on my portfolio. I'm phoning from Edinburgh. Do you have a local office?"

"Holistics does not have high street outlets. You can obtain a comprehensive review of our products online. Have you visited the money management link on our website?"

"Yes, but it doesn't really answer my question. I'm in London next week. Is there somebody I could make an appointment with?"

"I'm afraid not, sir. But we do have a live chat line facility. You can access it from the homepage." The call handler had moved up to a higher level of brusqueness. I had been categorised. I was a vexatious crank caller. I would be off the line in another minute. I persisted, "There's no way I can meet with a Holistics representative across a table?"

"I'm afraid not, sir." A suspicion had crept into her voice. I was a Luddite. "I take it you are online?"

I decided to kill the call. "No."

"You could still access the website through your local public library." Now, she was speaking to an old-age pensioner.

"That's what I'll do."

"Thank you for your interest." It was the sort of thing people say to you when your job application has been, on this occasion, unsuccessful. "Have a nice day."

While online, I discovered Sir Roger had been a castaway on *Desert Island Discs*. I delved into the BBC Radio 4 programme's archive, put on a pair of headphones, and listened to Eric Coates' familiar melody to the accompaniment of sea birds on the seashore. "My castaway this week... soldier, decorated war hero, entrepreneur, man of ideas, politician, dare I say gambler, a true Renaissance man... Sir Roger Hollis: what drives you?"

But I never really found out. Sir Roger was charming, but elusive. If there was a grotesque portrait to be unveiled, he kept it concealed up in the attic. I sat the programme out. Again, I had that nagging sense of guilt that I was on a diversion down some dead-end cul-de-sac, and I was wasting my time. But I persisted, jotting down his choice of eight records on a scrap of paper. As a matter of fact, I still have it.

First record: *The Cantus in memoriam Benjamin Britten* by Arvo Pärt. A descending melodic minor scale rendered ever more complex by multi-layered strings. And the tolling of a bell. Hypnotic. It occurred to me that this might become the signature tune of my research. I might listen to it if I wanted to get in the mood.

Potted biography. Early life: born in Dorset, the son of an Anglican vicar and a music teacher. His mother very loving, his father rather distant, and strict. Only child, solitary pursuits. Educated Winchester, a choral scholar. What was it like to be packed off to boarding school at a young age? Difficult. He had been gauche and withdrawn, unpopular, a figure of ridicule. Bullied? Yes, bullied, certainly. How did he deal with it? Did he tell his parents? His teachers? Did he seek help? No. He carried out a single, audacious act that was so insane as to border on the suicidal. He challenged his chief tormentor to a duel. As you do.

Second record: *When I am laid in earth*, from Purcell's *Dido*, sung by Ferrier. That dark, haunting, beatific voice.

Gap year. Europe, languages, skiing. Home, Oxford (First, PPE), friendships, first love.

Army. The Falklands. *Esprit de Corps*. Tremendous enthusiasm for the modern service and its peace-keeping role inside NATO and alongside the United Nations.

Third record: Vaughan Williams *Sinfonia Antarctica*, the last movement, prefaced by lines from Robert Falcon Scott's last journal, spoken mellifluously, almost sung, by Sir John Gielgud.

I do not regret this journey; we took risks, we knew we took them, things have come out against us therefore we have no cause for complaint.

This provided the interviewer with an ideal 'in' to explore Sir Roger's act of heroism, but Ms Laverne got nowhere.

Fourth record: The theme music to the 1963 film, *The Great Escape*. It has become a kind of anthem for England football supporters abroad – a solo trumpet emanating from the terraces. There was a brief discussion about football hooliganism. Hollis was remarkably indulgent. "I'd love to get hold of some of these chaps. I could make soldiers out of them."

It occurred to me that he was choosing nothing but English music or music closely associated with England. That thought must also have occurred to the interviewer. "You really do believe in the greatness of England, don't you?"

"You mean the greatness of the United Kingdom. In the Falklands, I was never so happy as to have a Gordon Highlander by my side. Sublime." This led to a discussion about the position of the UK in the world today. Our relegation to the role of 'junior partner' was surely taken as a given. Not a bit of it. "The

British Empire remains the most remarkable empire that has ever existed on earth. We were entrusted with the title deeds of civilisation, and it is my view that we surrendered them with unseemly haste. Frankly, it has been a failure of nerve. Mr Pitt – I mean the Earl of Chatham – must be turning in his grave. Would you not prefer the *Pax Britannica* to the appalling conditions of strife that have overtaken many of our former possessions?"

"Some people," remarked Ms Laverne, "would say that we are not the solution; we are the problem. But is this not merely academic? Then, we had control of the high seas, dominated by a Royal Navy, in turn powered by the Industrial Revolution. Has that not all evaporated?"

"There is no reason why there should not be a new Industrial Revolution in these islands."

"What would that consist of? Financial services? Service industries? Or do you have another ace up your sleeve?"

"Lauren, if you hold an ace up your sleeve, you do not reveal it until the moment you play it."

Fifth record: It was William Walton's incidental music to *Henry V*, with the Shakespearean text spoken by Christopher Plummer. I was beginning to detect a pattern. Sir Roger was, and remained, a warrior. Henry's famous Agincourt speech preceded the intensely stirring music.

And Crispin Crispian shall ne'er go by
From this day to the ending of the world...

I confess I dislike Henry V. No, not the play, certainly not the music, but Hal. The man, himself. I thought he treated old Falstaff abominably. He chucked all his old mates as soon he had gained the crown. And it wasn't as if he was a reprobate who suffered a change of heart. It was all premeditated. Remember,

"I know you all, and will awhile uphold…" He had it all mapped out. The path to kingship. The Plantagenet brand. Or was it the House of Lancaster? And when he finally made it, it wasn't that he dropped a pose to show his real self. He just adopted another pose. "We few, we happy few…" Aye right. He really invented the idea of alternative truths. He may have stirred the hearts of men, but I have a sense he himself remained entirely cold. What a fake. I have this notion Shakespeare felt the same way about him as I did. I bet he read that speech to Ms Hathaway (there's that name again) and said, "Does it move you? Doesn't do a thing for me." Christopher Plummer was terribly good at playing Hal, just as he was terribly good at playing powerful American political elder statesmen who are completely charming, ruthless bastards.

It occurred to me that Sir Roger Hollis was, in fact, Henry V.

Sixth record: The Beatles! I love the Beatles. But Sir Roger managed to choose surely the ugliest track they ever recorded – *Helter-Skelter* from the Double White Album. Now what was the point of that? Maybe Sir Roger was preaching to his power-base. He had a constituency of crazies, people who might be driven to a frenzy when Sir Roger rendered the St Crispin's Day speech. Helter-Skelterers.

Ms Laverne moved to the absurd litany, the catechism demanded by the programme's premise.

"Are you practical? Would you be able to fend?"

"No, not really. I'm afraid I'm more a man of ideas. Nowadays, I tend to think them up and then get somebody else to put them into action. Mine's the easy bit. It's always more difficult to make things work."

"But you must have learned something of survival in the army!"

"Oh, absolutely. But I was fitter then." A good-humoured chuckle.

169

"Would you try to escape? Would you build a raft?"

"Yes, I would. I think my need for human fellowship would overcome my innate sloth, my impracticality, and my fear."

That was pretty rich, coming from a VC.

The interviewer tried once more to broach the subject of the feat of arms which had earned him this signal honour, but he skilfully parried all attempts with an admirable reticence and with the utmost tact. That, coupled with the fact that he couldn't remember the first decade of his life, made the overall impression oddly patchy. Plenty on Business, on Wealth, on the Business of Accruing Wealth. Not much on politics. ("This isn't really a political occasion.") In the end, the impression was of a very busy, a very active, and a very successful man. But what was his creed? What was his totem? What did he live by?

Seventh record: It was Holst. A Planet. Which would he choose? Perhaps the hymn from Jupiter. 'I vow to thee my country.' No. He opted for Neptune – the Mystic.

Then Ms Laverne tentatively broached a delicate subject. "I can't ask about your life without touching on an area of controversy."

"You mean fox hunting."

"No. I mean gambling.

"Oh. *Gambling*." Laughter, in unison.

"And gambling for huge stakes. Millions. Millions of pounds, that is. Las Vegas, Monte Carlo. Many people consider that a man prominent in public life demeans his office with such extravagance. What do you say to them?"

"That if they feel it to be an issue of conscience, then clearly they should not vote for me. But bear in mind that the British Empire was founded not in the cabinets of Whitehall but on the crap tables of Chelsea and Vauxhall. What is it Kipling says? Something about risking everything in one game of pitch and toss, losing, and starting over again. Remember, Winston was a gambler and kept the company of gamblers."

"Much to Clemmie's chagrin."

Laughs. "Yes, well, Imogen would sympathise with that. I've always been a gambler. I don't think it makes me any less of a politician, and I know it does not diminish me as a businessman."

"Do you think it could become a problem?"

"You mean like alcoholism or drug addiction? Yes, I suppose it could. But so far, I'm on a winning streak. We'll just have to accept that the jury's still out on that one."

"Are you addicted to risk?"

"I don't think I'm addicted to anything except maybe snooker. You know Steve Davis, the ex-world champ whom I run into from time to time, once talked about the state of mind you need to win a major tournament on the green baize. When you visit the table, the game must mean nothing to you, and yet it must mean everything. I've always played to win, and I've always risked losing. You can't have one without the other. I think that was my birthright. It was what became crystalised for me during the Falklands, and it's what I try to carry into every area of my life, political, entrepreneurial, recreational."

Final record? Vaughan Williams again. He chose the last movement of the Sixth Symphony. Utterly cold, utterly pianissimo. In the great Anglo-Saxon litotes tradition, RVW was famously dismissive of the idea that his music had a programme. It meant nothing. It was merely music. Arnold Bax used to say much the same. Tongue in cheek? Who can tell? It occurred to me that this music owed a lot to the music we had just heard. Neptune. Was RVW giving a nod to his friend Gustav? Even within the context of this Anglophile bunch of discs, RVW 6 seemed to me an odd choice. Was it a slip of the tongue?

I thought a lot about Sir Roger's choices. I developed the notion that they were key to his personality. Actually, they were key to *Whetstone*. If I understood them, I could solve *Whetstone*. I was particularly interested in his last two choices. Neptune from Holst's *Planets Suite*, and then the final movement of RVW 6. Music for a nuclear winter. Who could doubt it? RVW 6 finally fades into inaudibility, just as Neptune does. The orchestra plays two recurring chords – in E flat major and in E minor. E flat major is the key of Beethoven's *Eroica* Symphony. In its slow movement, RVW 6 has already alluded to the *Eroica*. It takes the three-note trumpet fanfare of the start of *Eroica's* finale and turns it into a nightmare. E minor is a soundscape of uncertainty and desolation. How will RVW choose to end his Sixth Symphony? With the affirmation and resolution of E flat major, or with the abject desolation of E minor?

He settles on E flat major. And then, just when you think you are there, and almost inaudibly, he drifts into E minor.

That is the key to Sir Roger Hollis.

One book (besides the Bible and Shakespeare). Thomas Hardy. *The Return of the Native*.

And one luxury? That's easy. An epée.

Extraordinary. You get banished to a situation whose defining characteristic is solitude; you are offered a single balm of solace, and you choose a weapon?

And, if you could only save one of your eight discs from the waves, which one? RVW 6. Clearly, it hadn't been a slip of the tongue.

Was I any the wiser about what made Sir Roger Hollis tick? If I were a halfway decent cryptographer, I would be able to decipher a musical message that would allow me to read Sir Roger Hollis, complete. The key was in the last movement of RVW 6. And also, quite inexplicably, I had the notion that Sir

Roger had left something out. Some piece of music, English again, and cryptic, had been omitted because it revealed too much. What could *it* be?

If you want to understand the man, study his soundscape.

XIII

When you write a letter to the papers, you need to check the following day for rejoinders, be they bouquets or brickbats. Sir Roger got back to me by return.

Dr Cameron-Strange may be affronted to be relegated to the role of 'bit-player' in Operation Whetstone, *but it is precisely because his role was so circumscribed that his overview must, of necessity, remain purblind. He does not have the first idea of what is going on around him, and it is for that reason that he would do well – I sharply remind him – to remember that he is a signatory to the Official Secrets Act.*

The good doctor needs to wake up and smell the coffee.

It was a terse riposte from a big beast designed to give me a fright. But to be honest, I was gratified. Sir Roger Hollis might have done better to ignore me. Now I knew I had struck a nerve. I read that letter while listening to Mishal Husain interviewing Sir Roger (the man was ubiquitous) on BBC Radio 4's *Today* programme. The tragic death of a hiker on the

Durness Peninsula had sparked a debate in Holyrood about the future of the northwest tip of Scotland. The First Minister was making the case that Cape Wrath had been neglected for too long, that it really ought to be opened up and developed perhaps as an outward-bound centre, that the road should be repaired and sealed and extended southeast so as to cross Durness Sound at its narrowest point and provide ready access to the Cape. Cape Wrath would become an Absolute Must on the bucket lists of people travelling the so-called North Coast 500. The leader of the Scottish Conservatives dismissed the FM's proposal, pointing out that we are currently living in a very dangerous world at a very dangerous time and that the Defence of the Realm was rather more important than the production of a tourist brochure for Planet Earth. The Labour leader found it remarkable that the FM's hastily concocted *flight of fancy* should coincide with HMG's well-developed plan to increase defence spending, which would guarantee jobs for the local community. The Lib Dem leader proposed some kind of compromise which appealed to nobody, involving a catamaran from Durness to the lighthouse. He was trying to be emollient, but the others got somewhat heated.

"Far be it from me," said Sir Roger, "to interfere in the business of the Scottish Parliament." I knew then that he was about to interfere in the business of the Scottish Parliament. He put the whole thing to bed by reminding everybody that defence was reserved and not devolved; ergo, the deliberations of the Parish Council at Holyrood carried about as much weight as would those of a High School Debating Society. In a single utterance *ex-cathedra*, he swatted Holyrood aside like a fly. Ms Husain moved on, taking the opportunity to ask for an update on *Whetstone*. Misgivings were still being expressed in the House about the handling of the operation. I pricked my ears up.

"Look. That situation had become very dangerous. We had to move. We gave the medic a chance. Actually, we gave him twelve hours. God knows we bent over backwards. He couldn't even get *one individual* off the plane. Then he started playing Cowboys and Indians. Our hearts go out to Mr and Mrs Fergusson, but we cannot allow…" I muttered under my breath, "Oh, *pul-lease…*"

Finally, a segment on *British values*. Sir Roger had this idea that everybody working for any government organisation must swear an oath to uphold them. Apparently, there was a White Paper. That could well mean that before too long, legislation would be drawn up. There would be a Bill. The government was minded to accelerate it through the House. The Bill would become an Act. I wondered if the NHS would be classed as a government organisation. If so, I would have to take the oath. I'd better find out what *British values* are. Ms Husain asked Sir Roger to name them, and Sir Roger *pshaw-pshawed* as if to say, "Don't be silly; everybody knows what British values are." Ms Husain, however, pressed him, so Sir Roger threw out a few pearls: Parliamentary democracy, fair play, and the rule of law. I wondered how other countries would react to the Brits taking ownership of them. Didn't the Greeks invent democracy? If the British are remarkable for playing fair, does that mean everybody else is playing dirty? With respect to the rule of law, is every other country intrinsically anarchic? What a load of tosh.

I was getting argumentative. A fresh idea had crossed my mind: a new model for a *modus operandi*. I would make it my life's work to goad Sir Roger, to be a pain in his neck and a thorn in his flesh. I would insinuate myself into his presence wherever he went and systematically and deliberately create a bad smell. If I could get him to lose his temper, he might give himself away. I would develop a persona. I would become a cross between John Buchan's loud-mouthed Yankee John Scantlebury Blenkiron and Peter Falk's depiction of the rain-coated LA detective Columbo. Blenkiron would stand up at political meetings and indulge in lengthy and inarticulate harangues. Columbo would cast himself as a dim-witted plod and persuade the suspects in his murder investigation that he was a harmless idiot. He would terminate an interview, make an exit, and, at the door, rub a knuckle into his temple and say, "Oh, there's just one thing I can't understand... Oh, it's nothing really..." Thus, the object of his interest would get careless.

So I resolved to become a stubborn and persistent letter-writer to the daily papers, like one of these disillusioned retired colonels whose glass is always half empty and who is perpetually returning his gong to the palace. I could put a tartan gloss on *Disgruntled of Tunbridge Wells. Curmudgeon of Kircaldy*, or *Bloody-minded of Breadalbane*. I would cast myself in the character of a barrack-room lawyer, somebody impatient of nuance who sees everything in black and white, who can solve all the world's problems on the back of a fag packet, and who can't quite figure out why anybody would view the world differently. I would come across as not very bright. I had a notion that if I started to stir things up in an indiscriminate way, the establishment would let its guard down and, just once, betray itself. Thus, I might find out why the powers-that-be decided to storm that aircraft. I knocked off another quick letter to *The Telegraph*. It was in the form of a haiku.

For British values?
Snobbery, obfuscation,
Hypocrisy, power.

I even started to tweet. I think the platform was still called

Twitter at that point. You can't imagine how anathema this was to me, but I gritted my teeth and got on with it.

Funny the way Whetstone *is disappearing off the radar. It's as if it never happened. The news junket has moved on. So sad.*

It was a modest enough start. Tweets: 1. Following: 40. (I didn't know I was following anybody.) Followers: 3. Likes: 0. Something to work on.

Inevitably, I got a phone call from Margaret Rowallan.

"What are you doing?"

"Glad you asked, Margaret. I'm conducting my own investigation into *Whetstone*. I'm stirring the waters to see what turns up."

There was a fractional pause. I fully expected her to order me to stop being a loose cannon, to rein me in and give me a sharp rap on the knuckles, but all she said was, "Be careful."

The real downside with Twitter is that people start to tweet back.

> *If you don't like it*
> *Here, why don't you bugger off*
> *Back to New Zealand?*

That was a haiku, too. Inevitably, the tweets became highly abusive.

> *What is it your SAS mate says? Check six. I'm going to shoot you in the back, then I'm going to smash your sis' beloved Strad, then chop her fingers off, then little Caitlin… 666*

And again:

> *We're on your case. We know where you live. We're outside your window. See you, maybe tonight, maybe tomorrow… 666*

And some of it I can't print here.

It wasn't all negative, my correspondence. I got some fan mail, including a brief letter of encouragement from somebody in London who called himself Smith.

Dear Dr Cameron-Strange,

If you want to understand Whetstone, *ask Sir Roger Hollis what* Palimpsest *is.*

Yours faithfully,

Smith

Palimpsest?

I had to look it up. Palimpsest *pal'imp-sest*, n.a manuscript in which old writing has been rubbed out to make room for new… Gr. *Palimpseston – palin*, again, *psaein* (contracted *psen*), to rub.

Then, one evening, I was driving home through Bruntsfield to find the road was up. As if Edinburgh wasn't congested enough. There was a diversion round by Grange, through the quiet streets around the old Astley Ainslie Hospital. I continued in ever-decreasing circles. Two minutes from where I live, I'd entered the police speed trap before I'd spotted it. For a split second, I had the crazy notion that the detector pointed in my direction was a firearm. But I wasn't really worried. I've attended to so many road crash victims that I'm a stickler for the speed limit. I gave the young female police officer an idiotic grin. A block later, I became aware of the flashing blue light in my rear mirror and pulled over. The police car parked obliquely immediately behind me, and the lights kept flashing. I lowered the car window, switched off my engine, and waited. There were two police officers. One stayed in the patrol car, and the other sauntered unhurriedly in my direction and leaned over the car window. I could hear a background prattle coming from the radio on his flak jacket. I took the initiative.

"Good evening."

The courtesy was not returned. "Are you aware, driver, of the new twenty-mile-an-hour speed limit?"

"Yes, I am." I hadn't broken it.

"Are you also aware, driver, that your central rear brake light is not working?"

Ah. "No, I hadn't realised that."

"A functional central brake light is a legal requirement."

"I'll attend to it."

"Would you step out of the car, please." I complied. Now, the second police officer approached and walked round the car, carefully scrutinising the tail lights, the tyres, and the bodywork, looking for defects. He took note of the registration number and radioed it through, presumably checking that the car was insured and had a valid MOT certificate.

Then I got breathalysed. The police officer looked at the dial on his machine and said, with evident disappointment, "No show there."

The second police officer completed his circumambulation. "Would you open the boot, please?" I did so. He rummaged within.

"Would you turn round, place both hands on the roof of the car, and spread your legs."

Stop and search. I was frisked. It reminded me of my similar experience on AA301. There was the same sense of breathless tension. Now I know what it is like to be a young black man in Brixton. I said, "If you were to tell me what you are looking for, perhaps I could help." There was no comment.

The staccato jabber from the second officer's radio announced that the car's documentation was clean. The officer scribbled a chit and handed it to me. He said briefly, "You have three days to fix the light. You are free to go." I smiled at him and replied, "Thank you very much." I got back into the car, put my seat belt on, started the engine, and drove round to Thirlestane with exaggerated care. The police car followed me all the way, lights still flashing. I parked in front of the entrance to my flat opposite Warrander Baths. The police car turned left into Spottiswoode and disappeared.

So!

Then I hit the Big Time. I was discovering that being National Medical Adviser to the Security Services, despite Sir Roger's best efforts, carried with it a certain *caché*. The BBC's *Question Time* was coming up to Edinburgh, and I got the invite to be on the panel. It was an ideal opportunity to convince all my colleagues and the world at large that I'd finally lost my marbles. The venue was the Signet Library, just off the Royal Mile, by St Giles. On the panel? I was delighted that the Government had despatched a suzerain to her northern outpost, a distinguished grandee, none other than Sir Roger Hollis. I suppose the Beeb must have decided to capitalise on *The Telegraph* spat twixt Enterprise Czar and N-MASS. MSPs from the bottom of the Royal Mile represented Labour, the Lib Dems, and the SNP. And then there was me, the joker in the pack. I knew I was there solely because of *Whetstone* and my brief moment in the sun. I might never get this opportunity again.

There were half a dozen questions. The first was related to international terrorism. Irrespective of all the other woes of the world, 9/11 still casts its long shadow down the new millennium. Is it justifiable to *take out* the warlords of the so-called Islamic State through drone strikes? This related to a recent US-led operation culminating in the demise of an enemy of the people, with some unfortunate collateral damage. I had thought Fiona Bruce might give me some time to find my feet, but no, I was invited to lead the debate. I made the point that I considered the execution of a suspected criminal without charge and without a fair trial not only morally reprehensible but politically counterproductive.

"Imagine if you were a guest at a wedding in Auchtermuchty" (I have no idea why I chose Thomas Carlyle's birthplace) "and the US drone dropped its payload on you and killed thirty guests, including the bride, in pursuit of a warlord who, as it turned out, wasn't actually in attendance. What better recruiting sergeant for radicalisation than that?" (Applause).

"I could never understand the US' triumphalism when they 'took out' Osama Bin Laden. They buried him at sea because they didn't want to turn his grave into a shrine. Actually, they just succeeded in turning the whole ocean into a shrine." (Heavy applause).

I just remember Sir Roger's expression of distaste at having to put up with my naïve liberal sentimentality.

A question, inevitably, about the NHS. Why were 'A & E' (sic) performances so dismal? I corrected the terminology and assured the panel that nobody in the field of Emergency Medicine paid the slightest attention to the four-hour rule.

We moved on. Ms Bruce consulted her *aide memoire*. "And the next question comes from Kathryn Hathaway. Kathryn Hathaway, please."

"Should the SNP have the right to call a second independence referendum?"

From my position, I couldn't see her, but I recognised that low-toned, limpid, North American voice. Why should I have been surprised?

Sir Roger: "Forget it." (I paraphrase.)

Moi: "Well, the clue is in the name. If you don't want a second referendum, stop electing the Scottish National Party to Holyrood and Westminster."

The various answers came back along predictable party lines. Of course, the SNP MSP was all for it, though a little coy about the timing. Ms Bruce threw it back to the questioner. What did Ms Hathaway think?

Ms Hathaway came out unequivocally in favour of a second referendum, to be held as soon as possible. She added, "I note that Dr Cameron-Strange made a general point while himself sitting on the fence."

I replied, "I think you'll find I answered your question directly, in the affirmative."

"Does that mean you are chucking your hat into the ring?"

"In what sense?"

"Last time we spoke, you were equivocal."

Ms Bruce, sensing a hidden agenda, intervened in good humour. "Stop flirting, you two!" There was laughter.

Trident next.

Sir Roger: "We live in dangerous times. Now is not the time to make well-intentioned but hopelessly idealistic gestures of unilateralism. Look at North Korea!" (They'd just fired an intermediate-range ballistic missile into the Sea of Japan.) "How else to defend ourselves against a rogue state that is, let's face it, bonkers."

Me: "Maybe they are bonkers, but are they any more bonkers than us? Indeed, we take pains to convey the sense to our enemies that we are just a little unhinged. Who knows what the Prime Minister has written in these *letters of last resort*. Trident is an abomination."

I can remember the government grandee looking at me with an expression of utter disgust. He patiently explained to the nation the necessity of retaining and upgrading the deterrent for the next fifty years. He had the air of a man who was carrying out a task that was well beneath him, doggedly and resignedly. A junior minister really ought to be carrying the flag on this paltry show, but I will bite my lip and do the state some service.

Next question. The Government had done a U-turn on the planned high-speed rail link, and terminated it at Birmingham. Shouldn't HS2 have been extended up to Edinburgh, the Athens of the North?

Sir Roger switched from disgust to enthusiasm in the blink of an eye. "HS2 is only the start." Apparently vacuum trains were the future. The government was pushing hard for research and development so that Britain could become a *world leader*. We were on the verge of making Japanese maglev technology look quite pedestrian. Apparently, you could get into a pod, be magnetically elevated and then fired off down a vacuum tube at speeds in excess of 4,000 mph. The entire length of the country could be traversed in less than fifteen minutes.

Ms Bruce: "Is this feasible?"

Sir Roger, "Absolutely."

Somebody in the audience interjected, "What happens if there are leaves on the line?" More laughter.

"Not an issue," said Sir Roger, "in a tunnel."

When the British mining industry collapsed in the mid-80s, apparently, his people diverted all these centuries of subterranean expertise into tunnelling. "Currently, I'm a bit out of the loop, but The Conglomerate have three long-term projects. Naturally, we call them Tom, Dick and Harry."

"But," said Ms Bruce, "didn't it take the Great Escapees years just to tunnel a few hundred yards?"

"Well, they didn't have Conglomerate technology. We can lay 100 metres of track a day. If we started thirty-odd years ago, well, as our American cousins say, 'Do the math.'"

Me: I couldn't understand this obsession with speed. Anything that travelled either along or under the ground really ought to travel sedately. Wasn't it pleasant to take some time out from our busy schedules and take the train down to London, admire the passing countryside (I threw in a quote from Philip Larkin's *The Whitsun Weddings*), read a book, and go to the dining car for lunch?

With four minutes to go, there was just time for a quickie.

"What are British Values?"

"...a reference, no doubt," interpreted the Chair, "to the recent proposal that employees of government departments and organisations espouse them. Roger Hollis?"

Sir Roger remarked wearily, "We've been over all this. Look, I'll spell it out for you." He scribbled on his notepad and, with a cheesy smile, held a sheet of paper up to the camera. There they were again.

Parliamentary Democracy, Fair Play, and the Rule of Law.

I pointed at the document and said, "It's a palimpsest."

Sir Roger Hollis' smile instantly vanished as if he had been slapped.

"What the devil do you mean by that?"

The Chair didn't intervene. The audience was still. There was a sense that the antagonism that had simmered beneath the surface between Sir Roger and myself for the duration of the programme was about to erupt to the surface.

"I mean that you have apparently rubbed out true British values and replaced them with your solipsism. But it doesn't matter how hard you try to conceal them; the original text is still there. British values remain unchanged."

"And what are they?"

Ms Bruce glanced at the clock. "Doctor. In a sentence?"

"Snobbery, Hypocrisy, and Obfuscation."

Well well! Next week we're in Solihull.

It worked.

After the programme broke up I ducked quickly out of the Signet Library. I knew it was rude; I really ought to have stopped to talk with Ms Hathaway. Indeed, a part of me, a lot of me, wanted to do just that. After all, for whatever reason, she'd gone to all the trouble of coming all the way up from London. But I argued with myself that I was only protecting her. I spelled trouble. Best to get away. I crossed over the Royal Mile and dropped down via the Playfair Steps from the Mound to Princes Street. I paused at the National Gallery before crossing to the north side of Princes Street, waiting for a tram to trundle by. It was followed by a sleek black limousine. It crossed my mind that Princes Street is now closed to all but commercial vehicles. Maybe it remains open to Members of the Inner Party. The limo hissed to a halt beside me. It didn't look like a fun car, not like these garish pink limos that ladette gangs sometimes hire for hen parties. Big-breasted women in scant frocks lean out of the windows raising champagne flutes and yelling jollities at you. No. This car looked like the armour-plated presidential conveyance of a dictator. It might have had little diplomatic flags fluttering over the headlights. It looked like a hearse. As it drew level with me, the nearside middle door opened, and a big man in an ill-fitting black suit, with a white shirt and a black tie, stepped out and obstructed my way. He looked like a bouncer, security at a London East-End gymnasium, dressed up to attend a gangland funeral.

"Step inside."

I made to walk past, but another figure in a dark suit had stepped up behind me and before I knew it, I had been firmly manhandled into the car. Up front, the driver looked like a desiccated old scrivener in a Victorian legal office. He stared rigidly ahead as if oblivious to the activity around him. He had the elongated contour of a Lowry figure but was as inhuman as a stick insect. I found myself seated in the middle of a plush black leather bench, facing rearwards. The rear seat had a sole occupant. It was gloomy in the car and uncomfortably hot. I could only discern a silhouette. There was a red carnation and a whiff of eau de cologne.

Now the limousine was sighing away from the kerbside. There was no audible engine note, and the vehicle's soundproofing completely absorbed any external traffic noises. The pitch of the bass voice was perfectly clear.

"I am Sir Roger Hollis. I am a rich and powerful man. I have influential friends. You are an impoverished doctor, young, inexperienced, and naïve. As of today, what little you possess is in danger of being forfeit. I am going out of my way to rescue you from your folly and now I will go further. I will hand you on a plate, gratis, the information that you and your colleagues will spend fruitless weeks trying to uncover.

"I am the person responsible for the initiation of the storming of *Aerolíneas Argentinas* Flight 301. The machinery of my intervention need not concern you. Suffice it to say that while you were engaged in rendering succour to a criminal – an undertaking in my view of dubious validity – preparations were already in place for a definitive curtailment to a protracted, pointless and decidedly messy negotiation. We cannot, and we will not, strike bargains with buccaneers and soldiers of fortune." The limousine crept round on to Shandwick Place in the direction of Edinburgh Airport. The monologue continued.

"Unfortunately, I now find that your quixotic attitude towards our political institutions strikes a populist chord. I do not propose myself to suffer the inconvenience of fielding the questions of a Parliamentary Select Committee, far less those of the hacks and scavengers from *The Guardian* and the *National*, a loathsome organ of whose existence I only became aware this morning. Therefore, it is time to close the file on this entire unhappy event. No doubt there will be a residual column inch spent on you in tomorrow's newspapers, but there will be none on the day following. You will doubtless be aware, however, that the medical disciplinary committee of the General Medical Council has taken a dim view of your shenanigans. I am given to understand that this is not the first time you have found yourself out of kilter with the ethos of governance in your profession. I have to tell you, however, that on this occasion, you have made such a thorough public nuisance of yourself that you must now be dealt with summarily.

"In short, Doctor, you will be struck off."

I said nothing.

"So I offer you a way out of your predicament."

The limousine drew to a halt. We were outside Haymarket Station. The silhouette on the rear seat produced a bulky white envelope and handed it over.

"Go back to your old stomping ground, Doctor. I can assure you that you are quite out of place in this environment. You will be happier in the colonies. I encourage it. Inside that envelope, you will find an open, first-class one-way ticket to Auckland, courtesy of Air New Zealand. There is also an extremely generous supply of money to cover any removal expenses. Enjoy."

I can't say I wasn't tempted. I opened the envelope carefully and glanced inside. There was a wad of red RBS £100 banknotes as thick as two packs of playing cards. I don't think I'd ever seen a £100 note before. I sealed the envelope back up. I smiled briefly at the man in the back of the car. I said, "I wish you hadn't done that." I made to hand the envelope back. The silhouette did not move.

"You are making a mistake."

"You took the words out of my mouth."

"You don't know me, Doctor."

"On the contrary, I know you only too well. I have met you many times before. Your persona is unchanging. You are the steel fist inside the velvet glove. You are the man who will not suffer opposition and who cannot bear to be thwarted. In short, Sir Roger, you are a bully."

I left the envelope with its brazen bribe on the black leather bench. I stepped out of the car. This time, I was unobstructed. I closed the car door gently, with the sonorous clunk of perfectly crafted coachwork settling into place. I glanced at the figure on the rear seat. The silhouette stared straight ahead and never moved.

XIV

Faith said, "You've got a visitor, Alastair. I didn't think you'd mind if I popped her into your office." Faith sucked in her cheeks, made a pout, and swept her hands down her sides and across the front of her thighs.

"What does she want?"

"Dunno. Medical student? Drug rep?"

But she was neither. I opened the door, and the woman in the white blouse and smart dark navy trouser suit rose hurriedly from the swivel chair parked at my desk. She looked as if she'd dressed for a job interview.

"Sorry! They said I could wait."

"It's fine, Ms Hathaway."

I was relieved to see I hadn't left my desk in a complete mess. Aside from a desktop computer and a telephone, there was only a Littman stethoscope and a framed picture of MacKenzie arm in arm with Caitlin, MacKenzie with her viola, Caitlin her oboe, both grinning broadly. The computer screen was blank. I rather like my office. I've tried to avoid clutter, give the place a little personality, and make it my own. In a busy hospital, I'm lucky to have a space like this to myself. It's about four metres square. The south-facing wall has a huge window so there's plenty of light. My desk sits just to the right of the window. I've got my framed diplomas on the wall above it. The west wall is essentially a bookcase and it is full of medical tomes. I'm a bibliophile. Opposite the window, to the north, there is an examining couch. Sometimes I consult in here. Hanging on the wall above it are two framed pictures, one of the Cuillin ridge in Skye, taken at sunset from Glen Sligachan; and the other of Cape Reinga, the top of New Zealand at sunrise. There is a chair for the patient positioned obliquely next to the desk. I sank into it. I gestured to the swivel chair. "Please." She resumed her seat. "How did you know where to find me?"

"It wasn't very difficult. Like it or not, you're a public figure. Besides, you left an audit trail. Dr Parkinson. You gave me his card."

"So I did. Incidentally, did I hear your voice in the Signet Library last night?"

"Yep, that was me. I tried to catch you after the show, but you'd slipped away."

"So how can I help you?" It amused me that the seating arrangements implied a role reversal. Maybe I was being a bit bolshie, putting her, as it were, in the hot seat. You've come to see me, so state your business. I could see her take a deep breath prior to putting into effect a plan she must have invested a little time and effort in.

"I saw your letters. When I read them, I realised you'd changed your mind." She spoke a little breathlessly, repeating herself. "When we spoke at Cockfosters, you said you weren't going to look at *Whetstone*, but when I saw your letters, I realised you'd changed your mind. So I came up. I've come to chuck my hat into the ring. I want to help."

I looked down at my fingernails. I was beginning to realise that her confrontational gaze was her defining characteristic.

"Ms Hathaway…"

"I can see what you're trying to do. You're throwing out a message in a bottle to see where it will drift and who will pick it up."

"More like pissing in the wind."

"Call it what you like. It's good. Keep going."

"Ms Hathaway…"

"Kathryn."

"Kathryn… I don't think this is a good idea."

"Why ever not?"

"I think you should stay away from me. I'm bad news."

"Because of Mary? Because of Suzanna?" I may have opened a dossier on Sir Roger Hollis, but Kathryn Hathaway had clearly opened a dossier on me. "Look. I appreciate your caution. But I'm a big girl. And I'm applying to join DAMASK."

"DAMASK?"

There was the hint of an amused smile. "Doctors Against Muddle and So-called Quality – with a capital K."

"You can't join unless you're a doctor."

"I'm reading for a Ph.D. You must have associate membership for students. So I qualify, don't I?"

I was momentarily distracted. It occurred to me that I didn't know the first thing about Kathryn Hathaway. "What's your field?"

"Apocalyptic literature."

"Oh."

"See. I'm nearly a real doctor."

"Nearly Dr Hathaway, DAMASK isn't a real organisation. It doesn't have a headquarters, or a constitution, or an AGM, or an annual conference, or a website, or even, for that matter, a membership. DAMASK is a figment of my imagination. It's my club, and it has a membership of one."

"In that case, let's double the membership. Propose me. Please."

"No. I blackball you."

"Why?"

"Because 'I am become death, destroyer of worlds.'"

"Oh gimme a break!" Yet it was at that precise moment – the first time I really took any notice at all of Kathryn Hathaway – that I saw her at her most vulnerable. Sometimes, very precious people carry with them an aura of premature mortality. If you don't know what I mean, listen to Eva Cassidy sing 'Autumn Leaves'. Kathryn said, with passion, "What earthly use is a club so exclusive it has a membership of one? Why do you persist in taking on the whole of the world on your own? It doesn't need to be that way. I'm offering to help."

"And what, precisely, would you bring to the party? The Revelation of St John the Divine?"

Then the phone went. "Excuse me." I leaned across and picked up the receiver.

Faith said, "Phone call for you, Alastair."

"Who is it?"

"They didn't say. Sounded urgent. Posh voice."

"Not the bloody palace again."

"Patching you through."

I punctuated the silence down the line. "Hello?" Perhaps it was a cold-caller selling me double-glazing.

The silence continued. Yet I knew the line was still live. Something told me not to hang up. I raised my eyebrows at Kathryn Hathaway and then looked up at the ceiling. She smiled briefly and politely turned away to gaze in curiosity at the picture of MacKenzie and Caitlin, while gently swivelling in her chair. I said again, "Hello?"

"Is that Dr Cameron-Strange?"

"Speaking."

"Dr… Alastair Cameron-Strange?"

"Who is this?"

"My name…

"My name is…

"…Smith."

"How may I help you, Mr Smith?"

"Would it be possible to meet with you?"

A host of possibilities shot through my mind: ex-patient with a grudge, *Daily Telegraph*, Channel 4 news, some crank.

"In connection with what?"

I had the notion that Mr Smith was standing within an aircraft fuselage, exit open, parachute strapped to his back, looking down at the terrain far below, willing himself, waiting for the nod from the jump-master.

"*Whetstone.*"

Now it was my turn to pause. Could still be Channel 4 news, incognito, teeing up an assignation, wired, with a hidden camera.

"Whom do you represent, Mr Smith?"

"I am a Civil Servant. I work within a certain government department." Now that Mr Smith had taken the plunge, he was appalled at the velocity he had already reached. "I have certain information." I envisaged Mr Smith as a slender middle-aged man of less than average height, dressed anonymously in a drab grey raincoat and a battered Trilby hat. He had eschewed his mobile phone, slipped unobtrusively out of Whitehall, crossed the river, and was making this call from a red telephone box, if such a thing still existed, somewhere in Lambeth. He had taken pains to disguise himself, to muddy the audit trail should anybody try to trace this call, and he had surely made an adequate job of it. But he was still frightened out of his wits. I decided to run with it.

"Where would you like to meet?"

"I'll come to you. But I would prefer a public place. Would you come out to Edinburgh Airport? I'll come off the London City shuttle. Would Wednesday suit?" He mentioned the British Airways flight number and the time.

"How will I recognise you?" Perhaps he would have a red rose in his buttonhole and carry a copy of *The Times*.

"If you wait at arrivals, I will recognise you."

"Very well."

I heard the receiver in the Lambeth phone box being replaced. I hung up. Ms Hathaway looked at me quizzically. I said, "Where were we?"

"I can be your sounding board. For Suzanna. We can think out loud. Two minds are better than one. Call it symbiosis. Or synergy. The whole is greater than the sum of the parts."

"Ms Hathaway… Kathryn. I got stopped and searched by the police yesterday. It was a set-up. They even went to the trouble of digging up the road and creating a diversion for my benefit. Just to lure me into a 20 mph zone. Would you believe it?"

"Did they find anything?"

"No. They tried hard enough. They even got me to open up the boot."

"Boot?"

"The trunk."

"Did they look under the hood?"

"You mean the bonnet?"

"Or in the glove box?"

"You mean the glove compartment? This is silly. Look. I thank you for your support and interest but believe me, you have no idea what you would be letting yourself in for. I must decline. Now, if you'll forgive me…" It was high time that this interview was terminated. I got up.

"Was she nice?"

"Excuse me?"

"The woman you're carrying the torch for. Was she nice?"

There was just no evading the directness of her gaze. Nor was there any purpose in prevarication.

"She was lovely. How did you know?"

"Because you've never even looked at me."

And she was quite right. I cut her dead. I was determined not to let her in. I wasn't going to have another Suzanna Fergusson on my conscience.

I went to see David Walkerburn, my lawyer. How very odd to retrace my steps of last winter, northwards down off Princes Street into the heart of the New Town, to 48 Heriot Row, just round the corner from Moray Place. It was very late in August, and it had been a particularly glorious summer, but the leaves were beginning to turn. The very tall, stooped figure gazed contemplatively at the trees in Heriot Row Gardens from the window of his book-lined study. "I did enjoy your performance in the Signet Library. Is it a case of *déjà vu* all over again?"

"In what sense?"

"In the sense that you have embarked on a personal mission for which everybody else lacks taste or enthusiasm."

I shrugged. "Same old, same old. But what I need to know is this: am I really giving away official secrets by telling the powers-that-be they fouled up?"

"That would depend."

"Upon what? The level of detail I made public?"

"No. The extent of the powers of your powers-that-be. I gather you sit on a committee. Do you have allies?"

"I don't know. I don't think so."

"Temperamentally, you are a loner? It's a pity you don't have anybody by your side."

"Funny you should say that, David. There's this American girl I know. Well, I don't really know. She was a friend of Ms Fergusson. She wants to come on board."

"You are disinclined to encourage her. Do I get the sense she is charming?"

I snorted. "To be honest, I haven't really noticed."

David raised an enquiring eyebrow. "You are concerned that she is vulnerable."

"Yes."

"You are vulnerable."

"I know."

"Is she over twenty-one?"

"Yes. Just, I think."

David turned from the window and faced me with an openhanded gesture. It was a mime. You know what to do. Why are you asking me?

Still I remained unconvinced. Actually, I was worried about my sinister internet trolls, the ones calling themselves 666. What was this 666 thing? Mark of the Beast. It was like something out of *Omen Damien 3*, something intended to send a shiver down your spine. It reminded me of that strange game of chess I'd played up in Easter Ross on midsummer's night. I even researched 666. I found the number theory to be far more interesting than the numerology. 666 is the sum of the first 36 natural numbers. 1+2+3+4+... etc. Numbers like this are called triangular numbers. 15 is a triangular number (1+2+3+4+5) and of course, add 6 and this gives 21, the next triangular number. 15 squared + 21 squared = 666. Is that just a coincidence? Silly question. It's like that old advert for *Dolmio* pasta sauce. *You ask me why? I cannot tell you. I only know that it is so.* But you can see why mathematicians are convinced that number theory is the Holy Grail, the answer to everything.

The Roman numeral for 666 is DCLXVI. There is a single occurrence of the symbols of value less than 1000 in decreasing order. Now *that's* coincidence.

In base 10, 666 is a repdigit and therefore a palindromic number, and a Smith number. A prime reciprocal magic square based on 1/149 in base 10 has a magic total of 666.

How do people get into stuff like this? I mean, why do they pursue these lines of enquiry? That old gentleman up north had told me that physicists were intensely practical people who were trying to solve earthly problems in the here and now. But surely the same could not be said for an Euler or a Galois, a Hardy or a Ramanujan. What drove them?

I knew what preoccupied me with the number theory relating to 666. I shied away from the apocalyptic stuff. 666 was the number of the devil.

Then the following day I opened *The Telegraph* letters page and got the hell of a fright.

Sir,

Sir Roger Hollis' heavy-handed attempt to put our chairman in his place (letters, August 29) was entirely misplaced. Dr Cameron-Strange is attempting to find answers to questions that Sir Roger, in his role as chairman of the Select Committee, has not even bothered to ask. What was the purpose of the hijacking of Aerolíneas Argentinas Flight 301? DAMASK will pursue this line of enquiry even if Sir Roger will not.

But then, Sir Roger is just a bit-player.
Sincerely,
Kathryn Hathaway
Honorary Secretary
DAMASK
(address supplied).

Oh my God. Not only has she joined the club; she's sitting on the board.

She wasn't wasting any time. I was sitting in the dining room in the hospital, quietly minding my own business, when Ms Hathaway slid on to the bench beside me and laid a hand on my sleeve.

"I've got it."

"Aw look. What is this? Harassment? Why are you stalking me?"

"Because it's so easy." That was true. Put on a smart suit and a determined look, and you can walk anywhere in a hospital, and nobody will challenge you. "But listen—"

"I'm calling security."

"Just shut up and listen. What was it you said about being stopped by the police?"

"I can't remember."

"You said they went to the trouble of creating a diversion."

"That's right."

"That's it."

"That's what?"

"*Whetstone*. AA301 was a diversion."

"Yes I know. They got diverted from Paris Charles de Gaulle to London Heathrow."

"No no. Not just the flight. I mean *Whetstone*. The whole thing. And that's the point. *Whetstone*'s not just the security response to a hijacking. *Whetstone*'s the whole shebang." She was actually quivering with excitement. "Don't you see? It had nothing to do with the Malvinas and opening old wounds and all that. They could have hijacked any old airplane. Just so long as they kept it on the ground at Heathrow for twelve hours and kept you lot busy. You've been putting all your concentration into AA301, but that's precisely what they wanted you to do. Because the stuff that they wanted

199

to conceal, the stuff that really matters, it was happening someplace else!"

I said dubiously, "That's just a hypothesis."

"Yes, but once you buy into it, everything else makes sense. Three postulates." She produced a notebook out of her ever-present satchel. It was the notebook, with the pastel floral covers, of the late Suzanna Fergusson. Kathryn Hathaway had carried on from where her friend had left off. "Look – I jotted them down." I found myself once more gazing down at that journal.

The purpose of *Whetstone* was to create a diversion.

The organiser of the diversion was Sir Roger Hollis.

The perpetrators of *Whetstone* were never going to be allowed to leave the aircraft.

Kathryn Hathaway might have sat and argued her case, but she was cleverer than that. She added her mobile phone number to Suzanna's journal and then left it with me. I could see it was a gesture of confidence that she would get that precious notebook back, because its content would convince me.

"Call me." And then she left.

I sat and scratched my head. Ms Hathaway was giving me time. It was generous of her because she was far ahead of me. These postulates perhaps begged more questions than they answered. If *Whetstone* was a diversion, from what were we being diverted? Presumably, from something else that was happening in Heathrow that day. What happens at airports? Aircraft take off and land. People come and go. Baggage comes and goes. While we had remained in the European Union, much of that could happen with the minimum of surveillance. What were the four great freedoms that underpinned the EU? The free movement of people, of finance, of goods and services. Now, with Brexit, things presumably were more complicated. Maybe that was why Hollis – assuming Kathryn Hathaway's hypotheses were correct – took immense trouble to create a diversion. While the security services were totally absorbed in AA 301, who, and what, were coming in, or going out? What was being exchanged? An individual, an expertise, a component or components of something? Was it a financial transaction? And at what cost?

I realised my use of the code word *Whetstone* had changed. We had thought of *Whetstone* as the response of the Metropolitan Police to a situation. But now I thought of *Whetstone* in a global way. *Whetstone* was also the operation as conceived by its planners and perpetrators. *Whetstone* was the entire scenario. *Whetstone* was a masque, an elaborate piece of choreography. Who was the choreographer? Sir Roger Hollis.

Was that merely prejudice on my part, to pin the blame on a guy I didn't like? No, it was more than that. Three times, Sir Roger had tried to put me in my place. First, in the Palace of Westminster before the House of Commons Defence Select Committee. Then, on *Question Time*. Finally, in his limousine. He saw me as a threat.

But why was I a threat? This brought me to Postulate Number Three. That gang was never going to get off that aircraft. They were, whether they knew it or not, a suicide squad. God knows how they were recruited. I had a notion they had been in waiting, in a state of preparedness, for a long time. For years, maybe for decades. It was ever thus. There's an element in our society, perhaps in any community, which just sits and waits. They are like sleepers, waiting for the call. They sit and wait for the lunatics to take over the asylum. The bad guys get in. Overnight, all our precious, fragile institutions of *parliamentary democracy, fair play, and the rule of law* are obliterated, and suddenly, the place is being run by a bunch of gangsters. Then James and Johnnie and Taff and Paddy report, *slouching towards Bethlehem*, for duty. Maybe they were told it was a suicide mission, or maybe not. Perhaps they didn't care. All they had to do was hold the fort and divert the attention of the authorities. Once the job was done (in their case, at approximately eleven thirty that night), the plug would be pulled.

But there was something else. One last piece of the jigsaw was missing. It was the reason why Sir Roger Hollis was paying me such close attention. What were we being diverted from? What transaction had taken place that day? I was convinced that Sir Roger thought I knew. Or nearly knew. It was like the psychological experience known as *presque vu*. I was back to my situational puzzle. I was the only person on earth who knew not only the *who* and the *how* of Whetstone, but I also knew the *why*. Except that I couldn't see it. It was staring me in the face, and I couldn't see it.

But of one thing, I was certain. In addition to Johnnie and Jimmy and Taffy and Paddy and all the other *compañeros* there was one other person who was never meant to get off that plane.

Me.

I called her.

"Okay. DAMASK. You're in. Where are you?"

"The Hilton in Grosvenor Street."

"Can a graduate student afford the Hilton?"

"Not really."

"You'd better come and stay." I gave her my Marchmont address.

"Golly! I couldn't presume…"

"You'd be doing me a favour. Besides, Madam Secretary, I'm going to give you a swag of work. Can you house-sit for the weekend? I've got to go to Royal Deeside."

"What takes you up there?"

"The 9.30 from Waverley. You can have the use of my car if you drop me off and pick me up."

"No. I mean, what are you going to do up there?"

"Take tea with His Majesty."

She didn't believe me. I got her back to the business of accommodation and persuaded her she would be helping me out. She said dubiously, "If you're sure…"

"That's settled then."

She added, "We need a name. For the operation, I mean. You know, like *Whetstone*."

"*Feuilles mortes.*"

"As in autumn leaves? Isn't that a tad melancholy?"

"Think of the magnificent colours of a New England fall."

"OK. *Feuilles mortes* it is." Kathryn asked me if I'd garnered anything further from my Hollis research.

"Not much. Just that he likes English music. He was on *Desert Island Discs.*"

"What's that?"

"Radio 4." I intoned, "*Desert Island Discs* was created by Roy Plomley. It was produced by Cathy Drysdale. Lauren's castaway next week…"

"What sort of accent's that supposed to be?"

"Caribbean."

"That's *awful*! Anyway, what's the format of the programme?"

"A celeb gets washed up on a beach with eight records of their choice."

"Records? As in vinyl?"

"Shellac."

"How are they going to play them?"

"I suppose they have a gramophone."

"What's a gramophone? Is it solar powered?"

"I think you are taking the premise too literally."

"It's a lousy idea. It won't last."

XV

Periodically, given a spare moment, I would turn my attention to the conundrum of the mole on the Witan. I spent an hour doing this on the train on my way back to Edinburgh from Insch since, apart from Ralph Parkinson, the entire Committee had been present at Balmoral, so they were all fresh in my mind. I was reminded of the time I first encountered these individuals on the improbable occasion of a Burns Supper, held on board a naval vessel on the Waitemata Harbour at the bottom of the world. Did I warm to any of them? Probably not, but then, I'm not a committee man. I sit on the Witenagemot, and I sit on ELSCOMF, and to be honest, I keep getting the personnel confused – *mea culpa*. I'm not a team player. I've always had trouble remembering people's names. With customary Latinate pomposity, we medics call it *nominal aphasia*. But I told myself, you can work at it and get better.

I wrote the individual names of the members of the Committee *sine nomine* down on cards, along with their code names, and I added brief aide-mémoires and hat-check descriptions. Then I shuffled them and laid them out, after the fashion of the nineteenth-century chemist Mendeleev, Dmitri Ivanovich, who, to all intents and purposes, devised the structure of the periodic table without knowing what half the elements were. Thus:

Archbishop Percy Mogadishu. *Somalia*. Sound. Sanctity of the confessional.

Lord Chief Justice Forteviot Dunning. *Silk*. Scottish – after a fashion. Not guilty.

Baroness Margaret Rowallan. *Sphinx*. Oracular. Headhunted me. Above the battle.

Chief Superintendent Harry Golightly. *Super*. Solid. An ally.

Chief Inspector Ronnie Slack. *Slacker*. *Au contraire*, conscientious. I'll cut him some slack.

Rear Admiral Sir Miles ('Otto') Mattick. *Scud*. Senior Service grandee. Seaworthy.

Air Vice-Marshall Johnnie ('Kipper') Herring. *Spitfire*. Airy.

General Iain Civil. *Sword*. Prime suspect.

Major Martin Forster. *Scimitar*. Friend. (I think.)

Sir Christopher Hotchkiss. *Spook*. Spooky.

Mr Jonathan Braithwaite. *Sports-Jacket*. Another Spook. Faux-bonhomie. Under a cover of grease paint, deeply inscrutable.

Dr Ralph Parkinson. *Shrink*. AWOL. Bonzer.

...and me.

It didn't take me much further forward. It occurred to me that I was more suspicious of the military personnel than of the civilians. And somewhere in the middle were the intelligence people, the public school, Oxbridge lot who got *the tap on the shoulder*. During the height of the Cold War, didn't the most *establishment* of them turn out to be a bunch of traitors?

Put a sock in it. Give it up. DAMASK, after all, is a fiction. Or at least, it was.

I got off the train at Haymarket, passed through the ticket barrier and walked briskly through the station concourse towards the east entrance. A tall young woman was standing with her back to me at a book stall, preoccupied in her perusal of the newspaper rack. The regulation smartphone jutted out of a hip pocket. I was momentarily lost in contemplation of her figure. I've discovered that when you are in an unrequited state, you are immune to the charms of all women save the one whom you are unable to forget.

That moment was when I knew I had emerged from my purdah. What a bloody relief. It was only when she turned round that I realised it was Ms Hathaway. She had plaited her long dark hair (I finally noticed the colour) into a ponytail. Her T-shirt featured the logo (inappropriate, all things considered), *Don't ask me to do anything – ever*, and her jeans bore extravagant slashes across the knees. She was one of *les sans-culottes*, dressed, literally, in rags.

I raised a hand in a laconic salute. "Hi." A hug would have been creepy. We hardly knew each other. I looked at my watch to cover my confusion. "Six o'clock. You hungry?"

"Starving."

"Good. Do you like Indian? There's a great Punjabi restaurant just across the road."

I visit the Omar Khayyam frequently enough to be greeted as an old friend. The *maître d'* shook my hand. I think Kathryn thought that was quite cool. It certainly gave me an absurd sense of self-esteem. "Your usual table?" We were directed to one overlooking Shandwick Place. She ordered a pint of Kingfisher lager for herself, briefly perused the menu and ordered, without fuss, a Punjabi lamb karahi, hot, and pilau rice. I took the chicken khushab karahi and

206

also ordered a pint. "Share a naan with you? It'll be as big as a Frisbee."

"'kay."

She handed the menus to the waiter, gave me a mischievous smile, and asked, with evident curiosity, "How was His Majesty?"

"Most gracious."

"Any other royals?"

"Just about the entire clan, so far as I remember. Who else? PM and spouse."

"Really? How fascinating. Any gossip? Did you get a selfie?"

"No. And no."

"You're not going to tell me anything, are you?"

I passed a palm swiftly over the crown of my head and vocalised an onomatopoeic impression of a ricocheting bullet. She said, "Aw yeah. It's all a blur." She was being sarcastic, but in fact, she was right. The whole weekend had had a surreal quality. I was left with a host of images, and I could hardly discern the real from the imaginary.

Kathryn said, "So typical. You're a republican, but at the first sign of royal patronage, you get star-struck. Now you're in the Firm's pocket."

"I don't know why you say I'm a republican. It's you who are a citizen of the Great Republic. I am a loyal subject and a churl. But I know why you're interested in stuff like this. I have this theory that the USA is a Kingdom and the UK is a Republic. Your President, with all his executive orders, he's like George III. Britain's stroke of genius was to render the head of state completely powerless."

"To hell with that. Spill. I'm very good at confidential."

"That's how leaks happen. Everybody's good at confidential. The whole world can keep a secret. But I can tell you the public bits. Hoppy picked me up at the station."

"Hoppy?"

"The King's equerry. Sir Hopcroft Metcalfe."

"Pal of yours, this Hoppy?"

"Bosom buddies."

Actually I'd rather taken to Hoppy. Predictively enough, he'd been a ruddy gentleman in three-piece Harris Tweed, driving an immaculately preserved wooden-slatted Morris Minor Estate complete with – what do you call them – duck boards? I was entering the world of the grouse moor, the salmon beat, the stag on the hill, populated by men in Ulsters driving shooting brakes. I recalled from something I'd read somewhere that if you nabbed a salmon, a grouse, and a stag, all on the same day, that was dubbed a *MacNab*. And if, for good measure, you threw in the Laird's daughter, that was a *Royal MacNab*. Probably apocryphal. I didn't mention it to Kathryn.

I'd expected Hoppy to be an urbane functionary and a snob, but I think he found the whole set-up to be quite as surreal and farcical as I did. He was clearly good at putting people at their ease. He helped me with my luggage. Saturday turned out to be a glorious summer's day, and the drive from Insch to Balmoral made me realise what a beautiful country I had come back to. So full of variety. My Scotland had always been the wild and savage west coast, but I couldn't help noticing that Royal Deeside was meticulously tidy, as if somebody had swept all the roadsides clean with a broom. And blessedly, it was full of trees, not imported conifers, but Scots pine and birch and rowan and aspen and juniper and oak and all the varieties of the ancient Caledonian forest.

This was Scotland as it might have been. As it might yet still be. We reached a section of straight road emerging from a glade to reveal a glen falling away to the left. Just beyond the 'No stopping' road sign, we took the left turn into an anonymous driveway and passed by the gatehouse. I asked Hoppy to brief me on protocol. Should I not speak until spoken to?

"Oh, don't worry about any of that. We're quite relaxed up here. Just be yourself." I resolved to take his advice. He himself gave the impression of holding everything at an ironic remove. The shenanigans of the court were hilarious.

My room was very pleasant and quite homely. It had none of the stereotypical anonymity of a luxury hotel. I might have been in a nice Speyside B & B, but for the art; the depictions of Highland landscapes looked expensive. I went across to the window and looked out over the land of the mountain and the flood. I loved it. But I could quite see it wouldn't be everybody's cup of tea. There was perhaps a hint of asceticism. No wonder a young metropolitan girl like Princess Di had felt trapped. Sir Henry Campbell-Bannerman, when he was Minister of War, used to come up here to be entertained by Queen Victoria. He would write letters to his wife complaining about the purgatory of it all. But I was more than happy to enter another world and have the experience, so long as it only lasted the weekend. Hoppy had encouraged informality (I sensed that his idea of informality had strict limits), so I took him at his word and went out for a walk. I merely strolled down to the river and back, and nobody bothered me. I had the sense that I had been clocked in, identified and vetted, and had the run of the place just as if I were a guest in a boarding house.

Kathryn asked, "So, how did you spend the weekend?"

"Saturday afternoon – walk in the park and then dinner. Sunday – church at Crathie. Lunch. Another walk in the park. Afternoon tea. Back to the station with Hoppy. And here we are."

"That's not a description. That's a report. Were you the only guest?"

"Good Lord, no. I sit on a committee. We were all there."

"Dr Parkinson?"

"No. Parkie's on the Big Sulk. He's in the huff."

"You were in the huff."

"I got over it."

"Did you discuss *Whetstone*?"

"I could tell you—"

"I know, but you'd have to kill me."

I was vaguely aware of a noisy table at the other end of the restaurant – half a dozen young men. I could just make out some colourful post-match locker-room banter. Football or rugby? The gentleman's game played by hooligans, or the hooligan's game played by gentlemen? I decided on the former. We were sufficiently removed from it that it didn't bother me. Then one of them got up and went to the loo, which happens to be down a staircase abutting *my table*. As he passed us, he whispered to me, "Wanker" and carried on.

I stopped chewing and held my fork in mid-air. "Forgive me if I'm mistaken, but I have the distinct impression that guy just called me a wanker."

"What's a wanker?"

"I don't know what the equivalent word in American would be."

The food came. We ate in silence for a bit.

"Did you speak to His Majesty?"

"Oh yes."

"What about? God, this is like getting blood out of a stone!" I think Kathryn was genuinely displeased with me, that I should somehow be amnestic with regard to huge tracts of that weekend. But truly, it was like a dream, only to be recalled in snatches. For a short time, I was in a completely different world. I remember at one point Hoppy holding open for me the front passenger door of *Saxe-Coburg's* Land Rover (the owner at the wheel, no seatbelt, PM and spouse in the back). "Welcome to Brans Hatch." At dinner on Saturday evening, over coffee and brandy and *petit fours*, and once the royal party had retired, General Civil got even more plethoric and obstreperous than usual. "Well, Doctor, that was the biggest load of Tommy rot I've ever heard you spout on *Question Time* last Thursday." He started to thump the table with a fist and shout, "What do you need to do to hear some tunes round here? Fetch a Jock!" It crossed my mind he was getting plastered. He started to make inane remarks about 'The Nats' and High Treason. I couldn't help baiting him. "What's to be done about these troublesome Scots, Iain? Tanks on Sauchiehall Street?"

"If that's what it takes!"

I said to Kathryn, "Shall I tell you the most interesting thing that happened to me during the weekend?"

"Yes, please."

"OK, but first you tell. How did you get on with your homework?"

The guy who had called me a wanker came back up the stairs and, this time, whispered to Kathryn. Or rather grunted.

"Bitch."

Actually he said something much worse.

There was a shocked pause. I put my fork back down on my plate, swallowed, and said, "Forgive me, but did that guy just call you—"

"Uh-huh."

I put my napkin down beside my plate and stood up. "Would you excuse me?"

"Please, don't, Alastair. He's not worth it. I get it all the time. You'd better get used to it."

I didn't get it. I said, "What do you mean *get it all the time*? I expected some brickbats when I went on a telly programme going out from this city, and that's fine, but I don't expect my friends to be insulted."

"Am I your friend?"

"Of course you are."

"Well, in that case, do your friend a favour. Give her this honour. Please don't make a fuss, at least not tonight. Forget him. Listen, I'm dying to tell you what I've found out." I sank slowly back down into my chair.

She pushed her dinner plate to one side and put in its place Suzanna's notebook. It had become a kind of talisman, that commonplace book. She put on an old-fashioned pair of stout, dark-rimmed glasses of the sort favoured by the late Buddy Holly. Now, she looked like a Ph.D. student. She opened Suzanna's book, perused her notes, and absently bit her pen.

"I found out a bit more about Hollis' early life. There was a scandal at his school. He was in a fight."

"Oh yes. He mentioned it on the radio. He called it a duel."

"That would be right. Guess the choice of weapons?"

"Pistols at dawn."

"The epée. Apparently, the protective guards on the sword tips were removed. He nearly killed his opponent. Somebody called Philip Crabtree. There was the hell of a stink."

"A hit. A palpable hit."

"Multiple palpable hits, more like. Crabtree needed a splenectomy." Kathryn read from her notebook. "Bilateral punctured lungs. Peritonitis from an injury to the large bowel."

"All that with an epée? Hollis must have gone berserk."

"Then I researched The Conglomerate. It's big. I mean, it's *huge*. I guess the clue's in the name. 'An industrial group made up of companies which often have diverse and unrelated interests.'" She had memorised a dictionary definition. "Well, so far, I've counted twenty companies, and still, they keep coming in." She rattled off a series of trade names vaguely familiar to me. "*Tapestry, Parvenu, Banlieue, Compeer-Ampulla, Nouvelle Riche, Carte Blanche...* The list goes on. They're all multinationals. And the thing is, if you add up the stock market values of all the individual concerns, the aggregate is in the gazillions. Their annual turnover is well in excess of GDP."

"UK GDP?"

"US."

"Oh my."

"They're all offshore. None of them seem to pay any corporation tax." I remembered the Holistics' telephonist's remark – "Holistics does not have high street outlets."

"That's not all. Once you start to investigate who sits on the Board of all these companies, you realise just how incestuous The Conglomerate is. For example, Hollis was MD of *Rapitrack* before he put it in a blind trust."

"What's *Rapitrack*?"

"Frictionless, high-speed magnetic transport. His daughters run it now. They also run *Platinum Seam*. But who ran it before them? Hector Harcourt-Beasley. Who is Hector married to? Hollis' oldest daughter, Patricia. Keep it in the family. You accrue wealth by making alliances through matrimony. It's positively medieval. Look."

She flicked over a page in Suzanna's notebook and showed me an extended family tree she'd drawn up. As I studied it, she asked, "Who do you think the family lawyer is?"

"Hugh Standish?"

"On the money."

I glanced at the broad outline of the genealogy. Some names I recognised. Some I didn't.

I couldn't help noticing that the bottom of the tree was more detailed than the top. The Gang of Three were all there, but if this really were a family dynasty, it wasn't clear to me who the great Paterfamilias figure might be. Who was the Big White Chief? Who was calling the shots? Kathryn closed the notebook. "How did I do?"

"You done good."

"Let's say The Conglomerate masterminded *Whetstone*. But we still don't know why. We still don't know what it was that was traded through Heathrow that day."

"I know."

"You *know*?"

"No. I mean, I agree with you."

She shook her head. "No, no. You *do* know. I know that you know. You've said it before. It's just buried in your unconscious."

"I know you know I know."

"Why don't you get Dr Parkinson to hypnotise you?"

I snorted. "This is silly. Shall we return to His Majesty?"

"Oh yeah." She rested her chin on her clasped hands, elbows on the table.

I recounted this anecdote in an offhand way so that Kathryn thought I was just kidding her on. It was the Sunday morning. Halfway through my scrambled eggs, Hoppy Metcalfe touched my sleeve. "The Archbishop has called for you. I'm afraid he's indisposed. We could send for the local GP, but since you're here…?"

"I'll get my bag."

As I retrieved my battered Gladstone from my room, it occurred to me that it had been quite absurd of me to imagine that I could ever have given this up. I carried the tools of the trade around with me, alert to the opportunities of off-duty medicine. Without a stethoscope, I was nothing. If spared, I'd probably go on well past the age of seventy and then finally have to be pushed out by colleagues who recognised my obsolescence long before I did. Only four decades or so to go!

I knocked on Percy Mogadishu's door and let myself in. I couldn't help noticing that the Archbishop could even vomit into a basin with a certain gracious air. I was amused that his pyjamas were purple. Maybe he, like me, was never off-duty.

"Archbishop."

"Doctor. Call me Perry. Please." He wiped his lips with a napkin.

"Alastair." I shook his hand. Moist, but not clammy. Temperature 37 degrees Celsius. I asked, "Are you poorly?"

"It's nothing, I assure you. Just a migraine. I get them occasionally."

"Me too. Do you recognise a trigger?"

"Preaching to His Majesty, I dare say! Crathie."

"Ah." I took out my stethoscope.

"That's not necessary. A short sleep, and I'll be fine."

"I thought you sent for me."

"I did, but not for a consultation. For a favour. Will you be my locum?"

"What?"

"Take the service. I considered the company in general and decided you were the best bet – good, sound Presbyterian upbringing. My input, granted, was supposed to lend the occasion a certain ecumenical flavour. Still, I'm sure the congregation, and indeed His Majesty, as King of Scots, will be pleased to find themselves in more familiar territory."

He looked at the appalled expression on my face and laughed gently. "Don't panic. I'm not asking you to compose a sermon. Merely read one out. The material is all prepared." He nodded in the direction of a purple A4 folder on the bedside table. "Fortunately, I like to have everything written out in clear, legible fourteen font sans serif. It's all there, along with an order of service. I've farmed out various bits and pieces to the rest of the Committee – prayers, readings and so forth. But I'd be grateful if you took the homily."

"You must be joking."

"I never joke about God's work."

"Jesus Christ."

"The man in question."

"But Archbishop…"

"Perry."

"Perry. I'm not qualified. Granted, I like to sit at the back of cathedrals, but frankly, I'm not a religious man."

"People attend church for many different reasons. I can tell you are a very spiritual person."

"Yeah, right. The more spiritual I get, the less I believe in anything."

"In theological parlance, that is known as *doubt*. I'm not asking you to make a commitment in public. This is not a Billy Graham rally. Much as I admired the Reverend Dr Graham. You may wish to intimate the circumstances. You might say, 'Don't shoot the messenger!' You could disown the whole content if you like. Start with a disclaimer and a limited liability clause. But I shouldn't make too much of it. Otherwise, you may hear the distant sound of a cock crowing. All I am asking you to do is read from a script."

"Shouldn't you be asking Crathie's incumbent minister?"

"I can't seem to raise him on the telephone, and I shouldn't like to drop this on him at the last moment. You, on the other hand, have a cool head and have time to peruse the material."

"I don't know…"

"I am asking you, I, temporarily indisposed, and feeling pretty wretched, importune you to do me this honour."

Ah. Importunity. He used the I-word. I had to relent.

"Well… if you put it that way. How can I do other than acquiesce?"

"Thank you." He said it lightly as if I'd handed him a glass of Highland Spring water. "Let us pray."

I clasped my hands in despair.

"Dear Heavenly Father, I give you thanks for your servant Alastair, who has come to us in an hour of need. I thank you for his kind-heartedness and open, generous spirit."

"Holy mother of God."

"I pray that you may give him courage and boldness to undertake this, your morning's work."

"Christ Almighty." (I sounded like a zealous participant in a Baptist church service in Montgomery, Alabama.)

"May he feel Your presence as he spreads Your word. May he touch the hearts of all, high and low, with Your message and Your grace. We ask these things in Jesus' name..."

I was completely undermined. I muttered, "Amen."

I've always suffered from Impostor Syndrome, but I've never felt a greater impostor in my life than when I eventually ascended that pulpit. Of all the crazy things I've ever done in my life, this had to take the biscuit. The church was packed. I surveyed the congregation. His Majesty was seated way over to my left so that I was barely conscious of the royal presence. I just made sure to avoid eye contact with Martin Forster, the person I considered most likely to give me a fit of the giggles. I'd had a quick word with Martin after I saw the Archbishop. "Perry's sick. I'm taking the service."

Martin looked very solemn. "He just gave me a reading. Guess you drew the short straw."

I have very little recollection of most of the service at Crathie. There was a brief announcement concerning Perry's indisposition. Then things got moving. Intimations, hymns, prayers... I just sat and tried to gather my wits. Margaret Rowallan read the Old Testament lesson. She read beautifully. Genesis chapter 3. The luring of Eve by the serpent to eat of the fruit of the tree that is in the midst of the garden.

For God doth know that in the day ye eat thereof, then your eyes shall be opened, and ye shall be as gods, knowing good and evil.

Anthem. I can't remember what it was. I was too busy rehearsing. I was completely out of my comfort zone. The order of events seemed to accelerate, and the moment of my own participation drew ever nearer. New Testament lesson. Major Forster looked very fine in his uniform. He read expeditiously as if he were giving out orders on the eve of battle. Trouble is, he read the wrong thing. I realised there had been a cock-up in the order of service. I glanced at the crib. The New Testament reading was meant to be from The Gospel According to St John, Chapter 6. The feeding of the five thousand. That had somehow been transcribed as the Revelation of St John the Divine, Chapter 6. I suppose I might have interrupted the Major and asked him to read the appropriate verses from the Gospels, but I didn't like to, because he was reading so well. I just let him continue. In fact, I got rather absorbed in the text. It was the King James' Authorised Version of 1611. What is it the Southern Baptists say? If it ain't King James, it ain't Bible!

> And I saw when the Lamb opened one of the seals, and I heard, as it were the noise of thunder, one of the four beasts saying, Come and see.
>
> And I saw, and behold a white horse: and he that sat on him had a bow; and a crown was given unto him: and he went forth conquering, and to conquer.
>
> And when he had opened the second seal, I heard the second beast say, Come and see.
>
> And there went out another horse that was red: and power was given to him that sat thereon to take peace from the earth, and that they should kill one another: and there was given unto him a great sword.
>
> And when he had opened the third seal, I heard the third beast say, Come and see. And I beheld, and lo a

black horse; and he that sat on him had a pair of balances in his hand.

And I heard a voice in the midst of the four beasts say, A measure of wheat for a penny, and three measures of barley for a penny; and see thou hurt not the oil and the wine.

And when he had opened the fourth seal, I heard the voice of the fourth beast say, Come and see.

And I looked, and behold a pale horse: and his name that sat on him was Death, and Hell followed with him.

I glanced ahead at the transcript of the sermon I was supposed to read out. It was all about the feeding of the five thousand. Oh dear.

Hymn.

I stopped rehearsing. I'd become preoccupied with the four horsemen of the apocalypse. I found myself conflating them with the members of the Commons Select Committee. Roger Hollis, Hector Harcourt-Beasley, Hugh Standish. Who was the fourth?

End of hymn. The organist closed the stops, left the organ loft, and sat down on a pew. I rose to my feet, trying to ignore the royal presence on my left, and shuffled Perry's purple A4 papers.

"Your Majesty, Your Royal Highnesses, friends, I start with an apology. Not only do you have the wrong pastor, you have the wrong text. Much as I'm tempted to pin the blame on Major Forster, it's simply down to a typo on the order of service." I waved it in the air. "For 'Revelation of St John the Divine' read 'Gospel according to St John'. Perhaps I should read you the relevant passage, and thus, we can make sense of Archbishop Mogadishu's pertinent remarks."

I opened a battered copy of the New Testament. Then I

closed it again. I picked up Perry's purple sermon. Then I put it to one side. I don't know what came over me. I started to ad-lib.

"To be honest, I'm relieved. I'm not comfortable with miracles. I've never come across one, and I rather hope I never do. From time to time, you hear stories of miracles occurring in some remote location. A pair of adolescent girls in a remote Andalusian village see visions and start healing the lame, the halt, and the blind. A team of cardinals go to investigate.

"Of the feeding of the five thousand, I prefer the interpretation that those in the crowd were moved to share amongst themselves that which they had. That is miracle enough. You may say that is a mere metaphor. But is metaphor mere? Metaphors get bad press. Metaphor is all we have. The late great physicist Richard Feynman used to say that we did sums with units of energy, called joules, without having any idea what energy actually was. That makes 'e equals mc squared' a metaphor. Fancy that!

"So why don't we consider Major Forster's four horsemen of the apocalypse from the point of view of metaphor and how they might be relevant to us now? I see that the seals of the four horses and horsemen are opened by four beasts. We often refer to our political grandees as *Big Beasts*. I will leave you to interpret for yourselves who these beasts currently might be." There was a ripple of laughter.

"I think of the rider of the white horse as being a metaphor for Empire, the urge to dominate and to conquer. The riders of the white horse and the red horse go side by side. You cannot dominate without suppressing opposition. You must unleash the dogs of war. Yet war, as an instrument of policy, is abject failure.

"The rider of the black horse relates to the gap between the rich and poor. The more penny-pinching the poor need to be, the more opulent the lifestyle, the oil and the wine if you will, of those in power. The rider of the black horse is the purveyor of a scam. He deals in humbug. I almost used a stronger word.

"And the pale horse? The pale horse is the inevitable end point for those who would aspire to be as gods. This wish for absolute power is ultimately a death wish.

"The great miracle of our existence is not only that nature obeys certain fundamental laws, but that we are able, albeit through a glass darkly, to decipher them. If we observe a miracle, that is, something that occurs in defiance of the laws of nature, it merely indicates that our knowledge is incomplete. Perhaps our knowledge will always be incomplete. It's the human condition. Our great error is to aspire to be as gods, aspire to certainty. Our greatest enemy now is the mindset that we are on the verge of solving the mysteries of the universe. Dear Heavenly Father, help us to replace lust for certainty with Faith, lust for domination with Hope and, at long last, lust for death, with Love.

"Amen."

I sat down to bemused silence.

I think it was following my homily at Crathie that my colleagues on the Committee *sine nomine* began to suspect I had mental health issues. They started to give me sidelong glances and a wide berth. Not that anybody said anything. Well, that bastard Forster did. He took the piss remorselessly. He used an expression of W. Somerset Maugham. "Here comes 'The Great Religious'!" Everything's a joke with Martin.

Word got back to Perry. "They tell me you gave an interesting homily! *Extempore*, I gather."

"Sorry."

"Nothing to apologise for." A pause, then: "I wonder if the tragic demise of Ms Fergusson has affected you very deeply."

"That would hardly be surprising."

"Indeed, it would be surprising if it hadn't. Let me know if you ever want to talk about it."

"You are very kind."

"In your own time."

Unlike my sister, I don't have a performer's temperament. I always suffer a reaction after any stage appearance. It is a sense of deflation that doesn't have any obvious connection to how well, or how badly, the performance went. I never had a greater sense of that than after Crathie. It almost incapacitated me. And I couldn't get that apocalyptic passage from Revelation, its exalted language authorised by King James, out of my head.

Later in the afternoon, I walked out of Balmoral Castle and went back down to the river. I was in a bit of a state. I guess Perry got it right. It must have been some kind of delayed reaction on my part to the sudden and violent death of Suzanna Fergusson. I hadn't processed it. In Emergency Medicine, you get inured to gore. You remain detached. You have to, otherwise you wouldn't be able to function. See all these lacerations and contusions? It's wonderful what can be done with theatrical make-up. See all that blood? Surely it's ersatz. See all these eviscerated organs…

But Suzanna had been real. And now, in the twilit nadir of my post-performance despondency, here at the river's edge, I came to an absolute standstill.

A Land Rover trundled down the gravel track on the opposite bank and, where the shallows of the river made a ford, crossed over. The vehicle drew up beside me. The driver leaned out of the car window. No seatbelt.

"Can I offer you a lift, Doctor?"

I was unable either to speak or to move.

He got out of the Land Rover. "Shall we let the dogs out for a moment?" I think it was a trick he learned from his mother.

I nodded.

So he let the dogs roam free for a while as we strolled by the riverside, and talked. Kathryn didn't believe that either.

XVI

Back at Thirlestane, I was still preoccupied with weird soundscapes and the four horsemen of the apocalypse. Kathryn had gone out to some late-night concert at the Queen's Hall.

Caitlin dropped by for a cup of tea. She'd fallen in love with the *cor anglais*, and was giving me a demo on the instrument she had recently acquired. The doorbell rang at about 9 pm. Caitlin answered it. She came back into my living room, wearing the portentous expression of a butler, and carrying a silver salver bearing Major Forster's calling card. I went to the door.

There they were, standing, waiting politely out on the landing, the odd couple, just as they had been on that first occasion aeons ago – the big gruff man in the off-white crumpled suit and the tall, slim, fit-looking military man. A host of memories flickered through my brain. I muttered ungraciously, "Not you lot again." I left the door open and turned and went back into my living room without bothering either to invite them in or tell them to go away.

Dr Parkinson and Major Forster followed me in, quietly closing doors behind them, and sat apart on the settee.

"Do make yourself at home. Thought you'd gone walkabout, Ralph."

"I had. I'm back." He sniffed the air. "*Amouage*. Ms Roy, your signature scent announces you."

I didn't contradict him. If Parkie married up the evidence of a lady's presence with that of my sister-in-law, it was fine by me. For all that Kathryn was now DAMASK's honorary secretary, I was still determined to be protective of her.

"Anyway, we need to talk business." Major Forster glanced at Caitlin and back at me. Caitlin took the hint and announced cheerfully, "I'll go and practise in the kitchen."

I waited until she had left the room, and then said, "What are you doing here?"

"Margaret Rowallan asked us to call on you. She's concerned."

"What's she concerned about?"

"You."

Martin Forster said, "She's worried." I'd forgotten about the dynamics of their double act. "Should she be?"

"I'm fine, thanks."

"She just thought you had become a little... preoccupied."

"Fey."

"Yes, *fey* was the word she used."

"I'm not fey."

"Good!" Ralph Parkinson clapped his hands once softly. "I'll let her know."

"Ralph, what have you been up to?"

"Usual business. Researching the past."

"Where've you been?"

"Antarctica."

"Weren't you there last summer?"

225

"Antarctica is a region of the mind."

Well, this and many similarly pretentious utterances are scattered about the pages of the Antarctic literature. For the famous explorers of the heroic age, the voyage towards the Pole was as much an epic spiritual as it was a physical journey. Everybody has their Deep South, said Shackleton. In recounting the details of his incredible ordeal, he spoke of the strong feeling that his exhausted party included an extra, intangible guest. I said, "It can't be very hospitable there just now, down at the bottom of the world."

"Cold and dark, but at least it was tourist-free. None of your cruise ships anchored in a huge gin and tonic with ice – no lemon – semaphoring one another because they've run out of Perrier water."

Parkinson lit a cigarette. He conflagrated half its length in a single concentrated inhalation, which he held within his lungs for ten seconds, the way people smoke a joint. Then he expelled billows of smoke through his nostrils. He looked like a dragon. He glanced at the glowing ember of the cigarette. "Mind if I smoke?"

"Have you considered vaping?" I fetched him an ashtray. "Anyway, what took you down there?"

"The *Francis Drake*. Scientific Research vessel. It's the successor to the *Captain Cook*, with whose wreckage you are familiar. Margaret sent me, directly after *Whetstone*."

"I thought you had resigned."

"We put that about. The fact is that the Committee, somebody on the Committee, is not to be trusted. Anyway, I took a flight to Buenos Aires. Lovely city. Paris of the South. Then, an internal flight to Ushuaia. The most southerly city in the world. I spent a week in Patagonia. Tierra del Fuego. The land of fire. Incidentally, *Aerolíneas Argentinas* are very good. Then we headed out on the *Drake*, skirted the Horn, and headed south across the Drake Passage. The *Drake* crossed the Drake. Ha!"

"What was the purpose of your trip?"

But Parkinson seemed in no hurry to come to the point. He just carried on puffing away. "Weather wasn't too bad. Short days, of course, but skies were largely clear. Bit of fog at the Antarctic Convergence. Oh! I won the bottle of bubbly for spotting the first iceberg. About the size of a Scottish castle. Looked like a huge prehistoric monster. Gnarled head and shoulders and a smooth sloping rump. Glistening with penguins. Had something of the hue of pale blue coconut. Did you know there are lots of varieties of berg – tabular bergs, bergy bits, brash, glacier bergs, growlers, frazil, grease ice, slush... Some as small as your G & T ice cube, others, well, as big as Belgium."

"Where's this going, Ralph?"

Parkinson put a fresh cigarette between his teeth, lit it with the butt of the last one, and stubbed the butt out in the ashtray.

"I was following in the footsteps of Sir Roger Hollis."

"I thought he went to the Falklands."

Parkinson shook his head. "Hollis was never at Goose Green."

"You mean he didn't see active service?"

"Mm? Oh, he saw active service all right, but he saw most of it in Ushuaia."

"Who sent him down there?"

"The dirty tricks department."

"And how did you get on his trail?"

"I have my sources." Parkinson nodded in the direction of Major Forster. Forster remarked briefly, "The regiment has a long memory."

"Once we sorted out his movements in Ushuaia, we got on his trail, on his wake, I should say. He traversed Drake's

Passage by ocean-going yacht – quite a feat, single-handed. We picked up the scent again at Admiralty Bay off King George Island. We visited Arctowski, the Polish base. Then we went to Belingshausen. Russian base. Geez, what a dump! I seem to recall it was sleeting, and there was a vicious wind the day we were there. Felt like I was standing in an abandoned Welsh mining village. This huge wet gravel pit studded with ramshackle huts and battered Lada trucks. Last outpost of the Gulag. Even the name has the ugly ring of a concentration camp, don't you think? I walked over to the Chilean base and met two charming Chilean children in a little wooden shed. They sold me a mug and a T-shirt. D'you know, they'd been there, in the gravel, for a year. One of them was so young that I wondered if she would recognise grass when she saw it."

"What do they do at these bases?"

"Squat."

"Squat?"

"Stake a claim. Anyway, our next port of call was Deception Island. Ah yes, Deception." He took another long drag. "Hanna Point was nice – penguin colony. I rather took to the penguins once I'd got used to the stink of ammonia. It's the tang of the guano. Pink excrement – krill in the diet. Adelie, Gentoo, Chinstrap. Sociable cobbers, taking their morning constitutional in pairs. They didn't mind us at all. Only got a bit uneasy if we got too close to their young."

"Where's Hollis in all this?"

"Oh, Hollis was everywhere. Telephone Bay, Pendulum Cove, Whaler's Bay – a vast volcanic caldera, and hot springs. But that wasn't the real Antarctica.

"The real Antarctica began around 63 degrees south. Melchnikoff Point, Melchior Island, and the Gerlache Strait, which separates Brabant Island and Anvers Island from mainland Antarctica." Parkinson stared absently into the remote distance. "Sky, ocean, rock, ice... Such vistas! Teeming with wildlife – dolphins, penguins, seals, whales, and albatrosses. Now your hills and glens are very grand, I grant you. Not unspoiled, but impressive. Just like the Outback back home. But this place is pristine. Privilege to be there, really. I reckon you visit Antarctica by privilege and not by right. The continent might tolerate your being there for a while, scrambling about the beaches, but it doesn't care a jot for your well-being. It's completely indifferent to you and, in the end, completely pitiless."

I remembered Hollis' third choice on *Desert Island Discs*. RVW. *The Sinfonia Antarctica*.

"You still haven't told me what Hollis was doing down there."

"Burying loot."

Parkinson told me this story. There was a man named Dieter Schweppenburg, born in Austria in 1920. So he was in his mid-twenties when the world, his world, completely fell apart. Waffen SS. He ran a death squad in Poland. The Allies wanted to get him, but when the Russians arrived, he headed west, and in all the chaos and confusion of spring 1945, he slipped through the net and vanished. He got out of Europe through Lisbon and eventually reached South America. He took with him a tonne of plundered gold in untraceable smelted ingots, and he disappeared into Argentina. He changed his identity completely. He was just another immigrant thrown up out of the chaos of the war. But he made a new life for himself, and his rise to power as a mining engineer and industrialist was a celebration of the idea of the self-made man. What was not widely known was that he had not started with nothing but the shirt on his back. He had started with collateral. By 1980, an anonymous immigrant had become a multi-millionaire living on an estancia that stretched from the River Plate halfway to

Chile. He had offices in Buenos Aires and far-reaching interests in mineralogy, metallurgy, beef production, mass media, and a soccer franchise. His business empire was named *Maldives Pty*. The name said much. He was an inveterate rightist on the side of the generals, and he saw the reacquisition of the Falkland Islands as a means of sustaining a crumbling political regime. More. He saw it as part of a plan to wreak vengeance on the old enemy – England. He became Galtieri's chief financial adviser and vowed to supply the collateral that might conceivably sustain a war effort. He began to negotiate with Rudolfo Baltiérrez, Galtieri's press secretary.

Galtieri, Baltiérrez, and who else? Mendoza... the hawks and the doves of the old Junta, names as resonant and as utterly defunct as Asclepius and Agamemnon.

HMG resolved to take him out.

"You mean," I asked in measured tones, "to assassinate him?"

Parkinson gazed at me unblinkingly. "To take him out of the equation."

"You mean kill him."

"You sound like Tam Dalyell in the House, hounding Mrs Thatcher over the sinking of the *General Belgrano*. I guess you weren't around when old Blighty despatched her armed forces to the South Atlantic on board the *Hermes*. You can't imagine – nor did the British public ever realise – what a dreadful risk that was and what a desperately near thing the conflict turned out to be. Talk about putting all your eggs in one basket. The whole of the expeditionary force was virtually aboard a single vessel. Lines of communication so long and so slender... Mrs T was at a banquet with the Royal Navy in Portsmouth when news of a potential naval engagement reached her. She turned as white as a sheet and asked a heavily braided First Sea Lord what to do. He said, 'Take her out, ma'am.' So, to get back to the Schweppenburg business, once you've overcome your qualms about sending a thousand men to the bottom, it doesn't seem too bad to sanction the despatch of one more. It was to be a commando job.

"Herr Schweppenburg had been known to be staying at his Patagonian lodge at the foot of the glacier high above Ushuaia. The operation was to be carried out by a three-man cell. Fawcett, Chepstow, and Hollis. An ocean-going yacht served as their forward HQ. They had the massive advantage of being able to anchor in the territorial waters of a contiguous nation ostensibly neutral but in reality hostile – Chile – courtesy of the obliging General Pinochet. The long approach up the bay to Ushuaia was done by Zodiac under cover of night. They landed to the southeast in land that has since been redeveloped as the airport. Then, there was the long trek skirting the township and homing in on their prey. They found and identified their target.

"Then who knows what happened? It's all lost in the din and muddle of war. War is nothing but a grand integral of personal animosities. It all started to go wrong. Schweppenburg saw he was cornered and sought to bargain for his life. The stake was precisely that which was to finance the Argentinian war effort – gold bars.

"Then there was a quarrel. Hollis was for making a deal. Fawcett was against it. Chepstow was ambivalent. There was a fight. Panic. Confusion. Shots. Schweppenburg died, but he took Fawcett with him. The upshot of it all was that it was Chepstow and Hollis who survived, who embraced the nightmarish task of hauling a tonne of gold down the mountainside to the harbour and getting it off. But somehow, they pulled it off, and they made it back into Chilean waters.

"Then they split the spoils and separated. Chepstow disappeared into Chile and never reappeared. Hollis, in a remarkably daring escapade, piloted the ocean-going yacht singlehandedly across the 800 kilometres of the Drake Passage. He was lucky with the weather and, within a week, was dropping anchor off the appropriately named Deception Island just off the Antarctic Peninsula. From there, Hollis began systematically to offload his treasure trove in discreet moieties that could lie untouched and undetected in specific and secretly documented locations. He buried his fortune. His nest egg, the means by which he would be able to found The Conglomerate. He would return for it at a much later date. In the meantime, he set sail for South Georgia with a cock and bull story about a bloody and sacrificial operation which had succeeded despite heavy losses. Poor old Chepstow and Fawcett had bought it. Not long after, Stanley was taken, and Mrs T was at the microphone outside No 10, crying, 'Rejoice, rejoice!' In the euphoria and overwhelming relief of victory, Hollis received his gong, shrouded in mystery, of course. The citation of honour remained heavily classified. It was to become a talisman, all the more powerful for that. Now Hollis had acquired two things – a couple of letters to his name that would guarantee entry into any exclusive club on earth; secondly, a treasure trove which he had put, literally, on ice."

I asked, "How did you find out all this, Ralph?"

"I reached Chepstow."

"Where did you find him?"

"In a care home in Punta Arenas. He's dying. I think he was relieved that we've finally caught up with him. He didn't want to carry his dark secret to the grave. So I just turned on a device and let him talk."

"Will the evidence hold up?"

"In a Court of Law? Nah. For that, we'd need to subpoena Chepstow, and we don't have the extradition treaty for that. Besides, he's too ill to travel." Parkinson carried on chain-smoking. "So let's see, we know that Hollis is a liar, a cheat, a murderer, a thief, and a thoroughly unpleasant fellow. But I still don't know why he ordered the storming of *Aerolíneas Argentinas* Flight 301."

"Me neither. I've been racking my brains. I saw something on board that aircraft, and I can't remember what it was. I go over and over *Whetstone* in my head, and I still don't see it. I'm missing something."

"Your trouble is, you're trying too hard. I think I can help you. I see no alternative. Alastair, I'm going to have to abreact you."

XVII

Well, hadn't that been precisely Kathryn Hathaway's idea? But I wasn't keen. In fact I wanted Forster and Parkinson to clear off before she came back from her Queen's Hall concert. "You're not coming anywhere near me with any sodium pentothal. None of your truth drugs and polygraphs. You're not wiring me up to the national grid."

"Don't be stupid. There's no quackery involved. It's really just a kind of informal chat."

I said dubiously, "I don't know. Isn't it a form of retrogression? What's the downside? Come on, Ralph. Outline the risks and benefits, and then I can sign the consent form. Or not, as the case may be."

"Every treatment," said Parkinson judiciously, "has its unwanted effects, just as every invasive investigation carries its modicum of risk."

"I dare say. And just what might that risk specifically be? What if you take me too far back, and I turn into a witch from

Massachusetts or a defeated cavalier from the battle of Edgehill or a galley slave in a quinquereme from Nineveh?"

"You're being silly. And your ignorance of history is as deplorable as your ignorance of psychiatry. Edgehill was indecisive."

"What if I get stuck? What if you can't bring me back?"

"That'll be a first. I'll write you up in *The Lancet*."

"What if I start getting flashbacks?"

"I expect you're getting them already. Abreaction," said Parkinson in a discursive tone, "is the resolution of a neurosis by reviving forgotten or repressed ideas of the event first causing it."

"Mm. I know. Like flooding."

"C'mon. You know the way to drive out the bogeyman is to confront him."

"So I've heard. Personally, I prefer to keep mine locked away in a cupboard along with all the other skeletons. As long as they don't bother me, I don't bother them."

"Right you are. Now that we've got all that out of the way," said Parkinson briskly rubbing his hands together, "let's get on with it."

Forster volunteered, "It worked for me. He cured my nail-biting."

"Well, I'm vastly reassured. Look, if we're going to do this, can we bring Caitlin back in?"

"Alastair, this isn't a slumber party."

"I know, but I think she might be able to help."

"What exactly is it that Ms Roy adds to the mix?"

"Perfect pitch."

"Whatever."

I slipped into the kitchen and paused for a moment to listen to the rich alto voice of the *cor anglais*. Caitlin stopped playing. "What are you talking about through there?"

"Soldiers in the SAS on a commando job. What are you practising?"

"You mean they weren't wearing any underwear? Slow movement of Ravel's G major piano concerto."

"It's beautiful. Will you come through and help me to remember another piece of music? Dr Parkinson's going to hypnotise me."

"Cool!"

Parkinson had got up and busied himself about the room. "Just a few minor adjustments. We'll switch the main lights off. We need just a little subdued lighting. That Anglepoise lamp would be good. Ms Roy, could you sit here? Major, we'll place you here. Just so. I'll just meld into the furniture here. Perfect. All set?"

I settled myself into the armchair. "No music hall stuff now, Ralph. I won't be made to bark like a seal."

Now Forster had drifted back into the room's gloomy recesses. Parkinson himself had slumped anonymously into an easy chair set at right angles to me. He was a grey silhouette. The lamp cast a limpid yet not lurid pool of light around me. My tone lost its banter. I said seriously, "Ralph, I don't want to get stuck on that aircraft."

"I know, mate. I'll escort you on, and I'll escort you off, safe as houses."

Caitlin said, "Are you going to use a watch and chain?" And, in an absurdly thick Teutonic accent, "You are feeling drowsy…" Parkinson smiled briefly and waited for everybody to settle down. He paused for absolute silence, as a conductor might before raising his baton, and then began.

"Now, Alastair, I want you to make sure that you are entirely comfortable in your chair." There was no hint of the soporific in his voice. It was a pleasant, melodiously pitched bass voice, beautiful to listen to. Funny how I'd scarcely noticed that before.

"Just make sure each muscle group is devoid of strain. Begin distally and work proximally. Mindfulness."

A cultured Melbourne voice.

"No strain in the quads or hamstrings. Bottom pushed well back in the chair." That accent came from east of the city centre, not too far from Port Phillip Bay.

"Back well supported. No lumbar strain. Your abdominal wall is quite relaxed and is not compressed by poor posture."

Take a tram from Flinders Street station over the Yarra Bridge.

"Your breathing is absolutely unlaboured and perfectly regular."

Pass the cultural arts complex on your right and the parkland leading to the Botanical Gardens on your left.

"Your neck is very free of strain. It's well supported by the cushion on the high-backed chair. See – you can rock it gently from side to side with perfect ease."

Past the rather grandiose war memorial high up on your left and swing into St Kilda Road.

"Your forearms are resting on the arms of your chair, and your hands are clasped across your midriff. That's a very comfortable position."

Take a left where the tramlines converge, cross Punt Road, and you're into South Yarra. Just a little further now.

"You are utterly relaxed, all the way from your toes to your fingertips."

There was dead silence in the room. Toorak. That must be it. Parkinson comes from Toorak, and he pretends to come from Footscray. That explains why he reminds me of Humphrey DeForest Bogart. Tough guy from a genteel background. Anyway, he obviously hasn't hypnotised me. I can think of whatever I like – stream of consciousness. I can hear a peat crumbling in the grate.

"Alastair, we're going to talk about *Aerolineas Argentinas* Flight 301, the hijacked aircraft you boarded at Heathrow in your capacity as emergency physician. I remember watching you cross the tarmac carrying a resuscitation crash box. You climbed a staircase to the rear exit of the aircraft. You were made to put the crash box down at the top of the staircase, and then you went aboard. Do you remember?"

"Yes."

"What happened next?"

"I was grabbed by two men in balaclavas."

"What else did you see?"

"Nothing else. I was blindfolded. Then they pushed me forward to the front of the aircraft."

"You could see nothing. Walk the length of that aircraft again. Have you started to walk?"

"Yes."

"How do you feel?"

"Tense."

"There is no need to be tense. You are revisiting this scene and experiencing it in retrospect. Therefore, you can change nothing. You cannot change the experience, and nor can the experience change you. It is a finished thing. You are like a time-traveller who can return to witness an event. But you are now insubstantial to that event. Or the event is insubstantial to you – like a hologram. You can walk about the hologram and view it from any angle you wish, but you cannot make any adjustments, only report what you see.

"But, of course, you see nothing. You are blindfolded, and I see that your eyes are now closed. How far down the aircraft have you walked?"

"Fifty, sixty metres."

"Can you touch anything?"

"My arms are being held firmly to my sides."

"Can you smell anything?"

"It's a very bad smell – of many frightened people who have been close together for too long in a confined space."

"What can you hear?"

"It's hushed. Remarkably quiet." As now. "A child crying…

"…seat belt being undone…

"…coming to the end of Economy now. Swish of the curtain as we are now about to pass forward into the First-Class Section…

"…ouch! Jarred my leg on the step. Arms released now to let me use the handrails. Up to the top, left, left again – stumbling a bit. Searched… intimidated… blindfold coming off."

I opened my eyes. Yes, it was all there before me in the monochrome twilight. The patient spread-eagled in his chair, the cabin crew, the sinister men in balaclavas. I could work my way through the thoracostomy procedure, then the catch-up resuscitation and the blood transfusion, the endless delay and the excruciatingly slow progress of the negotiation, then the assembly of the stretcher and the dismantling of all the paraphernalia of the Resus. I took one last look around the chaos of the Business Class cabin to see if there was anything I was missing. No, nothing.

I said to Ralph in a dreamy tone, "Let's go back downstairs now."

"Okay. What do you see?"

"I'm back at the top of the stairs. I'm walking backwards, holding the leading edge of the stretcher."

"Go on."

"Down the steps, we go. We have to tilt the stretcher very steeply. It feels almost vertical. Very heavy. I'm worried the patient slips down on top of me, but it's all right.

"We've got to the bottom. It's a little bit awkward

negotiating the corner. Now I'm walking backwards into Economy.

"The transit's shaken the patient up a bit. I thought he'd probably get quite hypoxic on the way down the stairs, but in fact his oxygen sats aren't so bad. Still, he's delirious. His hands are trailing along the cabin floor. I have to stop and balance the stretcher between one hand and one knee so that I can put Taff's hands back across his torso."

And yes. There *is* something different.

"They've got all the passengers strapped in. They're playing some music."

Calmly and unhurriedly, I hummed the tone row, the bleak plainsong chant of all these weeks ago, in a low undertone.

"There's a guy sitting in the first aisle seat on my right. I'm facing the front of the aircraft, and I see him quite clearly as I pass. I can even see the number of his seat above his head. 27D. He's wearing headphones. Something else. Something I didn't notice. He's got a laptop on the table in front of him. Suzanna told me they'd confiscated everybody's cell phones and electronic devices. So how come he's still got his laptop? He half turns when he hears the patient wailing deliriously. He's got a funny half-smile on his face. Middle-aged man. Middle height. Greying hair. Light-coloured grey suit. Utterly nondescript. He seems to look at us, look at me, look at the patient, look at Suzanna; then he carries on working with his laptop. I've seen him before. Elsewhere."

What is it that's different about Taff? It's his hands – the mangled hands with the tatts. I see what it is. His hands lack any sign of trauma. His hands are whole. His stigmata are healed. Then I remembered.

"Oswald."

I stared in wonder at Taff's hands.

"We carry on backwards down the aisle. Everything seems

to be going all right. All of a sudden, I feel a thump on the back of my calf. Suddenly there's smoke everywhere." I could feel its acrid bite searing down the back of my throat, tearing at my lungs. I began to cough.

"Okay mate, you can come out now. Fast-forward again."

"Can't breathe!"

"You are sliding down the escape chute onto the apron. You're out of the aircraft. It's over."

I heard Martin Forster say, "Maybe it's like sleepwalking. You're not supposed to wake somnambulists."

"He was never asleep." Parkinson slid off his chair, stepped forward, and gave me a hefty thump on the back. I gave my head a shake and cleared my throat.

"You okay?"

"Yes I'm all right. Phew. *A la recherche du temps perdu.*"

"Proust?" said Caitlin. "Yuck."

Oswald. I'd met him before, only for a few seconds. He was the man up in the northwest who had served that wizened old man and me, and recharged our glasses during our game of chess. His master had said, "Thank you, Oswald. You can let yourself out. The doctor and I can fend for ourselves."

"Thank you, sir. Goodnight, sir. Goodnight, Doctor."

It took me long enough to remember him, but he had remembered me. He recognised me instantly, and he realised that should I reciprocate, then I would have established a connection between *Whetstone* and his master. That was why, the day following *Whetstone*, I had woken to find myself preoccupied with that extraordinary midsummer night in Wester Ross. My unconscious had made the connection even when my conscious mind could not. And that was why Oswald, the point man by the bulkhead on the first row of Economy, had pulled the plug. It took me long enough, but now the connection was established. I had discovered my *éminence grise*.

And because of what I'd seen in Taff's hands, I knew that St John Pennington-Althorp was the Pale Horse of Death.

I yawned, stood up, and stretched. "God, I'm tired. Feel as if I could sleep for a week."

Parkinson said, "Did you get what you were looking for?"

"Yes, I think so. Did you get the theme, Caitlin?"

"Yes." She played it back on the *cor anglais* – that gorgeous, plangent, liquid, limpid alto sound.

"Do you know what it is?"

"Yes, I do. We had a run-through at the NYO."

"What is it?"

"It's Gustav Holst. Homage to Thomas Hardy. *Egdon Heath*."

XVIII

Kathryn came with me for the assignation with the man who called himself Smith. I wasn't sure whether the presence of another person might make him even more nervous than he already was, but I decided to risk it. Just before we left, the mail arrived. There was a letter from London, addressed in a neat hand and posted first class. I opened it with curiosity.

Dear Doctor,

I'm due to meet with you tomorrow, but it occurred to me to send this on to you just in case, for whatever reason, we fail to meet up. I should explain a little more, but time is short, and anyway, I hope to be able to do so face-to-face. I must thank you again for your willingness to meet with me.

Sincerely,
Dominic Sinclair. (Mr Smith.)
PS: re the enclosed, the password is

PALIMPSEST586248050015, upper case all one word.
    All you need to know really.
    DS

There was a memory stick, barely the size of a piece of chewing gum. We didn't have time, so I stuck the letter with its inclusion in my pocket, and we got going. Kathryn drove. She said she needed to practise driving on the wrong side of the road. Once we'd negotiated the bottleneck of Corstorphine (20 mph speed limit – "For heaven's sake, adhere to it."), we made good headway past the Maybury Roundabout and then under the RBS logo on the bridge at Gogarburn. Ahead on my right, I could see the elegant biconcave lighthouse of the airport control tower. The air traffic was landing from the east. We took the airport exit and, mindful of the exorbitant car parking fees at our destination, parked for free in Ingleston Park & Ride, jumped through a gap in the hedge, and took the brisk five-minute walk to the terminal.

He didn't show up. We checked on the arrivals board that the flight was on time, verified that it had indeed landed, and put ourselves in a prominent position at domestic arrivals. I'd even got a pad of foolscap from W H Smith and, after the practice of meeters and greeters of delegates to corporate junkets, had fashioned a placard that might catch his eye, bearing the legend *Mr Smith*.

We gave him fully forty minutes, just in case he had brought luggage and promptly lost it. Maybe he was hanging around some carousel. I found a British Airways helpdesk and enquired if anybody was still coming off the flight.

"I think they're all processed through, sir."

Mm. It must have been a crank, after all. What a waste of time. We sat in a Costa Coffee place for a bit longer, nursing our flat whites, reluctant to leave, just in case. To occupy the time, I told Kathryn about my visitation from Forster and Parkinson the previous evening while she was out at her late-night concert, about Parkinson's research in the Deep South, and into the recesses of my memory. I thought she might pour cold water on my notion of a connection between *Whetstone* and a house up north in the middle of nowhere, but she listened intently and asked, "What was the house called, again?"

"Egdon Heath."

"Funny name for a pile in the West Highlands. Isn't Egdon Heath in Dorset? Something to do with the Tolpuddle Martyrs. What took you there?"

"A Tomahawk. Light aircraft. I ran into bad weather and had to land on the beach. They put me up for the night. Actually, they were very hospitable. Bed and board. And a game of chess. And a bizarre conversation."

"What did you talk about?"

"The two cultures."

"C. P. Snow?"

"Spot on. I'm impressed."

"I read about it when I was a sophomore at Yale. But Dr Leavis, Cambridge lit crit, he wasn't impressed. Then again, he was kind of a hard guy to impress. Who do you suppose were his four favourite English novelists?"

I opted for Dickens, Hardy, and two Brontës.

"Totally wrong. Jane Austen, George Eliot, Joseph Conrad, and Henry James. Fancy that, two women and two foreigners. I think he'd have squeezed in D. H. Lawrence if he could. Dickens didn't stand a chance. Dr Leavis thought his only decent novel, actually his *only* novel, was *Hard Times*."

"Haven't read it."

"It's kind of a diatribe against Utilitarianism. You know? Bentham, Mill, greatest good to the greatest number and so on. Dickens may have championed the poor, but I don't think he would have welcomed the welfare state. There's a giant schism in English letters that cuts a swathe through Romanticism and *Realpolitik*. That's really what's at the back of the Snow–Leavis debate. Orwell got it. You might campaign in poetry, but you need to govern in prose. Isn't it the same in medicine? If your doctor weeps for his patients all the time, he'll be bloody useless."

I had to laugh. "I suppose Utilitarianism underpins Beauchamp and Childress."

"Excuse me?"

"The four pillars of medical ethics. Respect for autonomy, beneficence, non-maleficence, and justice."

"Sounds like a useful resource."

"Sounds like a load of bollocks. Tender loving care is not a calculus."

I remember Costa had Radio 2 on the blower and I was listening with half an ear to the sad litany of the news with its usual digest of man's inhumanity to man, industrial disgruntlement, runaway climate change, and, as if we didn't have enough on our plate, wars and rumours of wars. Then, the travel news. Something about disruption on the London Tube. Somebody had fallen off the platform and under a train at Canning Town. Strawberry jam. The line closed for three hours. Terribly upsetting for the other passengers.

After about ninety minutes, we had to give up. Kathryn drained her coffee cup. "So what now?"

"Back to the flat I guess."

"Let's not. Let's go up north and check out this mysterious house of yours. After all, here we are at the airport. Let's jump on a plane."

"The hourly shuttle to Ullapool? I don't think so. Besides, I can't remember if I locked the door to my flat."

"You did."

"Or if I've left the gas on."

"What is this? OCD? What's Home Insurance for? Are you never spontaneous?"

"I don't have a change of underwear."

"Me neither. Who cares? Can't we hire a plane, Squadron Leader?"

"I dunno…"

"You're back to this protective veil business again, aren't you? I've told you before I'm over twenty-one. Besides, may I remind you I'm Honorary Secretary to DAMASK, so you can't dump me. It would be unconstitutional."

And I thought, 'Let's go to Ullapool. Why the hell not?'

That was one of these forks in the road you sometimes encounter. We could go back to the car, and trundle back into my dreary Marchmont flat, or we could take the ten-minute walk round the airport perimeter to the Aero Club. What's that poem by Robert Frost about a bifurcation of ways? You have a choice, and one option looks much the same as the other. You might as well toss a coin. What difference does it make?

All the difference in the world.

So what do you think we did? I offer you two scenarios. Here is the first:

At the club, Aaron Jackson, New Zealander still on the big OE, cocked an amused eyebrow. "Special ops again? Take the Slingsby Firefly for old time's sake?"

"Golf Echo Charlie Kilo Oscar? Is she available?"

"Yep."

"We'll take her."

"Mint."

How lovely it was to be back in the familiar surroundings of the Slingsby's cockpit, snug in the five-point harness, talking to the tower, taxying out and taking off and vacating to the north. I've said it before: When you are flying an aircraft and loose yourself from Earth's *surly bonds*, you leave all your troubles on the ground. We crossed the Boundary Fault Line and got established in the cruise. I switched on the automatic pilot. Actually, the Slingsby doesn't have one, but every seasoned pilot holds a George somewhere in the deep recesses of the mind. Kathryn seemed very much at home and relaxed in the right-hand seat, looking out and enjoying the view.

"You never asked me about my illness."

"No."

"I mentioned it in my eulogy for Suzie. She looked after me in the ICU."

"I know."

"Aren't you curious? I mean, you being a doctor'n all. I thought you'd be interested."

"You had acute anaphylactic shock – late presentation. You nearly died. Upper airway obstruction. You were in ICU for weeks. Multi-organ failure. You survived."

She frowned. "You've been hacking into my record."

"Heaven forfend. No. I worked it out."

She snorted. "You couldn't *possibly* know about all of that."

"You're right. I couldn't know for sure. It was just an educated guess. To start with, you're wearing a MedicAlert bracelet on your wrist. Is it a peanut allergy? The bracelet's getting a bit worn, so you've had it for a while. Most nut allergies are diagnosed in childhood, so you've pretty much been living with this all your life. You carry an EpiPen. You probably carry two of them in that satchel of yours. You even took them with you to the lectern at Cockfosters. It's just a part of your routine. You're well organised. So, the time you got sick, you were out in the sticks somewhere. Lost way out in the boondocks. That implies a delay to presentation, and why you became so desperately ill. Bit of a panic in the Emergency Department. They had to do a cricothyroidotomy. I can see the scar on your neck. Actually there are two. The bigger one's for the more formal procedure in ICU. Tracheostomy. A surgical airway. So they ventilated you for some time. That was because the end organs took a bit of a hit. Kidneys, lungs… The brain's all right. The last bit's easy. You recovered."

She looked at me as if I were a Martian.

We landed at Dalcross, by Inverness, and dropped into the Aero Club, where I had hired the Tomahawk back at the summer solstice. They had forgiven me for my late return of their machine, largely, I think, because I'd brought it back in one piece the day following that bizarre game of chess. Getting airborne again off the beach had turned out to be less of a suicide mission than my previous departure from Talisker Bay, an age ago. So sure, I could park the Slingsby on the apron, tether it down, and leave it for as long as I liked. Nice to have you back.

Kathryn and I crossed to the commercial terminal and hired a car. A red Audi hatchback. Now that I'd fixed on Ullapool as a destination, I couldn't wait to get there. I love Ullapool. I love to walk along its beach front and go out on to the pier and watch the Caledonian MacBrayne ferry from Stornoway come in and dock. Or to slip into the Ceilidh Place and browse the shelves of their remarkable book shop. To stop there for dinner. Or to take a walk up Ullapool Hill behind the town and admire the view. I love to head north out of the town into the wilderness of Assynt and to spend a day among the scattering of isolated lunar peaks; then to return, at twilight, to the town. You ascend a long straight, come round a curve, and you are rewarded with a glorious view of the township on the harbour, its lights twinkling in the gloaming. It's a happy, rational, place of community and kindness; a place of sanity. I could live there.

But we still had fifty miles to run. In the terminal building at Dalcross, I caught sight of a television screen and a sequel to an incident that had occurred earlier that day. Or, more accurately, a prequel to our own proposed assignation at Edinburgh. At least, I had a suspicion it might be that. The BBC were running a story about a tragic incident on the Tube connection for the Docklands Light Railway. It turned out the victim happened to be a high-flying Civil Servant. Permanent Undersecretary in MOD. General expressions of regret and dismay. Wife and three kids. Speculation about suicide. Had been under great strain, etc.

It was a bit of a long shot, but I took my diary out and studied the plan of the London Underground system. Canning Town was a link to London City Airport. Either Mr Smith got stuck because the trains all stopped working, or, more likely, I suspected, he was the guy who fell off the platform.

So that was the prequel. It turned out there was indeed also to be a sequel.

We crossed to the Black Isle (confusingly not an isle) via the bridge that separates the Beauly Firth from the Moray Firth and skirted the bottom of the Cromarty Firth. After Contin, the street furniture began to thin out, and at last, we were a loan vehicle heading north-west across the blasted heath.

She broke the silence. "You hardly know me at all, do you?"

"What?"

"I mean, you don't know anything about me."

"No, I don't suppose I do."

"Do you want to?"

I didn't answer that. I thought about it. I wasn't sure. I was nervous. We continued in silence.

"Then again, I don't know much about you either."

"What would you like to know?"

She shrugged. "Dunno. Start with the easy stuff. Answer as soon as you buzz. Seconds out, no conferring. Beatles or Bowie?"

"Beatles."

"White wine or red wine?"

"Depends on the entrée."

"Favourite song."

"*Doppelgänger*."

"The Clash?"

"Franz Schubert."

"Signature dish."

"Hominy grits."

"You're just taking the piss."

"Well, in *Pride and Prejudice*, Miss Elizabeth Bennet makes the observation that you cannot understand somebody simply by knowing whether he prefers *Commerce* over *vingt-et-un*."

"Yes, but don't you ever lighten up?"

"My point is that this absurd *Hello Magazine*-style catechism will tell you nothing of substance."

"Perhaps you think of yourself as Mr Darcy."

"Ha! I'm more like Mr Collins. 'My dear, it only remains for me to express the violence of my affection for you.' Miss Eliza said to her father, 'Sir, can this man be sensible?' But have it your way. Anyway, it's my turn. Favourite meal?"

"I love seafood. But…" She held up her left wrist and gave her MedicAlert bracelet a shake. "You weren't quite right about the peanuts. Unfortunately, it's the mussels that are trying to kill me. My turn. Biggest hero of all time."

"St. Paul."

"Favourite night out."

"Orchestral concert."

"You really know how to show a girl a good time. Smoker or smoke-free?"

"Smoke-free."

"You just failed the lie detector test."

"Honest, I quit."

251

"Best sex."

"Mind your own bloody business. My turn. Signature scent."

"Chanel No 5."

"No. It's *Amouage*. I can detect it. Caitlin uses it."

"Can a girl have no secrets?"

I was in a teen rite-of-passage, come-of-age road movie – an unlikely alliance of a rock chick and a nerd. We just wanted to be two kids going out on a date. Looking back on it, that car journey westward to Ullapool might have been the last occasion in my life that could remotely be called *normal*.

I asked, "Where's home?"

"Boston."

"Your parents still alive?"

She laughed. "Yeah! They're both 47."

"What do they do?" I sounded like a physicianly elder statesman, one of the wise old men of Edinburgh Royal Infirmary.

"My dad's a journalist, and my mom's a human rights lawyer."

"Brothers and sisters?"

"Four. Two of each."

"Where do you come?"

"Smack bang in the middle. Now you tell. Parents?"

"Died when I was eleven."

"Oh no. What happened?"

"Plane crash."

"I'm sorry."

"It's a long time ago."

"Brothers and sisters?"

"One twin sister."

"Does she look like you?"

"You tell me. You've seen her photograph."

"On your desk? The girl with the dark hair. Yes, she does

look a bit like you. Who's the other one? The redhead. The younger one?"

"Sister-in-law."

"Ah. Mary's sister. What exactly *did* happen to Mrs Cameron-Strange?"

"Car crash. I told you I come with a government health warning. Which reminds me..." – I wanted to change the subject as much to help her out of her evident discomfort – "What happened to your wedding plans?"

"Guess I got cold feet."

"Meanwhile, a dejected Bostonian is pining for you."

"New Yorker. He'll get over it."

We took the briefest detour onto the A832 to Gairloch. I said, "You must come and see Corrieshalloch Gorge." We left the Audi in the car park, passed through the kissing gate and slalomed through the Moine schists down to the suspension bridge. (No more than six walkers at any one time.) We took a walk across to the footbridge's central point to stand in awe at the dreadful chasm, the cascading waters, and the rapids below. I had a moment of disorientation on the footbridge. Just a brief moment of vertigo. I know it's ridiculous coming from an aviator, but I'm scared of heights. In medicine, vertigo is defined as a hallucination of movement. Is it movement of yourself with respect to the earth or movement of the earth with respect to yourself? That's the point – you can't tell. It's a little bit like sitting on a train motionless at a station platform. The train on the line on the other side of the platform begins to move, and for a moment, you have no idea whether you or the rest of the world are moving. A wave of intense nausea can attend it. I put on a portentous thespian voice and declaimed to Kathryn:

"How fearful
And dizzy 'tis to cast one's eyes so low!

253

...I'll look no more,
Lest my brain turn and the deficient sight
Topple down headlong."

"What?"

"*King Lear*. Act 4, scene 5. You're pale."

"Sorry. I need to get off the bridge." She turned and walked back, grasping the bridge rail firmly and taking careful steps with exaggerated care. She ascended back up to the car without looking back. When I caught up with her, she was leaning against the passenger door of the Audi, her back to the gorge. The colour had come back to her cheeks.

"You okay?"

"I guess so. Funny – I'm not usually bothered by heights."

"Corrieshalloch is pretty awesome."

"D'you know, I'm not even sure it was the height. I got a funny feeling. I've been here before. But I haven't."

"Like, *déjà vu*?"

"Yes. But maybe no. I've *almost* been here before."

"*Presque vu.*"

"But never have."

"*Jamais vu.*"

"That was really weird. I don't think the French have a word for it. The words simply don't exist. It's like… I was having the initial experience that would later invest the future experience with the *déjà vu* sensation. Does that make sense?"

"Call it *avec prescience vu.*"

"Let's get out of here."

PALIMPSEST586248050015

All you need to know really.

Five hundred and eighty-six billion, two hundred and forty-eight million, fifty thousand and fifteen. Anything special about that number? Back in the Audi, and during the long descent to Loch Broom, we played around with it, to the hypnotic free-verse background of the "Shipping Forecast" on the car radio. *Viking, North Utsire, South Utsire, cyclonic five to seven at first, occasionally storm...*

It was like a conundrum that might be asked on a zany late-night Radio 1 talk-back show. 586,248,050,015 is the answer. What's the question?

Dogger, Fisher, German Bight, good, occasionally poor...

People would phone in with suggestions. Age of the universe in Mercurial years. Number of atoms in a carat of gold. As a denominator, chances of winning the national lottery. Cockroach population of the world.

Trafalgar, Sole, Lundy, Fastnet, cyclonic five to seven at first, occasionally storm...

Kathryn said, "Is it a prime number?"

"Divisible by five, so, not a prime."

Rockall, Malin, Hebrides...

"Does it sit between two primes – 0013 and 0017?"

"The first one is divisible by three."

Bailey, Fair Isle, west or northwest five to seven...

"What are you, an idiot savant? Twelve digit number. Maybe it's just a mobile phone top-up voucher."

Faeroes, Southeast Iceland...

"Of course!" I snapped my fingers. "It's a coordinate."

"Coordinate?"

"You know. Latitude and longitude."

Then she saw it. "Of course it is. Silly us. Which hemisphere?"

"It's got to be here, where we're at. Fifty-eight degrees north can't be too far away."

"But forty-eight? East or west?"

"No no. It's in degrees, minutes, and seconds. 48 seconds. Let's see... It's 58 degrees, 62 minutes, 48 seconds north, then

255

what was next? 50? East or west? East would be Siberia. West would be Cape Cod."

"Not fifty. Zero five. Five degrees east of Greenwich."

"That's going to be the North Sea. Try five degrees, no minutes and 15 seconds west."

If it had been up to me, I'd probably have waited until we got into Ullapool and then found a touristy shop with maps and laboriously trawled through them. Kathryn searched for it on her mobile and had the answer in a minute.

"It's Cape Wrath. It's exactly Cape Wrath. It pinpoints the lighthouse."

I had known it all along. Ever since that unfortunate lone hiker had got mown down during military operations, and Hollis had done his brief and merciless Obit to the camera, I had known *Whetstone* and Cape Wrath were inextricably linked.

We checked into the Royal Hotel. At the hotel reception, there was a momentary confusion. I said, "Two singles if you have them…"

"Isn't that rather an unnecessary expenditure? A double or a twin would be fine. Look, if you're prudish about it, we can sleep with a sword between us."

"Or I could sleep on the floor."

"Or we could both start on the floor and then move into the bed." As ever, the candid, unblinking hazel eyes – I'd finally spotted their colour – stared me out.

I grinned stupidly at the receptionist, who seemed unusually preoccupied with her computer screen. "Well, that's sorted!"

"Maybe you'd rather I was a guy."

"No. I'm not really a guy's guy."

"Not even one for a drink – what is it you say? – with the lads down the pub?"

"I guess not."

"Are you a lady's man?"

"You mean, like a gigolo?"

"A lounge lizard."

"A poodle-fakir."

"Poodlefucker?"

"Steady on."

XIX

We could walk back to my car and trundle back to my dreary old Marchmont flat, or we could take the ten-minute walk round the airport perimeter to the Aero Club. I told you of a bifurcation of ways and that I would offer you two scenarios. This was option two.

By the time ninety minutes had elapsed we had to give up. There was nothing for it but to walk back to Ingleston and pick up the car. Then, to add insult to injury, just as we were rejoining the main drag back into Edinburgh, next to the enormous field where they hold the annual Royal Highland Show, an agricultural vehicle spreading fertiliser appeared from behind a hedge and had the temerity to spray us with a tonne of manure. I cursed softly. Kathryn had a fit of laughter. At least we had the windows closed. "What a stench," I said. "We'd better put it through the carwash. There's a place at Maybury."

But it turned out their machine was on the blink. A gaunt individual with an Eastern European accent redirected us to another filling station somewhere between Bankhead and Saughton. They had some sort of arrangement. Just five minutes away. He gave us the postcode, and I tapped it into the satnav. Kathryn drove on, on automatic pilot, just following the bland instructions coming out of the dash. We entered a poorer neighbourhood.

"At the roundabout, turn left, second exit. Your destination is fifty metres on the right."

It was a garage forecourt, like any other garage forecourt. Bit run-down. Kathryn bypassed the pumps and drew up before an automatic carwash that was busily fussing over a BMW. She jumped out of the car and disappeared into the shop while I gazed vacantly at the giant brushes cascading over the bodywork of the black saloon. They gave the car one final titivation and then stood back as if to admire the handiwork. Now the drying fans passed, superiorly and laterally, from front to back. Then, the machine came to a stop. A red light on the left side at the car wash exit switched to green. I heard the engine of the BMW start up, and the car moved forward to vacate.

"Perfect timing. God, this crate stinks!" I remember Kathryn passed the strap of her satchel over her head and onto her left shoulder. She glanced at the docket in her hand, tapped the six-digit code into the keypad on a console on her right, and jumped back into the car. There was a beep, and a message on the screen of the console told us to move forward. Kathryn shut her window, and automatically, I checked all the other windows were closed. We moved forward.

Once we were inside the belly of the machine, the green light ahead on the left switched to red. Kathryn stopped the engine and applied the handbrake. Abruptly, the whole apparatus sprang to life and deluged us from above with a monsoon of water and detergent. Then, the enormous black rotating brush descended on us from above and methodically cleaned the car radiator grill and headlamps before ascending to cross the bonnet and approach the windscreen. At the same time, companion brushes at the sides similarly attacked the car doors. Now that the brush covered the windshield, the interior of the car grew gloomy, and the roar of the machine was deafening. It was like being clamped within the jaws of a gigantic and ravenously carnivorous prehistoric monster. How would a young child react to this experience if exposed to it for the first time and without a reassuring explanation? He would be either exhilarated, or terrified, or perhaps both in equal measure. The reassurance probably wouldn't make much difference. Children learn to distrust adults very early. What do *they* know? But it's funny how kids love things like dinosaurs. They love scary stuff, up to a point. I glanced at Kathryn. She was oblivious, absorbed in her smartphone, catching up with her texts.

Now, the process was being repeated back to front – more thunderous gloom from behind. As the brush passed over the hardtop, it was like being inside a washing machine on spin dry. The lateral brushes worked away conscientiously at the tyres and hubcaps. The car rocked gently from side to side. Then the thunderstorm was back over the front windscreen, the bonnet, the headlights.

A pause. I waited for the drying apparatus to commence its run. It didn't. I said to Kathryn laconically, "No drier. I should have got a shammy and done it myself." She was still absorbed in texting. "We're on drip-dry mode. We got the cheapest option. What's a shammy?"

I glanced at the red light. It should have changed to green, but it was stubbornly staying on red. "It's a peasant's version of chamois."

"Are you really a peasant?"

I said to Kathryn abruptly, "Get out of the car."

"What?"

I opened the passenger door. "Quick. Get out of the car."

"What the hell are you talking about?"

Suddenly, the machine sprang to life again, but it was as if the program had got mixed up, and every component was being supercharged and directed to act at once. Instinctively, I threw the passenger door wide open and got both feet firmly onto the ground so that I was able to reach back into the car, grab Kathryn round the shoulders, and haul us both away. It took considerable force to get her across the car's central console. I just remember her looking at me with an expression of complete bewilderment, as if she had suddenly discovered I was a violent rapist and serial killer. I dragged her across the passenger seat while being careful to stay on my own two feet and pulled outwards and upwards. She had no choice but to scramble to find her feet so that, for a second, we were face to face in an involuntary embrace. Now, a great commotion of freezing water at high pressure came at us from all angles and seemed to pin us against the side of the car while the great black brushes descended with their hideous roar. Despite, or perhaps because of, extreme danger, I couldn't help noticing the way Kathryn's soaking wet T-shirt clung to the contour of her body. Which way to go? Forward or back? More light emanated from the rear. I grasped Kathryn again round the shoulders and huddled her out of the maelstrom into the daylight. I tripped, and we both sprawled on the asphalt.

Now, Kathryn was outraged. "What the *fuck* are you playing at?"

I nodded towards the carwash. "Look."

For myself, I didn't need to look back. I knew the garage had turned into a demolition yard and the carwash into a machine designed to scrap and pulp old crates into compacted cubes of mangled metal no bigger than a child's funeral casket. I got up, pulled Kathryn to her feet, kept a firm grip on her right hand, and started running. I knew we had slipped through a wormhole, crossed a billion light-years, and entered an alternative universe.

How do you know you are having a nightmare while the nightmare is still ongoing? Now we are being followed by a host of zombies. We need to get out, fast. We need to hire a plane. But first you take the tram. Bankhead. Edinburgh Park Station, Edinburgh Park Central, Gyle, Edinburgh Gateway, Gogarburn, Ingleston Park & Ride… Do you remember that time you sat and read an Icelandic saga in a gate lounge in Keflavik, and emerged from your book to find the entire airport terminal building was deserted? You had the feeling you were on a film studio's back lot, and that all the vanished passengers had been film extras previously put there for your benefit. Well, here it is again, this time on an Edinburgh tram. All the other passengers – they could even have been the same film extras – stopped talking amongst themselves, stopped fiddling with their devices and gadgets, and looked up at us, their faces barely concealing their sense of amusement. Well, I hear you say, that is because you were sopping wet. No no. They'd been talking about me. About us. I could feel it.

Then there's a gap.

I was standing at the window looking out at the dawn over Ullapool Harbour when she came up behind me, put her arms round my neck, and said, "You have a beautiful body, but we need to buy you some clothes."

I didn't say anything. I was still in the throes of a bad dream.

Kathryn slid round to face me, looked at me quizzically, and said, "Are you all right?"

"I think I had a nightmare."

She pulled a face. "God! Surely I wasn't *that* bad!"

I put a thumb and forefinger on the bridge of my nose and tried desperately to separate fact from fiction. Am I losing the plot? Get a grip! None of that happened.

Did it?

Was I getting overwrought? Was I living in Cloud Cuckoo Land? Following that abreaction in Thirlestane, Ralph Parkinson had been very dismissive of my conclusions. "What makes you think something else was going on in Heathrow that day? Where's your evidence?"

"It's the only thing that makes sense. The man in seat 27D…"

"So you think you recognised him. Do you think this would stand up in a Court of Law? People are falsely fingered on identification parades all the time. Then there's this twaddle about the tune."

"I studied his soundscape."

"His soundscape. *Soundscape!* Listen to yourself!"

"All right, Ralph. So what's your formulation?"

"The most straightforward one. Have you heard of Occam's Razor? Of course, you have; you're a medical man. You go for the simplest explanation and don't overcomplicate things. You may not like it, but the tabloid version of *Whetstone* was right. A bunch of nutters go for a joyride. Then Hollis loses his temper and pulls the plug on them. Now, he ought not to have done that. His timing was terrible. You got that much right. I didn't like it any more than you did. Neither did Margaret Rowallan. The Enterprise Czar had no right to interfere. That's why she asked me to open a file on Sir Roger Hollis. Frankly, she wanted some dirt on Hollis so that she could put him back in his box. Now we can do that, and the case will be closed."

I replied. "The case is far from closed. It's only just beginning to open up. *Whetstone* is undoubtedly connected with a big house in the far northwest with the name *Egdon Heath*. We need to get up there and take a look."

"Here we go again. Old *Speedbird,* traipsing around the Scottish Highlands like some crazed Alan Breck, preoccupied with Sir Roger's taste in music. I don't need to remind you, Alastair, you've got form here. It's not the first time you've disappeared into the Celtic twilight on some madcap escapade."

"And I don't need to remind you, Ralph, that the last time you all thought I'd lost it, I was vindicated. Horribly vindicated."

"That was then and this is now. For God's sake. I ask you. *Soundscape!*"

Kathryn was still studying me, with a look of concern. "You know what? I think we'd better take a day off." From the dressing table, she picked up a bulky document in stout brown folders, opened the hotel guide on the menu page, and frowned. "What's a full Scottish breakfast?"

"Sausage, bacon, egg, tomato, mushrooms, beans, fried bread, black pudding..."

"What's black pudding?"

"Blood and oats, basically."

"I'll have everything but the black pudding. Toast and coffee. Then we'd better go shopping. Then let's go for a walk. I don't know, climb a hill or something. They say it's a good way of clearing the head. That way, we can decide what to do. What about that sugar loaf thing up at Lochinver?"

"Suilven? Bit of a trek, and it's a long walk in."

"What about the local, touristy one? Stac Pollaidh."

"Stac *Polly.* The dh is silent."

"Celtic spelling is weird."

"Gaelic orthography is perfectly logical and rational once you know the rules."

"If you say so. Anyway, Stac *Polly*, it is. Is it a Munro?"

"Not even a Corbett. It's just over 2000 feet."

"A Donald, then."

"The Donalds are all south of the Boundary Fault Line. No, it's a Graham."

"This classification system is way too complicated."

"If in doubt, call it a Marilyn and most of the time, you can't go too far wrong."

"Marilyn, as in Monroe? You've got to be kidding."

"We'd better take a look at this before we go." I handed her Mr Smith's memory stick. She sat down at the dresser, took her tablet out, and plugged it in. "So. What have we got? *Palimpsest Cape Wrath.*"

"What do you suppose *palimpsest* means?"

"It's a document on which an original text has been erased to be replaced by another one."

"I guess the monks must have been short of vellum. But I mean, what do you suppose Palimpsest *means*? It's got to be some sort of metaphor. You know, the new replacing the old. An obliteration of the old. Some kind of reinterpretation of the old. An act of concealment or an act of development. What does it mean in the context of Cape Wrath? What, if you will, is underneath Cape Wrath?"

The tablet detected Mr Smith's memory stick and a box popped up. 'What do you wish to do with File E?' Kathryn responded: 'Open.' The antivirus software ran a quick check and declared the data safe to examine. A fresh screensaver appeared. There it was – the lighthouse, on the edge of the world, and a wild and precipitous coast line. A box opened in the centre of the screen directly over the lighthouse. Kathryn typed in *Palimps—*. I said, "Upper case."

"PALIMPSEST586248050015."

The screen filled with icons. "Oh, Lord. This is going to take some time."

It proved to be a thankless task. Dominic Sinclair was a permanent undersecretary in the Civil Service, but he was clearly scrupulous about separating his professional and private lives. There was no trace of Whitehall to be found. The icons on the desktop screen seemed to refer to trivia. There were games of one sort or another. A programme that allowed you to land a 747 at various airports across the world. I would have been happy to play with that for a while. Email? We didn't have a password. Kathryn tried PALIMPSEST586248050015 again, as it was the only option we had, and was surprised that it actually worked. But it didn't really help. There were only a dozen messages in the inbox. Two, both from the previous day, were unopened. We opened them sequentially, both of us vaguely conscious of a sense of guilt, rummaging through the private affairs of a dead man. One was a circular from *Meet Up* – something about a forthcoming Pub Quiz. And a personal message: 'Hi Dominic. I wonder if my last went astray as you never got back, and I know how punctilious you are! Still on for Thursday? H.' I guess *H* now realised why Dominic had been so slow to reply. I trawled my way through the other messages, but they were entirely commonplace. Nothing.

Then Kathryn had an idea. She muttered thoughtfully, "PALIMPSEST… all you need to know, really."

"What?"

"A manuscript in which old writing has been rubbed out to make room for new. That's it! It's really perfectly obvious. What has been erased?"

She went back into email and pressed 'Trash'. There was a single document. PALIMPSEST. She opened it. We sat together and read through it in complete silence.

"Holy shit."

XX

"What are we going to do about *The Thing*?"

I said, "I think we should post it on the internet. It'll go viral. Tell the whole world."

"And have every copycat fifteen-year-old geek on the planet do their own *Thing*? I don't think so."

"Well, we can't just leave *The Thing* where it is, as it is."

Palimpsest had morphed into *The Thing*.

"Shouldn't we tell that committee you sit on? The Whippersnapperpot."

"Witenagemot. I don't trust them."

"None of them? What about Dr Parkinson? Or Major Forster?"

"I dunno…"

Abruptly, she made her mind up, stood up, and took me in both hands. "Then let's stick with Plan A and go up that hill of yours. We can call at the shops and pick up everything we need. They say brisk exercise is the best way to clear the mind."

I'm not very good at shopping, particularly getting snarled up in the petticoats of a woman traipsing round a clothes shop. But I have to admit she was so practical and expeditious that it was all I could do to emulate her example and keep up. Then, armed with our swag of booty, we swung back to the hotel to drop a few bits and pieces off and then drove the Audi north out of Ullapool to disappear amid the scattered outcrops of Torridonian sandstone peaks on their plinth of Lewisian gneiss. I hung a left down towards Achiltibuie, threading my way through all the interlaced lochs and lochans.

It wasn't a good day for a hill walk. I remarked to Kathryn that it was dreich.

"What is *dreich*?"

"*Gruamach*."

"I think I get the picture. Or lack of it."

The car park at Stac Pollaidh contained only two other cars. We parked adjacent (why are cars such gregarious creatures?), got geared up, and got going, crossing the road and heading north, through a gate and then uphill through shrub and young woodland to the open moor. I noticed the path was new and a lot better than when I'd last visited this heavily eroded hill. The old route, which once headed straight up the face of the mountain, had grassed over. I checked my compass. I'd already lost sight of the car and our landmarks, Sgurr Tuath, Loch Lurgainn, and Cul Beag to the east. Left or right? I ignored the path to my left, and we turned right, passing through another gate.

Now, the path curved round to the far side of the Stac. Where Cul Mor joins Cul Beag, we usually would have been rewarded with stunning views of Suilven across the wilderness of Assynt. Not today. We left the circular path, which passed around the base of the mountain and climbed steeply towards the lowest point of the ridge. It was a short, easy scramble to get to its high point on its eastern side, from where we could head up the col. It wasn't long before we reached the crags and buttresses that had been formed during the Ice Age when the ridge was exposed as a nunatak above the ice sheet.

We'd reached the tricky part. We could avoid most of the rocky towers ahead by staying to their north side, but the final one had to be negotiated. There was a short traverse above a steep drop. *An Stac* is a very popular climb, but in fact, its (true) westerly summit is a little tricky to attain. There is what is known as a 'bad step'. Kathryn took one look at it, shivered, and said it wasn't for her. I think she was having another Corrieshalloch moment. I wondered if I should negotiate it alone on this foul day – the acrophobic aviator. But the top was enticing and literally only ten minutes away. Kathryn said, "You go. I'll wait for you here."

"I'll be 20 minutes. Don't wander off and get lost in the mist."

She nodded. "Don't worry. I'll stay put, right by this rock. I'll give you half an hour." As an afterthought, I gave her the car key. "Just in case it really starts pissing down." She took it but said, "I'm not moving. Not without a compass. You're going to have to rescue me."

Today, the scarps and pinnacles assumed a sinister quality that reminded me of the sullen, oppressive and brooding stacks of the Quiraing in the Tolkienesque environment of Trotternish, Isle of Skye. There is a place in the Quiraing, the Prison, which always fills me with foreboding when I visit. I have a notion that something murderous once happened there, and that the presence of ghosts ensures that it continues to happen for all time. Now on Stac Pollaidh, I experienced that same sense of foreboding. I'd lost sight of Suilven, Canisp, Inverpolly Forest, or the Summer Isles out in the Atlantic. I tried to remember the names of the various pinnacles that now seemed to crowd in on me and menace me: The Sphinx, Tam O'Shanter, Andy Capp, Madonna and Child, Lobsters Claw. It was all I could do to stop myself from turning back, grabbing Kathryn, and running back down to the car.

I took a deep breath and, concentrating on where I was placing my hands and feet, ignoring the sheer drop, I made that last, swift, dangerous scramble to the top. There was a makeshift cairn. I cast around for a piece of rock, found a modest pebble, and added a few centimetres to the height of Stac Pollaidh.

"Fine day for a walk."

I nearly jumped out of my skin.

Major Forster was a hooded figure sitting motionless on the other side of the cairn. He had taken off a light rucksack and balanced it beside him. He was eating a sandwich and occasionally sipping from a hip flask. He proffered me some delicatessen. "These pork and pickle mini-pies are terribly good."

I took a moment to calm my nerves, then slipped round to the west, slid my back down the cairn and sat down beside him. I declined the pie but took a swig of his schnapps and said, "Well, you old bugger, what are you doing up here?"

"Baroness Rowallan asked us to keep an eye on you. We've got your back."

"But how on earth did you find me?"

"It's not difficult to follow somebody who keeps their mobile phone switched on."

"I take it your Doppelgänger is with you?"

"Dr Parkinson? Of course. We work best that way. It's a symbiosis."

"Synergistic, no doubt."

"Indeed."

"Symbiotic synergy seems to be all the rage these days." I

made a quick decision. The precipitous scramble to the peak of Stac Pollaidh must have made me impulsive. "Here. Take this."

"What is it?"

"It's a letter from a Whitehall mandarin named Dominic Sinclair, the late Dominic Sinclair, with an enclosed USB drive. It's the solution to *Whetstone*."

"What do you want me to do with it?"

"That's beyond my pay grade. But if I were you, I'd be careful who I share it with. Show it to Margaret Rowallan. Show it to Ralph if you like."

"Ralph doesn't think *Whetstone*'s a problem."

"Well, he's wrong. Tell him The Conglomerate has constructed a Doomsday Machine up at Cape Wrath. Probably deep underground. If it were up to me, I'd blow it up. Can you get hold of a bomb? Not just a damp squib, mind. Something with a bit of grunt."

"Oh my. Doctor, you've come a long way since you took the Hippocratic Oath."

"A dirty bomb. A neutron bomb. Something that will put the place off limits for a thousand years or so."

"Right you are."

"Thanks. Gotta go." I was conscious of the passage of time and that Kathryn would be waiting.

The scramble back across the bad step was heady and precarious. I always find coming down more difficult than going up. But I negotiated it unscathed and got back to Kathryn's rock just within her thirty-minute deadline.

She wasn't there.

ENDGAME

XXI

In Medicine, when you discover that you have made a mistake, you cross your fingers and hope for the best. In the Emergency Department you see a child with a headache. You diagnose something benign, like tension headache or migraine, and you send the child home. It's only subsequently that it crosses your mind that the diagnosis might have been something more sinister. With a gnawing sensation in the pit of your stomach, you realise that you might have overlooked some subtle pointers – the complaint of limb pain, the appearance of circumoral pallor. You take urgent steps to have another look. You make a phone call. Naturally, there is no reply. It's then that you cross your fingers. After all, you might still have got it right the first time.

But you know, deep down, in your heart of hearts, that you didn't.

I took a quick reconnoitre round the immediate vicinity. It was deserted. I cupped my hand and called her name. Nothing.

I turned from north to west to south to east and called out four times.

Nothing.

I stormed back up to the summit of Stac Pollaidh, negotiating the bad step quickly and without thinking about it. I reached the cairn where Major Forster had been eating his lunch. He had vanished into thin air. I rushed back down, over the bad step again, this time with careless, almost suicidal abandon, to Kathryn's rendezvous point. It was deserted.

That which I had most feared has come to pass. I had indulgently considered that my wish to protect Ms Hathaway came out of sheer altruism, an extension, if you will, of the Hippocratic Oath. Not at all. I wanted to protect her because I wanted to protect myself. I had known unequivocally, all along, that if I put her in harm's way, then I would lose the plot. And now the name of Kathryn Hathaway could be added to my list of spectral sylphs. A huge switch, like the lever a railway signalman must manhandle in order to change the points at a major junction, clicked in my head. My train of consciousness was about to be diverted from the main arterial route onto an exotic, meandering branch line which might lead anywhere, never to get back on track. I always knew that this was a lone mission and that I would end up conducting it on some remote, metaphysical plane.

I am become death, destroyer of worlds.

Simultaneously, like another click of a switch, my environment – it happens on the Scottish hills, it can turn on a dime – changed from benign to malignant. You become aware of a change of atmosphere. Nature and the great outdoors are suddenly sullen and inimical. I literally sprinted back down to the car park. It too was utterly deserted. The red Audi hatchback had gone.

Had she got fed up waiting for me and come back down

to the car herself? But why would she do that when she had actually said she wouldn't? 'I'll give you half an hour,' she'd said. I hadn't overrun my time. Even if I had, surely she would have waited for me in the car. She wouldn't have left me out in the middle of nowhere. She wouldn't just have driven off.

I stood in the middle of the road and looked first east, and then west. The world was silent and deserted. I noticed there wasn't even any birdsong. That was when I felt that cavernous emptiness in the pit of my stomach. Mary, Nikki, Suzanna, and now Kathryn. I kept trying to convince myself that there must be a perfectly rational explanation for her disappearance. She'd had to rush back to Ullapool. Had she taken ill? Had she had to inject herself with one of her EpiPens? I couldn't even text her. I hadn't saved her number on my mobile.

Maybe she hadn't gone back to Ullapool. Maybe she had driven off in the other direction. Maybe she had embarked on some insane mission of her own. She was going to 'pop down' to Egdon Heath, just out of curiosity, then pick me up on the way back.

Impossible.

I thought I could hear the sound of a motor vehicle in the distance. In the muggy silence, its direction was hard to discern. But the engine note was gradually getting louder. It was coming from the east. Well, Kathryn, I'll have something short and sharp to say to you if you've taken the Audi for a spin.

It wasn't her. For a second I thought it was, when a smudge of red puttered out of the mist. I recognised it as the post van. I stepped out into the middle of the road and flagged it down. The driver stopped, wound down his window, and looked at me enquiringly. Could I hitch a ride to the end of the road? He nodded and I climbed on board. We continued the journey, west, in silence. I sat in a stew, absorbing the inescapable fact that I had lost her.

We snaked along the B road and further into the wild bleak landscape, away from the direction of Ullapool, further out on the Achiltibuie peninsula. Stac Pollaidh's irregular crag receded into the mist. I had a strong sense of moving away from civilisation and into an undiscovered hinterland beyond the pale. An ancient chart might have warned me: here be goblins, the more so as I knew from the map that I was heading into a long, narrow cul-de-sac. The only way out was back. We drove all the way to the coast at Altandhu and then turned left again to head southeast, with the sea always on our right. The driver asked me briefly if I were heading for *The House*. I nodded.

On this September afternoon the sun never made an appearance. No beautiful vista of the islands floating and dancing on the sparkling water. The Summer Isles were invisible.

Horse Sound. We passed the turnoff to Badenscallie burial ground, down on the beach. Achduart. We were nearly at the end of the road. Culnacraig, under the lowering shadow of Ben More Coigach.

The postal van came to a stop by a deserted gatehouse. The driveway descended in the direction of the sea, through a dense copse into a natural hollow. From here, the house was invisible. I got out of the van and watched the driver make his delivery, pushing a few letters into the gatehouse letter box. He nodded briefly at me and restarted his vehicle. I watched him carry out a neat three-point turn and head back from whence we'd come. I walked down the driveway, which took me through the dense camouflage of the thicket. The house was west-facing. I took in a rather drab rear courtyard before the driveway veered right and widened into a substantial gravel forecourt on the house's coastal side. Now I could hear the boom of the sea. There was a single vehicle parked before the grand entrance, a battleship-grey Daimler. I walked past it and ascended the weathered stone steps to the front door. I remembered the tiny plaque on the entablature on the pillar on my right. *Egdon Heath*. In the porch there was an electric light burning, but the house showed no other sign of life.

Did I have any semblance of a plan? I had stopped thinking rationally and logically. I was only conscious that, in some sense, I had moved from the middle game to the end game, where the normal strategies of war, the maintenance of the redoubts and parapets and salients of attrition, would cease to apply. I was done with tactics and strategies. This was a distilled situation. The endgame merely had to be played out.

I pushed the doorbell located in the stonework on my left. I could hear nothing ringing out, and it was impossible to know if the bell was working. I gave it a minute and then pushed it again. Almost immediately the door was opened.

I was taken aback. I had expected to be greeted by a sober butler in tails, and indeed my host had a solemn face, but he also happened to be a cherub, about eight years old. I said, "Oh, hello!"

"Hello."

"Are your mum and dad at home?"

"Yes."

"May I speak with them?"

"Who are you?" An adult might have said, "May I say who is calling?" but children are so much more direct, and have no need of circumlocution.

"Tell them it's Alastair."

"Alastair who?"

"Alastair Cameron-Strange."

He turned, walked unhurriedly through the grand atrium to a door on the far right, opened it, and announced in a loud voice, without faltering, "Alastair Cameron-Strange is at the door."

The pause was only fractional. "Thank you, Torquil. Please invite him in."

Torquil returned to the front door, opened it wide, and said gravely, "You may come in."

The atrium was as I remembered it, with its ghastly accoutrements and military paraphernalia. I didn't think the drawing room into which I was led was the same room where I had once played a game of chess. Here was a jolly, chintzy scene. The adult company, three men and three women, sat amid the floral upholstery while the children, four of them, played a board game on the floor. It was a happy atmosphere, but there was something stagey about it. I might have stepped back in time a hundred years.

"Oh, hello!" Hector Harcourt-Beasley got up and addressed me with a look of amused bafflement. "This is a surprise. You should have come for dinner. We've just finished up, but I'm sure Cook could rustle something up."

"I'm fine, thanks."

"Drink?"

"Just a glass of water, thanks." My mouth was dry. I had a moment to study the company. It hardly came as a surprise to me that I knew the men. Sir Roger Hollis said, "You've come a long way, Doctor."

"It's quite a trek."

Hugh Standish asked me if I were staying locally.

"Ullapool."

"Two of the best bookshops in Scotland," remarked Hector Harcourt-Beasley.

"Indeed. I intend to have a browse."

I tried to marry the ladies up with the gentlemen. Lady Hollis would be the tall, slim, and rather severe matron in a pale green gown; Mrs Standish was a livelier, twinkling, rotund individual. Mrs Harcourt-Beasley, the youngest member of the group, was an English rose, very beautiful. Of course, I recalled, she was Hollis' daughter. Patricia. Hector was Sir Roger's son-in-law.

"Do sit down." I sat between Patricia and Lady Hollis. I resisted the temptation to sink back into the deep plush of the sofa but stayed on edge. The water came, in a tall, slim glass, with ice. I took a sip. There was nowhere to put the glass down. I held on to it.

There was no mention of any of our previous encounters and no further expression of surprise at my arrival. Nor was there any haste to ask me my business. The body language merely indicated a polite interrogative receptivity, so to say, "Just tell us what's on your mind in your own time."

In fact, they resumed the conversation I'd evidently interrupted. "Dr MacTavish said it was nothing to worry about."

"Did he make a diagnosis?"

"Hang on. I wrote it down." Mrs Harcourt-Beasley rummaged in her bag and produced a piece of paper. "*Molluscum contagiosum*. Oddly enough, he said, it's not that contagious."

"Did he give a treatment? Creams? Unctions?"

"He said it wasn't necessary. He said if you squeezed them with tweezers – he called it 'disrupting their architecture' – they would take the hint and go away, but he said it was rather a laborious task and could cause distress. And they would go away in their own time. Besides, they don't seem to bother Torquil."

Torquil was indeed sanguine, nay phlegmatic, seated over the Monopoly board with his cousins. There followed a rather rambling lay discourse about various skin complaints. It was all so commonplace that I knew if I didn't bite the bullet, I would lose motivation and forget why I had come. And they clearly weren't going to ask me. I'd just have to raise the subject.

"You haven't had a visit from a young lady today?"

It was such a non-sequitur and abrupt change of tack that it sounded prying and inquisitive. The dermatological discussion halted abruptly.

"Young lady? Let's see now. We had Torquil's tutor as usual, and somebody from the church about the flowers for Sunday. Anybody else, Patricia?" It suddenly occurred to me, they all spoke an archaic BBC received pronunciation as ancient as the BBC itself. I was taking part in some elaborate costume drama. I was Richard Hannay, played by Robert Donat.

Mrs Harcourt-Beasley considered. "That frightful woman from the WI, but I'm not sure I'd call her young." She looked at me with an amused expression. "Have you lost somebody?"

"Yes, as a matter of fact, I have. Her name is Kathryn Hathaway."

"What a charming name! Should we know Ms Hathaway?"

"I have a notion she may have called. She was driving a red Audi hatchback. Early twenties. Five foot ten. Long dark hair. American accent. Eastern seaboard."

Patricia Harcourt-Beasley considered. "I was out riding most of the day. Hector, you were in. Did anybody call?"

"Not that I know of. But I was doing my red box. What was her business, Doctor?"

I took another sip of water. "She would have been inquiring about Operation *Palimpsest.*"

"Is that another church fête?" He never skipped a beat.

"Mr Harcourt-Beasley, you know what Operation *Palimpsest* is."

"I dare say I've been told, but to tell you the truth, I get all these charitable institutions, worthy as they are, mixed up with one another."

"Perhaps Sir Roger could remind you, or indeed Mr Standish, or, indeed, perhaps most authoritatively, St John Pennington-Althorp, the Duke of Assynt."

There was a silence. For a moment, I thought the charade had come to an end, but the company was merely expressing its bewilderment.

"*Palimpsest*, Roger?"

"I don't think I contribute to that one."

"Hugh?"

"Me neither."

"Doctor, you are going to have to enlighten us."

"Very well." Conscious of a gathering sense of absurdity, I took another sip of water and then a deep breath. "Operation *Palimpsest* is a top-secret initiative. It is run by government ministers but it is not an official UK government enterprise. Most of the members of the Cabinet are unaware of its existence. It involves the purchase, the import, and the assemblage of a WMD the likes of which the world has never seen."

"WMD?" asked Patricia Harcourt-Beasley, frowning. Was it another offshoot of the WI?

"Weapon of Mass Destruction." I sounded ridiculous, even to myself, but I plodded relentlessly on. "It was brought into the British Isles, in component parts, much like a Meccano game, for subsequent assembly. It came through Heathrow on August 15th."

"August 15th?" Sir Roger said. "That, as I recall, was the day of *Whetstone*."

"Indeed it was. *Whetstone* was integral to *Palimpsest*. *Whetstone* served as a diversion."

"It certainly diverted you, Doctor, as I recall. Where does Ms Hatherton come into all this? Where, come to think of it, do we come in?"

"Hathaway. She is a very direct person. I'm sure she would have asked you where you'd put *Palimpsest*. To confirm our suspicion."

"What is it you suspect, Doctor?"

"*Palimpsest* is on the Parph."

"Parph?"

"MOD territory, just to the north. The road to Cape Wrath."

All their faces bore the same expression, that of people trying to observe ancient rituals of courtesy while realising they are dealing with somebody who has become mentally unbalanced. There was a tinge of sorrow and regret. But, behind it all, I felt sure, there was something else. I had seen it before, not so long ago, on the faces of that Parliamentary Select Committee. It was barely perceptible, but it was there. Just a trace of fear.

"Mind if I take a look around?"

Mrs Harcourt-Beasley put her drink down on the table and rose. "Well, I've often shown our guests round the policies, though I have to say, never on this pretext. Where would you like to start? That's all right, Hector. The doctor and I will manage perfectly well. Finish your drink."

We stepped out into the hall. "Where to begin?"

"Round the back, where the Audi's parked."

"I don't think we have an Audi. That's the one with the symbol like the Olympic Games logo, isn't it? Frightful, aggressive drivers. They tailgate."

I turned back to the drawing-room door and lunged it open. I wanted to get a quick snapshot of the company demeanour once I had gone. They looked up at me with polite perplexity. I had the farcical demeanour of an Inspector Clouseau. I gave them an appraising and cautionary glance. Just checking.

I wandered in a trance behind Patricia down a long corridor and into a spacious and well-appointed kitchen.

"That's all right, Cook. We're just taking a shortcut."

The sole vehicle in the back courtyard was a bicycle, an old Raleigh with a Sturmey-Archer gear, leaning up against a drainpipe. There were no cars. I took a walk round. Nothing. There was a double garage. I nodded towards the doors. Obligingly, Mrs Harcourt-Beasley opened them up. Inside, there were two cars: a smart, black BMW saloon and a sportier, red open-top vintage Mustang. She even opened up the car doors and the boots.

"We never lock anything here. So safe in the country. Where to next?"

I already knew my search would be futile. If there were any chance of my finding Kathryn, they would never have offered me the guided tour. Nonetheless, I took it. It might be worthwhile to master the geography of the house, to get a sense of where Kathryn had been, to try to reconstruct her last movements. I had moved beyond social awkwardness. I didn't care how this must look. I concentrated on the task at hand.

We started at the top of the house and worked down. Patricia led the way. She was very elegant. She placed each stiletto directly in front of the other in the runway walk of a fashion model. There was a percussive tap off the parquet flooring.

"This is Torquil's room. Sorry about the mess. Boys!

"One of the spare rooms. You are very welcome, if you are staying.

"I love this room. Such a view of the sea. I never tire of it…" I might have been her real estate agent, and she briefing me so that I might take prospective buyers round. *Oil fired central heating throughout, lots of power points, cupboard space…*

"You'd better look at the loft." A short spiral stairway led to a spacious rumpus room which seemed to serve as a gymnasium. There was a treadmill, a cross-trainer, a rowing machine, and some weights. Nothing else. We came back down the spiral stair and descended another flight.

"Billiard room. It's really Hector's only vice. Do you play?"

"Music room." It was dominated by a pristine black Steinway concert grand on a raised dais. There was room for an audience of perhaps twenty. The bookcases were full of sheet music and scores. There was a music stand erected within the curved contour of the piano, and a violin lay on the piano lid. I wondered who played.

"Private chapel. I know it's a bit of an indulgence." It was like a quiet room in an airport. There was even a small pipe organ.

More bedrooms. I opened a cupboard door.

"Oh yes, plenty of storage space." The litany went on. We moved from floor to floor. My antennae were out. I was looking for any remote clue, any hint of her presence. Meanwhile I was mapping out the house, counting the rooms, their layout with respect to the central stairwell, memorising the geography as if rehearsing for a quick egress during a fire. Patricia became quite chatty. It was as if she had forgotten the nature of our reconnaissance. "The house has been in the family for years. So many glorious summers we've spent, sailing mostly. Do you know the Summer Isles?

"Dining room. Rather OTT, I'm afraid. Frankly, it gives me indigestion."

I remembered it. We were back on the ground floor. I'd stopped listening to her running commentary. I even went ahead of her, darting from room to room, swiftly taking in each vista with a sweeping glance, oblivious as to how monumentally rude I must look. I kept thinking I would enter the room where I had once played a game of chess, but if I did, I never recognised it. By the time we were back in the main hallway, we had almost run out of options. Patricia asked me if I'd found what I was looking for.

"I'm afraid not."

"Has your friend been missing for long?"

I glanced at my watch. "I haven't seen her for a couple of hours."

"Perhaps she went for a walk. The countryside is so beguiling."

"No. We'd made an arrangement. It's very unlike her. She would have called."

"Perhaps she can't get a signal. We are remote."

"She would have worked round that. It's completely out of character."

"Oh, dear. It's very worrying when somebody seems to go missing. I remember I missed Torquil in a supermarket for five minutes. The store detective found him. I felt so guilty. Have you told the police?"

"Not yet."

"Perhaps you should. Would you like to use the telephone?"

"In a moment. Could we just conclude the search?"

"I thought we had done."

"No. There's one more room. That's if I've understood the internal geography. There should be one room directly under the Chapel. That would be…" I pointed. "This way." I pointed at a book-lined wall.

"Well, as you can see, Doctor, that is a wall lined with books."

"No."

"Sorry?"

"There is a room here."

"A room with no door?"

"Apparently not; ergo, the door must be concealed." I started to examine the books.

"This is getting ridiculous." For the first time, I detected a trace of irritability.

"I take it one of the books is the key. Which is it?"

"Doctor, I've gone out of my way to assist you. I've—"

x

287

I started to browse. "Dickens? Thackeray? Trollope?"

"Try Scott."

I hadn't heard Sir Roger Hollis join us. He took up a position beside his daughter and put an arm round her shoulder. "You mustn't think Patricia is being obstructive or devious, Doctor. She is merely trying to protect my granduncle's privacy. His den is his last sanctum." He leaned across and took a volume of Scott off the middle shelf. It was *The Heart of Midlothian*, in the Edinburgh edition. He replaced it immediately. The bookcase obligingly swivelled. I passed through. Sir Roger joined me, but Mrs Harcourt-Beasley stayed in the hall.

The Duke of Assynt was seated at his desk.

If I expected any sudden revelation, this was entirely anticlimactic. Here was a small, dull room dominated by a broad, heavy desk littered with papers and correspondence. There was a single swivel chair in front of a desktop computer that was currently asleep. A single small window in the wall opposite the desk afforded scant illumination. There was a stale aroma of tobacco smoke. This was a utility room where a man might deal swiftly with his correspondence. It was deliberately designed to be spartan and unwelcoming so that the occupant would not be tempted to linger but would discharge his tedious secretarial duties and then get out. That was all. Seated at his desk, with a letter in one hand and a silver letter-opener in the other, St John Pennington-Althorp looked absently in my direction. Sir Roger said, "How dare you interrupt the Duke."

His appearance was exactly as I remembered. He was so elderly and emaciated that I, in our previous encounter, had presumed he must be dying. Yet I could detect no evidence of any further physical deterioration. It occurred to me he would probably go on forever. The Duke of Assynt proffered a hand in my direction. "How do you do, Mr...?"

"Doctor. Alastair Cameron-Strange. We've met."

"Really? I have such a poor memory for faces."

"On midsummer's night. Here in this house. We played a game of chess."

"Chequers, surely. I'm not much good at chess."

"We used the Lewis chessmen."

"I thought they were in London. Anyway, what can we do for you, Doctor?"

Sir Roger said icily, "The doctor thinks we have kidnapped a friend of his."

"Lumme! Have we?"

"I think even the doctor, having ransacked the house, will have to conclude that we have not. He would insist on breaking his way into this room."

"Doctor, you mustn't mind Roger. He does tend to cosset me. Anyway, as you can see, I'm alone here. About your friend. When did you last see him?"

"Her. Her name is Kathryn Hathaway. As you very well know."

Hollis interjected again. "Look. You've searched the house. Exhaustively I think. Perhaps you should redirect your enquiries elsewhere. Enough."

"No."

"Doctor Cameron-Strange, I think you will admit we have bent over backwards to accommodate you, but I have to say now that you have exhausted our patience. I really don't know what else we can do for you."

But the veneer of civilised bonhomie no longer impressed me. You see, even behind the stale reek of pipe smoke, I could smell the merest hint, a memory, of Kathryn's perfume. *Amouage*.

"Where have you put her?"

"I beg your pardon?"

"She's been here. Within the last couple of hours, she was here. Where is she now?"

Hollis smirked at me. I dropped all pretence at civility. I cupped my hands, and I started bawling her name at the top of my voice.

"Oh you poor chap." Hollis gave me the gentlest of smiles. "You'll never find her." For a moment, he appeared to drop the role-play and speak without irony. In retrospect, I suppose he might merely have meant that she wasn't there, but it seemed to me at the time he was mocking me, and that was why I lost it. I went for him. I got my hands to his throat. But I didn't get a chance to hurt him. Instead, help – three burly retainers, as far as I remember – appeared from nowhere and half a dozen hands had me around the chest and midriff, and I was escorted, gently but firmly, back out into the hallway and placed in a solid high-backed chair. The help disappeared unobtrusively into the background.

Patricia reappeared. She looked worried and upset. "I've sent for the police."

I snapped, "Bloody good thing too. I shall have some stiff words to say to them. Kidnap is a very serious offence."

"My dear fellow, we are not kidnapping you!" I'm not sure if Hollis was wilfully misunderstanding my drift. "We are merely putting you into safe hands for your own protection."

Harcourt-Beasley said, "Roger, you're too much of a softie. This man has assaulted you. You must certainly make a complaint to the police."

"That won't be necessary, Hector. Anybody can see the doctor needs help. Doctor, you are overwrought. I think you need to seek professional advice. Maybe something good can come of your visit after all. Think of it as a gateway to therapy."

I was escorted back into the drawing room and made comfortable again amid the chintz. I was even offered another drink, which I declined. The children had all been put to bed. Now the blue strobe of the police car drew up in the forecourt.

Hollis went out to meet them. I could hear him at the door, explaining the situation in soothing and emollient terms.

There were four cops, young, tall, fit-looking guys. It crossed my mind that Sir Roger must certainly exert a degree of clout to summon such manpower so quickly in such a remote location. They might have said to me, "We can do this the easy way or the hard way." But I couldn't very well deny that I had tried to assault somebody. I would come quietly. I didn't fancy the humiliation of being led out in cuffs. Still, I wasn't prepared to stay silent.

"Guys, thank goodness you've arrived." I was gushing. "These people have abducted a woman named Kathryn Hathaway. I believe her to be in great danger."

"Alastair Cameron-Strange, I am arresting you on a charge of common assault. You are not obliged to say anything…"

"Gentlemen," interceded Sir Roger, "is this really necessary? I do not wish to press charges. The man needs help."

I said, "To hell with all that. I just want you to find Kathryn Hathaway."

"Come along with us, sir. We will take a complete statement from you."

I was escorted from the house. I remember as I got into the back of the police car, one of the guys laid a firm hand on the crown of my head as if to prevent me from banging it off the door sill. I glanced back at my hosts. They had assembled, three men and three women, at the front porch, watching me. They almost convinced me, and I could almost believe, that they were full of concern for my health and well-being.

XXII

"I'm absolutely convinced they took her. Abduction is a very serious crime. She was in that house. I know it. She might not be there now, but they are holding her somewhere."

I was sitting in the middle of the police car's rear seat, with a police officer on either side of me. They were extremely uncommunicative. It occurred to me that they didn't even talk amongst themselves. I sat and stared at the backs of the heads of the two officers in front.

What if they aren't policemen at all? I had a very bad moment when I thought of that. The prospect of a night in a police cell might not be the worst option.

"Where are we going?"

Silence.

The car travelled swiftly, and in what seemed a flash, we were back abeam Stac Pollaidh.

"Can you slow up? I just want to check if my car's in the car park."

They didn't, and it wasn't.

"It's a red Audi hatchback." I gave them the registration number. "Stolen. That's the least of the matter."

Now we had reached the T-junction at the eastern end of the Achiltibuie Road. It occurred to me that if we turned right and headed for Ullapool, I might be all right. If we turned left and headed north, I had all the trouble in the world.

We turned right. All might yet be as it seemed. As if to confirm this, the guy on the front passenger seat turned round and said to me, "Consider yourself lucky the Duke is not pressing charges."

"I wish he would. Then I could have my day in court."

"That's fine, sir. Let's get you back to your hotel, and we can get a full statement from you when we get there."

I recognised the judicious tone of somebody trying to fob me off in a conciliatory way. God knows I've used it often enough myself. Twenty minutes later, we arrived back at the Royal Hotel in Ullapool. They escorted me straight up to my room and watched me fumble with the door key. But the door was open.

"Visitors."

My sister hurried to me and embraced me as if frightened that I was somehow going to slip from her grasp and vanish away. Her face was drawn and tear-stained. She said nothing. Ralph Parkinson was lingering in the background, giving my sister time. I waved at him as cheerfully as I could.

"Ralph."

"Speedo."

A slim, bearded man entered the room unobtrusively, slipping past the police officers, who waited outside in the hallway. He was of middle height, casually dressed in blue jumper, fawn chinos, and brown suede shoes. Ralph said, "This is Mr Fotheringham."

"Denis." He shook my hand. "Social services."

I was so slow on the uptake. A family member, a psychiatrist, and a social worker. Why couldn't I see what this was going to be? MacKenzie sat beside me on my bed and held my hand. Ralph took the single chair, and Mr Fotheringham remained by the door.

I gushed. "Ralph, am I glad to see you! So much to tell you. You can't imagine how frustrating it is being banged up like this, when I've got the solution."

"Solution to what, Speedo?"

"Solution to everything! See, I've worked it out. It's all come together. It all fits!"

"How does it fit, Al?"

"Exactly as a situational puzzle should. All the component parts, necessary and sufficient. You have them before you, like pieces of a jigsaw puzzle. But you can't see how they can possibly go together. Not, at least, until you make that crucial mental leap. Lateral thinking. Then you wonder how on earth you never saw it because all the time it was staring you in the face! The fit! The fit of the parts!"

I remember my sister never said a word. She just held my hand and looked at the floor. Mr Fotheringham observed me with professional curiosity, like a taxidermist examining animal pelt. Ralph said, "What are the parts, Al?"

"Seven of them, Ralph. As you'd expect. They are the seven seals of Revelation. Four of them are straightforward enough. Of course they are the four horsemen of the Apocalypse."

"Who are the four horsemen, Al?"

"First up is the Chancellor of the Duchy. Hector Harcourt-Beasley. No great surprise there, eh? A foreign secretary in waiting. He sits astride the red horse – the one that brings war. Next is the black horse. That's the Minister without Portfolio, Hugh Standish. A Master of the Universe. The man holding the purse strings.

"Then there's the white horse. I must admit that had me

294

fooled for a long time. Naturally, I thought it must be Sir Roger Hollis, the Enterprise Czar. But that's not right. I just couldn't see it. I was up too close. So close, in fact, that I couldn't possibly retain perspective. It was only a recollection of a game of chess that told me the answer."

"What's the answer, Al?"

"Why, Ralph, it's me. Don't you see? I am the white horse!"

"Sure you are, Al."

"That just leaves the pale horse. I'll come to the pale horse in a minute, because the other three components of the jigsaw were what led me to him. Remember there was the theme?"

"What theme was that, Al?"

"The one you helped me remember during the abreaction. You deserve a medal for that! Sir Roger's *Desert Island Discs* helped. I told you I studied his soundscape. 'Neptune,' and the close of RVW 6. Doesn't that say it all? Can't you see? This is more than a death cult. The man is devoted to total and absolute annihilation! But it was the disc he missed out that really counted. Remember his book? *The Return of the Native*. Colossal and mysterious in its swarthy monotony! It's Holst's *Egdon Heath* of course. That's the fifth component. I couldn't recall it. Ever since *Whetstone*, I'd been trying to remember it. I couldn't figure out why. My unconscious was trying to get me to link Heathrow with *Egdon Heath*."

"Why would your unconscious want to do that, Al?"

"Because of the man in seat 27D! That was the other revelation of the abreaction. The man in seat 27D was the man who served *Writer's Tears* to me in *Egdon Heath*. Oswald. That was why they didn't want me to get off that plane. In case I linked Heathrow to *The House*. D'you see?"

"It's all one massive conspiracy theory, isn't it, Al?"

"Absolutely! Oswald is component six. I bet you've already guessed number seven."

"You tell me."

"586248050015."

"You're going to have to spell that one out for me, Al."

"Co-ordinates. 58 degrees, 62 minutes, 48 seconds north. 5 degrees, zero minutes, and 15 seconds west."

"Where might that be?"

"It's the lighthouse, Ralph, at Cape Wrath. Wrath in itself is a clue. *Day of Wrath*. That reminded me of Taff's tats. Remember D-I-E and I-R-A? I thought it was something to do with Irish Republicanism, but it was nothing of the kind. If Taff hadn't lost his fingers, it would have been obvious. DIES IRAE."

"Ah-ha."

"An *Ah-ha* moment indeed! That all takes us back to number four, the pale horse. I know who the pale horse is, Ralph. The mastermind behind the whole thing. The *éminence grise*. The man who is not in government but who has the ear of government. The man who has access to the highest circles and yet who is barely known to the public. The man so pale that he is invisible."

"Who might that be, Al?"

I paused, to give my pronouncement added gravitas.

"St John Pennington-Althorp. Yes – the Duke of Assynt."

There was a heavy pause. What a relief to get it all off my chest. Ralph was an astute guy. He wouldn't waste too much time. Quick phone call to London. Let Martin know, certainly tell Margaret Rowallan.

Ralph Parkinson asked me gently, "Alastair, is there any possibility that the girl you were looking for in that big house – that she wasn't actually there? I mean, could these people you called on, and who sent for the police, could they be right to say she hadn't visited them?"

"Not a chance. I know she was there. I felt her presence. I could smell her fragrance."

"What's her name?"

"Kathryn Hathaway."

Parkinson smiled. "I bet she hath. How do you know her?"

"I met her at Suzanna Fergusson's funeral. Then she came up to Edinburgh. She came to *Question Time* in the Signet Library."

"You met with her there?"

"No, I didn't see her there, but I did hear her."

"You heard her. You mean, like a voice?"

"Yes exactly. She asked a question. Then she visited me in the hospital. But you know all this. I gave her your card. She contacted you."

"Alastair, I wasn't contacted by anybody named Hathaway."

"What? She told me she had. I must have picked her up wrong."

"Where's she from?"

"The States."

"Which one?"

"Massachusetts, I think. But I'm not really sure."

"What's she doing over here?"

"A doctorate."

"What's her field?"

"Believe it or not, apocalyptic literature. How neat is that?"

"Where's she doing it?"

"I don't know. UCL?"

"Is that a guess? Has she met your sister?" MacKenzie shook her head. "Or Ms Roy? Or your boss?"

"No."

"You kept her to yourself. What does she look like?"

"She's tall, and slim, with long dark hair."

"That sounds an awful lot like that girl in Auckland you've been trying to forget."

"Nikki? If you were to see Kathryn, you would know she looks nothing like Nikki."

"Alastair, please don't be angry, and please don't take this the wrong way. Just stop a while and have a ponder. I'm asking you to think carefully before you answer this. Do you think there is any possibility that Kathryn Hathaway doesn't exist?"

I stared long and hard at my psychiatrist. "No."

Ralph Parkinson addressed Denis Fotheringham without looking round. "Did you get all that, Denis?"

"Yep."

"Heard enough?"

"Yes, I think so."

It was only then that my sister MacKenzie spoke for the first time. She squeezed my hand hard and began to explain to me in gentle, loving tones about the paperwork that was required to section me under the Mental Health Act, Scotland, that would allow me to be transported to a place of safety and looked after and, most important of all, treated, so that in due course I would get better. And get back to normal. Oh yes absolutely. No question. Mental Health issues these days no longer carried any stigma. It was just a piece of bad luck. I could as easily have been struck down with pneumonia.

Now, looking back on it, it was an inspired intervention of the community mental health services to recruit my twin sister. If anybody else had been the bearer of bad tidings, I might have made a scene. It could have turned nasty. Frankly, I would have done my best to tear the place to bits and break my way out. They would have needed six burly orderlies to carry out a controlled restraint. Physical followed by chemical restraint. Oh yes I know the lingo. God knows I've been on the other side often enough. I'd spent my entire professional career making sarcastic remarks behind the backs of the mentally infirm. "That guy? He's mad, bonkers, raving, barking, daft as a brush, mad as a snake, out to lunch, one sandwich short of a picnic..." Would I have used similar epithets for somebody who was decrepit, demented, vertically challenged, or for that matter, black, Roma, LGBTQI, or any of the myriad other social minorities forever getting it in the neck? It had never crossed my mind how heartless I had been.

Until now.

XXIII

September 6th

My sister is a very trusting person. After all, the crime rate in the Highlands is very low. And the police, having handed me over to the shrinks and consigned me to the bin, were no longer interested in me. As for Ralph Parkinson, he must have thought we should all have a night's sleep before I was escorted to some secure facility. So I didn't have to make a rope of knotted sheets and drop out of the window. All I needed to do was pack a light rucksack, wait until everybody had gone to bed, and then walk out of the hotel and over to my sister's Jaguar. She hadn't locked it. And I knew where she was accustomed to hide the spare key. I remember turning on the ignition, releasing the hand brake, and letting the car freewheel down the hotel's brief sloping driveway, quietly jump-starting the engine as I turned into the public highway. Thus I crept out of Ullapool and headed north into the wilds of Assynt.

I felt detached. It was as if I watched the sleek black Jaguar

300

from the air, following it, like a drone tracking its progress across the blighted moonscape, briefly hugging the coast, then turning inland to cross Strath Canaird, the driver slowing to glance to his left at the jagged rocky contour of Stac Pollaidh. Will he turn down in that direction and towards Coigach? No, not this time. He heads north. And all the while, like a musical worm, over and over again in my mind, that endlessly recurring and overlapping descending melodic minor scale of Arvo Pärt's *Cantus in memoriam Benjamin Britten*, anguished strings, and the tolling of a bell.

Durness was a ghost town, a huddle of buildings crouching round a T-junction at the top of the world. I never saw a soul. In my memory I can see tumbleweed floating up the main street but that is absurd; that is confabulation. I made a swift reconnoitre, then turned the car back round and drove south for a mile to Keoldale, hung a right and negotiated the single-track road down to the Kyle. The house up on the right was deserted and in darkness. The car park at the ferry crossing was empty. I drove in and stopped the Jag. I already knew what I had to do. I would swim the Kyle and then cross the Parph on foot.

A giant full moon rose abruptly somewhere between Kinlochbervie and Sheigra. It would help with the water crossing. I might even be able to swim up a kind of translucent, scintillating moon lane. I opened the car boot and inspected the contents, trying to plan ahead. I fossicked about and found MacKenzie's wet suit. Kiwi lass, every bit as outdoorsy as me. I struggled into it. It was a hell of a tight fit, but it was preferable to freezing to death. I took a change of my own clothes and double-bagged them in plastic, along with a few personal effects. Waterproof enough? I packed them in the rucksack. Travel light.

No point in hanging around. I put the rucksack on, pulled the straps tight, and walked gingerly down to the wharf. I paused and looked at an ancient, battered sign on the pier at the water's edge. It read MINISTRY OF DEFENCE TERRITORY. NO ACCESS TO THE PARPH WHEN SITE ACTIVE. There was then space for an insert. A single word in large red lettering occupied the space.

ACTIVE

Below this, KEEP OUT. LIVE ORDNANCE. EXTREME DANGER.

I waded out into the water. God, it was cold for early September, even with the wet suit. I picked out a feature on the opposite shore and took a bearing. How far was the swim? Maybe a kilometre. I launched out and got moving. Now there was a persistent inshore chop that made it difficult to settle into a rhythm, and I was conscious of the drag of the rucksack on my back. Ignore it. Just concentrate on the freestyle technique of your front crawl. The full moon is making navigation easier. Keep its orb on your left shoulder.

After ten minutes I was warmed up and could afford to take stock, pause and tread water. I turned and looked back at the solitary car where I'd left it in the carpark. I was halfway. Nobody knew where I was. I was the loneliest man on earth. I turned again, took another bearing, and got going.

I began discerning detail on the opposite shore, which thus far had been a dark shadow. Heavy, full-leafed trees on a steep single track climbed to the right. Below them, a shingle beach and the shadow of a wharf. Two hundred metres to swim. Minutes later, my feet touched the bottom. I gave it half a dozen more strokes and then stood up and waded out onto the beach. I had survived the most challenging part of the journey. I left the beach and walked up on to the edge of the track, absorbing the atmosphere of the Parph. I thought of the title page of Holst's *Egdon Heath*.

A place perfectly accordant with man's nature – neither ghastly, hateful, nor ugly; neither commonplace, unmeaning, nor tame; but, like man, slighted and enduring; and withal singularly colossal and mysterious in its swarthy monotony.

And I thought of Thomas Hardy's *The Return of The Native*.

The time seems near, if it has not actually arrived, when the chastened sublimity of a moor, a sea, or a mountain will be all of nature that is absolutely in keeping with the moods of the more thinking among mankind.

I took off my rucksack, and inspected the contents. I must have made a good job of securing the plastic bags because my things were dry. I took off MacKenzie's Lycra and put my clothes back on, jeans, T-shirt, pair of sneakers. I stuffed a few valuables, and my phone, into my pocket. I stooped to double-knot my running shoes. Then I stuffed the swimming togs into the double plastic wrap and put them into the rucksack. I searched round for a hiding place I would later be able to identify, thinking of how the place would look if I had to make the journey in reverse. Last tree on the right before the wharf. I walked across and wedged the rucksack between some roots at the back of the tree.

Wonder of wonders! There was a rickety old mountain bike parked precisely at the spot I'd chosen. I tested the tyres. Firm enough. Now the eleven miles to the lighthouse at the Cape didn't seem such a tall order. I took the bike and walked it up the initial steep slope of my route, observing that the wheels were turning freely, testing the brakes, making sure my newly-acquired vehicle was intact, all ship-shape and Bristol fashion. At the top of the hill, I mounted and started pedalling.

The track's surface was hellish, and even in the moonlight, the potholes came upon me unexpectedly. There was the ever-present possibility I would wreck the bike, wreck myself. Concentrate! And don't be tempted to go too fast. Just stay on the saddle. Make sure you get to your destination.

I wish I could convey to you how awful it was to feel this overwhelming compulsion to get to the lighthouse, and yet to be constrained, to be measured, to take time. I was back amid the night terrors of my childhood. My mother had soothed me and told me they weren't real, but I'd always known they were real. I'd always known they were some kind of rehearsal or dry-run for something my child self knew I would later encounter, in adulthood. And now, here it was.

The track followed the distant side of the Kyle for a couple of miles and then turned abruptly west. There was a descent to a bridge over a stream. I took it cautiously. A sign in red said 'Danger Area'. Now I was leaving Durness Kyle and biking inland on a heading which took many twists and turns but which more or less kept me on a northwesterly track in the direction of the lighthouse. The trees grew sparser, and I became more aware of the contours of the peninsula. I was flanked by thousand-foot hills, Fashven and Maovally to my south and Sgribhis bheinn to my north. A water feature appeared on my right. Loch Inshore, and here, the remnant of an ancient dwelling at Inshore itself. It was deserted. It was here that I suffered my mishap. The front wheel of the bike seemed to give way beneath me, and I lost directional control. Then the whole bike seemed to skid and buckle, and I fell off. Fortunately, it happened on the flat, and the only thing that got injured was my pride.

I sat still for a moment, collected my wits, then got up and inspected the bike.

Flat tyre. No bicycle pump. I wasn't even halfway. I was

now facing the prospect of a ten-kilometre run. It occurred to me, in a slow-witted way, that I was taking part in a triathlon. The notion made me grin like an idiot, inanely, at the moon.

Automatically, I parked the bike in the ditch clear of the track, and got going. There was a steady upward incline for about two kilometres. Now the countryside was bereft of tree or bush, gradually becoming bleaker. I was running on level ground and, a kilometre further on, I was conscious of a slight descent. It had been unlucky losing the use of the bike, but at least I hadn't hurt myself, and, more to the point, the lurid sign back at the Kyle about ordnance seemed to be a false alarm. Bit of a damp squib. Exercises presumably were over for the day, and they had merely omitted to change the sign.

When a Tornado comes at you from behind, passing 200 feet above your head at 500 knots, it does so absolutely without warning and with a deafening shriek. Instinctively, I dropped to the ground. Simultaneously a second whining scream terminated abruptly in a low-pitched crump that almost ruptured my ear drums and left them zinging and hissing and left me disorientated, vertiginous and nauseous. A kilometre ahead, the sun rose abruptly and I was in broad daylight for two seconds before it set again with perfunctory despatch. The sound of the Tornado vanished completely.

Ridiculous to imagine it had been firing at me. But the site was live after all. I remembered the hapless individual who had been strafed by the drone. Maybe there was going to be another *tragic accident* on the Parph. Sir Roger would have another opportunity for a set piece to camera. "The National Medical Adviser to the Security Services must have been under very great strain to put himself deliberately in harm's way. Our hearts go out…" Cut the schmaltz and get moving! Ignoring the tinnitus still ringing in my ears, I resumed the run and increased my speed. I became aware of the proximity of the sea on my right. There was a turnoff to the right, which I felt sure would lead quickly to a north shore inlet.

For a moment I had an episode of complete disorientation when I forgot where I was. I was no longer running from the Kyle of Durness to Cape Wrath. I was in Northland, New Zealand, running from Te Paki Station to Cape Reinga. The sea I could hear on my right was the surging surf of Spirits Bay, close to the convergence of the Tasman with the Pacific. Here was the turnoff to Tapotupotu Bay. I ignored it and stayed on a westerly course, crossing a bridge over a substantial stream, negotiating a few twists and turns, and then settling back on to my northwesterly heading.

With a flick of a switch in my head, I was back on the Parph. The track dropped down again to negotiate another stream. Now I could smell as well as hear the sea. I must be getting very close. The path backed southwest and then took me in a final arc towards my destination.

Now there was another sound overhead. It was intermittent, like the buzz of a rogue insect that somehow slips past the protective mesh of the mosquito net and disturbs your nocturnal slumber. I glanced up. The silhouette of the drone, no bigger than a portable campfire gas cooker, was perfectly delineated in the moonlight, hovering only twenty feet above my head. It monitored my progress, tracking northwest in parallel with me, looking down inquisitively. I ignored it.

I will never know for sure, but I imagine that the last kilometre of that triathlon resembled the sensations of going over the top against an enormous artillery barrage at Third Ypres. If I hadn't been frightened out of my wits, it might have been an exhilarating experience, like watching the Edinburgh Castle fireworks on Hogmanay. They always left the big guns to the end. There was such a cacophony of whizz-bangs and such an explosion of light that I lost all perspective of where I had come from, where I was or where I was going. I was merely a runner putting one foot in front of another and passing through a giant Catherine wheel, running a gauntlet of fire. I remembered the words of Winston. 'If you're going through hell, keep going.'

Abruptly the noise all came to a halt. There was complete silence.

There it was. A scattering of disused buildings and, overlooking the giant rock buttresses of the very top of Scotland, the lighthouse. Half a kilometre short of my destination, I stopped.

I don't know what I'd expected to find. There was absolutely no sign of habitation. Under the silver glare of the full moon, I was the sole inhabitant of an abandoned landscape on the edge of the world. What had I expected? A fence, barbed wire, a sentry post, signs of activity?

Nothing.

Maybe I'd got this all wrong. Maybe this was a wasted journey. What should I do? Finish the task, get to the lighthouse and touch it, have a quick look round, and then head back. I told myself, you're only turning a half marathon into a full one. Would I have enough energy for the water crossing? Maybe it would be better to find some shelter on this side of the Kyle, snatch a few hours' sleep, and do the swim in the morning.

I took the last few hundred metres at a gentle jog. Ahead of me, a nondescript single-storey building stood between me and the cliff edge. Behind it and slightly to the right, the lighthouse, unilluminated, was a dark shadow. Further to the right lay some elevated ground and, at its summit, was another derelict elongated single-storey building. I slowed to a walk, turned off the track, and climbed up to its entrance. This must be the old Lloyd's Insurance building, where they looked out for ships coming in off the North Atlantic. They would telegraph to London to say, "So far, so good," and the insurance premium would change.

I tried the door. It was locked and barred. This building had been out of use for years. I walked around its edges. The place was as quiet as a mausoleum.

Next, there was the building between me and the lighthouse. I strolled down to it. Though deserted, it seemed in a better state of repair. This must have been the destination for tourists intrepid enough to brave that potholed track by minibus before MOD closed the operation down. But again, there was an air of total desertion. You don't have to neglect a place for too long before nature begins to take over and obliterate bricks and mortar with weeds and lichen. I verified the door was closed and locked and took one clockwise turn round the building.

That just left the lighthouse. I don't suppose the latter-day mariners, with all their satnavs and ocean-sounding devices, have needed the succour of a lighthouse up here for decades. I sauntered down a remnant of path towards the cliff edge, as much wanting to touch my destination as a runner would, as complete any investigation. I was like a Munro-bagger adding a stone to a cairn on a mountaintop. Then I would turn and head for home. I'd got a bit dry with my exertions. No matter. Plenty of freshwater mountain streams to cross on the way back. I could hear the crash of the ocean four hundred-odd feet below me. The bulk of the lighthouse, with its elegant contours, loomed over me. I reached the entrance, locked fast, touched it, and walked, anticlockwise this time, round the base of the lighthouse to its northwest aspect on the edge of the ocean.

Quite suddenly, superimposed on the periodic crash and suck of the tide below, I felt as much as I heard a low-pitched grumble and the whine of a generator starting up somewhere beneath my feet. With a sharp crack the lighthouse came to life.

A white searchlight cast its broad beam out across the ocean. I watched the beam make one single, precise 360-degree pass, clockwise. The light source regained its original position, and then abruptly, its beam foreshortened and swivelled downwards in my direction.

I was bathed in its incandescent white light.

Mesmerised, all I could do was stare upwards at the source of the brilliant beam.

My assailants must have come at me silently from behind. The rough canvas bag was thrust over my head and shoulders, the light vanished, and I was in darkness.

XXIV

West Highland Free Press, September 9

Police Highland has, with reluctance, downgraded the search for the missing National Medical Advisor to the Security Services, Dr Alastair Cameron-Strange, from a rescue to a recovery operation. The search has to date focused on an abandoned black F-type Jaguar found three days ago at the Kyle of Durness jetty one mile south of Durness. A search of the Sound by a team of divers has thus far drawn a blank. A spokesman for the Government, Enterprise Czar Sir Roger Hollis, has issued a statement:

> *The National Medical Advisor to the Security Services has recently been under great strain. We fear that, despite timeous psychiatric intervention, he may have succumbed to despair. Our hearts go out to the relatives and loved ones of this outstanding public servant at this most difficult of times.*

XXV

1801. – *I have just returned from a visit to my landlord Marley was dead to begin with a truth universally acknowledged was the best of times it was the worst of times of Spanish rule and for many there was no possibility of taking a walk during the whole of a dull dark and soundless day in the autumn of the year while the present century was in its teens you have requested me my dear friend call me Ishmael*

When you receive a blow, a significant blow, to the head, you stop composing in paragraphs. You lose syntax. You can't even complete a first sentence but that it degenerates into a word salad. Your brain shuts down. Partly, it is a defence mechanism. Your central nervous system cowers in its lair like a frightened animal. You are concussed. Obtunded. From the instant of the blow, you stop laying down new memory. This is called *antegrade amnesia*. If the blow is more severe, you additionally lose memory that has already been laid down. This is known as *retrograde amnesia* and implies a greater degree of trauma.

Should you recover, you need to reconstruct all the bits that have gone missing. And, because you can only start at the point where you have rediscovered your identity, you need to proceed in a retrograde fashion. Think backwards.

I am in a pit at the bottom of the world. I can feel the pressure of the billions of tonnes of earth above my head. I am miles under the surface. I am convinced I have been here for three days now.

I was trying to resuscitate an unconscious patient, to rouse this inert man from a deep coma. How deep? He does not open his eyes when I squeeze his fingertip. Nor does he speak. Nor does he move. Therefore, he scores 3 on the Glasgow Coma Scale.

But then, you get a 3 for turning up. Sleep now. Try again later...

There are three men. One is vicious, one is vindictive, but the third? He is squeamish. He will not hold my gaze. He keeps visiting me in my cell, the way you might keep pushing on your own exquisitely tender abscess, to convince yourself it is still there. He insists I am a member of an illegal and proscribed organisation. DAMASK. With this I am charged. They told me as much when I sat before them, the horsemen. The white horse the red horse the black horse

But I am the rider of the white horse. The rider of the pale horse told me so.

This man who averts his gaze, who wishes to wash his hands of me, I cannot help him. He will carry on interrogating me until he extracts a confession, but I have nothing to confess and therefore I have nothing to say. He reiterates his accusation and all I can do is shrug and reply, "So you say."

The short-term memory is shot to bits, but in most respects the long-term memory is perfectly intact. I was such a screwed-up child, a somnambulist haunted by night terrors. I dreaded

312

any form of febrile illness, not because of the sore throat or the cough or the headache, but because I knew that every night I should go mad. I suppose they were nights of delirium, these awful flights into areas of darkness beyond my comprehension. *Acute confusional states*. Every dream is a psychotic episode. At night, we all become schizophrenic, lying abed with our rapid eye movements and fixed lunatic rictus. It doesn't matter how utterly crazy the dream's construct; during the dream, we just accept it for what it is. You may say we lose insight, just as a mad patient appears to lose insight. You say to him, during the psychiatric interview, "Do you really think it likely, that you are duty-bound to let the Prime Minister know that you are being pursued by a team of homosexual Russian spies?"

Well, yes, of course.

R D Laing thought that schizophrenics were not deluded at all but merely saw the world in a different way. If your way was original enough, then you were an artist, like Kafka or Dostoevsky. In other words, the one quality you did possess was insight. I always knew it. My mum would rouse me from my tormented *cauchemar*, wipe my damp brow, and say, "It's all right. It was only a dream. It wasn't real."

But I always knew it was real.

A nightmarish flight; the absolute necessity to get somewhere, and to stop something from happening, before it would be forever too late. I ran to my sister's room and woke her. I woke the whole house. I expected my mother to reiterate that familiar trope: it's okay, it was only a dream, not real. But I could see she wasn't sure. I could see the anxiety and worry knit in her brow.

"Were you sleepwalking?"

"I suppose so."

Does sleepwalking exist? I doubt if it does in the sense that is commonly understood, that is, of a person moving around unconsciously whilst in a deep slumber. The somnambulist is not *unconscious* but rather in a state of *altered* consciousness. Sleepwalkers are psychotic. But it is not true to say that we sleepwalkers lack insight. I realised even then that my darling mum was wrong when she said I was only dreaming. I had been granted more insight than I could bear. Mankind cannot stand too much reality. But need I tell you this? Maybe that which I regard as a highly unusual manifestation of an inner world is, in fact, perfectly commonplace, perhaps even universal. Everybody who is mortal is born to face, in the end, a Stygian moment. It is Robert Browning's *Prospice.*

Fear death? To feel the fog in my face…

I didn't tell my mother, I didn't tell anybody, that I had walked right down to the gates of hell. Yet for some reason, I was allowed to retreat, and come back up. I've known, ever since, that one day I'd be back. This was why I was granted that rare, and in its way privileged, visitation to the depths of Creation, so that I might prepare myself. Or rather, so that I might pray for guidance, and for a strength far beyond my own personal reservoir of courage and resilience.

And don't think for a moment that this is merely an episode to be passively endured. This is going to be a triathlon, one of the big ones, an Iron Man event. You are a lone pawn, fighting your way down the edge of a chessboard to the heart of the enemy camp. Just like that Lewis chessman that midsummer's night when, unwittingly, you supped with the devil. You may stay on your feet and survive the course, but that is not going to be sufficient. You have to win.

Try another painful stimulus. I'll push a knuckle into my patient's sternum. Still his eyes are closed; but he is muttering incomprehensibly. And what is this bizarre posture? Why is he folding his arms across his chest, like a corpse?

GCS 6. Try again later… Let us sleep now.

Who are you? The recurring question that Pastor Niemöller asked of himself. You still don't know who you are, but you know you inhabit the lowest tier of existence. And nobody knows you are here.

Once more, I attend my patient in his deep slumber and push my thumb into his right supraorbital ridge. This time, he opens his eyes. He mumbles like a drunk man. He tries to push my hand away. GCS 10. His consciousness remains diminished, but he is no longer comatose.

I need to get this montage of disparate and confused episodes into some semblance of order, like a Patience player endlessly shuffling and reshuffling the pack, then setting the cards out again to see if they stack up right and the game can be played out.

There was an incarceration. Before that, a gap. That must have been the time of the brain injury. Before that, a ride on the London Underground. Before that, a descent down a mineshaft. Before that, my arrest.

No. Something else between the arrest and the descent. Something of critical importance.

An Extraordinary General Meeting of the Conglomerate. What is that?

There was a girl named Kathryn. I lost her, then I found her again, but then I lost her again so that I began to think my finding her was just some kind of wish-fulfilment. Didn't my psychiatrist tell me that she had never existed? They had separated us. I was hooded again before leaving the court.

Court?

315

The descent. Mineshaft. We plunge with marked rapidity, the pain in my ears excruciating, and then suddenly, with a bilateral pop, gone. The persistent roar of air resistance at terminal velocity. Two minutes of rapid descent, the atmosphere markedly warmer. Three minutes.

Four minutes.

The Slingsby Firefly was in the grip of a steep and rapidly plummeting spin, right handed, and I was clawing at the controls, trying to get it to stop. Full left rudder. Push the stick forward. Why the hell won't it stop? Now the aircraft's trajectory is flattening out, but still she won't stop rolling and pitching and yawing, and now the ground's rushing up to meet me and to pulverise me into a million fragments. Oh God, I'm going to throw up. I broke out in a frosty sweat; I retched and retched until all I wanted to do was die. Let me just stop now, here in this prison cell of mine, and sleep forever.

The halt was as rapid as an emergency stop. How far have I fallen? Three, four thousand feet? Now I have left the shaft and am being propelled, as I imagine it, along the main artery of a deep plexus of subterranean corridors. Here it is as hot as a Turkish bath. We have walked, I think, for two hundred metres, I have no idea in which direction, but I have a notion we are now under the sea. The acoustic is flat and dry. Abrupt turn left, right, left again. A low rumble and a persistent draught of musky air coming from my left. Brought to a halt; hands and arms, heretofore held firmly behind my back, released.

I am back in the London Underground.

After the descent, a demonstration of the instruments of torture. A familiar voice in my left ear. "You would wish to know about *Palimpsest*?"

A voice from some half-remembered Committee that doesn't have a name. It's the mole.

"You would see for yourself? Very well. You will be shown. But mind, curiosity killed the cat."

I am on the platform of an Underground station. Characteristic oblong blue nameplate superimposed on a red circle. Aldwych. Piccadilly Line. On either side, anachronistic advertisements for Senior Service, Capstan, and Players (please). Trailers for movies and West End shows. *Gone with the Wind*, The Windmill Theatre (we never close), *In Which We Serve*. Snatches of wartime propaganda – *Make Do and Mend, Keep calm and carry on, Is your journey really necessary?*

Here's my ride. This can't really be the London Underground. The black truncated circular apertures of the tunnels disappearing from each end of the platform are barely two metres in diameter. And the carriage now appearing noiselessly out of the tunnel on my left, snug within the contour of the tube, resembles a bathysphere. It draws silently to a halt directly in front of me.

Now I am aboard.

Completely featureless interior, like a vehicle designed to transport passengers from an airport terminal building to an aeroplane, the transit so brief that there is no need to provide other than the most basic amenity – two benches in pale cream and a single vertical chromium handrail. I face rearwards. Opposite, an implacable jailer, and the mole. Beside me, a wraith.

"Hello, Oswald. Where are we off to?"

No reply.

Silently we leave the pool of light on the station platform, and the archaic advertisements fall away. In the violet gloom, I can perceive beyond the bathysphere the walls of a tunnel covered with complex arrays of multi-coloured pipes and cabling. I am passing through the innards of a prehistoric creature, or perhaps I've entered the doughnut aperture of a

317

state-of-the-art MRI scanner, except that its dimensions are immense. Suppose we are moving round a circular line. How big is the doughnut? Let's see. Aldwych station platform had a subtle curve. The hundred-metre arc of the platform might subtend an angle of – what? – a single degree at the centre of a circle? That equated to a circumference of 360 times 100 metres or 36 kilometres. My befuddled mind grapples with the arithmetic. Just a rough guess. A circle of diameter somewhere around twelve kilometres. Ballpark. Say the centre of the circle is directly beneath the lighthouse.

I've remembered the lighthouse.

Most of the circumference of this circle must be under the sea. It crosses my mind it is like the Large Hadron Collider. What does it do? Accelerate particles, presumably. But for what purpose?

Always, the striated and multivariate lumen of the tunnel wall hugs the bathysphere. Staring at it at close quarters is like looking down a microscope at a pathological specimen.

What's our speed? One kilometre a minute? The trip takes forty minutes, travelling so far as I can judge in a perfect circle, anticlock, the mathematicians' positive direction. So my arithmetic has not been too wide of the mark. Here we are back at Aldwych. The mole asks me if I admire *Palimpsest*.

I sniff. "Not much of a tourist draw. Needs a bit of tarting up. Why not introduce some Gothic horror, like a carnival ghost train? Could do with the odd shrieking ghoul."

And before the descent, the trial. Ah yes. The trial.

I went to the theatre – when? – two nights ago? Did I see a play, or was I a member of the cast? I was Claudio in Shakespeare's problem play, *Measure for Measure*. "Be absolute for death." But no. This was a Whitehall farce. It took place in a high-ceilinged rotunda. I was back in the ancient anatomy lecture hall of the old Medical School on Lauriston Place in

Edinburgh, with its steeply tiered seats, from which the students of yore might witness, at close quarters, the dissection of a cadaver. I occupied the position of the cadaver. The audience occupying the benches – I've seen them before. They were the crowd of film extras assembled for my benefit at Keflavik. I saw them all again somewhere between Gyle and Gogarburn on the Edinburgh tram.

But this was not a lecture theatre. Where there should have been a blackboard, there was a bench. Between it and the terraced seats, where there should have been a demonstration area, there were desks with chairs facing the bench. It must be a legal drama. This is a Court of Law. Kathryn Hathaway is in the dock.

But I have been told that Kathryn Hathaway does not exist. You have been ill. You are under the care of a doctor. He thinks my preoccupations amount to little more than a surreal mono-delusion. I can hardly contest the point. I am sure that that doctor was not only acting responsibly within the powers entrusted to him, and acting in good faith, but that, in placing me under a Control Order, he was availing himself professionally of the only course of action reasonably available to him. I cannot deny that I have entered a world of insanity, and therefore must be, myself, quite mad.

Act V Scene II:

Now, I, too, find myself in the dock. Surely this is pantomime. Perhaps it's a Gilbert & Sullivan operetta. *Trial by Jury.*

But there is no jury. This case is going to be heard *in camera.* The public gallery is empty. The defendants will not receive representation. This isn't even a show trial. There is only the triumvirate ascending to the bench, dressed in academic gowns as for a graduation ceremony.

They were hooded. This gave their procession a Druidical

appearance. In unison and with theatrical deliberation, the occupants of the bench swept back their hoods. They acknowledged the court with a brief bow of the head. Then, again in unison, the judiciary sat down. Staring straight ahead, I said to Kathryn in a stage whisper, "It's okay. I'm here. It's all right now."

I'm back in the Palace of Westminster facing a Parliamentary Select Committee. On the bench, the Minister without Portfolio sat on the left and the Chancellor of the Duchy of Lancaster on the right. Between them, in the position of Chair, I fully expected to see the Enterprise Czar. But no. The Czar was not present. His position had been taken by the frail elderly gentleman with the soft manners and the puzzled frown, now in the centre of my visual field, a seething, teeming migrainous aura, a shimmering apparition of such grim maleficence that I had to avert my gaze.

The Chancellor of the Duchy of Lancaster spoke.

"You just couldn't let it go, could you? You just couldn't resist sticking your nose into affairs that are no concern of yours. And now, see where it has landed you. See your situation."

The Duke of Assynt's phthisic visage winced briefly. "Sit."

We did so.

The Chancellor of the Duchy of Lancaster presented the case for the prosecution. I can only recall snatches, piecemeal. "In the long history of human conflict... this installation necessary... Defence of the Realm... function as a deterrent every day... necessity for secrecy... fifth column, spies, traitors..."

I stifled a yawn. Can there be anything more wearisome than the tedious *apologia* of a megalomaniac?

I was vaguely aware that, on my left, Kathryn had taken out of her ever-present black satchel the familiar notebook, in its pastel shades, of the late Suzanna Fergusson, and she was scribbling away, perhaps penning a farewell note to somebody, much as Suzanna had written one to her.

Next, the Minister without Portfolio. *Faux* case for the defence. "Sorry state of affairs… hapless individuals… no alternative… with regret…" He had qualms.

Next, back to the Chair for the summing up. They certainly weren't wasting any time. Summary justice, no doubt, to be followed by summary execution. It crossed my mind that somewhere towards the end of this charade, the Chair would be handed, on a sable cushion, a black cap. I forced my gaze to fix on the grim, baleful visage. The hooded eyes lifted themselves away from the brief and settled upon us. The mouth writhed.

"Stand up."

We got slowly to our feet. I found Kathryn's hand and held it.

"Is there anything you wish to say?"

I might have mumbled and stamped and filibustered. "What the hell kind of a Mad Hatter's tea party is this? What's going on here? I demand an explanation!" I didn't. I needed no explanation. I knew perfectly well what this was. This was a summons to the headmaster's study, for a brief and one-sided lecture prior to a caning. I said instead, "We do not recognise the authority of this court. We demand to be taken before a legitimate judge, in a legitimate public location, by writ of *Habeas Corpus.*"

"My dear doctor," said the Chair, "your erstwhile colleague Lord Chief Justice Forteviot Dunning might have told you that *Habeas Corpus* offers you no protection here, here as we are, north of the Border. You had rather invoke the Scot's Criminal Procedure Act of 1701. But even then, I have to tell you it would be useless to you. As soon as you entered this domain, you forfeited your *Human Rights*. Null and void."

"This is a kangaroo court."

"The defendant is contemptuous of this court. Make a note of that, bailiff. Do you really have nothing else to say?"

Here, at last, was my Final Departures Lounge. What was there left to do? Don't panic. It wouldn't help. Don't succumb to fear. Above all, don't grovel. Don't let them think that you are a broken man. Behave with manners. Assume aristocratic insouciance. Die like a man. I stayed quiet.

"Very well. We may proceed…"

"I have something to say."

"Ah. Ms Hathaway."

Kathryn rose to her feet. She had lost her apprehension. There was colour in her cheeks. I had the distinct impression that it was sheer anger that had brought her to this level of composure. I have an idea that she had composed a damning indictment of the proceedings and jotted down some bullet points in Suzanna's commonplace book. In fact, I know she did because the notebook and the bullet points sit before me as I write.

Demonstration of the absolute corruption of unbridled power.
Recall the words of the Duke in Shakespeare's Measure for
    Measure –
'He who the sword of heaven will bear
Should be as holy as severe…'
Both plead Not Guilty to all criminal charges, whatever they may
    be.
Gross abuse of power, wealth, and privilege…
Ridden roughshod over the rule of law…
Disregard of every standard of decency and humanity…
Ruthless pursuit of absolute power…
A crime so egregious it cannot be named.
…Theocide.
Despise you utterly. Beneath contempt.

Citizen's arrest.
Call upon these gaolers immediately to take you into custody.
Rest my case.

Coruscating, incandescent, and sublime.

In the event, she ditched it all and rather strayed off-*piste*.

"Why doesn't your Conglomerate take its fucking *Palimpsest* and shove it up its arse?"

The bench took a few moments to confer. Their whispers were barely audible. There was a general nodding of heads – a consensus. The whispering stopped, and the court sat back in repose. The Chair took a few notes and paused to read them over. He clasped his hands and cleared his throat.

Inevitably, with due solemnity, the bench found against us, balefully pronouncing our fate. Perpetual durance. "I should explain to you," remarked the Chancellor of the Duchy of Lancaster, not without relish, "that this installation, once active, is entirely automated. Henceforth, it will require no human oversight. Accordingly, this court, with the exception of the current occupants of the dock, will shortly return to the surface."

The Duke of Assynt stared straight through me.

"Checkmate."

He ended with a terse instruction, which I'd always taken to be a figure of speech but which I was shortly to discover was, horrifyingly, literally accurate.

"Take them down."

The guards closed in around us. The judiciary filed out. The Chancellor of the Duchy was the last to leave. On his way out, he issued a terse directive to the gaolers.

"Scourge him."

XXVI

"You would wish to know about *Palimpsest*? You would see for yourself? Very well. You will be shown. But mind, curiosity killed the cat."

I am Schrödinger's cat. The physicist Erwin Schrödinger proposed putting a cat into a box and sealing it up, along with a piece of radioactive material cunningly linked to a vial of poison, in such a way that should a single radioactive event take place, the vial of poison is broken, and the cat dies. We cannot know whether such a radioactive event will take place. We can only assign to it a certain probability – a probability in this case of one half. The point is that you can only know if the cat survives or dies by opening the box and looking. Now, I may fully explore the experience of being Herr Schrödinger's cat. So long as I, the cat, remain sealed and unobserved in this closed box, I am that unfortunate individual in Edgar Allan Poe's *Facts in the Case of M. Valdemar. "I say to you that I am alive and dead."*

Now I can remember the episode before the trial – the arrest. There was a lighthouse at the end of the world. I remember how its beacon surveyed the ocean across 360 degrees and then abruptly swivelled down in my direction to bathe me in its incandescent light. It occurred to me that the lighthouse had assumed the inimical appearance of a gigantic Dalek, and I couldn't help but laugh out loud. That was before the rough canvas bag was pulled over my head and neck, peremptorily, the way a condemned man on the scaffold is hooded, prior to the placement of the noose. Now I'm back on board *Aerolíneas Argentinas* Flight 301. Blindfolded, being pushed from behind; the exact same flat monosyllabic instructions.

"Walk."

Don't panic. You have no options; therefore, your life has become distilled into a condition of complete simplicity. Concentrate on controlling your rate of breathing. Live each moment. Stay absolutely alert to the sounds around you. Learn as much as you can. Stay alive.

"Stop."

I heard the sound of a heavy door being unlocked and drawn wide open on ill-used, creaking hinges. I tripped on the shallow lip of a kerb but was supported upright as again I was pushed forward. I heard the door behind me creak again, and then close with a dull thud. The acoustic timbre of my environment changed. I had entered an echoing vault. The musty odour was all-pervasive.

You have entered the lighthouse. You must be at its base, directly under its light source. You are under arrest.

That's it. I've pieced it all together. All I have to do is invert the order of events, and my amnesia will be cancelled. Arrest – trial – descent – demonstration – incarceration. Oh, and the *scourge.* I am back in my cell in the bowels of the earth.

I recall entering this cell. The incident of violence that

disrupted my memory has not yet happened because I am still able to think and act, more or less, rationally and logically. As soon as the heavy steel-studded door closed behind me with its terminal crash, I took out my mobile and composed the briefest of texts. It was my first opportunity, the only time I'd been left on my own since entering this catacomb.

Caitlin! De profundis. I am at 586248050015. Call Major Forster. Send the cavalry ASAP. Fail not. Al xxx

Why Caitlin? I remembered how she'd opened the door to Forster that night at Thirlestane. She had presented his card to me on a silver salver. Had she kept the card? In any case, I didn't have that many options. I store precious few numbers on my phone. I could have texted MacKenzie, but if MacKenzie is learning a new work, she just goes into hibernation for as long as it takes. She can switch her phone off for weeks. Caitlin, on the other hand, is a teenager wedded to her device. She once told me if she wakes up in the night, she checks her phone. I pressed send, simultaneously wondering why my captors had not confiscated my device.

No signal detected. Call queueing.

They didn't need to. Well. It was worth a try.

The mole from the Committee *sine nomine* dropped by – the man in the snazzy technicolour dream coat.

"*Sports-Jacket.*"

"*Speedbird.*"

I wasn't yet hopeless. I could still affect to-hell-with-you bravado. "Jonathan Braithwaite. I should have guessed it was you. Anybody with a dress sense as appalling as yours is not to be trusted. *Sports-Jacket*, isn't there a lady in your life who could offer you some fashion advice? Get yourself a new outfit, man."

He pouted apologetically. It occurred to me he was a little embarrassed. He hadn't much altered his demeanour. There was still the adopted, hearty bonhomie, the wheezy joviality, and the reek of cigarette smoke. He actually gave me a hug! That was why it was so easy to slip my phone into one of the cavernous pockets of that hideous garment. He avoided eye contact. He whispered in my ear.

"No hard feelings, old boy." For one excruciating instant, I thought he was going to kiss me. I think he found the idea of impending physical violence distasteful. He slipped furtively away. He didn't want to be a witness to it.

Viktor Frankl, the Viennese psychiatrist, a survivor of Auschwitz, who knew better than anybody about the realities of incarceration in the deepest pits of Creation, once remarked that your oppressors can take away from you every last thing that you possess, with one exception. They can't take away your attitude, the way in which you choose to view your circumstances.

I was lying in the sun on Ninety Mile Beach, beside the dunes and the *toi toi* grass, at the outlet of Te Paki Stream, my head cradled on a thigh and the smooth blue fabric of a girl in surgical scrubs.

"Mary."

"Ssshhh. It's okay." She stroked my forehead.

"Where's Kathryn?"

"She's okay. She's alive." A very strange thing happened. I can't explain it. All I can say is that I had an overwhelming conviction that wakefulness, awareness, consciousness, were all somehow profoundly beneficent. In a mood of serenity, and in my imagination, I wrote Caitlin a letter.

De Profundis
Am Parbh
Sutherland
Friday, September 9th

Darling Caitlin,
You mustn't worry about me. By the time you read

327

this, I will be beyond harm. I just wanted to thank you for
coming to stay with me last year in Edinburgh. I'm afraid
I wasn't very good company! I'm so glad you are back at
school playing music and enjoying life. It's as it should
be. You are the sort of person who lights up a room just
by walking into it. Whatever you do, please keep playing
the oboe (or, if you prefer, the cor anglais). If you and
MacKenzie ever get to play RVW's Flos Campi *together,*
as I'm sure you will, then you can bet I'll be there!

Love to Eric and Sally,
God bless,
Alastair x.

Time to sleep now.

In the morning, I applied some pressure to the patient's
right mastoid, but his eyes were already open, his thoughts,
and therefore his speech, had returned to normal, and his
movements were fully coordinated.

GCS 15.

I remember getting up with a preordained sense of purpose
that I couldn't quite comprehend. There was a pile of neatly
folded fresh linen lying beside my palliasse. I discarded my
filthy rags and got dressed, wondering if I were sleepwalking
again. I remember experiencing no surprise when I tested
my cell door and found it was open. I stepped out into the
passageway.

What next?

Next, a tall young woman with long dark hair appeared
out of the gloom. She was in a hurry. She didn't see me as she
passed. Maybe I was invisible. She stared in wonder at the open
door. She looked inside to verify the cell was empty. All she
would have seen was a pile of rags. Then she disappeared again.

The recovery from a brain insult is full of uncertainty. It

may not be complete. It may not occur at all. You hope it will be two steps forward, one step back, and not one step forward and two back. But you just never know.

"Fasten your lap strap."

Now I am back in the cockpit of my beloved Slingsby Firefly. I strap myself in using the five-point harness, comprising a stout metal disc snug in the midriff, holding a crotch strap centrally and two straps across the iliac crests on either side. Two further straps across the shoulders from behind. Yet this can't be the Slingsby. I lie facing upwards, almost supine, the attitude of an astronaut.

"Where are we going?"

"Not us. It's only a one-seater. So it's you."

"But—"

"Shut up and listen. There's not much time. Shortly – very shortly – you will be in London. You will worry and fret about me, but you must not worry and fret because you have things to do. Trust me that all is well, and all will be well. Everything is taken care of. Believe that, and don't allow yourself to be distracted, because you have one more duty to discharge. Do you understand me?"

I shook my head. "I'm not leaving this place without you."

"Alastair, look into my eyes. Listen. You are called…"

She hypnotised me with her eyes. Yes, I was right. They were hazel.

"…To see a World in a Grain of Sand
And a Heaven in a Wild Flower
Hold Infinity in the palm of your hand
And eternity in an hour."

She embraced me, kissed me on the lips and whispered in my ear, "Goodbye, my love."

The dark shadow who had conducted me from my cell

glanced in and ran his hand over the buckle in my midriff to double-check it was secure. Then he fitted an elaborate balaclava-style racing helmet, doubling as a neck brace, over my head, and now I fitted snug in my seat. Before me, a control console sat centrally, and there were several digital visual display units but precious few control levers in what was clearly a highly automated system. I wondered where my journey was about to take me. I hoped it would be back to the surface.

The departure was so silent and the initial acceleration so gradual that, for a moment, there was a vertiginous sense that the walls of the tunnel were moving while I remained static. Then came a sense of a deep-seated engagement of power, a declutching, and a sense of torque. A low rumble's crescendo to a roar was rapid. The acceleration, when it came, was as violent as a kick in the solar plexus. I think I passed out.

How long this new period of unconsciousness lasted I cannot say. Long enough to have this dream. I was in a strange vehicle back in the London Underground, decelerating towards the limpid pool of light of a subway station. The tunnel wall outside the carriage window became more distinct, and I had a sense of my velocity. Say forty miles an hour… thirty… twenty… Now, walking pace. A station platform came into view. Once again, there was the traditional circular sign of the London Underground, with its characteristic logo.

Trafalgar Square. Bakerloo Line.

We came to a halt. The pod's door opened automatically. I slipped off my helmet and turned the flange on the buckle of my harness through ninety degrees, and the straps fell away. I sat still for a moment. Then, with some difficulty, I eased myself out of the chair and pulled myself upwards and through the pod's aperture. I alighted in an extremely ungainly fashion. Actually, I crawled onto the twilit platform on my hands and knees. Then I got up. I felt a little uncertain on my feet. I paused on the platform and put my head between my knees and waited for my vertigo to settle down. I turned and watched the pod silently disappear back into the tunnel in the direction from which it had come.

The platform was deserted, and dimly lit. There was a single exit, a brief tiled corridor which took me to an endless, trundling wooden staircase. I stepped onto it and gratefully allowed myself to be transported slowly upwards past the adverts for Bovril and Woodbine towards, I sensed, the glorious sunlight.

I emerged, blinking, into the morning glare, staring at the pigeons strutting around imperiously under Nelson's Column.

XXVII

Proms-wise, I've never really been much of a fan of The Last Night. All that bunting in red, white and blue. You can picture me watching it, despite myself, on a dodgy telly with poor reception in some hovel somewhere deep in the Highlands, drinking a bottle of beer and staring morosely at the flickering screen.

But now that I'd managed to drag myself along to the Royal Albert Hall, I resolved to get into the spirit of the thing. The place was packed to the rafters. Six thousand souls, ready to have a party. Actually, I was lucky to be there. The only reason I'd been able to get the hottest ticket in town was that my twin sister happened to be one of the stars of the show. She'd said apologetically, "I'm afraid you're going to have to prom." But as a matter of fact, that suited my purpose ideally. I needed to be close to the stage.

I dressed for the part rather extravagantly. White tie and tails. And a red carnation. I felt like Fred Astaire. In any other context, I would have looked utterly ridiculous but I was able to wander around the precinct of Kensington Gore of a beautiful Indian summer's evening and be entirely anonymous. I remember strolling across the courtyard between the Royal College of Music and the Royal Albert Hall, and the hopeful crowd of people queueing for a last-minute ticket return didn't give me a second glance. I circumnavigated the hall clockwise, crossed the road to Hyde Park and walked all the way down to Kensington Palace, quietly planning the evening ahead. Unlike the BBC Symphony Orchestra, I wasn't going to have the advantage of a rehearsal. I just had to try and anticipate the evening in my mind like a thought experiment. It was clear to me that my intervention would take place late in the evening. I didn't want to spoil MacKenzie's special night. Interrupting the Baxes was bad enough; interrupting MacKenzie, the soloist, would have been unforgivable. I went back to the Hall, ascended to the Elgar Room and had a light supper, quietly reviewing the events of the day.

I'd staggered out of the Tube into the morning sun, crossed Trafalgar Square, found a Costa, and ordered a coffee. To sit in or to go? To go. The barista looked relieved. I went out and sat on the pavement and planned the day ahead. After I'd drunk the coffee, I'd absentmindedly put the paper cup down on the pavement in front of me. A few passers-by obligingly left some loose change in the cup, but to most people, I was invisible. That's not counting the guy in the sharp suit who got down on his hunkers and said, "Why don't you people take yourselves and your effing gypsy caravans back to Bohemia and stop littering our streets?" But then a man from St Martin in the Fields sat down with me and asked if I had a place to stay that night. I told him I'd made arrangements. He gave me a Mars bar, which I ate. Such is the kindness of strangers. I got up and started to walk in the direction of Regent's Park.

I fell in step with another couple of gentlemen down on their luck. We fellow mendicants must stick together. They didn't seem to mind my presence. I wondered if I were still some kind of insubstantial ghost because they kept looking round at me as if to figure out whether or not I was actually there. Perhaps I was the hooded figure in Eliot's *Wasteland*, or like that supernumerary individual accompanying Shackleton's exhausted crew across Antarctica. We passed another tramp, lucky enough to secure a zero-hours contract, wearing a sandwich board.

Drowned N-MASS horribly vindicated.

Then a waif, a street urchin, carrying a pile of newspapers. He didn't actually call out, "Read all about it!" I'm making that up. I used the loose change collected in my paper cup to buy a copy of *The Times*. I couldn't yet focus on the newsprint, but I could see quite clearly my own image on the front page. They had printed this photograph of me before. I suppose it was the only one of me they had in the archive. It was the picture of me emerging from Heathrow, after *Whetstone*, blood-bespattered.

I handed *The Times* to one of my fellow travellers and ventured, "What's all that about?"

"It's that trouble in the North."

"What trouble?"

"A kettle of stinking fish." The man with my copy of *The Times* was remarkably well-spoken. It just shows you, homelessness can happen to anybody.

"What... kettle, precisely?"

"Haven't you heard? Where've you been? What planet are you on? But nobody really knows. There's a huge police operation. They've called the army in – bomb disposal. The media are going berserk. They say we've been invaded – the first time in nearly a thousand years. But the government are very tight-lipped. At any rate, they've queered their pitch, whoever they are. Apparently this guy saw it all coming." He pointed to my picture. "Poor fellow. Drowned."

So. The juggernaut of misinformation and disinformation was already trundling down the highway. I slowed my pace and quietly detached myself.

"Not drowned," said the other wayfarer. "Social media say that guy's been spotted. Wait up a sec." He grabbed *The Times*. He studied my photograph more closely. I could see him make a double-take. He looked back at me, then again at the paper, and again back at me.

But by then, I had disappeared.

We were into the second week of September. Autumn had officially begun, but it was still very hot in London. All the doors and windows were lying wide open in the Langham, opposite the BBC, and that was how I'd managed that morning to walk unchallenged up to a mezzanine floor, cross a ballroom and go out onto a balcony, and then pass through a set of French windows to find myself in a casement, behind a curtain, in my sister's suite. She had just received a visitation. Dr Ralph Parkinson and Major Martin Forster were being fastidiously polite, coughing into fists and making sympathetic noises. This was a bereavement visit. I really ought to have burst in and disillusioned them, but I wanted to see my sister on her own. So I waited, still inhabiting my alternative universe.

Martin Forster explained, "We found your car the following day, Ms Cameron-Strange."

"The Jaguar," said Parkinson.

"...up at Durness Sound. We conducted a search."

"We put frogmen into the water."

"Nothing."

"In the end, we had to presume that he had followed his instinct and gone to the lighthouse."

"It turns out he was right all along. He managed to get a message to us."

"Via his sister-in-law."

"God knows how. God knows how he got a signal."

"Down there."

"But he was right. There is something at Cape Wrath."

"An installation."

"We're still searching it. It's very deep."

"Deep."

"It will need to be eradicated."

"Extirpated."

"Completely and utterly destroyed."

"Of course, we will make every effort to find him before we…"

"…extirpate."

My sister knit her brow and said in a distracted way, "There was a girl. Is she safe?"

"We don't think there was ever a girl."

"Oh."

"We think she was…"

"…a figment."

My sister said dully, "Go away."

There followed profuse effusions of sympathy and much doffing of caps. I had the impression of two powdered, bewigged courtiers walking backwards out of a royal chamber. I waited until they had gone and then stepped into the room.

"MacKenzie."

She didn't recognise me. Hardly surprising. I'd grown a beard in the interim. I was an absolute down-and-out. Or maybe she thought I was the window cleaner.

"MacKenzie, it's me."

I saw the look of recognition finally dawn. She gave a scarcely human howl and attempted to cling to me. But I took a step back and said, "Better not." I think she thought I meant it wasn't right that we hug, because I was amid some mysterious process of spiritual purification, but all I really meant was that I was desperate for a bath.

I pass over her endearments. They are very precious to me. After the tears, principally, I remember her laughter.

I said, "Are you playing tonight?"

"I cancelled."

"Can you cancel the cancellation?"

"I don't know. I mean, Sir Andrew will have made alternative arrangements."

"Can't you call him? I bet you get reinstated."

She glanced at her watch. She bit her lip. "There's a band call at two." She suddenly made up her mind. "Okay. I think we can do this. Yes!"

For my second manifestation, I followed Parkinson and Forster across to the anonymous building just off Storey's Gate. The day was getting hotter and sultrier as it wore on. I entered and walked up to the first floor unchallenged. It was the same board room that the Committee *sine nomine* had occupied when it last convened. They may have thought they had locked themselves away securely, but I had no difficulty in slipping unobserved into an anteroom. The last time I was here, they had conducted business as if I were *in absentia*, so I was not surprised to be ignored once again. I was able to hear and to observe proceedings.

"I always knew there was something weird about *Sports-Jacket*. Anybody who dresses like a pansy has to be a security risk." Civil sniffed. "Where is he anyway?"

"Golder's Green. The police station. Plea bargaining."

"Plea bargaining?"

"Some sort of extenuating circumstance." Harry Golightly said, "*Speedbird* had it right all along."

337

"Serendipity." Civil waved a dismissive hand.

"Call it what you like. But the fact is, there's a ghastly contraption up at Cape Wrath."

Baroness Rowallan said, "It will shortly be destroyed. Without trace."

"Who's going to tell *Speedbird*?" This, from Forster.

"Now let's not get over-sentimental about this." Civil was being brisk. "The doctor may have done himself as much as all of us a favour."

"Do I sense, Iain," remarked Forteviot Dunning, "that you are about to prepare a breakfast soufflé that involves the cracking of eggshells?"

"*Dulce et decorum est*, don't forget. The doctor was never happy amid the Witan."

I stepped in and said cheerfully, "Peace and joy."

Well! General Civil went ballistic! He was absolutely furious that I should have had the temerity to come back from the dead. I thought he was going to burst a blood vessel. *"Where the devil have you been? Who the devil do you think you are? What the devil do you think you're playing at?"*

"I have been a canary, a harbinger, in a deep mine." He ranted on, but I'd stopped listening. Margaret Rowallan abruptly adjourned the meeting but bade me stay behind. We had a confidential and deeply mysterious chat of the sort that can really only be had in the United Kingdom.

"Once again, Defence Advisory Notices 03 and 05 are being applied to the Fourth Estate."

"Uh-huh?"

"The details of the events that are about to take place in the far north will not be made public for fifty years. In the interests of national security."

"I see."

"Of course, something will be put about. There will be

concerns about unusual seismic activity in the North Atlantic. These will be addressed. There will be rumours of a radioactive leak at Dounreay. These will be quelled."

"Of course."

"The Prime Minister will announce a radical and courageous cabinet reshuffle by which his party and his government will reclaim the political centre ground."

"I look forward to hearing the PM's announcement."

"The Monopolies Commission has decided to split The Conglomerate into its multivariate parts. The Conglomerate will essentially cease to exist."

"For the best, I am sure."

"It may turn out to be surprisingly difficult, however, to construct a case specifically against the Enterprise Czar, such that it would stand up in a Court of Law. A preliminary review already suggests that Sir Roger Hollis has taken great pains, has gone to extraordinary lengths, to cover his tracks."

"That's unfortunate."

"In addition, it would be difficult to explore these issues in a public forum while maintaining the fifty-year veil of secrecy deemed necessary."

"I'm sure it would."

"Much as the Committee *sine nomine* would wish to pursue this, we are all, as you are well aware, bound by the Official Secrets Act. Still, it is unlikely The Conglomerate will be resurrected, and I think we must assume that it is, as of now, a spent force."

"Then we must choose success over victory."

There was a pause.

"On the other hand, there might be a way of ensuring that Sir Roger is… finished. For example, a person of imagination and flair, and with a rising reputation as something of a maverick, and with a track record for, so to speak, *stirring it up*, might find a way of exposing Sir Roger Hollis to the world."

"That would be felicitous indeed. How would you imagine such a maverick person would achieve this?"

"I couldn't say. But I imagine such a maverick person would use his vivid imagination to bring about the desired effect in a manner quite beyond the scope of my own creativity."

"Well, I hope to see it."

"Of course, you must understand, the Chair of His Majesty's Witenagemot the Committee *sine nomine* could not possibly condone publicly any such behaviour, or activity, coming from such a maverick person."

"Of course not."

"Much as she might privately admire it."

That was the end of the substantive part of our conversation. I got up and headed for the door.

"Alastair."

I turned. "Mm?"

"Something I don't understand. How did you get out?"

"I don't know, Margaret. Some sort of miracle I guess." I went away and got cleaned up.

After supper in the Elgar Room, I visited the Gents and checked my appearance in the mirror. MacKenzie had put me in touch with the BBC Symphony Orchestra management, and I'd got kitted out, perhaps rather more extravagantly than she might have anticipated. I straightened my white bow tie, and entered the auditorium. It was 7.15 and the hall was already well filled, but I was able to work my way unobtrusively down towards the front of the promenade area, to position myself close to the conductor's rostrum and a little to the left, so that I should be close to my sister. The orchestra members were taking their place. The stage was brilliantly lit for the benefit of the unobtrusive and silently moving TV cameras. While there was a sense of excitement in the air, the atmosphere within the auditorium was still relatively restrained. It was only really in the second half

340

that the party proper would start, that the conductor's rostrum would become festooned with streamers, and the promenaders would grow lively, if not obstreperous. By then – and this was the critical thing from my point of view – the worldwide television audience would have tuned in. That was why I had dressed to the nines and why I had taken up my position so near the front. I needed my moment in the sun. I wanted that moment to go viral. It had to reach the eyes and ears of those occupying the furthest reaches of The Conglomerate, the foreign investors, the invisible movers and shakers of *Whetstone*. They needed to understand that somebody in whom they had staked a major investment had become a bad risk.

Meanwhile, there was another reason why the atmosphere for the moment remained somewhat restrained and formal. For the first time at a Last Night, the Royal Box would entertain a royal party.

I glanced at my watch. 7.28. Now, the hall was filled, and the orchestral presence nearly complete. The combination of audience chatter and orchestral warm-up was intoxicating. At 7.30, I turned and looked up at an area behind and above me on my left where the BBC announcer – I think it was Katie Derham – was doing her intro. Now the house lights dimmed across the hall, except for the Royal Box. An expectant hush fell across the auditorium. The orchestra's assistant leader rose to supervise the tuning. A plangent oboe A. I thought of dear Caitlin. Brass, winds, strings. Now complete silence. Ms Derham completed her spiel, and then Stephen Bryant, the leader, entered to applause and took his seat.

Then the entire assembly, orchestra and audience rose as one.

The King and Queen worked their way carefully down to the front of the box at its mid-point and remained standing while the rest of the royal party assembled around them.

I counted an assembly of twelve. Six royals, two ladies in waiting, an equerry – yes, it was Hoppy Metcalfe – and three representatives of the great and the good. I recognised them. There was a philanthropic captain of industry, a diplomat, and the Enterprise Czar, Sir Roger Hollis. He occupied a front-row position, separated from the King by two other royals. Once the company had taken their places, His Majesty acknowledged his subjects with a barely perceptible nod of the head and a smile and sat down.

The entire assemblage sat. I had a sense of being present at some long-lost ceremonial event of great historic importance. I might have been in an imperial palace in Tsarist Russia.

A beaming Sir Andrew weaved his way through the violins, bowed gracefully toward the Royal Box and then to the company at large. Then we were off into the *William Tell Overture*.

Well received.

For the first time that evening, I experienced a sense of anxiety. Was I really going to rain on their parade? Then I remembered I had another reason to be nervous. Some minor adjustments were being made to the seating arrangements as the first violin section moved back a little to allow space for the soloist. Aside from that, there was little change to the large orchestra that had been assembled for the Rossini. Now once more, the orchestra was reseated, and there was a moment of hush.

MacKenzie wore a long sleeveless evening gown in forest green, Celine by Hedi Slimane. The mysterious chatoyance of the Phoenix Stradivarius' deep brown varnish glowed under the arc of the television lights. She shook hands with the first violin front desk, briefly checked her tuning, and flashed Sir Andrew a smile. All my nervousness fell away.

Andante tranquillo.

So, my sister embarked on the journey of William Walton's

Viola Concerto. I began to appreciate what an extraordinary instrument had fallen so fortuitously into her hands. The Phoenix was a huge voice. Full-bodied, earthy at its lower reach, mellow and mellifluent in its characteristic middle register, and extraordinarily expressive and passionate in its upper echelons. I also came to realise that the Phoenix had found its ideal exponent. As MacKenzie had once said to me, she had tamed the beast.

At the end of the movement, she took a moment to let her shoulders drop and release all the tension from the muscles. She scanned the prommers unobtrusively, caught my eye, and gave me an imperceptible wink followed by the cock of an eyebrow. She had spotted my attire. I thought she might take a fit of the giggles. You never know with MacKenzie. But instead, she took up her viola, turned back to Sir Andrew, and gave him a nod.

Vivo, con molto preciso.

Indeed! This concerto was first performed at a London Prom in 1929 by Paul Hindemith, with the composer conducting. MacKenzie had big shoes to fill. At the movement's close, there was spontaneous applause.

Allegro moderato.

The epilogue stays with me. Dark, poignant, tragic. On the viola, a pair of falsely related major sixths, accompanied by the orchestra's barely audible minor sixths, faded to silence. MacKenzie's bow reached its end. Sir Andrew held the rapt silence for an age. Then MacKenzie began to emerge from her trance, and Sir Andrew's arms slowly began to drift down to his side.

Four curtain calls. At the last I thought I might get another wink and a grin, but her look was more interrogative, as if to transmit telepathically, "Now, what are you up to?"

Then the interval came, but I didn't retire to the bars. It was vital that I not lose my ringside seat. Twenty minutes later, the hall began to refill, and there was a palpable lightening of the atmosphere. Conductor's rostrum duly bedecked, the whole arena was a blaze of colour with streamers and bunting. The members of the royal party had resumed their positions unobtrusively. I glanced up. Yes, Sir Roger was still *in situ*. Now I was feeling nervous again.

I can't say I remember much of the rest of the music that night. Brahms, Strauss, and then all the old chestnuts and war horses. Sir Henry Wood's Fantasy on British Sea Songs. Rule Britannia. What next? Of course. *Pomp and Circumstance March No 1*. Sung with great fervour. But not, according to Sir Andrew, perfervid enough. Obligatory encore. Last lap. Rapturous applause. Here we go.

Sir Andrew regained the rostrum. A floating streamer landed on his shoulder, to general amusement. He brushed it off, beamed across the house, and took up a microphone. "Your Majesties, Your Royal Highnesses, My Lords, Ladies and Gentlemen..." (Toot, parp, whistle, laughter...) There followed the usual household announcements. Sir Andrew expressed his relief that he was no longer obliged to provide the audience with a set of statistics relating to the season. He did, however, propose a vote of thanks to our soloist Anne Strange, to the BBC, BBC Chorus (brought to its feet), the BBC Symphony Orchestra... I wondered how long to let him go on for. I decided that if he embarked on a panegyric to the healing power of music, then that would be my cue.

And he did. I started to edge towards the short staircase on my left that would allow me access to the stage.

"We live in a querulous age..." (Very loud bang, laughter and cheers...)

"...and at a time when, more than ever, we are in need of music..." (General calming of the mood of the house...)

"...and of its power, in the world, to be a force for good.

344

Do I say that Rossini, and Walton, and Strauss, and Brahms, can solve the problems of the world? Of course not."

I took the six steps up on to the stage and walked centre stage between the first and second fiddles.

"Yet we who love music cannot fail but be aware of its extraordinary power to communicate, across language, across cultural barriers…"

I believe the appropriateness of my attire was the crucial factor that stopped people, stopped security, from realising that there had been a breach.

"…and we can and must believe that our devotion to music and our resolve that it survive and flourish, particularly amongst our youth, will live on…"

Even when I reached his elbow, he still believed it was just a part of The Last Night jamboree.

"That is why my final vote of thanks tonight is to you, dear listener…"

He even let me take the microphone from his hand with little more than a quizzical frown. I felt like Eamonn Andrews, with the big green book, on an ancient episode of *This Is Your Life*. Here was something unscripted, but in the happy atmosphere, Sir Andrew could easily ad-lib and take it in its stride. The whole hall, chorus, orchestra, and audience thought precisely that. It occurred to me to motion to the conductor to step aside so that I could take his place on the rostrum, but that might have been pushing my luck. Instead, I occupied that part of the stage, between conductor and leader, which my sister had occupied an age ago. I looked up at the audience and took in a sea of faces in one single sweeping glance. Yes, no sense of alarm there, no recognition that we were about to wander off script. How long would it take them to twig that I was an impostor? Ten seconds? So choose your words carefully. Make them count.

"Your Majesties, Your Royal Highnesses, my Lords, Ladies,

345

and Gentlemen, and, if I may be specific –" looking up towards the Royal Box now –

"Sir Roger Hollis."

Across the gulf of the auditorium, our eyes met. He was watching me with fixed intensity. "Your Junta is dissolved, and the dark satanic mill at the top of this island will shortly be entirely destroyed." Something odd was happening to my perception. It seemed to me that Sir Andrew had disappeared, as had the BBC Symphony Chorus behind me and the BBC Symphony Orchestra around me. I occupied an empty stage. Now the promenaders had left the hall, and it seemed to me that the seats and the boxes all across the auditorium were emptying, and that the Royal Box itself had emptied, all but for one individual. Sir Roger Hollis and I had the entire Royal Albert Hall to ourselves. I was the sole performer, and he was the sole member of my audience.

"It's no use, Hollis. You are finished. You see, we've reached Chepstow."

The Royal Albert Hall was deathly quiet. Why should it be otherwise, when only occupied by two individuals? I took a compact disc, in its case, out of my pocket, and waved it in the air.

"Chepstow, terminally ill, has unburdened himself. This is a copy of his deposition."

Silence.

"Accordingly, you will now apply for the Chiltern Hundreds."

I had to admire Hollis for his *sang froid*. He raised a hand in salutation, gave me a brief smile of acknowledgement, and a nod of the head.

Then it seemed as if the occupants of the hall had returned from the bars and restaurants and passages and had retaken their seats, the Royal Box had once more filled, and the performers had returned to the stage. I smiled and mouthed an inaudible "Thank you" to an astonished Sir Andrew and handed the microphone back. I found myself surrounded by a group of well-dressed but very robust, fit-looking individuals. In my memory, they were all wearing short white smocks and disposable gloves in lurid violet. They all looked like dentists. One of them coughed into a fist and said to me in an undertone, "We don't want any trouble, do we?" I nodded in acquiescence and allowed myself to be escorted from the platform, as if by a bodyguard. The audience gave a bewildered and reflex round of applause. As soon as we had left the auditorium and found ourselves in the huge circular passage that circumnavigates its way around the Royal Albert Hall like a Large Hadron Collider, I was dealt with more robustly and frogmarched through – I computed – two radians. From the hall, I could hear an echoing rendition of Parry's setting of William Blake's *Jerusalem* in Elgar's orchestration, played by the orchestra and sung by the entire company. I was turned abruptly into a disused bar, where two London coppers were waiting.

The police officers took note of my immaculate attire and grinned broadly. They were enjoying themselves hugely. "Well well, *Maestro!*"

Cuffs were produced. I said, "Is this really necessary? I'm not planning an encore." The policemen found this equally amusing and put the cuffs away. The dentists in white smocks withdrew. I said, "Would you mind leaving the door ajar? I'd rather like to hear the National Anthem." It was the Benjamin Britten arrangement, in two verses, the first quiet and reverent, the second fervent and *maestoso*. No third verse. Something about troublesome Scots.

My preoccupation with music seemed to confirm the police's assessment of me as a fruitcake rather than an international terrorist. White tie and tails doubtless helped.

I was perfectly harmless. They might even let me loose on the streets without further ado. Now, one of the policemen walked across to the bar and started to speak into the lapel of his uniform. There was an angry crackle of static and a brief exchange. I suppose it would have been with *Sarge* back at the station. The constable returned to his colleague, and they held a brief conference. They turned to me.

"We're going to the car now. Coming quietly?" And then a familiar trope: "We can do this the easy way or the hard way."

I was still holding on to the CD of Chepstow's deposition in my hand. I put it in my pocket. I didn't want the cops to confiscate it. To tell you the truth, it was actually MacKenzie's recording for *Naxos* of the Viola Sonata by Arnold Bax.

We left the building to the strain of *Auld Lang Syne*, or at least a bastardised version of it.

"I'm all for the quiet life. Where are we off to?"

"The Maudsley."

It wasn't cuffs they were holding in reserve. It was a straitjacket.

XXVIII

I'm bound to say I was treated with the greatest courtesy and kindness in the Maudsley. Private room; fed and watered – cuisine not bad. I was a little taken aback when they removed my cummerbund and shoelaces, but I was too tired to argue. In fact, I crashed and slept soundly and dreamlessly for ten hours – no foul fiends and flibbertigibbets. In the morning, I had the usual difficulty reassembling my memory banks – you can't recover from an insult such as I had received that quickly. And, of course, the old angst came flooding back with the memories. I pressed a buzzer by my bedside table, and a male nurse attended promptly.

"Can I use the phone? I'm really worried about a friend of mine. She might be in danger." I remembered the way Kathryn had said cheerio. She didn't say, "See you later." I think she said, "Goodbye, my love." It sounded awfully terminal.

"We'll bring a phone for you once Dr Parkinson has finished the ward round. He'll be along shortly."

"Can't I just make a quick call?"

"We'll organise it as soon as we can." That judicious tone again. The nurse sounded exactly like the policeman up at Achiltibuie, who had similarly fobbed me off. I lay in my striped NHS pyjamas, fidgeting in my bed, looking like the inmate of a concentration camp.

At length, the heavy man in the crumpled suit shuffled through the door.

"Shrink!"

"Speedbird."

"Ralph, I need to use the phone."

"That's fine. Just let me finish my ward round." He glanced around, pulled up a chair and sat down on my left.

"That was quite a performance you gave in the Royal Albert Hall last night. I saw it on the telly. His Majesty looked quite bemused."

"Certain things needed to be said, and somebody had to say them."

"You're all over the morning papers. Opinions seem to vary according to the political complexions of the various organs. You're quite the darling of *The Guardian*. *Doctor diagnoses a festering cancer.* Not so the *Daily Mail*. *N-MASS flips his lid.*"

"Which one is the more accurate?"

"I incline to nuance. Something else you might want to know. Jonathan Braithwaite has hanged himself."

"I'm very sorry to hear that."

"Terrible shock for his mother. Found him hanging from an oak tree in her garden. A harlequin, gently rotating in the dawn breeze."

"Still in his sports jacket, you mean?"

"Never out of character. Suicides are such selfish people, don't you think?"

"I don't suppose there is any more acute agony than the agony of remorse."

"Either that, or the prospect of an eternity in Wormwood Scrubs was not palatable to him."

"He shouldn't have done that. Where there is life, there is always hope."

"You would know."

"What was that you were saying about nuance?"

"Ah yes. Back to the mental state examination. Insightfulness in one area does not necessarily imply insightfulness across the board."

"Well now. Didn't I tell you there was a connection between *Whetstone* and a house in the far northwest? And did that enquiry not lead on to the identification of an installation that is indeed, in the words of *The Guardian*, a festering cancer?"

"Correct."

"So precisely what nuance do you have in mind?"

"I'm talking about your state of mind. You must know that when we last talked, in Ullapool, you were a little overwrought."

"Of course I was. Who wouldn't be?"

"And you still are."

"How d'you mean?"

"Well, for example. Why is it that you want to make an urgent telephone call?"

"Because I fear Kathryn Hathaway remains in danger."

"That's what I thought."

I twigged. "You still don't think she exists."

"Put it this way. She's not integral to the story, as it is panning out. We're back to Occam's Razor."

"But she rescued me!"

"You were released, so far as I can make out, because a government minister had a change of heart, and a member of the Committee *sine nomine* realised his cover was broken. Ms

Hathaway is redundant. Don't misunderstand me. You were right about *Whetstone*, but you need to appreciate that a severe ordeal can take its toll. I think you need time to recover. Trust me. Things will fall into place."

"We don't have time. Kathryn doesn't have time."

I think it was at this point that Parkinson became a little impatient with me. Looking back, that was not very professional of him. The trouble was, he knew me as a colleague as well as a patient. So exasperation crept in. It's called *transference*.

"God Almighty, you're still banging on about your imaginary friend."

There was a knock at the door. Parkinson ignored it.

"I've said it to you before. Stop and think. See it from my perspective. Do you think there is any possibility that you made Ms Hathaway up?"

I have a notion that Parkinson hoped this might be the moment I would have a flash of insight. Could he be right? After all, as he had said, none of my friends and colleagues had ever met her. And he was absolutely right when he said that I had been emotionally overwrought. I was quite prepared to admit that, for a time, I had been as daft as a brush. I remembered the words of Oliver Cromwell: "I beseech you, in the bowels of Christ, think it possible you may be mistaken."

There was another knock on the door. Persistent. Again, Parkinson ignored it.

"Alastair, nobody is saying that you haven't done sterling work. You happened to receive a head injury in the process, and, in my opinion, you have also received a psychiatric injury. I'm trying to alleviate the latter. I say again: Do you think it possible that Ms Hathaway never was?"

I stared long and hard at him. I batted the options to and fro. Yes or no? Yes might get me out of here quicker. Parkie cocked an eyebrow.

"No."

There was another soft knock on the door. Knock, and the door will be opened unto you.

Parkinson bellowed, with frank exasperation, *"What?!"*

The door opened. A tall girl in a smart navy-blue trouser suit, with long dark hair, carrying a slim black satchel, stood on the threshold.

"What do you want?"

She stepped into the room. I was so utterly overwhelmed, and so utterly relieved, that for a moment I was speechless, completely undermined. I remember she glanced softly in my direction, smiled, and turned to my psychiatrist.

"Dr Parkinson?"

"Yes?"

"I'm Kathryn Hathaway." She stepped forward and proffered her right hand. "I tried to call you, but I never got an answer. Now I've just learned from your registrar that, in the opinion at least of the psychiatric faculty, I don't exist. So, in the interest of the avoidance of any doubt..." She opened her satchel and produced her American passport. "Here's my ID."

Parkinson took the document, befuddled, and, for lack of anything better to do, examined it quizzically.

"I've come to collect Alastair. If any doubt as to my existence is the reason for his remaining here, then I think there can be little cause to perpetuate his restraint order. Don't you agree?" Her smile was very sweet.

For the one and only time in my life, I saw Ralph Parkinson, that embodiment of ocker machismo, wilt. He was intimated.

He handed the passport back. Then he frowned. I could see him trying to join the dots, trying to put the jigsaw together. He was struggling. It is the most difficult thing in the world, to cast aside a deeply held belief.

"Were you at Cape Wrath?"

"Oh yes. I can fully corroborate any depositions Dr Cameron-Strange puts forward."

"How did you get out?"

"I negotiated. Rather more successfully than you, I think. Saying that, I have to admit it came at a cost."

I was already out of my bed, grabbing my stuff and slipping into the *en suite* to clad myself improbably in full white tie evening dress. When I emerged, they were still talking about the trials and tribulations of negotiation.

"I would dearly have loved to leave on the same capsule as Alastair. But it was not to be. I had to hang around and discharge... further duties. But I was ready for that. To be honest, I was ready to lick their boots so long as I might be spared to extract revenge."

Ralph Parkinson looked down at the floor and then said, in a subdued tone, "I owe you both an apology."

I resisted the temptation to say something lofty, like, "Blessed are those who have not seen, and yet believed." Instead, I said, "Don't be daft. Anyone could see I was mad as a snake, one raven short of an unkindness, one pilchard short of a shimrer..."

"I still can't quite figure out how you got out."

Kathryn said, "I used whatever bargaining tools were at my disposal. You see..." She rummaged again in her satchel and produced Parkinson's own embossed business card and held it up. She intoned its mantra.

"You don't get what you deserve, you get what you negotiate."

XXIX

"Good heavens," muttered Forbes, over morning coffee, head buried in *The Scotsman*. "There's been an earthquake just off Durness. During the night. 4.2 on the Richter Scale."

"4.2? That's nothing," I said. "That's just rock-a-by baby in Paraparaumu."

"Windows were smashed and one gable end collapsed onto a car. There were no casualties."

I proffered the swear box. "One pound sterling for the C-word."

"Unfair. I was quoting." Forbes read on. "Concerns have been raised over potential structural damage to the decommissioned nuclear power station at Dounreay. Officials from the Atomic Energy Authority were observed combing the beach with Geiger counters."

"Place never seems to be out of the news. Where was the epicentre?"

"Cape Wrath, apparently, but very deep within the earth's

crust. Very unusual to have such seismic activity amid such ancient geology."

"I guess the tectonic plates are shifting."

It was three months later. Here we were, into December. Nothing had changed. Everything had changed. The *feuilles mortes* had fallen. Yet, for once, I had a spring in my step. Kathryn and I were going to New Zealand for Christmas. I was going home. But in the meantime, I was still embroiled in Edinburgh medical politics.

Back at ELSCOMF, Professor MacTaggart muttered to me in a barely audible *sotto voce*, "Should be able to do something for your cellist chappie. Got to keep the Baxes on the road. Seems to be responding to the medication, even at a paltry dose. Incidentally" – his voice almost faded to inaudibility, and he avoided eye contact – "that was a clever spot diagnosis of yours. Sharp." He called the meeting to order and moved briskly on. He was delighted to announce that the Health Minister was insisting that the GPs stayed open 8 am to 8 pm, seven days a week. If they didn't, they would lose revenue. "That should help to take some of the pressure off Casualty."

I said, "I doubt it. Apart from anything else, the GPs won't stand for it. It will go down like a lead balloon. As it should."

MacTaggart raised his eyebrows. "Alastair, I'm surprised. I thought you would have been happy for them to share the load."

"They are working every bit as hard as we are. Besides, what does the Minister think he's doing, micromanaging the NHS like this? Sometimes I wonder why we have a Health Minister at all. I would dearly love to depoliticise medicine. Why doesn't the government hand over the budget and tell us to get on with it? Actually, the rot set in with the new contract way back in 2005. The Health Boards took over out-of-hours care. They had no idea what they were taking on. Of course, the GPs handed it over with alacrity. Cynical move, really. They should have kept control. They should have said, 'We will look after the patients 24/7, so long as we are financed so to do, and then be allowed to get on with it as we see fit.'"

Faith knocked on the boardroom door and stuck her head round the corner. "Phone call, Alastair."

"Who is it?"

"It's the palace."

"See, Forbes, I *told* you this wouldn't work."

I took the call in the department. "Dr Cameron-Strange."

"Alastair, it's Hoppy."

"Hoppy!" I was lightheaded with euphoria.

"Can you spare a minute?"

"Two minutes for you."

"Anybody sitting near you?"

"One or two."

"Then don't react. His Majesty has asked me to sound you out. He understands you are, under normal circumstances, very much a private person, not one to search out the limelight, and more than happy to pursue your profession in a low-key fashion."

"Where is this going, Hoppy?"

"Indeed, he would perfectly understand if this proposal did not immediately have an appeal for you."

"And your point is?"

"Sorry. Just paving the way. Yes, indeed. Well, it goes without saying that His Majesty is pleased with the outcome following your various exertions and not a little impressed as we all are. He wonders if you would be interested to have your contribution to the safety and well-being of the realm marked by a token of recognition and, indeed, of royal esteem?"

"Sorry?"

"I'm not making myself clear. His Majesty wishes to invest you with an Honour."

"Honour?"

"An Order."

"Me?"

"Yes, Doctor. You."

"You mean, like, a gong?"

"We don't use that word at the palace."

Fair enough. Perhaps *gong* to Hoppy was like *casualty* to me – red rag to a bull.

"What sort of gong? Sorry. Order."

"His Majesty would be pleased graciously to bestow upon you the Order of St Michael and St George."

"What's that?"

"You mean, what is its historic heraldic significance?"

"Well, yes, I suppose that's what I mean."

"It would take some time to explain. I could send you some materials. Perhaps the most important point is that this investiture – should you accept – would not arise through His Majesty receiving advice from any political source or alternative form of patronage. That is to say, it would be the personal gift of His Majesty."

"Hoppy, I don't know…"

"No need to make a snap decision. Think it over. Take your time. Have a chat, if you like, with close family. Advise them, however, to respect confidentiality. Such awards are usually only made public on the eve of investiture. Give me a call at your leisure."

"Okay. I'll think about it." It sounded very ungrateful. I added, "Thank you so much. I'm – well – honoured." I hung up and once more sat staring vacantly at the phone.

Anyway, I took Hoppy's advice and asked around, sharing it only with people whose firewall of confidentiality I knew was impregnable, or at least as impregnable as our world of uncertainty allows. I started with Forbes. For Forbes, observance of the sanctity of the confessional is as natural as breathing.

"You're accepting it of course."

I won't say it sounded like a directive; but I sensed the irritability just under the surface, that would come up if I showed the slightest desire to falter.

"Why do you think I should?"

"Because it is an honour not solely to you but to those around you. To decline is not merely to disrespect the Sovereign; it is to disrespect all those who have believed in you and supported you. I have no doubt you will receive this honour with dignity and grace, remembering you do so on behalf of this worthy institution and its Emergency Department."

No pressure, then. But I asked myself if Forbes' formulation was justified. If, in all humility, I declined the honour for whatever reason, did it really mean I was disrespecting my profession and my colleagues? Hardly.

I asked David Walkerburn. Confidentiality assured again, and David would have no axe to grind. He would be entirely even-handed. It crossed my mind as I entered his office that he might bill me for this. And why not? It was professional time. I outlined my dilemma. He shook my hand.

"I take it congratulations are in order?"

"If I could answer that, I would not be seeking your advice."

"What is it you fear about being a member of this ancient and most venerable order?"

"I fear the establishment, David. I don't want to be in their pocket. D'you know, I once had a coffee with an acquaintance of mine in a café in Sicily. I went to the counter to pay the barista, and he said, 'No. Everybody here pays for himself.' He pointed out to me that that was how the mafia worked. They bought you your lunch, and that was it. They owned you. You might not think they owned you, but that no longer mattered. It was their opinion that mattered. There is no such thing as a free lunch."

"You think the British establishment resembles the mafia?"

"Every conglomerate shares common features."

"How do you view Professor Pearson's point that in this, you do not merely represent yourself, but also the colleagues and friends who support you?"

I've said it before: why is it that when you seek advice from a lawyer, they just bombard you with questions?

"It sounded convincing at the time, but, in retrospect, I think it's balderdash. I need never have told anybody about this. Then they would have been none the wiser."

"Do you think the order is beneath you?"

"For goodness' sake no. Believe me, I can see it's an honour to be asked. Actually, I'm pleased. Who wouldn't be? But I'm suspicious of my own pleasure. I don't like to think I have a price."

"It's a kind of inverse vanity?"

"Is that what self-respect is? Do I need an honour in order to feel worthy?"

"They say that every man has his price. Do you think you might go for something if it were inordinately high? Order of Merit? Companion of Honour?"

"Now you're teasing me."

"I bet you'd take the Nobel Peace Prize."

"And now you're being preposterous. Me and Dr Kissinger? Come on. Give me an opinion. I promise I won't hold it against you. Should I accept or decline?"

"I think you should follow the combined instincts of your head, your heart, and your gut."

I paid him fifty guineas for that.

Lastly, I asked the three women in my life. MacKenzie, Caitlin, and Kathryn. In retrospect it was probably a mistake to ask them all simultaneously.

Caitlin said, "Cool!"

"I'm thinking of giving it the body swerve."

"Cool!" Good for Caitlin. She couldn't care less.

"Stop being such an arse and take the bloody thing." This from my sister. "The Emergency Department will have a piss-up for you, and everybody will have a spring in their step. Stop being morbid."

Kathryn's onslaught was the worst. "Do you really want to hold your family back in the doldrums with your leftie scruples? You might feel smug about being a gong *virgin*, but you'll be smug on your own. Who wants to hang around with a guy in a donkey jacket? How're you going to explain this to your daughter?"

My who?

For a short period after The Last Night, our relationship had come under a subliminal strain whose nature I couldn't quite identify. I wondered if I were about to have morning coffee and another valedictory of the sort I'd experienced down at the bottom of the world, in the dim and distant past. She went through a period of being monosyllabic and morose, almost sulky. I kept trying to cheer her up with remarks which now, in retrospect, strike me as being completely inane. "How did you manage to persuade that gaoler of yours – was it Oswald? – not only to open your cell door, but also mine?"

"Pure charm."

"I've been trying to figure it out. Somebody must have got cold feet, or had a change of heart or something. I'd guess it was either Hugh Standish or Jonathan Braithwaite. The Minister without Portfolio really didn't have the stomach for it. As for *Sports-Jacket*, he probably discovered I'd sent a text to Caitlin, and so his cover would begin to run."

"Something like that."

"Well, whatever it was, I can't think what sort of magic

you worked to get us out of there!" (I was that thick.) "But it certainly paid off! What a rollercoaster ride was that!"

"Mm."

"D'you know, it's even possible they had a genuine change of heart. You were terribly eloquent from the dock, even if you dropped the bit about Shakespeare's *Measure for Measure*. Eloquent but brief. The Shakespeare had been on my mind. I felt as if I were taking part in a performance, and then you quoted it. The Duke of Vienna out-duked the Duke of Assynt!"

At last, she grew weary of my effusions, took me to one side, and said, "Look, you idiot. Stop banging on about it. What sort of magic do you think I worked? Listen to me." She put her hands on my shoulders, fixed me with that extraordinary penetrating gaze of hers, and once again hypnotised me.

"What character did you play in *Measure for Measure*?"

"Claudio."

"Uh-huh. Well, I was your sister, Isabella. Only I didn't have Isabella's scruples."

"Ah." I couldn't help wondering who had cuckolded me. The wraith, the ex-minister who had definitely lost his portfolio, or the worst-dressed man on the planet?

It couldn't be the wraith. Too subservient. It had to be Braithwaite or Standish. I have a notion that Kathryn thought I was going to ask, but she cut me dead. She muttered under her breath, "It was the worst forty-five seconds of my life."

I guess I'm just a jealous man. I decided not to go there. Instead, I shrugged and pouted and made an openhanded Gallic gesture. "God moves in a mysterious way."

She laughed, and, mysteriously indeed, whatever problem there had been seemed instantly to evaporate.

In the meantime, I was so taken aback by the idea that our relationship might be developing a sense of – well, call it continuity if not permanence, that I completely failed to hear what she was telling me. I suppose I was still too tied up in the affairs of the world to pay any attention. Sir Roger Hollis and the rest of them had applied for the Chiltern Hundreds. That's what mattered. And St John Pennington-Althorp? Well, no. He is, for the moment, beyond my reach. In fact, I am given to understand he has disappeared off the face of the earth. Some people think he is dead. But I don't think so. I haven't seen any funeral notices, nor obituaries, in the broadsheets. I know he exists, somewhere, in some corner of the universe as equally obscure as ours. He sits there, in his private den, hunched over the chess board, watching, waiting. Well, leave him to it. If I have been a small cog in the big wheel that still turns, then that's enough for me.

It is a great relief to me that my family remnant has fallen in love with Kathryn as much as I have. I was a bit nervous about Caitlin. I almost felt I had to ask her permission. I said, "Are you okay with this?"

"I love her. I love her skin. I'm swooning with envy. Why didn't you tell me she's black?"

Can I possibly go back to the day job? Is it possible ever again to go for a walk along the beach, to have a picnic, to kick a ball around?

To create new life? You see? Zero emotional intelligence.

The Royal Hotel
Garve Road
Ullapool IV26 2SY
December 21st

David Walkerburn and Hester Cardwell
Cardwell Walkerburn, Writers to the Signet
48 Heriot Row
Edinburgh EH3 6HR

Dear David and Hester,

Greetings from the wastes of Assynt. I thought I'd better let you know that the erstwhile Enterprise Czar, once Knight of the Realm, Roger Hollis Esq., has been in touch. Daft though it may sound, he has challenged me to a duel. Do you think I should take my epée?

I know it sounds rash, but I accepted. I agreed to meet, if not to duel. Just we two. I don't know. I just feel it right and propitious that we cross swords (so to speak) one final time. Our appointment is for midday tomorrow at a location (rather melodramatic, I thought) just to the southeast of Ullapool overlooking Loch Broom. It is at the footbridge over the Corrieshalloch Gorge.

I'm going along without any agenda. I feel that his machinations have been well and truly disrupted and that my task in that regard is done. Therefore, I have nothing to fear. I feel like Martin Luther King Junior: "I have seen the Promised Land." And as Dr

King said, "I'm not worried." So don't worry about me. Remember, I have a talent for brinkmanship.

Nevertheless, I thought it prudent to drop you a line. I'm trying to remember my 'final arrangements' that I think mostly involve my sister MacKenzie and my sister-in-law Caitlin Roy. All of that stands. But I think I may have neglected a modest account I hold in the Bank of New Zealand (BNZ). My account resides in the Otahuhu Store on Great South Road in Auckland. I dare say this garbled message will cause no end of legal ructions, but would it be possible to make it over to one Kathryn Hathaway? MacKenzie and Caitlin won't mind for a moment, and they will give you Ms Hathaway's contact details.

Thank you so much for all your help and advice over the years. But I mustn't get maudlin or morbid. And truly, I'm not. Au contraire, I'm full of hope.

Hope! It's a kind of nostalgia for the future.

Catch up soon

Alastair.